"YOU'RE HURTING ME!"

Genny tried to jerk her arm away from the Indian. "And you speak English! You despicable liar!"

"That's right, I do," Gus said quietly. "And I hurt people who pull knives on me. Did I scare you, lying flat on my back with a book in my hand? Pretty savage, wasn't it?"

"Let go of me!" Genny ordered.

"Do you know what would happen to you if I wanted to hurt you, Miss Stone? Do you think that puny blade would stop me, or anyone else?"

"Don't underestimate me, whoever you are. I can stop anyone I want to."

"So stop me now," he said laughing, pulling her close against him . . .

STORM DANCERS

ALLISON HAYES

AVON BOOKS 🔺 NEW YORK

STORM DANCERS is an original publication of Avon Books. This
work has never before appeared in book form. This work is a novel.
Any similarity to actual persons or events is purely coincidental.

AVON BOOKS
A division of
The Hearst Corporation
1350 Avenue of the Americas
New York, New York 10019

Copyright © 1991 by Lynn Coddington
Published by arrangement with the author
Library of Congress Catalog Card Number: 91-92070
ISBN: 0-380-76215-3

First Avon Books Printing: December 1991

AVON TRADEMARK REG. U.S. PAT. OFF. AND IN OTHER COUNTRIES,
MARCA REGISTRADA, HECHO EN U.S.A.

Printed in the U.S.A.

RA 10 9 8 7 6 5 4 3 2 1

Prologue

Chadds Ford, Pennsylvania, March 1864

The last time Genny Stone's escapades had gotten out of hand, she'd been sent to France to repent at her leisure. For nearly two years.

This time, she was determined that things would be different. Her father was playing chess with old Mr. Vernon at the Vernon estate, and Aunt Augusta was miles away in Philadelphia. They were not going to find out about this afternoon's activities.

In the secluded corner of the grounds at Riverwood, the Stone family's country residence, Genny glanced up from her canvas to behold a motionless man in a dark blue Union Army uniform. His arm was raised so that his palm rested against a stone archway, his tall form framed by the whisper green of barely budding willows. Beyond the arch, the heavy yellow bloom cloaking the forsythia hedge set off the color of his uniform like a golden ring encompassing a gem. The air was still and warm, the sky clear and soft with lamb's wool clouds and a bright sun. Blackbirds sang back and forth, intent on collecting twigs and bracken for their nests, while bees droned among the early blossoms.

"Oh, fiddle, Lieutenant Mercer!" Genny exclaimed, lowering her paint brush in feigned exasperation. She caught Nicky Mercer's interested gaze and shook her head. "Propriety is such a hindrance when one quests

1

after true art. I don't see how I am to paint you in a classical pose when you are fully clothed, but I can't think of a decent way for . . ."

She let the suggestion dangle.

Nicholas Mercer gaped at Miss Stone's request before the lascivious twinkle with which Genny was all too familiar leapt into his cobalt eyes. She'd seen Lieutenant Mercer ogle her younger sister, Beth, with the same eager grin he wore now. She'd been right about him. He didn't care for Beth any more than he cared whether he had lemon curd or strawberry fool with his afternoon tea; both were sweet, and either would satisfy.

Genny watched impassively as Nicky's fingers began to work at his collar.

"Say no more, Miss Stone. I'm happy to abet your artistic endeavor," Nicky's hands slid rapidly to the gold buttons of his jacket. He tossed the blue coat to the bench, then went to work on his shirt buttons. A moment later he peeled off the shirt and lifted an eyebrow, inviting her comment.

"That's better, I'm sure," she said blandly.

Nicky Mercer was an ungodly handsome rogue, with deep blue eyes, and jet black hair and mustache. He was tall, muscular, and inordinately aware of his physical charms. Genny watched him puff out his chest a bit and tighten his stomach muscles. Unmoved by his beauty, she focused on the task she had set to accomplish.

"Nicky," she began again, watching him smile at her use of his first name. "Please put your hand back up on the arch and lean your weight forward onto your left leg. That's good," she continued as he settled back into the pose she had chosen.

"I look all right?"

"Like Zeus himself," Genny answered.

"My scar isn't too unsightly? I wouldn't want to offend you, Miss Stone."

"It's barely a scratch. It adds to the image I'm creating of a Greek warrior." She was certain Nicky was envisioning himself as Achilles, Heracles, and Zeus, all rolled into one.

The lieutenant had been convalescing at the Stone country home southwest of Philadelphia for the past few weeks, after having taken a nearly spent bullet in his right shoulder. He'd received the small wound in a minor skirmish with Confederate troops in Virginia, and managed to talk himself into an undeserved medical leave. Genny imagined his commanding officer had gotten so sick of Nicky's lazy self-indulgence that the man had jumped at the chance to be rid of him. Nicky hadn't felt like traveling all the way home to New York, couldn't abide Army medical care, and decided it was high time he met those Stone girls his father was always going on about. His father and Genny's had been close friends in college at Princeton, so David Stone had welcomed Nicky when the Lieutenant wrote to ask if he might recuperate at the Stone country home outside of Philadelphia.

Genny's eighteen-year-old sister Beth had promptly fallen in love with the young officer. Thanks to her time in Paris, Genny had had frequent opportunities to observe young rakehells at work, and she promptly recognized Nicky Mercer as a long established member of that international brotherhood. She had subsequently spent the past two weeks trying to keep the lieutenant from taking advantage of Beth's cheerful naivete and innocence.

Beth, however, was certain Nicky returned her affections and wouldn't listen to Genny's warnings. No argument could convince her that Nicky was less than a serious suitor, and Genny's frustration had grown in direct proportion to Beth's increasing certainty that Nicky Mercer was about to propose.

The afternoon before, Genny had interrupted Beth and Nicky in this very spot in the garden. The passionate nature of the kiss she had intruded upon convinced her that something had to be done about Lieutenant Mercer.

Immediately.

"You know, Nicky," Genny said slowly, glancing at the watch pinned to her sleeve, "I do hate to embarrass you, but your pose still isn't quite suggestive enough of the classical for me to adequately capture the lines that will evoke the passion of Greek statuary. I think the line of your boots is interfering with the classical lines I'm after. It raises your heels, changing the whole line of your legs and back. The Greeks wore sandals, you know.''

Nicky was instantly seated on the stone bench beside the archway, tugging at his gleaming black boots. His stockings followed, tossed carelessly upon the ground. The flush in his cheeks told Genny that he was enjoying himself.

She took a deep breath and smoothed a hand over the full skirt of her cornflower blue dress. The timing for the next step of her plan was critical.

"You're being such a cooperative subject," Genny continued, picking up her brush again. "That's really much better. Do you know, though . . ."

She paused, suddenly embarrassed by what she was going to say. She'd done many reckless things in her time, but the request she was about to make was shocking, even to her own unconventional way of thinking.

"Do you know, lieutenant," she repeated, praying she wouldn't blush, "that in classical portraits the thighs are very important. The muscles must be depicted accurately and cleanly to communicate the power and beauty of the human form."

When she said the word "thighs," Nicky looked her straight in the eyes, a wicked, knowing smile spreading slowly over his face.

She waited, listening carefully to the sounds filtering in from beyond the forsythia bushes that screened off the corner where they stood. The blackbirds still sang, and sparrows tittered below the bushes. Nicky was silent, wrapped up in the smoldering glances he was directing at her.

Genny cleared her throat. "Well, I guess what I was trying to say was that the heavy material of your trousers makes it difficult to discern the form of your legs."

She felt a rapid heat suffuse her cheeks, but she suddenly heard the faint whisper of a skirt over the grass. Nicky didn't appear to have noticed it.

She forced herself to continue. "I mean, I could fill in the details based on the models that I painted in Paris, but then it wouldn't really be a portrait of you, would it?" Genny put down her brush and moved away from her canvas, toward Lieutenant Mercer.

"Miss Stone, am I correct in believing that you wish me to remove my trousers?" Nicky asked intently.

A twig crackled from beyond the hedge as Genny nodded.

"I know it's dreadfully improper, but it is for the sake of art," she all but whispered, staring at the ground.

Nicky was still for a moment. "For the sake of art," he repeated, slowly slipping his braces off his shoulders and setting the top button of his trousers free.

In another moment his trousers were around his knees. When he lifted one leg to pull them off, Genny took a step closer to him, holding out her hand to support his elbow. Just as he looked up in question, a loud shriek caused both him and Genny to start violently.

Genny recognized that shriek of indignation immediately, and it froze her blood. She nearly missed seeing Beth altogether, for her sister took one look at the lieutenant, cast an accusing eye at her, then turned to flee back toward the house.

Genny's attention was riveted instead by an imposing female with whom she was all too familiar.

"Oh my!" she gasped. "Aunt Augusta!"

Her aunt's appearance was about as welcome as Confederate troops in the White House. A knot of apprehension formed in Genny's middle as she realized there would be consequences from her afternoon's endeavor, after all.

A quick glance at Nicky Mercer dressed only in a pair of all-too-revealing white cotton drawers assured her that there would be dire consequences, indeed.

Chapter 1

Nebraska Territory, July 1864

Genny walked slowly to the crest of the hills that rose behind her small cottage and looked out at the sea of rolling earth that stretched far away to the horizons. The yellowy-green grasses had dried in the hot southerly winds of the past week, the landscape slowly shifting from the green and flower colors brought by wet spring rains to the drab dun that heralded hot summer. Her brown winsey skirt plastered itself to her legs, driven by the ever-present wind. Genny's fine brown hair was always a mess now; it wouldn't stay in a knot with the wind constantly tugging at it, and if she left it loose, it tangled so badly she spent hours combing the snarls out. Her skin was dry, her lips were chapped, and her eyes stung from the incessant sun and wind.

Staring at the empty land and the enormous, cloud filled sky, Genny felt lost.

She knew there were people six miles to the south, at Rivier's Ranch, a nearly abandoned way station along the North Platte River. Roger Rivier did a little trading with his mixed-blood wife's Cheyenne relatives and kept a few horses, mules, and oxen to trade with the odd travelers who still took the northern leg of the Overland Trail. Few passed the ranch anymore, most of the pilgrims following the more southerly route through Julesburg. The North Platte was virtually uninhabited between

Fort Laramie in the west and the forks of the Platte in the east.

The river itself and Rivier's ranch were hidden from Genny's view by a line of low, ragged hills. Beyond that, many miles to the south, lay the main Platte River Road and all the thousands of people who passed through on their way west to California, Oregon, Idaho, and Utah—but Genny couldn't see them, either.

For all intents and purposes, she was alone in a void of plain and sky.

Closing her eyes, she thought back to the day a few months ago when she had asked Nicky Mercer to undress himself as he posed for her in her father's garden.

The worst of recalling that day in March was that for once, she had done an excellent job of defending herself against Aunt Augusta's tirades and pronouncements. Her father, as usual, had not been helpful. Beth had locked herself in her room, Lt. Mercer had left for New York in a hurry, and Genny had suffered through a long recitation of her faults, past and present, without losing her temper once.

And then her cousin Paul Conrad had shown up. Naturally, he had felt it necessary to add his opinion though he had to wait for his mother to finish her say.

"I do not think I can tolerate the continuance of such brazen, ill-conceived adventures." Aunt Augusta left her post in front of the mantel, her right forefinger extended in a condemning gesture. "I do not care to spend my old age keeping watch over a reckless girl who should be married and raising a family of her own!"

Genny darted out of her aunt's way, ducking behind a wing chair. "You know how I feel about getting married, so let's please not bring that topic into this discussion, as well! I refuse to turn my life over to some man simply to appease social expectations, when I can manage perfectly well on my own!"

Aunt Augusta's shoulders rose in indignation at Genny's tone, but before she could launch a new attack Paul butted in condescendingly. "Mother, relax. You know how she'll go on if you get her started. I know exactly what would put her in mind to settle down permanently.''

Her cousin was tall and handsome, with china blue eyes and brown hair similar to Genny's. Dressed in dark brown riding breeches and matching jacket, and an open-collared white shirt that highlighted his sun-browned skin, Paul settled himself on the sofa, propping his feet up on the glass-topped, mahogany coffee table. Mud and bits of grass clung to the sides of his boots.

No one appeared to be listening. Genny and her aunt continued to glare at one another, while Genny's father, David Stone, sighed morosely.

Paul wasn't deterred by the lack of response. "Paris obviously didn't exert much of a reforming influence on my willful little cousin.''

Genny spared Paul a withering glance, then shifted her angry gaze back to Aunt Augusta's black grosgrain collar.

"In retrospect," he continued, undaunted, "it seems more of a reward than a punishment. Now if you really wanted to put Gen into an environment that might cause her to think twice about some of her wilder schemes, I've got the answer.''

"Spare us the histrionic buildup and spit it out, Paul," Genny drawled, sounding interminably bored.

"Don't use such vulgar language,'' Aunt Augusta ordered.

Paul ignored them both. "I think it would be good for Gen to accompany me when I go back west.'' Paul ran a freight company that carried goods from the Missouri River to the Rocky Mountains. "Nebraska Territory is just the place for an excitable young woman to work out some of her kinks. It's done wonders for no end of wild young men. It'll do the same for Genny.''

Paul grinned at his cousin, settled his hands behind his head and rocked back, a smug expression on his face.

Aunt Augusta turned to face her son, and even Genny's father swiveled to look at him.

He continued in a lazy tone. "Out on the prairies, Genny couldn't execute any of the half-cocked operations she's come up with in the last several years. There isn't anyone around to get into trouble with, or who needs saving from themselves. All her energy would have to go into good old, plain and simple hard work. Milking cows, cleaning out the chicken house, growing a garden, cooking for herself. No time for shenanigans like undressing unsuspecting army officers.''

No one said a word.

"I'm only offering what I think is a reasonable solution to an ongoing family problem," Paul explained with a slight shrug.

"I will not be referred to as an 'ongoing family problem'!" Genny thumped her fists on the back of the chair in front of her.

"The idea may have some merit," David Stone mused. "What do you think, Augusta?"

"I think it's absurd," Aunt Augusta snapped, surprising Genny entirely. "It's far too dangerous on the frontier for a young woman alone."

Genny bristled. She was hardly some hothouse flower to wilt before a little adventure!

"There's lots of women on the trail. And besides, Genny wouldn't be alone. I'd be there," Paul returned with a smile.

"Same difference," Genny shot back at him.

"I suppose you're right, Mother," Paul said, dropping his feet to the floor. He rose and sauntered to the fireplace, where he began scraping his dirty boots with the poker.

Genny glared at him. Paul continued scraping.

"Genny hasn't got the fortitude to survive a month on the plains. Sipping tea from Sevres china cups in a Parisian salon doesn't take the same kind of character frontier women need. It was foolish to think that Gen could survive in Nebraska. Even though it would be good for her, if she were up to it." He replaced the poker and grinned at Genny. "Too bad you're such a priss, cuz."

"I am not a priss," Genny corrected tersely. "I can handle anything you can, and don't you try to tell me I can't! You know well enough that there aren't any frontier women who have any more fortitude and character than I do!'' Her voice rose with every sentence. ''There is nothing out on your precious Nebraska frontier that I am not more than equal to! Not wolves, not Indians, not chicken houses, nasty old mules, prairie fires, dust storms, nor an army of smart-alecky, boorish males like yourself!'' She slammed her fist down on the chair back again.

''Then prove it, Gen.''

''Take my word for it,'' she warned.

''Prove it,'' he challenged. ''Prove it by coming back with me, Gen. Prove it by staying for a year on the frontier.''

The gauntlet had been thrown. Genny stepped from behind the chair and moved to stand in front of her cousin. An idea sizzled through her head.

''Might we by any chance be discussing a wager, now?'' she asked with soft fury.

Paul started briefly, then recovered his smile. ''If you wish. State your terms, Gen.''

Genny looked away from him to her father. He was leaning against his large, mahogany desk, his long legs crossed at the ankles, examining his fingernails with an expression of combined alarm and discomfort.

Genny put as much censure into her regard as she could as she stared at him. He glanced up at her, and his startled expression told her that he wasn't processing what was happening very quickly. She caught his gaze, but spoke to Paul.

''I want my art academy.''

Her father flinched and looked away.

''If I go west with you to stay for a year on the frontier, I want you to give me the money to start my art academy as soon as I get back.''

''I thought Uncle David was sponsoring your efforts there,'' Paul said, watching his uncle flush guiltily.

''He will, but he insists I wait until two years after the war has ended. I believe,'' she continued accusingly, ''he harbors the futile hope that I will marry and abandon the idea of opening my own school.''

''Which would be the best thing for you,'' Aunt Augusta added. "You ought to obey your father, young lady."

"All right, Gen, I'll put up the cash to get you started if you stay a full year on the plains. But if you skedaddle it back here one day before that year's up, you'll pay my price."

"Which is?" Genny asked, wary of Paul's uncharacteristically easy acceptance of her terms. She didn't trust him any more than she'd trust a rat in the pantry on baking day.

"My dagger," he said, suddenly serious.

"You mean *my* dagger," she corrected, smiling now. "I won it fair and square."

"That remains a matter of opinion."

"That's all you want?" She didn't trust him.

He nodded once, looking more sincere than Genny had ever seen him.

"Then the dagger for you, or my art academy for me." She extended her hand toward her cousin.

Paul took her hand in a firm, almost bruising grip. "One year on the frontier, Genny. Not a day less. Agreed?" he asked, gleefully.

"Agreed, you rat." Genny pumped his arm once as hard as she could. "This is going to cost you a pretty penny, cousin, and I'm going to relish every second of making you regret your impulsive generosity." She tried to draw her hand back, but he didn't let her go.

"We'll see," he laughed. "We'll just see."

Within a week, Genny had packed her trunks and begun the journey west.

Lifting her leather goggles from her neck to adjust them across her eyes, Genny gazed at the treeless prairie, wondering what she could have been thinking during that week that had kept her from realizing the folly of undertaking Paul's challenge. In all honesty, she knew she hadn't been thinking at all. She'd been acting single-mindedly out of pride and anger.

Throughout the trip, first by rail and riverboat, then in a wagon accompanying one of Paul's freight trains heading up the North Platte, she hadn't wavered in her determination to show Paul that she was every bit as strong as he was. When wolves had tried to steal a sack of bacon left near her campfire, she'd chased them off and retrieved the meat. When the wind had blown sand and dust into her eyes and nose, she'd gotten out her goggles and wet her handkerchief to wear over her face like a desert Arabian. When skunks invaded her new barn, she'd learned to live with them. Frontier hardships that would have discouraged most women she had met as challenges to her character and creativity, and she'd managed. So far.

Paul had brought her to the little valley he called White Rock Spring on May 27th, and by the end of two weeks, a crew of his teamsters had built her a three room cottage and a dugout barn for Trixie, her horse, and the half-dozen chickens Paul had carted west with them from Nebraska City. Genny had hung curtains, arranged her furniture, and set up the front bedroom as her painting studio. She'd unloaded the supplies Paul had hauled in for her, and undertaken the chore of learning to cook.

Paul left as soon as the house was finished to meet one of his trains on the way to Denver, and Genny had spent much of her time since then visiting at Rivier's ranch, learning basic housekeeping skills by helping Martha Rivier, the trader's wife. She had churned butter, mended stockings, dusted, beaten a rug, hauled water, boiled laundry, and mastered cooking bacon, fried potatoes and scrambled eggs. She was pleased with her progress. Paul had been as wrong as he'd ever been in thinking that she couldn't handle the hard work necessary to survive on the frontier, and Genny was looking forward to showing him how well she was coping.

But this was the third day since she had last walked over to the Rivier's, thinking that Roger and Martha might need a break from her constant presence, and wanting to see if she could manage completely by herself. The days alone had made the true difficulties of frontier life manifestly clear to her. It was only now, more than a month after Paul had left, that she had begun to appreciate the greatest obstacles she would face in the coming months: boredom and loneliness.

Turning back toward the draw in the rolling plains that hid the spring and her tiny house, Genny shook her head, willing herself to think of something else. As she came in view of her plain little house, the grass torn and trampled in a circle all around it where the teamsters' heavy boots had ripped up the sandy soil, she wondered if there was anything she could possibly find to take pleasure in in the bleak, lonely prairies of Nebraska.

Walking down the broad, sloping hill toward her house, Genny heard her mare, Trixie, nickering from where she'd been staked behind the dugout barn. Genny whistled in response. As the black mare came in sight, Genny heard another horse answer. She turned toward the house, thinking Paul had returned, then stopped abruptly.

Leaning against her porch rail, the evening sunlight falling bright upon them, stood two very large, nearly naked Indians.

Genny's throat went dry. Indians roamed throughout the Platte Valley, but Paul had assured her she didn't have to worry about them in her new home at White Rock Spring. In spite of their increasing dissatisfaction with the whites, he told her they'd stay away. He wouldn't elaborate further, and when asked, neither would Martha Rivier. But Paul and Martha had been wrong. Two absolutely real and utterly wild-looking Indians now stood watching her with undisguised curiosity.

Approaching cautiously, Genny stopped several feet short of the men. Each had a rifle at his side, and a knife at his waist. Wiping her suddenly damp palms against her dusty cotton skirt, Genny stared at them, her heart pounding.

"Hello," she managed, her voice breaking. "Can I help you?"

The larger of the two men grunted unintelligibly, drawing Genny's eyes to his craggy face. He was tall, at least six feet four she guessed, in his middle years, and heavy. His large stomach sagged over the top of his leather breechcloth. When she met his coal-black eyes, she caught an unexpected glimmer of wariness. He jerked his chin toward her goggles and nudged his companion.

Genny pulled the goggles off self-consciously, dropping them into her seam pocket.

"My name is Eugenia Stone," she said, voice shaking. "This is my house." She pointed to the cottage. "Do you need something?"

The large Indian spoke in his own tongue, then thrust his right hand toward her. Brushing her palm across her skirt once more, Genny tentatively offered her hand, eyes fixed on the dark palm and fingers held open to her. When she finally placed her hand in the Indian's, his grip was gentle. Genny's startled gaze rose to meet his. He nodded briefly before releasing her hand.

He spoke again, this time pointing to the man beside him. Genny shifted her gaze to the other Indian; her heart immediately doubled its furious beat. Whatever meager reassurance she'd received from the first man's manner fled in the face of his companion's unconcealed interest. This man scanned her face before his eyes dropped to her breasts, one eyebrow raising fractionally in approval before he caught her gaze again.

A flush mounting her cheeks, Genny gazed boldly back, putting as much challenge in her eyes as she could muster. Though shorter than his friend, he was far from small. He was also several years younger, and terribly, terribly handsome. Dark eyes gazed intently from beneath straight black brows, and his bone structure was gracefully masculine with a firm, squared jaw and chin. The only features distinguishing him from the artists' models she'd seen in Paris were his even brown skin, shoulder length black hair, tied back in a neat tail and his buckskin trousers with the blue and red beaded strip down the side of each leg.

Genny let her gaze drift down over his well-muscled arms and bare chest, mimicking his appraisal, but not the open approval he'd granted her. When she glanced back up, his eyes were laughing, though he didn't move a muscle. The knowing anticipation she read in those brown eyes raised her hackles. That look was unmistakable. Genny knew instinctively she faced a formidable rake.

Confirming her assessment, the man reached for her hand, halting her backward step away from him. His touch was warm and dry, his palm rough. Genny sensed his confidence, and she felt his strength; for a split second she almost enjoyed the simple contact. In confusion, she sought his eyes again, frowning. She tried to pull away, but he held her hand firmly, tugging her a fraction closer. When her eyes widened in alarm, the ghost of a smile hovered on his lips. Lordy, but he was handsome! Too handsome, if past experience was any judge.

The second time Genny tried to disengage her hand, he let her go. Still blushing, she turned her attention to the older man.

"What do you want?" she asked. She wasn't going to look at the handsome one. She knew exactly what he wanted, and she knew he wasn't going to get it from her.

The older man looked at her without answering.

"Do you speak English?"

This time he shook his head.

"Oh." She'd been afraid they didn't. "Are you Cheyenne? Sioux?"

The older Indian nodded once. "Sioux," he repeated. "Sicanġu," he added.

The word sounded to Genny like he was clearing his throat.

"Friends?" she queried, glancing doubtfully at the handsome one.

"Friends. Sioux friends," the other man told her. "Supper ready?" he asked. "Sioux friends hungry." His smile was as gentle as his handshake had been.

Genny relaxed somewhat. "I guess you know enough English to get by," she commented. Releasing her pent-up breath, Genny decided to risk inviting them in. "I was on my way in for supper. Why don't you follow me."

She stepped around the men onto the porch, holding

the door open, ushering them into her main room, a combination kitchen, dining room, and sitting room. Watching the Indians cross her threshold, she prayed she wasn't making a mistake. Martha had told her Indians often stopped by the white settlements and forts along the Platte, usually for a meal, sometimes to steal horses. If they were after the latter, Genny would give them her blessing. Trixie was far more trouble than she was worth.

"Go ahead and sit down," Genny said, pointing to the table when the men looked at her uncomprehendingly. She walked past them to pull out a ladder-backed chair. "Please sit down while I get supper," she repeated, motioning the older Indian to take a seat. He did so slowly, laying his rifle across the round oak table.

Genny looked at it a moment, then decided to let it be until she had their plates ready.

"Make yourselves comfortable," she said. Whether or not they could understand her, at least it was a change of pace to have someone to talk to. "You're my first guests here in Nebraska," she went on, lifting plates and cups from the cupboards. She turned to stir up the coals in the new stove and throw a few sticks of wood into the firebox. "I'm afraid my provisions leave a little to be desired for entertaining, but I'll put on some coffee, and I got some bread at Martha Rivier's a few days ago. It's still fairly fresh. And there's some cheese, a little leftover beef, potatoes, pickles, and jam." Genny ducked into the pantry, reemerging with her arms full. "I hope this'll be enough."

She looked at the Indians. The gun no longer rested on the table. Both rifles were propped against the wall, while the men sat expectantly at the table. The younger man followed her closely with his eyes. They flicked down the length of her body, then returned to her face. Stiffening, Genny met his gaze briefly, then turned back to the counter.

"I wish you wouldn't look at me like that. It's rude, and doesn't impress me in the slightest," she muttered. She was suddenly relieved they couldn't understand each other.

Trying hard to ignore him, Genny pulled her iron frying pan from its hook above the stove and set it on the fire. She let it heat while she sliced cold cooked potatoes, then scooped up a dollop of lard from the can beside the stove, dropping it into the hot pan. As soon as it melted, the potatoes followed with a sizzle. Salt and pepper completed one of the few surefire dishes in Genny's limited culinary repertoire.

Half an hour later, Genny judged her first frontier dinner party a success. The cheese remained untouched, but her crispy potatoes had been devoured, along with every scrap of cold meat and bread, and most of the butter. The biggest hit, however, seemed to be the plum jam. Genny watched in fascination as both men poured spreading pools of it onto their plates, dipping their bread into it and gobbling it down with gusto. They looked so disappointed when they discovered the jar was empty that she got another from the pantry. When the bread ran out, Genny stared as the younger Indian began eating the jam alone with his spoon. His blissful expression made her smile.

The light had faded rapidly during the meal. By the time the Indians had finished the second jar of jam, the low rumble of thunder sounded in the southwest. Genny rose from the table to look at the sky, and the Indians followed her onto the porch. The sky was dark in the southwest, broken by flashing lightning that threw great bolts between the clouds and to the prairie below. Most of it was still too far away to hear, but even as they watched, the first breath of cooler air slipped over the dry hills to tease the hair off their foreheads.

"I wonder if it will rain this time," Genny mused out loud. There had been thunderstorms every evening for a week, but no rain.

The Indians were talking quietly. The older man caught Genny's attention, pointing to their horses, tied near the cottonwoods alongside the creek, then to her dug-out barn. He raised his eyebrows, clearly asking permission to move the horses out of the weather.

Genny didn't answer right away. She didn't mind giving the Indians supper, but she wasn't sure she wanted them to stay any longer. Things had gone all right so far, but there was no predicting what might happen if they hung around. Her eyes mirroring her hesitation, she looked involuntarily at the younger man.

Dark eyes met hers in a challenge that was for the first time devoid of sexual intent or appreciation. His gaze was knowing, but not of the ways of a handsome man with a pretty woman. Instead, his expressive eyes spoke of the ways of a white woman with a red man. Genny recognized the difference at once. Starting guiltily, she glanced back at the approaching clouds. Her country was in the midst of a war being fought over Negro slavery, an effort she supported on moral grounds; it would be hypocritical to treat these men any differently from men of her own race.

"Follow me," she said resignedly, walking past the Indians. "Bring your horses to the barn. I have to get Trixie inside, too." She motioned them to follow.

Meeting them in front of the earthen structure, she wrinkled her nose in distaste as she caught a fading whiff of skunk. The creatures were everywhere around the spring. One of them had accidently gotten shut up in the barn one night with Trixie. The horse and the visiting skunk had had quite a time of it, the end result being an unhappy horse and a very smelly barn.

The handsome one stuck his head through the door, but backed out immediately, muttering under his breath and scowling. He pushed his big dun gelding's reins into his companion's fist, then bolted. The older Indian laughed heartily. He looked at Genny, pinched his nose, shook his head and pointed at his friend. She grinned, wondering what the Indian's reaction would have been the morning after the skunk's visit.

Genny and the older Indian settled Trixie and the other horses. While they worked in companionable silence, Genny realized that she might have a problem, depending how long the storm lasted. She'd thought the Indians could bed down in the barn with the horses if they had to spend the night, but it was obvious that the younger one wasn't going to like that idea.

The storm was closer when they left the barn. Thunder boomed, trailing the stabs and flashes of lightning by scant seconds. Huge drops of cold rain splattered to the ground, leaving tiny craters in the exposed dirt. In the last light of day, Genny saw the handsome Indian standing on her porch, watching an advancing curtain of rain.

He turned to smile at her when he heard her step on the floorboards.

She didn't smile back.

Hours later Genny lay in her bed, wide awake with the covers thrown back. The diminishing rain outside fell in a summer whisper. Intermittent lightning cast silvered images through her bedroom window, but no sound of thunder marred the soft sigh of the nearly spent storm.

A small thud from beyond her closed door drew Genny upright. Her hand closed over the Spanish dagger beneath her pillow as she strained to hear any further sound. There was none. Unexpectedly, a faint light shone through the crack under the door.

Easing off the bed, Genny slipped to the door. She knew she shouldn't have let the Indians stay in her spare room. It was begging trouble, but the storm had been violent, lasting far longer than she'd expected. Now one of the Indians was up and about in the night, and she didn't doubt for a minute which one of them it was.

Unbidden, his image filled her mind, and in the quiet privacy of midnight, she allowed herself to enjoy the warm eyes beneath raven brows, the fine straight nose, and gently sculpted bones of his cheeks and jaw. His lips were beautiful: firm, yet full, easily cast in smiles, suggestive in equal parts of strength and soft surrenders. Genny shivered at the thought, not sure where it came from. She wondered if she could capture half the complexity she read in his face on canvas. Surprisingly, his was a face of character, not empty beauty, and she wondered if there was more to him than his suggestive behavior indicated. There was certainly something that set him apart from other handsome men she'd known; her response to him was alarmingly visceral, and all without so much as one shared word between them. It was unnerving. Nevertheless, if he was skulking about her parlor, she wanted to know why. She didn't mistake aesthetic appreciation for trust or the safety of familiarity.

Ever so softly, Genny turned the brass door knob and slid the door open a hair's breadth. An astonishing sight met her eye as she pressed up against the narrow opening. Her handsome Indian lay on his back on the sofa, three candles behind him on the occasional table, a book balanced in his left hand. On his naked chest sat a saucer. Genny watched him dip his right forefinger to the plate, then lift it to his lips. His tongue snaked out to capture a drop of something before his lips closed over his finger to suck it clean. Unconsciously, Genny held her breath while he repeated the process, an unaccustomed heaviness settling low in her stomach. Her own lips dropped open in sensual fascination.

Jam, she thought. He's gotten into the jam.

He paused to turn the page, then dipped into the saucer once more. Genny watched him lick his finger clean twice more before rational thought intruded with the force of a fully stoked steam locomotive.

The lying bastard! He was reading!

Chapter 2

Gus Renard couldn't believe his luck. Miss Eugenia Stone, the unlikeliest settler he'd seen yet, had a small bookcase crammed full of recent novels and the latest periodicals. He'd seen it the instant he walked into her house, tucked away in the corner between the sofa and an olive green armchair. Whatever the hell the well-educated, obviously well-fixed Miss Stone was doing set up in her nicely appointed cottage in the middle of Indian country, he hadn't the faintest idea, but he meant to take advantage of her library. After the girl retired, reluctantly leaving Walks in Thunder and himself to work out their sleeping arrangements in her guest room, with a single narrow daybed amidst a clutter of easels, paints, and canvas, Gus slipped back into the sitting room. The thick wool carpet, patterned with pink and yellow roses and green leaves on a wine-colored background, was soft enough to sleep on by itself, but he lay down on the brown velvet upholstered sofa to catch a few hours sleep.

When Gus woke up shortly after midnight, he lit three tapers, and settled down with the periodicals, most of them women's publications. When he'd looked at all the fashion drawings and read articles on transplanting tulip bulbs, the importance of writing uplifting letters to the brave young men fighting against the Southern Confederacy, and how to launder stains ranging from blood to blackberries, he reached for the Dickens novel that had caught his eye during supper. *Great Expectations* had

21

been published three years before, but he hadn't read it
yet. After raiding Eugenia Stone's pantry, helping himself to a fistful of raisins and a saucerful of strawberry
jam, he stretched out on the sofa again for a good read.
Grinning, Gus remembered nights he'd stayed up as a
boy, reading until dawn. A comfortable familiarity settled over him as he dipped his finger in the jam and
commenced to share Philip Pirrin's adventures.

Within minutes Joe Gargery was warning Pip that his
sister, Mrs. Joe, was on the rampage, looking for him
with Tickler, a willow switch.

Suddenly the book was ripped from his hands and flung
across the room, where it hit the cupboard before dropping to the floor. Reacting from long years of training,
Gus leapt to his feet. The saucer of jam catapulted off
his bare chest and bounced off the bosom of the angry
woman in front of him. It fell to the carpet and rolled
under the sofa.

"Oh!" Eugenia Stone blustered, pulling her nightgown away from her chest with one hand. She glanced
at the jam streak across her front, then raised her other
fist and shook it. Clasped in her hand was a small dagger.

Gus reared back. Instinctively his left hand shot out,
clamping hard around her wrist. He squeezed until the
blade fell to the floor. Miss Stone stared at his fingers,
wrapped painfully around her wrist, then at the dagger
on the flowered carpet. Her lips parted in shock, and her
eyes flew to the Indian's. Their eyes locked in furious
outrage. Genny found her tongue first.

"You're hurting me!" she shouted, jerking her arm
away from the Indian. He didn't let go. "And you speak
English! You despicable liar!"

"That's right, I do. And I hurt people who pull knives
on me. Why did you do that?" he demanded, forcing
Genny onto the defensive. He pressed his attack. "Did
I scare you, lying flat on my back with a book in my
hand? Pretty savage, wasn't it?"

"Just shut up and let go of me!" Genny ordered,
unable to sort her chaotic thoughts fast enough to voice
them.

"When you tell me why you came at me with the knife," the Indian insisted. He leaned closer in an attempt to frighten her.

"I heard a noise and saw the light under my door, so I picked up my dagger. What was I supposed to do? Roll over and go back to sleep? I was so startled when I saw you reading, I forgot I had it."

His fingers eased on her wrist, but he didn't let go.

"You were willing to use that knife on me?" His eyes flashed with sudden anger.

"Yes, I was!" she snapped. "Let go, now!"

"Do you know what would happen to you if I wanted to hurt you, Miss Stone? Do you think that puny blade would stop me, or anyone else?"

"Don't underestimate me, whoever you are," Genny replied with soft certainty. "I can stop anyone I want to."

He laughed. "So stop me now," he drawled, pulling her close against him.

His arms wound around her, pinning her arms and pressing her jam-stained nightgown against his chest. Genny caught her breath in shock as her breasts flattened against him. He was hard and warm, and his breath fanned her cheek as he searched her eyes. The scent of strawberries hung in the air around them. He was far too close for comfort.

She had to get away. Setting her jaw, she pushed at his chest while she groped for her dagger with her right foot.

"You smug bastard," she gritted under her breath. She tried to twist out of the embrace, but succeeded only in eliciting the rakish grin she'd seen earlier. "I suppose you think I don't want you to stop, don't you?"

He settled her a little closer, still grinning. "Your words, not mine, *istatola*. I guess your criticism of my manners at supper was just for show."

She grasped the narrow-handled dagger precariously between her toes. "Don't bet on it."

Genny brought the blade down on the Indian's foot as hard as she could, given her feeble grip.

With a howl, he released her and collapsed onto the sofa. As he went down, his leg tangled in Genny's nightgown. When she tried to back away, she tripped. Scrambling to her feet, her knee came in sharp contact with the point of the dagger where it had fallen.

"Ouch!" she winced, grabbing for the blade. When she had it firmly in hand, she retreated to an armchair and sat.

"Serves you right, you accursed little devil," the Indian said, examining the bleeding slash on the top of his foot.

Genny hauled her nightgown up to look at the stinging nick on her kneecap. Blood streamed down her calf. She pressed her fingers against the cut to stanch the flow. When she looked up, the Indian was gazing at her legs and ankles.

"Will you stop looking at me that way?" she snapped, tucking one leg beneath her and arranging her gown more modestly.

"Probably not. Old habits die hard," he said easily. "Don't take it personally. I always look at women this way."

"Why? Do you enjoy being rude?"

"No, I enjoy looking at women. I take it you don't approve." He absently rubbed his foot.

"Not particularly," Genny replied. "Do you have a name?"

"Several of them." He leaned back into the sofa, dropping his injured foot on his opposite knee. "Do you have some soap and a bandage? I don't want to get an infection in this little cut."

"That 'little' cut effectively halted your demonstration of my vulnerability, didn't it, Mister . . . ?" She waited for him to supply a name.

"Mister to an Indian. My, my. Such formality."

"All right, have it your way. The soap's over there." She pointed to the kitchen. "Why did you pretend you didn't speak English?"

"Indians alone on the prairies have to be careful. White people can be pretty dangerous."

"Why, of all the ridiculous notions . . . !" Genny began.

The Indian cut her off. "You don't think so? Do you have any menfolk around?"

She nodded.

"Who?"

"My cousin, Paul Conrad."

He shot her a piercing look. "Conrad's your cousin? As in Conrad and Crofts Freighting?" She nodded again. "Where is he?"

"Somewhere along the Platte. Do you know Paul?"

"I know who he is. What do you think he'd do if he walked in here right now?" the Indian demanded.

"He'd probably shoot you," Genny answered, though she doubted Paul would do anything beyond laughing and telling her he'd warned her she was in over her head.

"Exactly, Miss Stone. White people are dangerous. Predictably so."

Genny didn't care to argue his logic, so she flounced from her chair and limped to the kitchen. She rummaged around for a towel and some clean rags, then ladled warm water from the stove reservoir into a basin.

By the time she'd gathered a washcloth, soap, and the rags for a bandage, the Indian had moved to the table. She carried the bowl over to him.

He took it from her and set it on the table. They looked at each other in grudging silence until another unholy grin blossomed on the Indian's handsome face.

"I'll tell you my name and how I came to be educated, if you'll tend my foot and clean the jam off me, Miss Stone," he purred.

Genny snatched the clean towel off her shoulder and threw it to the table, pivoting away from the Indian. He grabbed her nightgown and hauled her back.

"Hey, hey, hey, come on, now. I'm really quite harmless," he insisted, settling a hand in the middle of her back in a soothing pat. She shrugged him off, not believing that for a second. "Come on, Eugenia Stone, I know you're curious about me." He handed her the washcloth.

Genny took it reluctantly. "This is extremely improper," she intoned righteously. "Not to mention stupid."

Instead of arguing, he guided her hand to the basin, dipped it into the lukewarm water, then brought it back to his chest.

Genny resisted, frowning mightily, but he pulled her hand toward him until he had it trapped against his breastbone. Then he began moving it in small circles, his large hand warm and damp over her own, his hairless chest hard and smooth beneath the cloth. Slowly, Genny began to ply the cloth herself, washing the sticky sheen of jam from his bronzed skin.

"Auguste René Renard, at your service, mademoiselle," he said softly, releasing her hand. "You can call me Gus."

"You're French?" she asked in surprise, stilling the cloth.

He gave her hand a nudge and she resumed washing.

"My father's Canadian. My mother was Sicanġu, or Brulé Sioux," he answered.

"Where did you grow up?" Genny rinsed the cloth and wrung it over the basin.

He didn't answer until she hesitantly touched it to his chest again. Honestly, she thought, how had she allowed him to talk her into such reckless behavior?

"I lived with my mother's people until she died. I was five. My father took me with him to Montréal then, and I stayed there until I was about twelve. Then I came home."

She had the feeling he'd left a lot unsaid.

"Did you go to school in Montréal?" Her hand feathered over a dark nipple and she felt it tighten beneath the cloth. When he sucked in his breath in obvious pleasure, Genny moved her hand away quickly.

"I went to school for a year. Mostly I had tutors. That's how I learned English," he explained. "The tutors were always Americans. My father likes Americans. He admires their morals." His voice was as warm and smooth as his dark skin.

"And did you learn any?" Genny arched her brows doubtfully.

He watched her hand slide across his stomach. "Any what?" he asked belatedly.

"Morals."

"I learned what they were."

Her hand stopped. "But not how to practice them, I take it."

He looked at her face, his eyes coming to rest on her mouth. "I have my own code of ethics. I make my own rules."

"Doesn't everybody out here?"

"Only the strong, Eugenia Stone. Only the strong." He touched a finger to her lower lip.

She backed away abruptly. "Stop that," she ordered.

She rinsed the cloth again, then used it to swab at the jam on her gown. Auguste Renard watched her in silence. Horrified, she felt her nipples contract as the damp fabric brushed against her breasts. When she dropped her nightgown, he would see them and think . . . Oh, God, what was she doing in the middle of the night with a strange man, a mixed-blood, nearly naked Indian, and without even a dressing gown on? It was every bit as brazen as undressing Lt. Mercer. And far more disturbing.

"I'll . . . uh, I'll get clean water for your foot," she stammered, turning away from him. "Keep talking."

"What else do you want to know?"

"Well, what do you do?" she asked, groping for any question to keep him talking while she refilled the basin.

"Not much. What do you do?"

Genny returned, holding the basin defensively before her. "I'm an artist. I plan to open an art academy as soon as I return to Philadelphia." She set the bowl on the floor and crouched before Monsieur Renard. "May I have your foot?"

"You can have any part of me you want." He grinned. Miss Stone scowled fiercely at him. "All right, I'll mind my tongue. You grew up in Philadelphia?"

She nodded, stroking the wet cloth over his foot. "I didn't realize I had a strong enough grip with my foot to actually cut you. I intended only to prick you hard.''

Gus stifled the off-color pun that rose to mind, contenting himself with a cheeky grin. "What are you doing out here, Miss Stone?"

"What?" His grin made her frown. "In Nebraska?" He nodded. "That's a long story," she hedged. She dried his foot, then began wrapping a bandage around it. His toes were brown and square, the nails neatly trimmed. "I have a wager with my cousin that I can live out here for a year. If I win, he'll provide the backing for my art school."

"Sounds like a foolhardy undertaking to me. Why do you need your cousin's money? This place looks like you've got plenty of your own."

"My father has plenty," she clarified, "but he won't release any for my school until at least two years after the war is over. He has it in his head that I'll marry and forget about the art academy," she said, tying off the bandage.

"So you're the headstrong, impatient type," Gus concluded. "Why doesn't that surprise me?"

Genny didn't respond to that. She put her hands to her thighs and pushed to her feet. "Repairs completed, Monsieur Renard. I bid you good night."

"Not so fast, Miss Stone," Gus chuckled, pulling her arm back and settling his hands at her waist. He stood, then boosted Genny up onto the table so fast she didn't have time to protest. "There's still your own injury to see to. Lift your hem."

"I certainly will not!" she gasped, too startled to jump down.

When she didn't comply, Gus pushed the white cambric up past her knee, anchoring it with a tuck under her thigh. "Why of all the . . . !" Genny sputtered, pushing at his hands. "Monsieur Renard, I insist that you . . ."

"Nice accent, but call me Gus, *ištatola*," he said, cutting her off as he batted her hands aside. "This is pretty deep." He ran his thumb over her knee, sending gooseflesh up her leg. He noticed, and grinned again. Genny looked away into the shadows beyond his shoulder. "You'll have to keep an eye on it for a few days."

"Stop calling me that, whatever it is. My name is Genny. I have an aunt named Augusta, you know," she informed him darkly. "There must be something about that name that renders its bearers, male and female, impervious to other people's wishes."

"Gives you a hard time, Aunt Augusta does?" Gus ran the wet washcloth over Genny's knee, scrubbing gently at the drying blood. "So that's where you got so back-talky."

"Oh, hush! You never told me what you do," she said, curious in spite of herself.

Gus caressed the back of her calf with the damp cloth. There was no other word for it. The unrepentant flirt was caressing her leg!

"I'm an Indian, *ištatowin*. I don't work in a bank, drive freight wagons, teach school, or preach the gospel. What do you think I do?" The cloth stroked her ankle gently, while his thumb rubbed her heel.

Genny stared at the dark head bent over her foot. "I suppose you hunt a lot," she guessed, her mind only marginally on the conversation. She couldn't fathom what he was doing to make her enjoy his touch so much. "Mmmhmmm." He worked the cloth back up her leg.

"And I suppose you fight a lot," she said, thinking of the lurid stories she'd read about Indian wars in the newspapers. Gus's hands stilled for a moment.

"Sorry to disappoint you, Genny Stone, but I'm no warrior," he said tautly.

He dropped the cloth into the bowl, then ran both hands up Genny's legs to rest behind her knees. The angry light in his eyes disintegrated into a mischievous twinkle.

"But we do lots of other things you might be interested in." He squeezed her calves and Genny's blue eyes widened. "In fact, maybe you'd better lock your bedroom door tonight unless you want to find out a whole lot more about those very things."

Genny was off the table and through her door in no time flat, slamming it hard. Gus heard the lock turn, and something that sounded suspiciously like "burn and be damned, you good-for-nothing flirt."

He laughed as he stooped to retrieve the copy of *Great Expectations*. Miss Stone had him pegged just about right, he thought. He'd burn, all right, thinking about her soft skin and wideset blue eyes, and he'd known for long years that the rest of her epithet was nothing less than God's own truth. He was without a doubt damned, and a more worthless half-breed flirt had never been spawned.

At dawn Walks In Thunder still slept soundly in the guest room, and all was silent behind Eugenia Stone's locked door. Gus rummaged through a flowered cloisonné box atop the bookshelf, extracting a long hatpin. He picked up the note he'd written and crossed the room to Eugenia's door where he inserted the pin into the keyhole, deftly catching the lock and releasing it. He swung the door open and stepped inside.

The room was shadowy in the dim light seeping through the open window, but the polished steel blade of Genny's small dagger glinted from the bedside table. Gus picked it up, and anger surged through him as he felt the cool ebony and silver etched handle against his palm. He rounded the bed and stared at the sleeping woman. She lay curled on her side, one arm cradling her middle, the other hand tucked under her cheek. So innocent and peaceful, so safe and trusting. His anger grew. She shouldn't be so trusting. Didn't she know he could hurt her? That she was vulnerable? That for all she knew he might be a man of violence? What if he let loose the part of him that taunted him to show her what a fool she was?

Still clasping the dagger, Gus gave in to temptation and lowered himself onto the bed beside her. Lightly, his hand quivering with restraint, he ran the point of the blade down her shoulder and across her forearm, just below her breasts.

The demons Gus normally held in tight check raced within him; his muscles twitched with his effort to control the violence inside. He both did and didn't want to hurt Eugenia Stone. She was beautiful, she'd been more hospitable than most white women would have been, and she was attracted to him. As he was to her.

And that, he knew, was the problem.

The tiny dagger clenched in his fist represented all the limits society set for him and those he'd set for himself as the result of his parentage. It had been a long time since he'd lost control and given in to the rage that rocked through him now, pushing him toward actions he didn't want to take.

Gus wanted to wake her with a warm kiss upon her sleep-softened mouth. Instead he laid his hand on her hair where it spilled across the pillow, rubbing the fine strands between his fingers. He breathed in her fragrance, flowery and faint, and watched her breasts rise with her slow, even breath.

He wanted to undress her and see her pale flesh naked before him. He wanted to touch her, to make her cry out in passion. He wanted to make her want him, need him with a throbbing, all-consuming, and blinding desire that cast aside all doubts and scruples.

Instead he fought his anger. He willed his body to relax, hard flesh to soften, rapid breath to slow.

Rolling onto his back, Gus gazed sightlessly at the ceiling as his emotions ebbed. He was shocked at the intensity of his desire and his anger. He thought he'd mastered these feelings years ago.

A minute later he rose and removed the beaded knife case his sister had made him from his belt. He slid the dagger inside it and placed it on the pillow. Remembering the note he'd written, he picked it up off the floor and slid it under the knife.

Then he left the room and Eugenia Stone without a backward glance.

Genny awakened slowly. An early morning breeze washed over her, bearing the sweet scent of grass and sage. She opened her eyes to watch her lacy curtains billow with the gentle rush of air. Yawning, she stretched her arms out straight, then let them flop back on the bed.

Her left hand connected with a solid object on the pillow next to hers. There, atop a folded piece of her stationery, rested her dagger, encased in a beaded knife sheath.

Genny jumped out of bed as if she'd been bitten by a rattler. The door she'd locked in the dark of night stood wide open. Why, that degenerate! How dared he enter her room! Genny started through the door, remembered her robe and went back for it, then sailed into the kitchen, thrusting her arms through the sleeves.

The Indians were gone. The door to the guest room stood open, and upon investigation, Genny found a damp towel neatly hung over the back of a chair. The washbasin had been rinsed, and a stack of blankets lay folded on the daybed.

She marched back to her own room, and snatched up the note beneath her dagger. Unfolding it, she read its contents quickly.

Dear Miss Stone,

Thank you for your hospitality, and especially for your excellent jam. I took two jars. And some raisins.

It isn't safe for you to stay here. There will be hostilities in the Platte Valley before the summer is over. Go to Rivier's Ranch. Then have your cousin take you to one of the army posts as soon as possible. And keep your dagger handy. You ought to learn to handle that rifle over the door, as well.

I hope we meet again someday, so I can return your book. I took it with me. Regretfully, I have a weakness for stories that begin with rampaging women.

                                        Auguste Renard

Of all the cheek! Stealing her book and her food, then telling her to leave, learn how to take care of herself, and implying that she indulged in rampages! Genny thought angrily that she'd love to show him just exactly what she could do with that rifle over the door. She'd go see Martha, all right, but she wasn't leaving White Rock Spring, not because some cocky, overeducated half-breed said so.

Scowling, Genny glanced at her dagger in its new case. The sheath was pretty, she admitted grudgingly, with a beaded blue and red geometric design on a white background. Though it was too big for Genny's small knife, at least Gus had left something in exchange for the things he'd taken. She reached for her knife, stopping suddenly.

There on her pillow, as plain as day, was the shallow indentation of another head.

"Oh, my heavens!" Genny whispered, snatching up the pillow to eradicate the damning evidence that Gus Renard had lain in her bed. She pressed her burning cheek against it, mortified beyond measure. When she caught the faint scent of strawberry jam and smoky leather, she hurled the pillow across the room. It sailed right out the open window, landing with a soft plop in the mud outside.

The gall of the man! He'd lain beside her on her bed while she slept! She hadn't thought it possible, but he was worse than Lt. Mercer!

And what was wrong with her, for pity's sake, that hovering beneath her scandalized indignation swam a tremor of illicit excitement. All too easily she conjured up the image of Gus Renard in her bed, his long hair dark against the white linen of her pillow slips, and his hand gliding up her calf as it had done last night. It was a far from horrifying picture. Lord help her, that realization simply didn't bear examination.

Flopping back onto the bed, Genny had only one clear thought: Thank heaven, Aunt Augusta is in Philadelphia!

Chapter 3

Martha Rivier looked up from her churning when she heard her name called from across the expanse of struggling buffalo grass that spread between her squat adobe house and the ramshackle corral that was home to a sorry collection of trail-weary mules and oxen. She raised her hand to wave at the slight figure walking toward her with the huge black mare in tow.

As usual, Genny Stone was smiling. Martha wondered how the girl could look so happy and carefree; there certainly wasn't much to smile about out at the place Genny called White Rock Spring. Paul Conrad had no conscience whatsoever in leaving his inexperienced cousin out there alone, and what were the girl's other relatives thinking to let him do it? What was wrong with them? No Indians Martha knew, not her own Cheyenne relatives, nor any of the Sioux, Arapaho, or even their Pawnee enemies would treat a woman so.

"Hello!" Genny called again, leading Trixie into the shade near the porch where Martha worked. "How's Lillian doing?"

Lillian was the cow Paul had bought with Genny's father's money, leaving her at the Rivier's since Genny didn't know the first thing about cows. She had her hands full with the half-dozen hens Paul had left her.

"She's fine, Genny Stone. Roger got me a dried calf's stomach for rennet over at Julesburg, so I can make cheese for you now," Martha said over the thump of the butter churn. "We should be able to sell whatever you don't want."

"That's good. I brought four eggs for you. Those hens aren't laying too well, yet. I must be doing something wrong," Genny said, tying Trixie's reins around one of the posts supporting the porch roof. She stepped up into the deep shade with a sigh of relief. "It's nice to get out of the sun. It's hot!"

"You ought to get a horse you can ride," Martha advised, tucking a loose strand of dark hair behind her ear. "Walking six miles in the heat of the day is crazy, Genny Stone."

"I know," Genny agreed with another sigh, "but I like Trixie. I'm sure it's only a matter of time before she'll let me ride her."

"That horse does what she wants, and she wants to run like a wild thing or be led around like a prize greyhound. Roger can get you a better mount if you ask him, although the traffic over on the main trail's down to a trickle. There's not much to choose from right now." Martha stopped churning to wipe her brow on a handkerchief she pulled from her cuff. "I worry about you out there alone. Word came in yesterday that the army's restricting travel on the trail. Only parties with at least a hundred armed men are being allowed through. The Sioux are headed home from Fort Cottonwood and their latest parlay with the bluecoats. It went as badly as the first two did, and my Cheyenne cousins tell me nothing will keep the young men off the warpath. My cousins can keep their people away from you, Genny Stone, but there are too many Sioux." She resumed churning, thumping the paddle a little harder than necessary.

Genny watched her in silence. "That's why I came to see you. A couple of Sioux stopped by my place yesterday," she finally said.

"Do you know who they were?" Martha asked, looking up again. Concern drew her generous lips into a taut line.

"A big man named Walks in Thunder and a mixed-

blood called Auguste Renard,'' Genny answered, taking
a seat on the steps.

"Aahhh. Monsieur Renard,'' Martha said, relaxing.
"So that's why you're here, Genny Stone. He's a handsome man, isn't he, half-breed or not?''

"I don't hold his Indian blood against him any more
than I hold yours against you, Martha, but handsome is
as handsome does. In which case he leaves a lot to be
desired,'' Genny replied, unwilling to admit any attraction to Gus Renard.

"Most women wouldn't think so.''

"Be that as it may. Do you know him well?'' Genny
asked, unable to resist her curiosity.

"Not well, but he stops sometimes to talk to Roger
and sell a horse. He brings good horses and he can ride
anything he can saddle.''

"I should have given him Trixie,'' Genny said, watching the mare stamp flies from her hooves.

Martha looked disparagingly at the black horse. "Even
Renard might have trouble with that one.''

"He told me his father is Canadian. Is he a trader?''
Genny asked.

"He was, long ago, but now he lives in the east. Gus
doesn't say much about that side of his family.''

"Haven't you ever asked?''

Martha didn't look up from the churn. "I don't need
to ask, Genny Stone. My father's family in St. Louis
pretends his half-Indian daughter doesn't exist. When
Renard doesn't speak of his past, I respect his silence.''

"I'm sorry, Martha,'' Genny apologized.

"I know that, Genny. You don't understand yet how
it is here. A single drop of Indian blood makes a man a
savage. It isn't as hard for mixed-blood women if we
have men to take care of us. My mother's people treat
me as one of their own, and except for the four years I
spent at the convent school in St. Louis, I've been happy.
My husband is good to me, and my cousins care for me
as they do their sisters. I manage to fit between Roger's
and my father's white worlds and my mother's Cheyenne
world without too much fuss. It's harder for a man,

though, to be caught between Indian and white ways. Especially when he's educated, like Renard.'' Martha paused and frowned. ''You should be careful if you see him again. Sometimes he . . .'' she trailed off, shrugging.

''You mean he's a ladies' man?'' Genny'd known that the instant she set eyes on the man.

''He is, but that isn't what I meant. He's restless. Unsettled. Be careful of him.''

''I'm always careful of overly handsome, arrogant rogues,'' Genny assured her, but she was surprised by Martha's warning.

''Did he kiss you, Genny Stone?'' Martha asked, with the barest hint of a smile.

Color climbed from Genny's neck to her hairline. ''He most certainly did not, though he had atrocious manners. He stole my jam, my raisins, and a book I was planning to read. Then he left me a note telling me to leave because there was going to be trouble before the summer was over.''

She wasn't saying a word about his visit to her bedroom.

Martha's slight smile disappeared as she looked back down at her churn. ''He's right. I'm surprised he took the trouble to warn you.''

''Why?''

''Gus Renard has been heard to say that any settler caught between the Indians and the army is only receiving his due,'' Martha said softly.

''Oh.'' Genny acknowledged a certain truth in his sentiment. ''I'm not really a settler, though. I'm going back after a year's up.''

''How would anyone know?''

''I told him. Nevertheless, I'm staying at White Rock Spring. There's a lot at stake. Besides, I can take care of myself.''

''How did you handle Gus Renard?'' Martha asked, her coffee-brown eyes serious.

''Well, he didn't kiss me, though I think he might have been considering it,'' Genny confided, smiling. ''I stopped him most effectively with my little dagger.''

Martha laughed. "Genny Stone, do you really think you would have stopped a man as big and as smart as Gus Renard if he wasn't willing to let you stop him?"

Genny shifted uncomfortably. The same thought had occurred to her on her walk in to the ranch.

"Let me tell you something," Martha continued, her tone suddenly harsh. "Gus is easy. He speaks English, he's educated, and he knows as much about white ways as you do. What's more, for all his big talk and wandering hands, he leaves white women alone unless their favors are for sale. Flirting with Gus Renard isn't the same thing as facing a war party of young men who've watched their families slaughtered by the bluecoats. Men who have hunted in vain for meat to feed their starving children and old people won't be stopped by your little dagger, and they won't respect you enough to keep their hands to themselves before they kill you. Genny Stone, you risk your life to stay at White Rock Spring. This isn't your father's parlor, where you can make light of danger and live to laugh about it tomorrow. Take Renard's warning seriously. He knows what he's talking about."

The color drained from Genny's face. "But Martha, how can I leave?" Genny whispered. "What about my art academy?"

"Dreams die when we do," Martha pointed out with cold realism. "Don't base your decision to stay on saving your pride in front of that worthless cousin of yours. He doesn't deserve it." She let the handle of the churn go. Her voice was softer when she spoke again. "Come now and help me. Grab one side of this thing and help me get it inside. We'll have a cup of buttermilk, then we'll wash and salt the butter. If I don't miss my guess, you're out of butter after a visit from Gus Renard."

"And jam," Genny added in a subdued voice.

"I'll send a little butter home with you tonight, but you should decide soon what to do. I wouldn't wait longer than a week."

"You're right, Martha. I know you are, but I hate to leave."

"Only out of pride. You're not happy here."

Genny gazed out at the drab hills and hanging dust that hid her house from view. "I'm bored."

"And lonely," Martha added.

"Yes," Genny agreed. So lonely that even a rake like Gus Renard seemed attractive.

"Come help me, Genny Stone. Busy hands relieve many burdens," Martha said, grasping one side of the heavy churn. "Come."

Genny left the small collection of dusty ranch buildings early that evening, fully intending to pack a few dresses and necessaries and return to the ranch the next day. When morning came, however, the day was uncommonly clear. The air was still, the dust had settled, and light pulsed and shone on the buttes and in the shimmering cottonwoods. Genny took her easel, watercolors, and brushes out onto the hills, along with a canteen of water, some bread and cheese, her dagger, and her carbine. That evening she returned for a supper of boiled eggs and crackers, then sat on the porch with her sketchpad, drawing until the light faded. Ideas and memories demanded expression, and for the first time since Paul had settled her at White Rock Spring, Genny felt she was accomplishing something.

The next morning, working from her sketches, she began a more ambitious painting than she had ever attempted from memory. She worked in her yard—if the expanse of trampled prairie could be called that—gradually recreating the image of two Sioux Indians lounging against her porch rail.

The oil painting took three days to finish, and even then Genny wasn't satisfied with it. The men's faces, as interpreted through her brush, seemed flat, lacking in emotion and complexity. Unable to determine what was missing, Genny put the canvas away on the fourth day. She turned her attention back to her watercolors, a medium for which she had greater affinity. By the end of the day, she had several small paintings she was happy with, including one of a plump feather pillow resting on the rain dampened grass outside her bedroom window.

The days passed. Every evening Genny told herself she would go to Rivier's the next morning, but when dawn came, White Rock Spring was quiet and peaceful. It seemed impossible that there was any threat in staying long enough to finish just a few more canvases.

So as July passed into August, Genny Stone remained at White Rock Spring.

Gus Renard frowned down at the plain of the Platte Valley from a low bluff on the north side of the river. After leaving the Platte Valley with Walks in Thunder ten days past, he'd returned to his Lakota camp up along the Smoky Earth River. Over the course of the week he'd been there, small groups of men had steadily ridden off without comment. Gus didn't need anyone to tell him what was happening. Trouble had been in the offing for months; the Lakota and their Cheyenne and Arapaho allies had had enough of the *wasicus* traveling through their lands. With more and more of the whites from the east building ranches and homesteads in Indian country, the Indians were ready to strike back.

Looking out at the deserted valley, Gus knew something was wrong. It was a fine, clear day but there was no traffic along the trail. An ominous smudge of grey smoke hovered in the southeast. He was thirty miles east of the forks of the Platte and the new army fort at Cottonwood Canyon on the south side of the river there. As he watched, a cloud of rising dust appeared over the hills north of the valley. Gus's dun gelding turned his nose into the wind and pricked up his oversized ears.

"What is it, Harv?" Gus murmured, straining to see what was causing the dust. Harv, the big horse Gus had bought from a secesh pilgrim from Tennessee, leaned into the wind and arched his neck. "Let's go see, you ugly old mule," he said, shaking the reins and guiding Harv into a gallop across the low hills.

In a few minutes the dusty cloud sorted itself into a stampeding herd of the large, highly valued American horses used by the Overland Stage Company. The racing animals were wild-eyed and flecked with foam and dust. Straggling along in their wake rode a lone Indian on a flagging red and white pinto. There were at least twenty horses in the herd, and Gus's eyes snapped with anticipation as he estimated their worth.

"Serendipity, Harv," he breathed as he bent low over the gelding's neck, urging him to a faster pace. "Sweet serendipity." Harv obliged eagerly, hurtling toward the other horses.

Gus signalled the other rider with a raised hand. When the man responded with a wave, Gus pointed to the north, toward a box canyon, and turned Harv onto a course that would drive the herd through the break in the bluffs. The other rider waved and gave a piercing cry, faint across the distance.

"Okay, Harv, let's get 'em," Gus shouted.

His blood surged through his veins as they approached the lead horse, a powerful bay stallion. Gus shouted and yipped and yowled for all he was worth. He waved his hat and screamed, and when the bay turned, veering into the canyon, he bellowed triumphantly. He followed the herd a distance into the box, then rode back to guard the narrow entrance.

The other rider was waiting for him. Gus recognized him as a Sicangu, one of his sister's husband's relatives, a young man named Afraid of Hawk. They greeted each other with satisfied grins.

"A good chase, *tanhan*," Afraid of Hawk said. "I was losing them when you showed up."

Gus nodded, panting. "They'll run themselves out in the canyon, but they won't get out. We can round them up after they settle down. Where'd they come from?" He unstoppered his water bag and took a long drink.

"The stage station down by Plum Creek." The younger man drank from his own water skin. "We attacked right as the stage horses were being unhitched and the ranch hands were bringing the fresh ones out of the corral. Broken Nose got inside the fence and chased all the other horses out behind them, so we got them all. A good morning's work, eh, *tanhan*?" Afraid of Hawk's dark eyes shone with pride and excitement.

Gus lowered his water skin. "Attacked? You attacked a stage station?" An uneasy feeling skittered through his chest.

"Mmm," Afraid of Hawk grunted, nodding as he drank. A trickle of water slid down his chin and across his chest. "Broken Nose and I joined up with some Shahiyela. I wanted the horses so I don't know what happened after I took off after them. Last night White Tail and some others told me there were attacks planned for the length of the stage road and on the Blue River, along the road the *wašicus* take to the Missouri. It's about time we did something to show these *wašicus* that they can't take everything they want. We've had enough."

"I know," Gus agreed, but the sick feeling grew inside him. "They aren't content to pass through. They're staying in our country now, taking it piece by piece."

Afraid of Hawk nodded. "Today we're taking a few pieces back. Starting with some fine American horses." He grinned.

Gus expelled a breath. "How far west were the attacks planned for? As far as Julesburg? Fort Laramie?" He'd known this was coming, but not when. It bothered him that no one had told him, even if it was generally known he wouldn't participate.

The younger man answered quickly. "The whole trail, I heard."

Gus thought about the white people he knew along the nearly deserted trail through the North Platte valley. They were his people too, even though he usually thought of himself as Lakota. The knot in his chest tightened as he envisioned the destruction that might be waiting when he rode back west along the river. Most folks knew trouble had been brewing all spring and summer and would have gotten safely to one of the army encampments. He hoped Paul Conrad's pretty cousin had taken his advice and gotten herself to one of the forts.

"Well, how are we going to divide up these horses? I saw a gray one I know I want. What about you, cousin?'' Gus asked, determined not to dwell on the consequences of the day's attacks.

"They would have gotten away from me without your help. You take the first picks, but if you want to let me choose, I won't argue,'' Afraid of Hawk told him. "Now, I liked the looks of that bay. That's one good-looking animal.''

"Good choice,'' Gus nodded approvingly. He grinned at his young cousin conspiratorially. "He'd make a big impression on a family with a pretty daughter.''

Afraid of Hawk grinned back at Gus.

An hour later a portion of Afraid of Hawk's war party rode into the mouth of the box canyon. Along with Broken Nose, a Sicaŋǧu from Afraid of Hawk's camp, there were six Cheyenne warriors. In hopes of finding the horses that had run off, they'd left a larger group of Cheyennes who were headed south. Disappointment ran high when it was discovered that Gus had captured the herd. By rights, most of the horses were his now.

Broken Nose walked to his and Afraid of Hawk's spare horses and unstrapped several heavy packs that had been slung across the Indian ponies' backs. "What's in the packs that's so heavy?'' Gus asked, walking over to help.

"Some of the *wasicus'* yellow metal and their green paper. There was a lot of it on the stage, and the ranch people got excited when I took it, so I thought it must be valuable. It's too heavy, though. I want to get back to camp fast, and the horses can't run carrying so much weight,'' Broken Nose explained.

"Can I look?'' Gus requested, kneeling in the grass beside the discarded canvas packs. Broken Nose assented, then went about tending his horses. Gus opened one of the packs and dumped the contents on the ground.

"Holy shit!'' he exclaimed in English. He reached for the other packs and looked through them, calculating rapidly. There had to be at least twenty thousand dollars in gold and greenbacks in the packs. "I think you got the Overland Stage Company's payroll. There's a fortune here!''

"Not to the Lakota or the Shahiyela,'' Broken Nose

replied with a burgeoning smile. "Now those horses back
there are pretty nice . . ." he hinted broadly.

"We just might be able to arrange a trade," Gus replied, laughing.

Afraid of Hawk shook his head in disbelief. "Only a
wašiču would trade good horses for a couple of packs of
worthless paper and rock," he proclaimed.

"Bad blood tells every time," Gus agreed ruefully.

Gus pulled the wide brim of his hat low on his forehead, shielding his eyes from the August sun as he walked
north, leading Harv along the narrow creek.

"It's not much further, boy. Then I'll get those heavy
packs off your back and see if we can't find some oats
for lunch," he promised, wondering what in tarnation
he was doing with the Overland Stage Company's payroll
instead of a herd of good horses. He couldn't turn it over
to the army without getting himself hanged, and he
couldn't haul it around with him. It had to be hidden,
and one place had sprung to mind as the ideal cache:
Eugenia Stone's house at White Rock Spring, or, as it
was known to the Lakota, Bad Spirit Creek.

The girl had to be long gone by now, and if she had
any sense at all, she wouldn't be back. Rivier's Ranch
had been deserted when he'd stopped there an hour ago
with Afraid of Hawk and Broken Nose to transfer the
payroll from their spare horses to Harv. The Sičangus
had headed north, away from the trail and the army,
refusing to accompany Gus to Bad Spirit. The place was
widely believed to be haunted by the ghosts of more than
twenty Cheyenne warriors who had been massacred there
by Pawnees a generation ago. Gus grudgingly admired
Paul Conrad's savvy in placing his pretty cousin there.
Under normal circumstances, no Indian would bother her
there. The present hostilities, however, were far from
normal.

Undeterred by superstition, Gus wound his way
through the hills to Genny Stone's place. He'd bury the
payroll in her pantry floor, then take off north to the
summer camps along the White River. It would be pru-

dent to stay away from the Platte Valley for a while, and he needed some time to think about what to do with the stolen payroll.

Genny stared into the gently bubbling water of the spring near her house. It lapped over the white limestone ledge that gave the spring its name, trickling through a bed of sand and pebbles to form a creek that meandered through the prairie bluffs down to the North Platte River. Cottonwoods, willows, ash, box elders, and chokecherries created a small thicket of cool, moist shade. Thick green moss grew over the rocks at the pool's edge, and pretty purple corn flowers still bloomed in the deep shadows. Overhead, a redheaded woodpecker perched high in one of the ash trees, drumming out an erratic rhythm, while blackbirds sang as they feasted on the ripening chokecherries.

The peace and tranquility of the spring left Genny's heart untouched. She was worried. Two days ago, Roger Rivier had ridden out to tell her that Indians had closed the Overland Trail and that he was taking Martha south to Julesburg. He had wanted her to go with them.

Genny still hadn't figured out exactly why she'd refused. It had seemed like giving up to leave, like admitting that Paul was right and she couldn't handle living on her own in Nebraska. There had been Indian troubles along the Platte for years, and people managed. She would, too.

But now, though she rationally doubted anything would happen to her, loneliness and nerves were getting the better of her. At odd moments she found herself uneasily checking over her shoulder, and she imagined all sorts of dramatic scenarios in which angry war parties of hostile Indians figured prominently. She'd never realized how much she relied on the Rivier's presence over the hills to assuage her sense of isolation and exposure. With them gone, she didn't feel safe.

Her stomach grumbled, reminding her that she hadn't eaten that morning, and that it was well past midday. Genny rose from the thick grass and waded through the bushes, scattering the indignant birds as she went.

When she came in sight of the house, she stopped dead in her tracks. A familiar dun-colored horse stood tethered to her porch rail.

Gus grunted as he swiveled an unopened barrel of flour back into place over the uneven spot where he'd buried the Overland Stage Company's payroll. It ought to be perfectly safe in the earthen floor of Eugenia Stone's pantry until he could figure a way to return it without getting himself hung for armed robbery and murder. *If* he decided to return the gold.

An idea had taken shape as he'd walked in from Rivier's. Long years ago, when he'd run away from his father's home in Montréal, Gus had spent a night with a young Irish Catholic priest in Chicago. Father Gilpin had hauled Gus in off the street, cleaned his hands and face, and fed him, mistaking him for a street urchin. Gus had been delighted. After a meal of boiled cabbage and potatoes, the priest read to Gus and a sorry congregation of immigrant and orphan boys in the musty basement of the Most Precious Blood parish church.

The experience had impressed Gus deeply, as had his brush with the poor city boys. Having lived on the prairies and in an elegant house in Montréal, he had never seen squalor like that he saw in the lake cities he passed through on his way back to his mother's people. More than the hunger and the filth, the empty faces of boys and girls who had no visions, no knowledge of their relation to the whole of life, and no joy in that knowledge haunted him. They were children without a place, and without family. For a Lakota boy, even one who had lived away from his people for many years, it was a chilling concept.

Father Gilpin had thought Gus was one of those boys, and offered him a place where he was welcome. The priest hadn't known that Gus had plenty of money sewn inside the waistband of his filthy trousers, or that his ragged attire was a disguise to keep his father from finding him.

Gus doubted that Father Gilpin remembered the dirty, mixed-blood orphan he'd claimed to be, but he had never forgotten the kindhearted priest. He'd looked Gilpin up when he'd been in Chicago after his disastrous year in Montréal when he was nineteen, and found him still struggling to care for Chicago's lost boys. From time to time, when Gus had had a good run at the gaming tables, or sold some horses for an especially good price, he'd anonymously sent a little money to the priest.

He wondered what the father could do with the payroll hidden beneath the flour barrel, and he considered *not* turning it over to the authorities.

There wasn't much inducement to give the money and gold back. Broken Nose had told him that all the whites at the Plum Creek station had been killed in the attack two days before, and Gus knew the army well enough to know that walking into a fort with that payroll now would be suicide. Even in six months, there was no guarantee that an Indian showing up with that money wouldn't be swinging from a rope by sundown, no questions asked, no consciences troubled.

Gus settled the barrel firmly into the dirt and rose to his feet, putting the payroll out of his mind for the time being. He brushed his hands on his leather britches and scraped the dirt from beneath his nails as he took stock of Miss Stone's pantry. His eye fell on the tin of raisins he'd dipped into before, and he reached for it. Miss Stone was clearly gone; no food was left out, everything was neat as a pin, and the house had been shut up tight. She'd never miss the raisins, he thought, tucking the tin under one arm and stuffing a handful into his mouth. He snagged a string of dried apples hanging from a nail above the sugar bin on his way out the door.

Elbowing his way into the kitchen, Gus was brought up short.

Miss Eugenia Stone stood before him, her mouth set in a firm line, her eyes narrowed. She held a brand new Spencer repeating carbine, one of the deadliest guns ever made.

And she looked like she was about to use it.

Chapter 4

Gus acted on instinct, loosing his brightest, most devastating, most intimate smile, the one he usually saved for the moments just after he'd divested a woman of her virtue. It was the smile that had saved him in more than a few tricky situations.

It had no effect whatsoever on Eugenia Stone. Her eyes narrowed to slits, and her lips thinned to the point of disappearing.

"What are you doing in my pantry?" she demanded coldly. "Put the raisins on the table. The apples, too." She waved the gun barrel toward the oak table.

Gus complied with her orders, thanking the saints he'd picked up the fruit before leaving the pantry. It was far better to be caught stealing raisins and apples than hiding a stolen twenty-thousand-dollar payroll.

He eyed the rifle Genny held awkwardly before her. Could she really use that thing? Would she? On a man she knew?

Or on a half-breed thief? If she was like most white women in these parts, Gus had his answer.

Like a rush of prairie fire, he felt the anger he'd experienced in her bedroom ten days before rising from his gut. If he'd been white, she'd have lowered the gun by now, dropped it as soon as she recognized him. Filching sweets was no killing offense, and they both knew it. He stood motionless before her, striving for control as his emotions took hold, driving rational thought from his mind. The knowledge that he had to keep her out of the pantry and away from the payroll lodged clearly in his mind, but beyond that, only impressions and feelings registered.

The soft blue of Genny's fashionable dress accented her eyes and her narrow waist, cinched with a wide black satin sash. God, but she was beautiful. He wanted to touch her, and that fueled his anger. What in hell was she doing wearing clothes like that out here in the middle of nowhere? And why in the name of Saints Peter and Paul was she still here? Why was she here at all?

"What are you doing in my house?" she repeated. Her bravado was slipping, though, and the tiny catch in her voice snapped Gus out of his stupor.

He flexed his hands slowly, and his anger flared suddenly in his eyes. "Indulging my sweet tooth," he bit out, his voice soft and menacing. Genny's eyes widened at his tone. "Why are you still here? Bucking for disaster?"

"I live here."

"More likely you'll die here."

Gus lunged, batting the rifle up, then wrenching it from Genny's hands. He tossed it onto the table and whirled her into his arms, pulling her back against his chest. He held her immobile, his arms wrapped like a vise around her rib cage, squeezing the breath out of her.

"Thunderation!" she swore, going limp in his arms.

He felt the tension drain from her body, and it seemed to channel straight into his arms. What was she up to? Why wasn't she fighting him? He gave her a quick shake.

"Aren't you afraid?" he rasped close above her ear.

His breath sent shivers rippling down Genny's neck. He was warm, smelling of dust and horses and sweet raisins. "No," she managed to respond, surprising both of them.

"You ought to be," Gus said grimly.

"I don't like you," she assured him. "But I'm not afraid of you."

"Why not?"

"I don't know. I just know you won't hurt me."

"I don't know how you can know that. I sure as hell don't." He released her abruptly, shoving her away from him.

"You don't have to be rough!" Genny staggered a step before gaining her balance.

Gus shot her a warning look. "You haven't seen anything, yet, darlin.' "

He reached for the Spencer, keeping his eyes on Genny. "Nice piece of work," he noted, lifting it to his shoulder and leveling it at Genny's midsection. "I hear these can shoot seven rounds in a few seconds."

"You wouldn't dare," she breathed, the color draining from her face.

"Oh, yes I would." He fingered the cartridge clip. "I don't know what the hell you're doing out here, or what Roger Rivier was thinking to leave you behind, but I'd be doing you a favor to shoot you clean and quick."

"You're insane." Her heartbeat stopped before racing with an adrenal surge, sparked by the first inkling of real fear she'd felt since she'd discovered his horse outside. This was not the same Gus Renard with whom she'd traded midnight banter a short time ago. Martha had been right; he wasn't stable.

"Not me, *istatola*. You're the one that doesn't seem to care what could happen to you if a war party rode in here. If you're so all-fired set on dying, I'll make it a lot easier for you."

He raised the barrel and aimed at her head.

"This isn't funny, Renard." She pressed her hands into her stomach to still a spasm of unease.

"It's not supposed to be, Eugenia Stone."

They stood in silence for a minute, searching each other's eyes. He had to be bluffing. She was sure of it. Almost.

Then she caught a flash of regret in Gus's dark eyes, and a flutter of panic shuddered through her. With an effort, she thrust the fear away from her. She refused to let him frighten her.

It was a bluff. She turned her back on Renard and started to walk away.

The gun exploded like thunder.

Genny dropped to the floor, curling around herself, head shielded by her arms. The tang of black powder caught in her throat as she struggled for breath. It was a long moment before she realized she hadn't been hit.

Gus stared at the blackened hole in the wall, shocked at what he'd just done. A split second after firing, he wasn't even sure why he'd pulled the trigger. Now what was he supposed to do?

Reluctantly, he realized he was going to have to take Genny Stone with him if he didn't want her to find the payroll. It was the understatement of the decade that she wasn't going to come willingly.

"You aren't hurt," he said flatly, striving to regain control of the situation. "If I'd have meant to hit you, I would have. Get up."

Slowly, Genny relaxed her arms and raised her head. There was a splintered hole in the wall beside the stove, right behind her. Sitting up, she tugged her skirt from underneath her and stared at the scorched powder burn over her left hip.

"You bastard!" she hissed, glaring at Gus. He still held the rifle, and he was still pointing it at her. "Put that down!"

Gus looked away for a second, struggling with his conscience. He was going to have to push her hard. When he caught Genny's eye again, anger flashed hard and bright in his dark eyes.

"Get up," he commanded, advancing on her, the rifle firmly in his right hand.

Genny scooted backwards away from him. "Martha told me you were dangerous, but I didn't believe it."

"Martha's a damn sight smarter than you are, *istatola*. Now give me your hand and get up." He reached his left hand toward her.

Genny backed into her bedroom door.

"Get up!" Gus reached for her arm and jerked her to her feet.

She tried to push away from him, but he crowded her

into the wall. "Now, you just stop this!" Genny pressed her back against the door.

Gus turned her around and motioned toward her door with the rifle. "Open it."

"Oh, no, you don't. This has gone plenty far enough, now . . ."

"That's right, it has! Open the damn door!" he bellowed. "Now!"

Genny turned the knob. Gus pushed the door open and thrust her into the room. When he released her with a little shove, she skittered away to hover by the window.

He leveled the rifle at her again. "All right, *ištatowin*. This is it. You're going to do what I say, or you're going to start losing fingers, one at a time."

"Don't you threaten me, you . . ."

"Arguing will lose you more than a finger. Get over here." His gaze traveled down her body, coming to rest on her hips.

"You're not going to lay a finger on me," Genny warned, inching away from the window.

"When you held the gun, you gave the orders. I've got it now, you do what I say. Quit dawdling and get over here."

Genny reluctantly took four dragging steps and stopped a yard from him.

His dark eyes flickered between her face and her bosom. "Closer," he insisted.

She went rigid when his eyes came to rest on her breasts. He couldn't. Dear God, don't let him do this, she prayed.

"Closer!"

She took a halting half step more. "You shouldn't do this," she said, her voice pitching higher. "My cousin Paul will be incensed when he finds out, and he's . . ."

"Your cousin wouldn't do a blessed thing, and you know it. He's the biggest louse on the Overland Trail," Gus ground out. "Closer."

If Renard wasn't completely devoid of sense, it wasn't any consolation at this point. "Oh. Well, you still shouldn't do this." Her chest felt tight and she wanted to run, but she wasn't so sure anymore that Renard wouldn't hurt her if she did.

"What shouldn't I do? Say what you're thinking, Genny Stone," he taunted. She was definitely scared now, and all it did was make him madder.

"Threaten me. Shoot at me. Manhandle me. Take your pick."

"That isn't what you meant. I've already done those things. Be more specific."

Genny didn't like the predatory glint in his eyes in the least. "Well, you shouldn't try to kiss me, or . . . worse . . ." She broke off, color flooding her face.

He smiled unpleasantly, his teeth white against his skin. "Worse, huh? I would have thought it was better."

"Well, you're a man." Her eyes fixed on the rifle in his hand. "That's how men think."

He raised a mocking eyebrow at her.

"I assume." Oh, Lord, this was no time to blither.

"I've had enough small talk, *ištatola*."

Gus brought the rifle up so that the barrel rested under Genny's chin. His left arm snaked around her, grasping her arm and pinning it against her back. He brought her up against him, the rifle hard and cold between their bodies.

"I'm not going to kiss you. Or worse. Yet. I won't make any promises I can't keep, and we're going to be spending some time together. Who knows what might happen?" Genny tried to pull away, but he held her firmly. "For right now, you're going to listen, and you're going to do what I tell you. Understand?"

Genny nodded once, feeling the cool metal of the rifle press into her chin. Could she believe him?

"Good. I'm taking you with me. Do you know about the attacks along the trail?"

"Yes," she whispered.

Gus stared at her in disbelief. "You knew and you didn't leave?" She shrugged. "God Almighty, you're a fool!"

When she didn't respond with more than a challenging glare, Gus took a deep breath. Genny felt his chest expand beneath her breasts, pressing the rifle more solidly against her.

"You're going to put on your most practical clothes, and pack a saddlebag with whatever necessities will fit. Then we're going to saddle that black horse of yours and we're getting our tails away from that river and any war parties or army camps. And you're not going to give me any trouble, because I'll give you more than you've ever imagined if you do. Any questions?"

"No. Just a statement. I won't go with you."

"I've just been explaining that you don't have a choice."

"But you . . . you aren't . . ." She fumbled for words. "You aren't safe!"

Gus smiled coldly. "Believe me, you'd do well to remember that, and that you gave up your chance to get out of here safely days ago."

"But you . . ."

Gus filled in the words she left unsaid from past experience.

"That's right, *ištatowin*, I'm a half-breed Sioux, and that makes a difference, doesn't it?" he gritted out, jaw clenched.

"The difference is that you just shot a slug into the wall not a foot from where I was standing because I caught you stealing from me! And for the second time, mind you! And you snuck into my room and lay on my bed while I was sleeping! What kind of man behaves that way? I don't care if you're a hippopotamus! You're a criminal, and I can't trust you! You've no regard for decency!"

Gus gave a throaty chuckle. "No, I don't. Not where pretty girls are concerned. For the sake of argument, I'll point out that Paul Conrad isn't well known for his regard for decency, and you followed him all the way from Pennsylvania to this God-forsaken wilderness. And he's been known to permanently borrow more than a little fruit from what looked like an abandoned house. But I'll say it again." He tightened his grip painfully on her arm. "You don't have a choice. You're coming with me."

The angry determination in his eyes left little doubt in Genny's mind that he spoke the truth, but she wouldn't give up. "What about Paul? He'll wonder where I am, and then he'll . . ."

"If he notices you're gone." When Genny started to protest, he shook his head, cutting her off. "I'll leave a note. I'm tired of arguing. We're both going to be a lot happier if you come along with a minimum of fuss."

"Do I have a choice?" she snapped.

"You always have a choice, but some ways are easier than others."

"Oh, shut up! And get this gun away from me if you want me to change clothes!" Genny would never admit that one insane part of her was almost relieved he was taking her away. Gus Renard, even as angry and crazy as he seemed, was a known quantity. He spoke English, even if he looked like an Indian, and almost anything seemed preferable to waiting alone for disaster. "Where are you taking me?"

"North. Away from the fighting." The gun remained in place between them.

There was nothing to the north, not even a trading post. "Into Indian country?"

"Indians head for Indian country."

"Will it be safe?"

"Isn't it a little late for you to start worrying about safety?" He laughed derisively. "Nothing is safe out here, Genny Stone. You ought to have figured that out by now. But as long as you're with me, you'll be as safe as you can be."

"That's such a comforting thought."

"Changed your mind about me?" He raised an eyebrow sardonically.

"Not at all," she said. "I just want to know what to expect."

Gus assessed her for a long moment, his expression grim. Releasing her arm, he pushed her a little away from him.

"You haven't got any idea what to expect. Now get your bags and get packing."

His eyes and the rifle barrel followed her as she opened her wardrobe to pull out a pair of saddlebags. She thought about trying to overpower him, or get hold of her carbine, but the knowing expression in Gus's dark eyes stopped her. He was a lot bigger than she was, and he'd already proven more than once that he could disarm her handily.

As unpleasant as the fact was, Gus Renard might well be her last chance to get away from the Platte Valley. With great reluctance, she acknowledged that accompanying Gus was probably not the worst thing that could happen to her. Not by a long shot.

But she didn't have to be happy about it.

"You have to wait outside so I can change," she informed him coldly, pulling her leather split skirt from a hook.

Gus shook his head.

Genny gaped at him. "Well you certainly aren't going to watch me disrobe!"

"If you don't hurry up, I'll undress you myself. Now hustle!"

"Of all the . . . !" Genny huffed and crossed her arms over her chest.

Gus glided across the floor on soundless moccasins and laid the barrel of her Spencer alongside her cheek once more.

"Do you really want to do this again?"

She shook her head. "I'd prefer it if you would find a few manners. You've made your point. I'm going with you. But you're not going to watch me change my clothes."

Their eyes locked. Seconds stretched into more than a minute. The minutes began to mount. It took every ounce of Genny's will to face the hostile arrogance in Renard's gaze.

Suddenly his gaze lightened. He smiled and his eyes crinkled at the corners.

"I'll grant you this skirmish. I won't watch, but I won't leave the room. Take it or leave it."

Genny took it. When he gave her his back, she hurriedly changed into her riding skirt and a collarless tan broadcloth shirt.

Gus turned back to face her. "See? I'm a man of my word. Don't forget it, and remember that you could end up a lot worse off than with me. Now get your boots and whatever else you need," he ordered, hovering at her shoulder, watching her closely.

With a mutinous scowl, Genny tugged on her boots and slung her goggles around her neck. In another couple of minutes she had assembled a few practical shirts, a skirt, stockings, underdrawers and camisoles, a brush and comb, a washcloth and a small towel, a bar of soap, and some hairpins and ribbons.

"That's it," she announced, clutching the collection of clothes to her chest.

Gus nodded, his unpleasant grin firmly in place. He glanced down at her underthings and raised an eyebrow speculatively, before his eyes lit on the blue satin ribbons.

"Hair ribbons?" The other eyebrow shot up.

"I have to tie my hair back with something," she said, shoving her clothes into the saddlebag. Gus shook his head, then flung the quilt from her bed and pulled off the top blankets, deftly rolling them together. When Genny picked up the saddlebags, he handed her the bed-roll.

"You'll need a jacket."

"It's in the other room."

"And this." He tossed her the small dagger that had been sitting on her bedstand.

She caught it deftly, holding it a moment in her palm. "Don't even think it."

"I'll think whatever I want to," Genny snapped. With a huff, she glanced once more at Renard's arrogant, willful expression, and tucked the dagger into her boot. "You may be sorry you gave that to me."

Gus chuckled softly. "I don't think so, *istatowin*. Pretty soon you're going to realize I'm doing you a favor by getting you out of here. But more to the point, you can't make it across the sandhills, or anywhere else, by yourself. You need me. So, let's go."

"You are the most arrogant, low-down, sneaking, thieving rat it's been my displeasure to encounter! I have never in my life been subjected to . . ."

Gus moved in on her, crowding her out the door, one of those nasty little, self-satisfied smiles plastered on his face. "And I think you're sweet, too, *istatowin*," he said, placing his free hand on her backside and pushing.

"Stop it! Don't touch me!" She darted ahead of him to get her jacket.

Gus scrawled a brief note for Paul and left it on the kitchen cabinet before picking up the extra provisions he'd taken from the pantry, adding a box of crackers and some cheese. His eyes and the rifle never seemed to leave Genny for more than an instant.

She glanced around the large room. Suddenly it looked familiar and comfortable, even inviting.

Gus Renard nudged her toward the door.

"Come on." He slung the bag of food over his shoulder and pointed to the door with the rifle. "We've got a lot of miles to cover before dark."

"I can't ride that horse," Genny announced, watching Gus tighten Trixie's cinch. The chickens he had let loose scratched at the ground underfoot.

Gus snorted. "I should have known. Look, a side-saddle isn't going to work for the kind of riding ahead of us."

"I can ride astride," she explained tersely. "But I can't ride Trixie. Nobody can."

"Don't be ridiculous. Is the horse saddle broke?" Gus ran a hand up Trixie's withers, patting her. The motion soothed him as much as it did the horse. He'd been glad to get out of the house and not have to look at the hole he'd blasted in the wall. And Genny wasn't giving him as much trouble as he'd expected.

"Oh, yes. She just doesn't like to be ridden. Is this overgrown mule of yours fast?" Genny shooed a hen out of her path and walked over to Gus's gelding.

"He's plenty fast. His name's Harv," Gus said, scratching Trixie's ears.

"Harv?" Genny laughed derisively as she shortened the dun's stirrups. "You named him Harv? Somehow I never pictured you riding an ugly old horse named Harv."

When she'd finished, she lifted her foot into a stirrup, and with a hop and a swing, she was up and over. She looked down triumphantly at a frowning Gus.

"He came with that name." He glanced up, not liking the gleam in her blue eyes. "Hey! What do you think you're doing? Get off my horse!" He left Trixie and reached for Harv's bridle. "For your information, Harv is as fine a horse as ever rode the plains. So his ears are big. He's smart, and he's loyal." Gus rubbed Harv's nose. "Looks aren't everything. Now get down and take your flashy mare."

Trixie nudged Gus's elbow, batting her long lashes at him when he turned toward her.

"She likes you," Genny observed in a sugary tone. And you're going to be sorry you did this to me, she thought to herself.

"Females always like me," Gus returned in the same tone, stroking Trixie's neck obligingly.

"So what does that make me? The last time I checked, I was most definitely a female, and I don't like you a bit."

"Yes, you do. You just don't know it yet."

"Are all Sioux men as insufferably arrogant as you seem to be?"

"Just the other big, smart, good-looking ones." He scratched behind Trixie's ears and clicked his tongue soothingly, but he watched Genny carefully.

"Flirting won't get you any farther with Trixie than it will with me, but you're welcome to try. I hope Harv isn't too tired."

"He's fine. He's as strong as the north wind."

"Is everything tied on Trixie's saddle good and tight?" Genny scrutinized her saddlebags.

Gus looked up at her in irritation. "Get off my horse," he repeated. If she thought she was going to run off alone, she was a fool. He'd catch her in a minute. One look at Trixie's long legs and powerful chest told him she was easily as fast as Harv. Besides, Harv wouldn't let her get out of sight of his master. If Genny wanted to play games, he'd play. Until she learned who was going to win.

Genny touched her heels lightly to Harv's sides; instantly he moved away from Gus and Trixie.

"Which way? Due north? Get her pointed that way, Renard." She nudged Harv to a trot. "Oh, you are a sweetie, aren't you?" she crooned, when he turned with only the slightest pressure on the reins.

"Damned horse-thieving woman." Gus rapidly lengthened Trixie's stirrups, and mounted from the left, American style. "All right, girl, go after them. Your mistress wants to play."

Chapter 5

Trixie crouched back on her haunches, then sprang forward. She laid her ears back and took off at a dead run.

"What in the name of . . . !" Gus yelled, catching his hat as it flew off his head. He crammed it down on his ears as he streaked past Genny, who already had Harv galloping northward.

"We'll follow as close as we can," she shouted after him.

He could have sworn she was laughing, but he didn't have time to turn and look.

Gus hauled back on the reins, but Trixie ignored him. He pulled until the muscles in his arms shook with the effort, unable to believe the horse wasn't responding to the bit that had to be digging into her mouth. Christ, he was going to kill that woman!

When Trixie hit her stride she was smooth and as fast as summer in high mountains. Once Gus gave up trying to slow her down and focused his attention on simply staying on, he almost enjoyed her fluid strength and grace. He conceded that Genny Stone had scored a bull's eye with this maneuver, and he had to wonder what other little tricks he was going to have to field as he ferried her across the sandhills.

It was two hours before Trixie slowed to a reasonable pace. Even then she didn't respond when Gus tried to guide her with the reins. She chose her own path, and

61

Gus had to acknowledge that he was simply along for the ride. Genny and Harv caught up with them and both horses eased into a walk, their sides heaving.

"Nice ride?" Genny asked breathlessly. Her hair had fallen out of its braid and her cheeks were flushed from the heat and exertion. The triumphant smile on her lips made Gus shake his head.

"Why didn't you just tell me?" he asked, panting. He took off his hat and wiped his brow on his sleeve. His hair was loose and blowing back from his face, the tie that held it having jostled loose many miles back. He gathered it on top of his head and replaced his stained and dusty gray hat.

"I told you I couldn't ride her. You asked for it when you didn't believe me." Gus didn't argue. "Martha says I'm foolish to keep her, but I admire her spirit."

"You would," he said easily. The ride had driven his violent mood from him, and Genny seemed more subdued, as well. "I've never seen a horse with a tougher mouth. Where'd you get her?"

"Paul bought her from an army officer east of Julesburg."

"I might have known this was Conrad's doing. Genny?"

"What?" She glanced sideways at him.

"I knew what I was doing with the rifle. You needed to be scared to get out of that place." He looked straight ahead, avoiding her gaze. Painting himself as a hero might turn her into a more amenable traveling companion.

Was he apologizing? Genny wasn't certain. It was plausible, but not in character with what she'd seen of him so far. "Maybe you can convince yourself that's what happened, but I'm not a fool, Renard. You lost your temper when you saw that gun in my hands. You can't expect me to believe your behavior was part of a plan to get me out of there."

"I didn't ask you to." Damn. She was astute. But he didn't have a better line. He'd play this one out awhile and see what happened.

"Why were you in my house, anyway?"

"I wasn't sure you'd left. I was just checking," Gus lied. Even if she didn't believe him, she'd never guess the truth.

"Out of concern for my welfare, no doubt," she drawled sarcastically.

He'd let that one alone. It wouldn't do to push her credulity. "More out of curiosity, I'd say."

"And a desire to indulge your sweet tooth," she surmised.

Gus grinned and shook his head. "You don't know what you're up against, *istatola*. This isn't your daddy's garden we're trailing through. I'm sorry it was necessary to scare some sense into you, and I'm sorry I put a hole in your pretty new wall, but I'm not sorry a bit to see you out of there. You can be as mean and prickly about it as you want, but it won't change anything."

"I am not mean and prickly," she corrected sharply, but some of her anger subsided with this more clear-cut apology. "Are you always so hotheaded?"

Gus looked at her pensively. "No, I'm not," he answered quietly. Then his expression lightened. "But I've been told that I'm always a handful," he added with a spreading grin.

Genny groaned. "I don't doubt it."

They lapsed into silence. Genny studied the landscape of rolling, golden sandhills dotted with marshy ponds. There were birds everywhere. Meadowlarks and blackbirds, flycatchers and kingbirds, swallows, buntings, ducks, grebes, a few hawks, and a small flock of pelicans. Their calls, cheeps, and chirrups filled the warm afternoon air with an avian symphony. The grass was high and thick, speckled with the deep golds and purples of late summer prairie flowers. There wasn't a tree in sight. Light breezes ruffled the surface of the grass and skimmed across the blue water in the ponds.

"Where are we going, and how long will it take?" she wanted to know.

"My camp is up around the Smoky Earth River northeast of here. It should take us a few days to get there."

"Where will we stay tonight?" Genny wondered aloud, watching a pair of blackbirds chase each other noisily across the hills. "This is such open country."

"Somewhere where the ground's dry and the water's good." Through lowered lids, he watched for her reaction. There was none. He tried again. "Snakes and the weather are the main inconveniences out here."

She'd forgotten about snakes; the worry in her eyes wasn't pretense now. "Are there a lot of them?" she asked mournfully.

"Enough," Gus said cheerfully.

"As many as there are skunks?"

Gus straightened his shoulders and grimaced. "Lots more. You seen any skunks?" He hated skunks. He doubted there was a worse smell in hell itself.

"One or two," Genny replied lightly, pleased that her sally had found its mark. "I've gotten pretty used to them in the last month. They're all over the spring. They come right in the house if I don't keep the doors and windows closed up tight. They're very friendly."

Trixie interrupted their baiting conversation by coming to an abrupt halt. Harv patiently stopped a few paces beyond and turned his big head to look back at her.

"What's the problem?" Gus tugged on the reins and dug his heels into Trixie's sides.

"She wants you to get off and walk," Genny supplied helpfully. "I'm surprised she let you ride this long. Once she stops running, that's usually the end of it. We walk home."

"How many times have you ridden her?"

"Twice. The first time she carried me out into the hills at a breakneck pace, I thought it was because she hadn't been ridden for a while and needed the exercise. When she did the same thing the next morning, I decided I'd had enough," Genny explained. "So we keep each other company. If I ever have to get away from White Rock Spring in a hurry, Trixie might eventually prove useful."

"Maybe. If she doesn't run you straight into trouble," Gus said. "Come on, Trixie. Let's go!"

The horse didn't budge.

"You're going to have to get off," Genny maintained patiently.

"Well, I'm not getting off." He slapped the reins and dug in his heels again.

"I wouldn't do that," Genny warned, but it was too late. Trixie dropped to the ground and started to roll, as if Gus and the saddle on her back didn't exist.

"Damn!" Gus hollered, jumping clear before his leg was pinned under the big horse. Trixie lay on her side, batting her eyelashes up at him.

"That isn't going to work on me, girl," he told her caustically.

"She's just giving you some of your own medicine, Renard. Pick up her leads," Genny advised, leaning on one forearm on the saddlebow. "She'll follow you like a puppy if you're on foot."

"Great," Gus said, disgusted. He looped the reins over Trixie's head and stepped back. Sure enough, she lunged to her feet. Gus led her to Harv's side. "Will she follow another horse?"

"I don't know," Genny said, watching as Gus tied Trixie to Harv's saddle. Then he took his saddlebags from Harv and tied them onto the black's saddle. "What are you doing?"

Genny gave Gus a puzzled look when he came to stand beside her and pulled her foot from the stirrup. He let it out, then rounded to her other side, doing the same to her right stirrup. When he straightened and placed his hand over hers on the saddlebow, she shook her head vigorously. "No, I don't think this is a good idea," she stated firmly.

"Too bad. Scoot forward, *istatowin*." Gus caught the stirrup and swung up into the saddle. Settling himself behind her, he put his hands on her waist. "Lift up a little." His hands tightened as he raised her bottom and adjusted her so that she sat partially atop his thighs.

"It's too hot to ride double," Genny cried in alarm, trying to hold her back away from his chest. He was warm and hard, and far too close. She didn't like it when he got so close to her. It made her feel so odd, all nervous and squeamish. His arms came around her to take the reins, and he pulled her back against him. She lurched forward again.

"This'll be more comfortable if you sit back against me. I don't feel like holding a woman who's as stiff as a preacher's collar for the rest of this ride. Relax." He pulled her back again.

"I can't relax," she said tightly. "I don't like being so close to a man who shot at me. It isn't intelligent, and it certainly isn't proper."

Gus laughed, his stomach and shoulders shaking under Genny's back.

"Since when has propriety become one of your concerns? Not two weeks ago you attacked me in the middle of the night wearing no more than a nighty and your indignation. You let me touch your bare legs, and, as I recall, you touched my bare flesh, as well. You didn't seem too worried about propriety then. And don't try to tell me now you didn't enjoy our little encounter."

"You've got a lot of nerve, Renard!" She squirmed, swatting his hands from her waist.

"To my mind, that was far more improper than riding double. This is a practical measure," he continued. "Not that it matters. Nobody but us knows anything about either incident, and since we both enjoyed ourselves, there's no harm done."

"I did not enjoy myself!" Genny insisted. The saddlebow against her legs effectively kept her from gaining any distance from Renard.

Gus pressed Harv's sides with his knees and they started moving, Trixie following complacently behind. The horse's ambling gait bounced Genny lightly on his lap, and Gus momentarily doubted the wisdom of such a ride, but he'd be damned if he was going to walk all the way across the sandhills.

"Deny it, then. Tell me you act this way with all the men you know, and it's nothing out of the ordinary." His voice was close in her ear.

"It was very much out of the ordinary!" she retorted hotly. "What way do I act?"

"Like you like it when I touch you."

"You are insane. Stark raving crazy, plumb coon dingy, and utterly half-witted. For mercy's sake! You shot at me with my own rifle, and you think I like it when you touch me?! Let me down, I'm going to walk!" She flailed about, trying to get a leg up over Harv's withers.

Gus hauled her back against him again. "No you're not. You can't keep up, and I'm not going to slow down. Come on, Genny. Admit you might enjoy it when I touch you, just a little bit."

Genny could hear the smile in his words as his hand drifted precariously close to the underside of her breast. She lifted her shoulders, throwing herself back into him to get away from his roving hand.

"I admit nothing of the sort," she said primly, denying the giddy sensation dancing through her belly. "I hardly know you, and what I've seen, I don't like."

Gus chuckled again. "I wonder what Aunt Augusta would think of these conversations we have?" His hand crept upward half an inch more.

Genny pushed at his hand and strained forward again. "You close your mouth and leave my aunt out of this," Genny ordered. "And stop laughing so much. I can't sit on top of someone who's constantly jiggling around."

He laughed harder. "You can't, huh?" He nudged Harv into a trot.

Genny's leather-clad bottom bounced down hard on his lap and his thighs came up firm beneath her. Clasping his left arm more firmly around her waist, he pulled her tight against him, and dipped his head to speak directly in her ear. The brim of his dusty, low-crowned hat brushed her temple.

"That's too bad, *istatowin*," he said without an ounce of regret, his lips moving seductively against the curve of her ear.

Goosebumps shivered down her neck and arm. Straining out of his reach, she sighed in resignation. "I take it this is your more usual *modus operandi*? If you can't terrify a woman, seduce her?"

"What a perceptive young lady."

"Do other women really like this sort of attention?" she asked tightly, her voice stuttering with Harv's choppy stride.

"They love it," Gus assured her, his breath washing over the sensitive skin on the back of her neck. "What's wrong with you?"

"Nothing a little sincere honesty and respect couldn't cure."

"Oh, honey, it's my honest appreciation that's got you flustered, and when was the last time a man's respect gave you goosebumps? My way's more fun." He nipped at her shoulder through the heavy material of her shirt, and she threw her shoulder up, clipping him in the jaw. He sat back, still chuckling. "You're going to enjoy this ride, Genny Stone," he predicted with maddening confidence.

"Lord help me," Genny groaned. "I think I liked you better when you were threatening to shoot off my fingers."

By the time Gus halted for the night, the sun was already below the horizon in the northwest, and Genny was ready to take Trixie and walk all the way back to White Rock Spring to face whatever dangers presented themselves. She'd been pinched, prodded, tickled, and stroked until she wanted to scream. The lout had even licked her! Right on the neck, just below her ear. She could still feel the path he'd traced with his silky tongue, ending with a tiny bite on her earlobe. Gus Renard was the most daring, infuriating man she'd ever met, and after the likes of Nicholas Mercer, that was no mean distinction.

Genny surveyed their campsite. Gus had stopped in a cleft in the hills above a pretty lake. There was no shelter, and the only good thing about the place was that it was upwind of the insects that hovered in the air over the water. She was too exhausted to care where she slept, wanting nothing more than a quick wash, a bite to eat, and her bedroll. It had been a long day, and Gus Renard

had worn her out. He'd started the afternoon out by
breaking into her home and stealing her food, shot at her
with her own gun, and forced her to accompany him on
this dash across the prairies. He'd ended it with his hands
all over her, and his lips in her hair, murmuring about
how soft she was. She'd started it wanting to see him
committed to an asylum for the feebleminded or interred
in a stockade as a criminal, and ended it with shivers
coursing through her when his fingers strayed too close
to her breasts.

Something was not at all right.

Genny picked up her soap and towel and headed for
the water as soon as the horses were taken care of. Kneeling on the marshy bank to dip her cloth in the water, she
considered that her attitude toward Gus this afternoon
seemed to have spurred him on. She was having a hard
time keeping up with his rapid mood changes, and it was
difficult to reconcile the angry man she'd met coming
out of her pantry with the rake who'd held her in front
of him in the saddle for hours. If he thought a few pretty
words and smiles were going to make her forget the
earlier part of the afternoon, he was dead wrong. He'd
treated her abominably, and losing his temper was no
excuse, whether or not he admitted that's what had happened. She believed him when he said he hadn't meant
to hit her, but she wanted to see him pay for frightening
her so badly. It had been satisfying to see him fly past
on Trixie, clutching his ridiculous old hat in one hand,
and the useless reins in the other, but it wasn't enough.

She had to find a way to deal with his glib tongue and
bawdy sense of humor. Maybe if she followed Trixie's
example and treated him to a little of his own teasing,
he'd ease up. And if Martha was right about Gus's restraint toward respectable white women, she should be
safe from any untoward consequences.

She puzzled for a minute about the inherent contra-
diction in relying on Martha's word that he was both
dangerous and no threat to her virtue at the same time,
but her instincts still told her that Gus Renard wasn't
going to hurt her bodily. Giving him as much sauce as

he gave her was worth a try, and he was probably right—
it might well be more fun.

Gus watched Genny slip away for a wash, debating
whether to follow or not. Her cheerful confidence irritated him; nothing seemed to affect her sense of safety
and her trust that everything would work to her advantage. Being possessed of spirit was one thing, and Genny
Stone certainly had her share, but reckless stupidity was
another. After everything he'd put her through that day,
as soon as she was left to her own devices, she was
traipsing off alone without a weapon, and apparently
unconcerned about possible dangers. Gus let her get a
good distance down the hill before he trailed after her.

He didn't follow too closely. After hours in the saddle,
holding her fidgeting, wriggling body in front of him,
he needed a little distance. If he didn't relax, he might
be tempted to disregard his rule against sharing his pleasures with white women. There was little enough to stop
him as it was: they were alone and isolated, he wanted
her with an intensity that startled him, and he sensed
Genny was far from immune to him, though he doubted
she'd admit it.

Crouching in the high grass, Gus watched Genny approach the water without so much as glancing around
her. She wet her washcloth and ran it over her face and
neck, oblivious to his presence a hundred feet behind
her. A warrior could have sauntered up and had her scalp
before she was aware anyone was there. Gus's brief flare
of anger gave way to disgust; he vowed he was going to
permanently shake Genny Stone's naive sense of well-
being.

He rubbed his chin in thoughtful anticipation. The best
way to rattle Miss Stone had become apparent during the
afternoon's ride; he suspected his outrageous flirting had
discomfited her almost more than being shot at. If he
made her think he was going to seduce her, he could use
her unacknowledged attraction to him to undermine and
challenge her attitudes and actions. He'd push her to the
edges of her well-bred eastern respectability, showing

her in more ways than one that she was out of her element
in the west, and that she had a lot to learn. The task of
keeping his own physical urges in check would only add
to the challenge. Overall, pretending to seduce Genny
Stone ought to substantially enliven an otherwise dull
ride through the lonely sandhills country.

As if in invitation to exactly such a course of action,
Genny stood and pulled her shirt from the waistband of
her skirt, proceeding to unbutton it. She slipped her arms
from the blouse and set it neatly on the ground, then
worked the buttons on her split skirt, shedding it as well.
Dressed only in her wrinkled white cotton camisole and
drawers, Genny lifted her arms and stretched, then shook
her hips back and forth, stretching first one leg and then
the other. Gus got a tantalizing glimpse of her violet-
colored stockings when her long drawers lifted above the
top of her boots, and he looked on appreciatively as she
ran her hands briskly over her backside, before reaching
again for her wet cloth.

Gus made no attempt to be quiet or disguise his movements, as he closed the distance between them. When
he stopped, she was still unaware of him, sluicing water
over the upper part of her left arm, head tilted back in
sensual enjoyment. Gus sighed appreciatively. It was
going to be hard to control himself, but there were most
definitely going to be certain compensations.

"I'd be glad to help you, *istatola*," he offered softly,
his voice carrying in the twilit calm. "You've already
had a taste of what we can do together with a little water
and a cloth. Care to broaden our repertoire? You can do
my legs this time, and I'll do your chest."

With satisfaction, he watched her back stiffen. He was
unprepared for the knowing grin she flashed him over
her shoulder a second later.

"That sounds intriguing," she said, her voice uncharacteristically low, and ripe with sensual considera-
tions.

She laughed when he stopped, and turned halfway
toward him, an arm coquettishly draped across her

breasts. "I think I'll take you up on it another time, though, Gus."

It was the first time she'd used his name; it sounded strange to both of them.

"You will, huh?" So she'd changed her tactics. Things might get interesting, he noted. Very interesting. "How about tomorrow?" he suggested, walking to her side. He reached out his hand and touched his fingers to her cheek. It was soft and damp.

Genny turned away from him, heat suffusing her chest and face. "We'll see," she answered, laughing lightly. This sort of thing seemed fairly easy, even if it was embarrassing.

"Yeah, won't we," Gus agreed, his smile wide enough to span the Platte. He chuckled merrily. "Don't take too long, Genny Stone. You never know what monsters may be waiting for you in the darkness." He slid his fingers down her neck to rest against her collarbone for a moment, then walked away.

Genny caught her breath at his light caress, and watched him retreat back toward their campsite. She hadn't stopped him from touching her, nor had she stayed her inordinate physical response to him, but she had surprised him, that much was clear. She smiled.

Gus wasn't the only one she'd surprised; she'd never have believed she could behave in such a manner! Maybe with a little practice, she'd actually be able to nettle him.

When she returned to the campsite, it was nearly dark. Gus sat on his bedroll, leaning against his saddle with legs outstretched, eating a handful of crackers and some buffalo jerky.

He pointed to his saddlebags with a cracker. "Get yourself something to eat. I brought your cheese for you, or you can have some *papa*. That's Lakota for jerky."

"What? No raisins?" she asked archly, putting her soap away and draping her towel across her saddle.

"Not for you," Gus returned cheerily. "I'm going to eat them all myself. My greed knows no bounds when it comes to anything sweet," he added suggestively.

Genny had to hand it to him. His skills with *double entendre* were definitely beyond her own.

"They're my raisins anyway," she argued. She shook out her bedroll. The blankets fell to the ground in a disorganized heap.

"Not any more, they aren't. I took 'em, and I'll fight for 'em." He grinned at her through a mouthful of cracker. "Want to arm rassle me for the raisins?"

"Not tonight," she replied, arching a brow to let him know she wasn't utterly naive. "All I want is sleep. Aren't you going to build a fire?" She straightened her blankets, then helped herself to a chunk of cheese and a few crackers.

"What with? Seen any trees that I missed?" he snorted.

"No. Can't you burn buffalo chips? Martha told me about that." Witty comments and snappy rejoinders were not leaping to mind.

"We don't need a fire. If you get cold, you can pull your bedroll over here and snuggle up to me, *istatola*. I'll keep you plenty warm," he promised, eyes twinkling.

Her eyes narrowed. She didn't like this man. Not one little bit. "Would you, now? Well, I'll keep your offer in mind, Gus. But who'll protect me from the wolves?"

He laughed. She was getting the hang of it. "Guess you'll have to take your chances there."

"Somebody told me most of the wolves in these parts are a pack of cowards anyway, so I probably shouldn't worry. They hang around camp, howling up a storm, but they don't attack." She popped a cracker into her mouth to keep from smiling, and sat down cross-legged on her blankets.

"Don't be too sure about that, *istatowin*. You're in Indian country now. The wolves up here aren't as tame as they are down along the river. You never know what might happen," he warned cheerfully. He stood, shaking cracker crumbs into the grass.

"I'm not worried."

"Maybe you should be."

"What's that word mean?" Genny asked, changing the subject. "What you call me. Is it Sioux?"

Gus crossed the space between their bedrolls in two long strides. He caught her gaze, then bent at the knees until his face was only a foot or so above hers. He reached out to brush a crumb from her upper lip. She didn't move when he ran his finger down the corner of her mouth to her chin, but her pupils widened. His hand fell away slowly.

"Here's your first lesson in Indian language and customs. First, we don't use the name Sioux except with *wašicus*, or white people. Those of us west of the Missouri River call ourselves Lakota. Those east are divided into two more divisions, the Dakota and the Nakota. The languages we speak bear the same names. Within each of these larger groups there are smaller ones, each with its own name. My mother belonged to the Sicaŋǧu, or as the *wašicus* call us, the Brulé. Sicaŋǧu means 'burnt thigh,' and it's an old name with a number of stories attached to it. *Ištatola* means 'blue eyes'; *ištatowin* means 'blue eyes woman.' "

"I thought it was an insult," Genny admitted, her eyes caught in his dark gaze.

"I know," Gus said gently. "There are going to be a lot of things you're going to misunderstand over the next several weeks. Try saying 'Lakota.' "

"Lakota," Genny tried, but the "k" didn't explode in her mouth the way it did when Gus said it.

He nodded once. "Try Sicaŋǧu."

She tried, but all that came out was a gargle. "I can't say that," she admitted self-consciously. "Say it again for me." He did, and she tried again with only marginally better results. Her eyes wandered over his face, lingering on the curve of his lower lip. He was too handsome for his own good. Or her peace of mind. "Nobody speaks English where we're going, do they?"

He shook his head. "Just you and me, Genny."

Uncertainty assailed her with the sudden chill of a September snowstorm as the realization hit her that she was going to have to rely on this crazy man for a lot longer than a couple of days.

"This is the biggest adventure I've ever been on," she told him, more to buck up her own quailing spirit than anything else.

"I hope you think so in another month."

"Oh, I will," she assured him.

"We'll see." He rose and strode past the horses out into the night.

"Where are you going?" Genny called after him.

"For a walk. Go to sleep, *istatola*. I'll be back soon."

Genny finished her supper and brushed the crumbs away, then wandered a short distance beyond the horses to relieve herself. When she returned, she took off her boots, unbraided her hair to comb it out, then flipped open her blankets, made a quick check for snakes, and burrowed inside. She slipped her dagger under her saddlebag pillow, and adjusted herself to the hard ground, shifting and twisting until she began to relax. Before drifting into sleep, she reflected that Gus Renard had seemed a little more manageable during their last conversation, despite his attempt to frighten her again.

As to her attempts at flirting, she thought she'd gotten in a few good remarks, and the suggestive postures and looks were easy, but her mind didn't naturally lean toward such silly dalliance. It could become a strain to maintain such behavior for long, and she truly hoped it wouldn't be necessary.

Listening to a cricket chirping in the grass somewhere nearby, she stared up at the clear night sky. The stars were bright and close, and she traced the ragged line of the milky way with an outstretched finger. She could hear Harv and Trixie breathing close at hand, and in the distance, a few wolves and coyotes started up a mournful chorus. She shivered, but knew they wouldn't hurt her. She'd grown used to their cries along the trail westward, and it would take a lot more than a few wolves to keep her from sleeping this night. She closed her eyes, and breathed deeply of the soft night air as she drifted into sleep.

Gus sat atop a sandhill less than a quarter of a mile from camp, staring at the dark horizon, hoping that Genny was getting nervous by herself. When a coyote yipped from another hill, Gus returned his call. They exchanged yowls for a few minutes, before more coyotes joined the song and Gus bowed out. He waited as they came closer to him, curious about the man sitting in the middle of their range, howling along with them. They sounded sad and sinister, he thought. When he'd come back to the plains after living in Canada as a boy, he'd thought there was no more tragic and intimidating sound than coyotes and wolves on a moonless night. Their cries still had the power to send a shiver up his spine.

Rising, Gus gave one last call, then walked back to camp. It would have done his heart good to see Genny Stone curled up in a terrified ball in her clumsily arranged bedroll. Instead, she was sound asleep, snuggled into her bed with her nose half-buried beneath her red wool blanket. She was lying on her side as she had been the morning he'd slipped into her room at White Rock Spring.

The memory sparked an ignoble, but attractive idea. Grinning, with wicked anticipation, Gus picked up his bedroll in one hand and pushed his saddle ahead of him with his foot until he stood over Genny.

Carefully, quietly, he arranged his blankets and lay down beside her.

Chapter 6

Genny dreamed she was walking outside at River-wood. It was winter; the ground was cold and bare, and naked tree branches rattled in a brisk wind. Her ears were freezing. She had forgotten her hat, and the wind nipped at her through her jacket. When she came to the archway in the garden, she saw Nicholas Mercer standing there without a stitch of clothing on. His pale flesh was tinged blue with the cold and he stared at her in shock, though he made no move to cover himself.

Embarrassed, Genny turned to run back into the house, but she lost her way and couldn't find it. It had disappeared in a tangle of clattering branches, biting wind, and pelting snow. She ran until she'd lost all sense of direction and space. Fear grew from a niggle in her belly to a tight, screaming tension in her lungs as the ground disintegrated beneath her feet. Cold and alone, she was left standing on a point of air, terrified to move lest she fall into nothingness. There was no landscape at all, only a watery blue sky that faded into mists where the ground should have been.

A man appeared in shadow form. He was half-dressed, and his hair was wildly long like a savage's. Genny started to scream, but he held up his hand, stopping her.

"Ssshhh," he whispered. "Everything's all right, *is-tatola*."

Solid warmth surrounded her, though the man remained in the shadows.

"Gus? Is that you?" she murmured softly. " 'Blue eyes,' you said. I have blue eyes. Will you give me your hand so I won't fall?"

"I've got you, Genny. I won't let you fall."

"My head is cold." Something stroked her hair, and there was warmth beneath her cheek. "That's better. Can I stay here for a while?"

"Yeah. For a while."

"Just a little while," Genny repeated.

Within seconds she was sleeping peacefully in his arms. Gus didn't think she'd ever been fully awake; he wondered if she would remember what she'd said in the morning, and what she'd think when she woke up sleeping close beside him. Her head rested in the hollow of his shoulder and he felt her soft breath like a feather brushing against his chest. Curled close beside him, she felt small and fragile, her body softly feminine. It pleased him that in dream-disturbed sleep she was wise enough to know she needed him, and he took a measure of satisfaction in her vulnerability. Gus pulled her tangled blankets on top of both of them before he, too, returned to sleep.

Genny tried to roll onto her back, but her arm was caught under a heavy weight. She tugged to no avail. Disparate sensations filtered through the semi-conscious haze of waking; smooth skin, warmth, a rhythmic sigh of breath, and a light scent of smoke and musk.

The inventory tallied suddenly into sharply focused reality. She was snuggled flush against Gus Renard, her cheek on his shoulder. His bare arm was pressed between her breasts, and one hand rested intimately on the inside of her drawn-up thigh. Her arms cradled him, one beneath his shoulder, the other thrown across his stomach. Somehow their blankets had coalesced into a single bed, though when she'd gone to sleep, his bedroll had been a good ten feet away.

"Oh, my heavens!" she said aloud, lifting her head to stare at her arms wrapped around Gus's sleeping form. Her skin showed pale against his in the starlight. She looked up to his face. His eyes were open, and he wore the unholy grin she was learning to dread.

"This could pass for heaven in a pinch," he agreed with quiet enthusiasm.

He lifted his shoulder and Genny pulled her arm free quickly, rolling away from him. Strong arms caught her from behind, drawing her back into the curve of his body. His knees came up under hers, and his thighs pressed into her bottom. She strained against arms that held firm.

"I see you took me up on my offer to keep you warm. I have to confess, I didn't think you'd do it," he murmured in her ear, his voice still thick with sleep.

Genny's inclination was to protest violently, collect her blankets and put as much distance between herself and Gus Renard as she could, but that was what he was expecting. She knew he was. Well, she wasn't going to let him rile her. Instead, she'd try to shock him. If such a thing could be done.

With an effort, she relaxed into him. His muscles froze briefly before he settled her more closely into his embrace. She felt him smile against her neck, but she knew she'd startled him again.

"You don't know me very well, Gus," she whispered, placing her arms over his where they wrapped around her. She ran her fingertips experimentally over his forearms; his flesh was firm and resilient to her touch. She repeated the caress with more confidence. "I have quite a reputation at home. Do you know why I'm in Nebraska Territory?"

"You said something about a wager with your cousin." Gus closed his eyes and concentrated on the tiny movements of her hands on his arms. He decided he liked it. Very much.

"Strictly speaking, yes, we have a wager, but that came about almost incidentally. My father was already prepared to send me out here for what had happened," she explained, exaggerating freely. "You have to understand that it was merely the latest of my escapades. I'd already been shipped off to France for a particularly inspired series of adventures two years previously. In fact, I'd only recently returned home. Father and Aunt Augusta had hoped that I'd reformed.''

"So you make a habit of adventures, do you?" Gus nuzzled her neck, inhaling her fragrance. "Your hair smells nice."

"Thank you." She arched her neck away from him. "You're tickling me."

"Sorry." He nipped at her earlobe.

"Gus, stop it. Don't you want to know what happened?"

"Oh, yes," he groaned against her neck.

"Then be still and listen. You're distracting me."

"That's the idea, *istatola*. But I'm intrigued. What atrocity did you commit to get yourself banished to lonely Nebraska Territory?"

Genny's laughter rippled seductively in the darkness. "It was hardly an atrocity. A little risqué, perhaps, but not at all fatal." She gripped Gus's arms lightly, running her hands rapidly across them. "I asked an officer of the Union army to undress for me so I could paint his portrait in a style reminiscent of Greek statuary."

Gus gasped. "Tell me you didn't."

"Oh, I did. And he did. Undress, that is." She felt Gus's laughter shaking his chest beneath her back. "You're jiggling again," she complained.

"My apologies. Did you like what you saw? Of the officer?"

He was too smooth. Genny wanted to see him with his feathers ruffled up a bit. "Oh, yes. Nicky is the most handsome man I've ever seen. Thick black hair with a beautiful wave in it, sparkling blue eyes, and as handsome as Adonis. His shoulders are broad and fine, his waist firm, and his hips . . ."

Gus stuck his tongue in her ear. She swatted him away immediately. "Don't do that!" she exclaimed, abandoning her description of Nicholas Mercer's imagined charms.

"Were you painting him or making love with him?" Gus laughed again, but there was an edge to his laughter that gratified Genny.

"Painting him, of course," she purred, copying a tone she'd learned from him and Nicky Mercer. Let him think what he wanted.

"I see," he replied archly, and Genny knew that he didn't at all. She didn't bother to suppress the giggle that bubbled triumphantly in her throat. "So what happened? Did Daddy catch you at this?" He began a series of small kisses along her shoulder.

It took a measure of concentration to force enough air through her constricted lungs to talk, but she did it. "Oh, no, it was much worse than that. It was Aunt Augusta, Paul's mother." She shuddered, as much the result of Gus's lips nibbling along her skin as for dramatic effect. "It was quite horrible."

"I'm sure it was," Gus consoled, his hands moving in small circles over her midriff and stomach. She felt a tension in him that hadn't been present a moment before. "So that's the real reason I'm in Nebraska Territory."

"I was right about your lack of concern over propriety."

Between the warm caress of his breath on her neck and the movements of his hands at her waist, Genny was sliding into an abyss of physical pleasure. "Not in all cases," she insisted.

"Were you in love with your army lieutenant?" he murmured, rubbing his chin along her shoulder.

"Nooo," Genny said slowly, opting momentarily for honesty. Her attention was centered on the enervating lassitude Gus provoked within her.

"So you pursued your dramatic course with what goal in mind? Perhaps to satisfy your curiosity about the male form?" His chin rasped along the material of her shirt and along her upper arm, while one hand slid down the outside of her thigh.

Genny gasped softly at his touch. "I know what males look like. I am an artist, and I've studied in Paris where there are fewer restraints on the artistic educations of serious women students." Delicious tingles shivered down her arms to meet the warmth upwelling from her middle.

"Then I fail to understand why you put Lieutenant Whoever-he-was into such a compromising position, and with such obviously detrimental result to yourself." His lips returned to her neck, bestowing kisses once again. "Unless," Gus continued in between pecks, "you hoped to spark a situation akin to your present one."

"Your mind slides along in a single rut." Oh, she had lied when she said she didn't like his touch. She had lied shamelessly.

Gus's hand came to rest on her ankle, then slowly worked its way up her bare shin beneath the wide leg of her split skirt. "I'm beginning to think yours does, too, *ištatola*." She arched beneath his touch, driving her buttocks back into his groin. "Be careful, Genny Stone," he hissed on a swiftly indrawn breath. "Is this what you wanted from your lieutenant?" He slid her onto her back, tucked her legs between his own, and ran his hand low over her stomach.

"No." She shook her head. "You don't understand."

Gus chuckled. "I'm not so sure about that. What do you want from me?" His hand glided up over her stomach to rest between her breasts.

She flinched from the intense pleasure that accompanied the touch of his hands on her body. With her eyes closed, her muscles tensed and straining against themselves, Genny realized she'd utterly lost control of the situation. She grasped for any idea that would enable her to set Renard back on his heels. When one came, she acted, covering his hand with her own, then raising it to her lips where she kissed his fingertips.

"I want to kiss you," she said, disentangling her legs from his and sitting up. One small hand pushed him onto his back, and she bent over him, her hair falling in disarray over her shoulders, spilling onto his chest. Before her bravado failed, Genny dipped toward him, her heart thudding.

Slowly, gently, she pressed her mouth to his.

His lips were soft, and his chest hard beneath her palms. She rubbed her mouth across his, then lightly plucked at his lower lip. Fascinated by the feel of him,

Genny repeated her motions, completely forgetting her purpose in precipitating the kiss.

Gus went absolutely still, even his breath suspended, as he accepted her inexperienced kiss. When she cupped his cheek in one hand, he caught her shoulders, and his lips moved suddenly across her own.

The liquid fire that had built between them erupted into passion. Gus took over the kiss with greater skill and certainty, and Genny met him with an ardor that caught both of them broadside. His mouth demanded pleasure and was received with welcome. When he sucked her lower lip, she followed suit, mimicking the delightful motion. When his tongue flickered at the corners of her mouth, she smiled and did the same to him.

Long, slow tremors rippled through her with his every touch, focusing tension in her lower body. Unexpected excitement fanned the fires she found in his embrace, so that when he rose to hold her in his lap, her back supported by his arm, she drew him to her once again. She sought a fuller kiss, and placed her hands upon his face, one finger brushing back a night-dark lock of hair.

She pressed for more without knowing exactly what it was she sought, darting her tongue along his lips. He groaned and touched his tongue to hers, startling her with the new sensation. She drew back, but he pursued, chasing until she accepted his moist, warm caresses. Deepening their meeting and the power of the kiss, their hands wandered. Large, strong fingers touched the small of her back, her waist, her hip, while small, sensitive fingers glided at his nape, his crown, his throat.

Foremost in awareness, sensual pleasure raged between them, while underneath, like a base for fine perfume, emotion smoldered into precarious fire. An elusive promise of security shattered Gus as it slipped past his logic to lodge inside his heart. Like a finely honed blade, it cut through him, quick and clean, leaving an unexpected sting in its wake. He groaned aloud, thrusting his tongue deeper into Genny's mouth, seeking more pleasure to still the burgeoning pain.

A temptation to trust beckoned Genny as she absorbed

the depth of feeling that brought Gus surging against her. The feeling was new, offering a promise of profound satisfaction. It split her attention, tearing her away from the single-minded pursuit of physical pleasure. Frustration wrung a small whimper from her.

With a ragged cry, Gus retreated, leaving a last, searing kiss upon her open mouth.

They broke apart, staring at each other in the pale light of the old moon rising. Questions filled their eyes as each sought confirmation of the strength of feeling that had surged between them.

Genny didn't know what to think when Gus closed his eyes and frowned. A second later he dropped his forehead against hers and sighed.

"What's wrong?" she whispered. "What happened?"

He shook his head, moving hers with him, but didn't answer. He held her in his lap, one hand lightly at the back of her head, the other at her waist. Silent and motionless, heads bowed together, they sat for many minutes.

Genny knew that she'd succeeded in disrupting Gus's equilibrium beyond her wildest imaginings, but she hadn't bargained on knocking the foundations out from underneath herself in quite so thorough a fashion. She had not kissed this man as if he were a thief who had fired a rifle at her and kidnapped her. She had kissed him as a man. As a lover.

Inexperienced as she was, she was not naive; the power of what they'd shared went beyond their physical attraction for one another. It both surprised and frightened her. The knowledge that this mixed-blood Lakota rake was not someone she was going to be able to handle with a pretense of flirtation held her silent.

Gus lifted Genny to her feet and rose to stand beside her. Away from his warmth she drew her arms in close, shivering in the predawn chill.

"It's near light," he said in quiet, clipped tones. "We might as well get moving. That horse of yours will slow us down enough as it is."

Genny nodded, hurt by his withdrawal, but not surprised. She bent to separate her blankets from Gus's and roll them hastily, venturing a single question.

"Why are you angry?"

He stood apart and rolled a smoke. She hadn't seen him smoke before, though she'd smelled tobacco on his clothes.

"I'm not upset with you." He struck a lucifer on his thumbnail, and held the flame to his tobacco. "Eat something if you're hungry. I'll be back in a few minutes, then we'll saddle up." The rosy-gold flare of light revealed his taut expression. He strode out past the horses, the glowing tip of his tobacco smoke visible long past the point where his sketchy silhouette blended into the night.

Genny sat back on her heels, staring after him. Gus Renard was proving to be far more of a handful than any one man had a right to be.

The sun rose red in a cold, clear sky about an hour after Gus and Genny resumed their journey. Gus set a northeasterly course and had Genny ride Harv, while he walked beside them, with Trixie following. When the sun was well up, Genny dismounted to walk as well. Neither of them said a word, and Genny concentrated on the subtle play of changing light as the sun rose higher. At mid-morning the wind picked up, blowing from the southwest. The temperature rose rapidly, and within a few minutes Genny had discarded her jacket and stopped the horses to tie it on the back of Trixie's saddle.

"You're getting sunburned," Gus observed, breaking the mutual silence. Genny turned to look at him. The censure she met in his eyes made her look away quickly. "You should have brought a hat."

"I was forced to leave in rather a hurry. It's inevitable that something should have been forgotten," she replied shortly, stroking Trixie's flank.

"Wear mine," Gus said irritably. He dropped his beat-up hat onto her head. Automatically, she reached up to pull it down firmly and their fingers collided on the brim. Genny jerked her hand back.

Gus stood beside her, radiating displeasure, but he didn't speak. Finally he started walking again, and Genny followed silently.

The heat built rapidly, and soon tiny clouds appeared, sailing in from the west, growing gradually from seedling puffs to substantial clouds that cast irregular shadows over the dips and rises of the sandhills. By noon, the sky above the puffy clouds had grown hazy, and without shade or shelter, the heat was unpleasant and draining. They stopped to eat and rest beside a lone cottonwood next to a marshy pond, and when they continued, Genny gladly followed Gus's suggestion that she ride.

Gus didn't like the feel in the unsettled air, and he didn't relish the prospect of being caught in a thunderstorm so far from shelter. He looked at Trixie, considering whether or not to repeat yesterday's race, but he knew that with the heat, it wouldn't be good for the animals to run so hard again today, especially not when he'd been pushing Harv for two days to reach White Rock Spring quickly. He wasn't going to sacrifice the best saddle horse he'd ever had, so he resigned himself to their plodding pace. At this rate, it would take a week to reach his camp on the Smoky Earth. He glanced up at Genny, annoyed with her for owning such a useless horse, and a lot of other things.

He laughed aloud at the sight that greeted him. In place of the pretty woman he'd deposited in the saddle half an hour ago sat a creature more akin to a gaudy insect than a lady. She had on his dirty old hat and her goggles, and she'd tied a yellow and red striped silk scarf around the lower part of her face and neck.

"What's so funny?" Her voice was muffled behind the scarf.

"I wish you could see yourself," he chuckled appreciatively. "You look like a big old bug up there, with a red and yellow throat and gigantic eyes. Walks in Thunder would get a laugh seeing you now. He'd never seen anyone wearing goggles, and you really shook him when we first saw you. He thought you might be a monster until you took them off. That's partly why he was so polite.''

"Unlike a certain other party," Genny reminded him. "I happen to like my goggles. They've proved the most useful thing I brought with me, though I originally brought them along as a memento of a wonderful day I had in Paris.''

"And what was so special about this day in Paris?" Gus asked.

"Well, I took a hot air balloon ride with a wonderful gentleman named Henri and we ended the day in a brothel because we needed to borrow money to get back to Paris from Henri's friend Anne, who worked there.''

"You don't worry much about your reputation, do you?" He started teasing to take his mind off his feelings and the darkening sky. The sun had disappeared yet the heat was oppressive.

"No, I can't say as I've ever given it much thought.''

"Why not? You're going to make it tough for any guy who wants to marry you, *istatola*." A more genuine smile creased his cheeks as he looked up at her. "How old are you, anyway? Shouldn't you be married already?''

"I'm twenty-four, and I have no intention of marrying. You're beginning to sound like a member of my family.'' She lifted her hair off the back of her neck and sighed. "It's abominably hot.''

"I never met a white woman who didn't want to get married," Gus said easily. "Except for ladies like your friend Anne. Is that what you've got in mind?''

"Oh, for heaven's sake!" Genny completely forgot her intention to tease him right back. "I don't wish to marry for a number of reasons.''

"Such as?''

"My older sister's recent marriage, for one. When I left for France, Freddie had been married only a short time, and already she was losing the ability to speak her own mind and think for herself. She is an intelligent, capable, and energetic person, but by the time I returned from France, she'd changed. All she thinks about now is her husband, Joe, and his health, and her baby. Joe was badly injured at Gettysburg and nearly lost his arm, so I can understand that somewhat, but I don't like to see her abandon all her interests, meekly standing at Joe's side, deferring to every word that falls from his lips. It's nauseating. Freddie used to write poetry and essays for a friend of hers who was a printer in town, but Joe disapproved. He thought it was frivolous, so she stopped. She used to deliver baskets of food to needy families in poor neighborhoods, but Joe insisted it wasn't safe and forbade her to continue. Everything she used to do of her own interest has been replaced by activities that Joe supports and approves of. The most disheartening part of it is that I like Joe perfectly well. He's a kind man, and a good father. But no matter how nice a man is, in marriage he's got the reins, and he believes it's his right and duty to train his wife and children to his will. I've absolutely no desire to enter into such an arrangement when I find my own will so acceptable. That, in a nutshell, is why I will not marry.''

She paused to look assessingly at Gus. ''What's your excuse, Renard? You look old enough to have collared some poor female and provided her with several offspring. Why aren't you married?''

Gus scowled briefly at the horizon, then subjected Genny to one of his less pleasant smiles.

''I tried it once and didn't like it.''

Chapter 7

"What did you say?" Genny's eyes widened.

"I said I tried it and I didn't like it."

"I heard you the first time! What happened? Did she die?" Genny asked in alarm. "Oh dear. I didn't mean to bring up a painful topic . . . ."

Gus waved his hand to cut her off. "Slow down. She was still alive, last I heard."

"Then you're still married!" Genny exclaimed in horror. God save her, she'd kissed a married man!

"No, I'm not. She left me. Her brothers came to visit us, and I went off hunting to feed them. They eat like a couple of starving horses. When I got back, I found my clothes in a pile where our lodge had been, and White Shell and her brothers were long gone. So, I don't have a wife anymore."

"That's all there was to it?" Genny asked incredulously. "Your wife left so you're not married anymore?"

"That's it. Straightforward. To the point."

"Goodness," Genny breathed. "It seems almost . . ." she hesitated.

"What?" Gus demanded sharply, anticipating her remark.

"Immoral," she snapped.

"That's a fine sentiment coming from a woman who visited a French whorehouse."

"That's different!"

"Would your Aunt Augusta think so?"

"Never mind about her."

"How about the rest of civilization?" he snorted. "Never mind them, too? So you have one set of rules for you, and another for everyone else. That would make you a hypocrite, wouldn't it?"

"I am not a hypocrite! I was simply visiting at Mademoiselle Chermont's and I in no way participated in any activities of a questionable sort! And I certainly wouldn't up and leave a husband if I'd been so foolish as to make a commitment of marriage before God and man," Genny intoned righteously.

"Lakota ideas about marriage are going to give you fits," Gus predicted. "I hope you're willing to work on increasing your tolerance for difference."

"Why did your wife leave you?" Genny pressed, ignoring his comments.

"Wouldn't you leave if you were married to me?" he taunted.

It was a singular thought, being married to Gus Renard. Genny laughed, picturing how that would go over on the home front. Ridiculous as the notion was, she appreciated that an alliance with Gus might have certain attractions. But she wasn't going to let her mind wander off in that direction. "I wouldn't be married to you or anyone else, so the answer is immaterial. I assume she had a choice to marry you in the first place?"

"Yeah, she was real excited about it. So was I." He sounded tired suddenly.

"What happened?"

"That's kind of personal, *istatowin*."

Genny leaned back in the saddle, embarrassed enough to blush, but not so much so that she was going to let her curiosity go unsatisfied.

"I'll bet you were unfaithful to her," she said solemnly.

Gus had to chuckle. "That would be the logical conclusion."

"Weren't you?" Genny asked in disbelief.

He shook his head. "No, I wasn't. I thought about it, but I wasn't. She got tired of me, *istatowin*, and she missed her family. She wanted me to go north to live with them, but I couldn't do it. So she went back home without me.''

"I would have thought if you loved each other, you might have worked things out," Genny said, faintly reproving.

"Now you sound like a self-righteous romantic. And here I thought you had no room for love in your plans.''

"We're talking about you, not me, and besides, love and marriage aren't necessarily the same thing. I don't have room for marriage. I haven't decided about love yet," she said. "Did you love your wife very much? Were you devastated when she left?''

Gus twisted his mouth in an irritated scowl. The glib announcement that Genny would consider a lover but not a husband rang discordantly. More to the point, her sincere concern and the hint of pity in her voice grated on him, pushing him into answering with brutal honesty. He stopped walking, caught Harv's bridle to stop Genny too, and pierced her with an intent gaze.

"Honey, I don't know what love is. My wife was a beautiful woman. I wanted a wife, I wanted her in my bed, and she wanted to be there. The only problem was that when our passions were sated, there wasn't anything left between us. The only thing I felt when she left was relief. Does that answer your questions?''

She nodded dumbly.

"Good," he said curtly. "End of discussion.''

Genny stared at him, but she found no words. No man had ever spoken so plainly to her, and the cold reality of Gus's failed marriage settled with the weight of granite in her mind. Their eyes held, and she read bleak acceptance in Gus's dark brown gaze. She was shocked, but more than that, she had the absurd desire to comfort him.

Slowly, Genny became aware of a low roar somewhere in the background, and that the constant sounds of the many birds had ceased. Harv stamped nervously, his ears twitching, and Gus's eyes shifted beyond her to fix on the sky. When he frowned, she turned to look over her shoulder.

Behind them in the southwest a huge storm cloud loomed, yellowy gray, obscuring the horizon, and moving rapidly. The wind gusted suddenly cooler, and swallows arrived out of nowhere, diving and careening in the currents above their heads. A low, steady thunder reached their ears.

"We have a problem here, *istatowin*," Gus informed her grimly. He quickly untied Trixie from Harv's saddle, and in another second, swung onto the gelding's back behind her, urging Harv into a gallop.

"What's wrong?"

Gus pushed her low over Harv's neck, his chest molded to her back. The saddlebow dug painfully into her stomach.

"We've got a hailstorm behind us, and it looks like a wild one." He spoke directly in her ear. "We've got to find some cover fast."

"Where, for mercy's sake?" The country was as bare as an open palm.

"I can't answer that one," Gus muttered.

He hadn't been paying as much attention to where they were going as he should have.

"What's causing that noise?" Genny asked. The wind rose, pushing them along, blowing their hair forward, even as fast as they were racing ahead of it. Trixie stayed even with them.

"It's the hail." The roar was getting louder. Gus scanned the low hills, praying for a gully, but he didn't see any place where they could get out of the way of the storm. In another minute, the tall reeds of a lake came into view, and Gus sent Harv toward the water in desperation.

When they reached the edge of the lake, Gus hauled back on Harv's leads, bringing him to a sudden stop that would have caused most mounts to rear in protest. The gelding's hooves plowed short furrows in the soft ground, but he didn't throw his riders. As soon as he was still, Gus leapt from his back, pulling Genny with him.

"Quick! Get the gear off Trixie!" he ordered.

Genny did as he said, loosening the laces that held

their saddlebags. Gus quickly removed Harv's saddle, then Trixie's, pulling it free as the last saddlebag fell at Genny's feet.

"Get 'em out of here!" he shouted over the wind. "There's no shelter for them. Their best chance is to run for it!"

Genny slapped Trixie hard on the rump. "Hyah! Go on!" The mare needed no further urging. She took off into the northwest, the gelding close on her heels.

"Help me dig these into the ground. Hurry, Genny!"

The wind blew his hair across his face so that she didn't know how he could see, but he was on his knees, using his knife to cut into the sod. Genny knelt beside him, and together they lifted a heavy section of grass and sand. Gus stuffed their saddlebags, blankets, and rifles into the cut, then replaced the grass, weighting it with their saddles. The roar was deafening as he rose, pulling Genny to her feet beside him. They turned to look behind them.

The prairie had disappeared in a churning, gray-brown cloud that thundered like a hundred locomotives. Above the constant din, peals of thunder clapped behind sharp bolts of forked lightning. Genny leaned into Gus, and his arm went around her automatically.

"What are we going to do?" she asked, trembling. They were completely exposed, with water at their backs.

"We'll wait to see how bad the hail is. If it's small, we'll shelter in the reeds," he told her, glancing toward the thickest area of growth.

"It isn't going to be small, is it?" Fear made her voice sharp and thin.

Gus looked down at her, and smiled with grim apology. He pushed a piece of hair away from her eyes. "I doubt it, *istatola*. There's too much noise."

"What will we do?"

His expression grew serious. "Just do what I tell you to and stay right with me. If you do, we'll have a good chance of coming through this without either of us getting hurt too badly. All right?"

Tiny bits of ice began to bounce in the grass ahead of

them, and Gus pulled Genny back with him to the shore of the lake before she could answer. Within seconds the hail reached them, stinging against their hands and faces as it hurled into them, and the sound of the storm drowned out their voices. The hailstones were the size of peas for a few seconds, but when the first jagged piece the size of a walnut hit Gus on the shoulder, he stepped into the water.

Hailstones pelted them painfully, growing larger by the minute, and hitting with the force of cannon fire. Gus pulled Genny with him into the lake until they were up to their waists in the slimy water. Genny froze when she realized what he intended.

"There's lightning!" she screamed, pushing hard to break free of his arms. "We can't go in the water!" A jagged hailstone the size of her fist splashed beside them, barely missing Genny, and the surface of the water roiled with the impact of the hurtling ice.

"Genny!" Gus dragged her with him into the center of the lake where the water reached her chin. "Don't fight me! We have to get *under* the water. Place one arm over your head, take a deep breath, and hang on to me! These stones will kill you if you don't!" he shouted in her ear. "Breathe, damn it!"

There was nothing else to do. She breathed deeply and closed her eyes, commending her soul to God. Gus pushed her under, moving into the deepest part of the lake.

It was strangely silent under the water, and Genny felt cold ice bobbing around her, but the water absorbed the impact of the hailstones. The stones traveled downward for some distance before they returned to the surface of the water. She clung to Gus, burying her face against his chest, eyes squeezed tightly shut. When her lungs were about to burst, she dug her nails into his shoulder. Immediately, they rose and broke the surface.

"Breathe!" he ordered, shielding her head with his arms. They were only up a second. Genny didn't open her eyes, but she heard and felt the sharp stones driving into the lake and pelting her shoulders. Gus drew her down with him into the water a second time, and the silence was almost a relief.

They rose to breathe a third time, a fourth, then a fifth. Genny lost track, concentrating on holding her breath as long as she could, and on the solid, secure feel of Gus's body against her own. She began to grow dizzy, unsure she could stop her lungs from opening any longer. When her fingers closed convulsively on his arms again, he propelled them to the surface, breaking through a layer of floating ice. This time they were met by the sting of cold rain, and the sound of water beating all around them in the air.

"It's over," Gus gasped between deep, rushing breaths. "It's just raining now. Are you all right?"

Genny looked at the white chunks of ice surrounding them in the murky water and nodded. Her lungs burned, and rain streamed through her already sodden hair, running in rivulets to drip from her chin. A blue-white flash of light startled her, and when thunder cracked a bare second behind it, she cringed, wrapping her arms around Gus's neck and dropping her face against his shoulder.

She raised her head as quickly as she'd hidden it. "We have to get out of the water!" She thought she screamed, but her voice came out small and frightened.

"Hang on." Gus kicked through the water, sweeping the ice chunks aside with his forearm, drawing Genny with him. He struggled for footing in the soft bottom, hauling her to her feet beside him. When she slipped, he lifted her into his arms and lurched toward the water's edge. Panting heavily, he left the lake, staggering under the pull of their wet clothes until he dropped Genny to the ground a dozen feet from the water.

They faced each other in the downpour, standing on an uneven layer of icy white hailstones. Genny looked helplessly at him, then down at herself. They were drenched and covered with slimy pond muck that stuck to their clothes and ran in streamers over their faces and arms. So much thick, sticky mud clung to Genny's boots that she couldn't see the leather underneath, even though the rivers cut into the mass by the driving rain.

"My boots are ruined," she murmured.

"And you lost my hat, but you've still got your goggles," he said, the ghost of a smile creasing his face. "We're going to stink like a couple of Indiana hogs if we don't get these clothes off and let the rain clean the muck off them and us." He reached for the buttons at her neck, fumbling to push the slippery buttons through their water-swollen holes.

Instinctively Genny grabbed his wrist to stop him. His cold fingers closed over hers, and he shook his head at her. "We just came out of an alkali pond full of bird muck. If we don't let the rain beat the filth and alkali out of these clothes we're going to have to throw them away. And your skin's going to itch and burn like all hell if you don't get rinsed off." He pushed her hands to her sides and resumed unbuttoning her blouse. "I'll try not to take undue advantage of the situation," he added dryly.

"You'd better not," she warned in a trembling voice, allowing him to undress her down to her drawers and cotton camisole, too shaken to object further. He tugged her shirttails free of her waistband, then drew her close as he worked the buttons at her waist. Supporting her elbow, he helped her out of the split skirt. She looked at it mournfully, rain streaming over her bare arms and soaking through the already wet cotton of her undergarments. "I'll have to throw it out anyway," she whispered. "If we ever get out of this storm."

Gus ran a finger along the reddened vee on her neck where her shirt had been open and the sun had burned her fair skin. "At least you won't die of sunstroke in weather like this." He smiled faintly, but a hint of concern furrowed his brow when he felt how cold Genny's flesh was. Placing her clothing in her arms, he turned to remove his own.

Numbly, she stood in the rain, her underclothes plastered to her, watching Gus remove his shirt and britches till he stood naked but for a leather breechcloth. A chill shook her and she shivered, her breath coming in ragged gasps.

Gus draped his clothes over his arm. "Come on, Genny. Follow me and move quick. Don't let yourself get any colder."

She did as he commanded, nearly running to keep up with his rapid pace, her boots crunching and slipping on the scattered ice. He led them away from the lake, then instructed her to spread her clothes over the thick grass, brushing away the litter of melting hailstones. "Scrub as hard as you can. Get the muck out of your clothes. Don't worry about your boots," he said, stooping to help her out of them, then peeling her stockings down her legs. Turning to his own garments, he scoured his shirt ruthlessly with his fist, rubbing so hard his shoulders and back strained with the effort. "Work, Genny!" he commanded when he looked up to find her watching him blankly. "Do it! It'll warm you up. The last thing I need is for you to get sick on me."

His sharp tone jolted her out of the stupor she was falling into. "We're going to catch a lung fever anyway, so I don't see what difference it makes!" she snapped, her temper breaking, but she spread her shirt and started scrubbing. There was nothing else to do, and nowhere to get out of the rain.

"I knew it would take more than a hailstorm to curb your tongue," Gus called to her, laughing.

"How can you laugh right now?" Genny shouted incredulously. She picked up a hailstone the size of a goose egg and hurled it toward the lake. "What are we going to do? The horses are gone, we can't get dry, and we're absolutely in the middle of nowhere! What are we going to do?" she repeated, pommeling her shirt.

"I don't know," Gus hollered back. "This is the biggest adventure of your life, remember? It didn't come with a player's guide."

"Ooohh! I hate Nebraska!" Genny exclaimed furiously. "Adventures are supposed to be exciting, not life-threatening!"

Gus threw his head back and laughed. All it had taken to shake Genny's cheerful confidence was the worst hailstorm Gus had seen in years. "Welcome to the west,

Genny Stone. Think what grand tales you'll tell of this day. It might even make a better yarn than the balloon and bawdy house story."

"If we survive," she retorted angrily.

Gus's smile was wry. "That's the challenge," he concurred. "I hope you're equal to it, because I wasn't kidding when I said I didn't know what to do."

"Don't tell me that! And wipe that stupid smirk off your face! Because of you, I'm going to die in the middle of this wilderness, and all you can do is laugh and grin like one of Paul's freighters with a dozen bottles of Plantation Bitters under his belt!"

"Would you rather I threw a tantrum, like you're doing?" he hollered back, flipping his soggy woolen shirt with a noisy slap.

"Oh, hush up! Just hush!" She pounded her fist into the ground. "And stop smiling!"

Gus and Genny pounded at their clothes, working their muscles, trying to warm their chilled flesh. When the rain lightened and the lightning and thunder moved off, following the destructive force of the storm northeast across the exposed country, Gus began looking for their saddles and buried gear. Genny straggled after him, her wet clothing draped over her arms in front of her. Her anger was fast giving way to unmitigated fear.

The saddles were lying on their sides several yards from the sod cut where Gus had hastily dumped their bags, guns, and blankets. The leather seats were marred with cuts and scarred white in many places from the sharp hailstones. Nicks were visible along the stirrups, and the straw padding stuck out of Genny's saddle along the cantle.

"We would have been cut to ribbons," she whispered.

Gus didn't comment, stooping to heft his saddle under his right arm. Genny bent to her own. "Leave it. Take my clothes," he said, transferring them to her arms and retrieving the second saddle.

He dropped the saddles near their gear, stacking them one atop the other. "Spread the clothes on the grass, Genny," he instructed, pointing a short distance away from the saddles. Then he lifted the sod to pull the saddle blankets and their bedrolls free.

"These aren't too wet," he said, spreading the heavier blankets on the ground in front of the saddles. "Strip off your underclothes, wrap yourself in this," he tossed her the red blanket, "don't argue, and hurry."

He loosed the string at his waist and turned away from her, wrapping his own blanket around his waist so fast she saw only a flash of paler skin at his hip. Moving with an economy of motion, he whirled the other blankets around him, and sat, his back to the saddles and the lessening rain.

"Hurry up," he repeated sharply. "This is no time for one of your fits of propriety."

She badly wanted to argue, but her instincts told her she needed to warm up and get as dry as she could, no matter the circumstances. Reluctantly, she turned away from Gus and shucked her drawers and camisole, mentally daring him to make a comment about her naked backside. As fast as possible, she wound the blanket around her. It was blessedly dry except for a couple of spots along the edges.

"Get over here. Don't stand there letting the blanket get wet," Gus ordered. "Drop your things clear and sit down. Quickly." He held the blankets up, tent fashion, and beckoned her to sit in front of him.

She reluctantly did as he directed, muttering under her breath. As soon as she dropped onto the saddle blankets, he made room for her between his knees, drew her none too gently into his embrace, and folded the blankets over her head and down over her feet to encompass them in a woolen cocoon.

"This is awful," she complained, her voice muffled beneath the heavy wool, as she thrashed about to find a comfortable position. "It's dark, damp, and it smells like a wet horse."

Gus grunted as she caught him in the ribs with her elbow. "Sit still and stop being a grouser. Settle back against me and help me get these blankets tucked under our feet."

"You're naked, for heaven's sake! I'm not going to lean back any farther!" Her backside was already only a hairsbreadth away from him, and his legs were wrapped around hers, his flesh damp and cool, the hair on his thighs rasping lightly against her fingers when she accidently knocked his blanket aside. He wiggled his icy toes against her feet, burrowing until he got them under the soft flesh of her calves. She tried to dislodge them, but he wouldn't budge. "Fix your blanket. It's coming loose around your legs," she said, dropping her hands primly in front of her.

"All sensitive parts are amply covered," he chuckled. "The more you move, the more the water will leak in, but the closer we get, the warmer and dryer we'll be. Try cooperating for once in your life, *ištatola*."

He pulled her back, arranging the blankets so the rain couldn't get through, with the outer one tucked under the edge of the saddle blankets they were sitting on, and the inner one under their feet and legs.

"You are so vulgar, Renard. This won't keep us dry for long."

Shivering, she helped him anchor the blankets. Her knees kept bumping into his thighs, and her fingers touched his ankles as she secured the blanket folds in front of them. She remembered the night when he had run his hands intimately over her legs under the guise of tending her cut knee, and this morning when, lying in a close embrace, he had run his hand up her ankle again. Her stomach fluttered at the memories.

"It may not rain much longer, and we're only dealing with one crisis at a time. Future planning is for speculators and bankers. Adventurers take life moment by moment." Gus wrapped his arms around her shoulders, his forearms crossing over her middle, and tucked his hands between her arms and her body. "Let me warm you up."

His hands felt like ice against her, and she stiffened at his touch.

"What do you mean, warm me up? You're colder than

I am." She shivered violently. "What do you know of bankers, anyway?"

"My father is a banker." He flexed his fingers, curling them under his palms, chafing them lightly against the scratchy surface of Genny's blanket. His movements sent darts of pleasure through her breasts, leaving an ache pulsing in their peaks.

"Really?" she asked, attempting to act as though his touch meant nothing to her. "In Canada?" It wasn't working. She clamped her arms to her sides to get him to stop, but only succeeded in trapping his hands against her breasts. Quickly, she gave him more room.

"Yeah." He nodded, and his chin rubbed the side of her face. He resumed chafing his fingers.

"Tell me about your family." Tingles ran down her neck to tickle ever lower into the core of her. Her attention wavered between her fears and the distraction Gus presented.

"Now? I want to get warm. I don't want to talk," he said, shivering against her. He wanted to concentrate solely on the warm tension that was building in his muscles as he touched Genny and savored the feel of her in his arms.

Her chest expanded with a rapid, ragged breath that caught audibly in her throat. "Please, Gus," she whispered, suddenly overwhelmed by how close they'd come to serious injury, her worry about what might have happened to Trixie and Harv, and what was going to happen to them without the horses.

"I don't like to talk about my family." Gus's voice was almost as cold as his fingers.

"I'll sit still and be cooperative," she pleaded tiredly, snuggling her shoulders against his chest, seeking the feeble warmth that was returning to his body.

Gus felt the slight tremors Genny was striving to subdue, and he knew she was fighting to control her emotions. Knowing it would help if he talked, distracting her, he still didn't want to remind himself of the rejection he'd suffered as a child, and later as a young man. Perhaps if he could divert her in other ways, as well, he could avoid giving her more than a perfunctory outline.

"All right," Gus sighed, deliberately fanning his breath over her shoulder. She straightened her neck and her shoulder twitched, bringing a smile to his mouth. "I'll make a special exception and tell you about my family. My father's name is René Renard and he's the President of La Banque Française Nationale de Montréal."

Chapter 8

"I thought he was a trader," Genny interrupted in surprise.

Thinking back to what he'd said about his father hiring tutors for him, she knew she shouldn't have been surprised. His articulate, well-accented speech and educated vocabulary alone marked him as a member of a family of means, but she had been willing to accept the pretense he cultivated of being the mixed-blood offspring of a simple trader. She didn't consciously examine why she'd done so as readily as she had.

"He did some trading at one time. There's only a difference of scale and attire between bankers and traders."

"How did he go from being a frontier trader to a big city bank president?"

Gus sighed, shifting his shoulders against the itchy wool that was draped over them, and wishing he hadn't gotten started. "It's a dull story. Don't you have any adventures to relate?"

"I want to hear this. You've got me intrigued, so you have to go on."

He fidgeted, inadvertently pulling the blanket closer over Genny's face. She put up a hand to push it back, and he finally settled his chin against her head. The darkness and the soft weight of the blankets over their heads increased her sense of intimacy. When he spoke, his voice was soft and low, just above her ear, and she could feel each movement of his jaw.

"My grandmother's family had managed the bank in close association with the Jesuits in Montréal for a couple of generations. She didn't have any brothers or male cousins, so my grandfather took over when my father was a boy. As a young man, René, my father, left to find adventures in the west."

"What does he look like?" she interrupted.

"He's as tall as I am, a little heavier, fair skinned and blond with light blue eyes. For all the difference in our coloring, we look a lot alike."

Genny easily envisioned an older version of Gus, but she had trouble seeing him as a blond Canadian. "Did it seem strange to you when you were a child that your father's skin was so fair when yours is so dark?" she wondered aloud.

Gus shook his head and chuckled. "No. He was my father, and I couldn't imagine him being other than as he was. I used to laugh about the hair on his face and chest, though. None of my mother's male relatives had hair on their bodies like he did, and my cousins and I all thought that he was half bear."

"Your chest is smooth," Genny said, flexing her shoulder blades against his firm muscles. She felt him tense under her movement.

"Like an Indian." He fell into silence.

Genny thought he was going to say something else, but when he didn't, she drew him back to his tale. "Did your father find his adventures?"

"Of course he did. This is the west, isn't it?"

Genny felt his smile against her ear as he dipped his head and continued, speaking so that she felt the movements of his lips on her jaw.

"He came in the twenties, at the height of the fur trapping days. My father traveled all through the mountains, between the big rivers in the east and the Pacific ocean in the west, far up into the north, and down into Texas. He visited California, and I think he maybe went down to Mexico. When he got tired of wandering and trapping, he set up a trading post for the American Fur Company on the Missouri, near the mouth of the Smoky Earth River.

"There he met a pretty Lakota widow whose husband had been killed in a fight with the Pawnees a couple of years before. Her hair was long, as black as midnight and as soft as silk. Her eyes were round and deep brown like an otter's pelt, and she was the most beautiful woman my father had ever seen. He fell in love the moment he laid eyes on her, but it took him months to convince her that a *wasicu* would make an acceptable husband. He gave up the trading post and followed her, learning to live as a Sicangu with her people. Finally, she consented to have him, and they were married." He bent and nuzzled Genny's neck, allowing the blanket to drop onto her head.

"She was your mother?" Doubting that a protest would stop him, and not certain she wanted to, she tried hard to ignore him and the currents of sensation that rippled through her.

"Yes." He lifted one hand to push her damp hair aside, then brushed his lips across her nape. He smiled when she gasped softly.

"What was her name?" She ought to stop him. She knew she should, yet somehow she didn't.

"We don't speak the names of the dead. It calls them back from the world beyond, and Indians have no liking for ghosts." His hand drifted down over her shoulder.

"Do you believe in ghosts?"

"No." His hand halted briefly, then resumed its path downward. He wondered if Genny had any idea of the legends about the place she lived, but he decided to pursue it another time. "But I honor my mother's memory by observing the customs she believed."

"You loved her. I can hear it in your voice."

His voice was as gentle and easy as an autumn leaf descending a breath of warm September air. His hand brushed her breast as he tucked his arm back around her, and Genny inhaled sharply; the feelings Gus's touch aroused were far more akin to the wild chaos of the passing storm than the tranquil beauty of falling autumn leaves.

"Yes. So did my father. My mother had a daughter from her first marriage, and he loved her little girl, Good Shield, as if she were his own. Then my mother welcomed René Renard's first son a year after she accepted the *wasicu* as her husband."

"That was you," Genny said, shifting her hips a little.

The blanket slipped open across her legs, and the outsides of her thighs slid along the insides of Gus's. Both of them held their breaths for an instant.

Genny rapidly tugged the blanket into place again.

"Yeah, that was me," Gus said, expelling his pent-up breath, and forcing his attention back to his tale. "And I was, by all accounts, a model infant. I never cried, I slept peaceably most of the time, and I was the smartest boy in camp. I also showed early signs of great talent, killing my first game birds at four and a half, and I was unstintingly brave, once saving one of my younger cousins from an angry crow who was determined to remove some beads from her cradleboard." He hugged Genny to him, rocking her lightly as he chuckled.

"And modesty was your foremost virtue." Shivers scattered pleasantly along the nerve endings in her arms and back as she moved with him.

"Absolutely. We were happy during those years of my childhood. Then my mother died when I was five years old." There was sadness in his voice that spoke of acceptance and regret, and he fell still. "She was on her way to visit some relatives in a nearby camp when a late spring blizzard caught her party out on the plains without shelter."

Genny shuddered involuntarily. "These prairies aren't an easy place to live, are they?" she asked softly, placing her hand over his forearm.

The question she didn't voice hung in the air: what would happen to them without horses or shelter?

Gus shook his head and sighed, leaning more heavily into her. "None of them made it, and my father took it hard. He stayed in the camp for a couple of months after her death, but he was so unhappy he had to leave, to go somewhere he wouldn't be reminded so much of her. So he returned to his family in Montréal.''

"What happened to you?"

Thinking of him as a small boy who'd lost his mother made her want to offer comfort. She tucked her fingers between the crook of his arm and the scratchy wool covering her breast.

"He took me with him. Remember? That's where I learned to read.''

"What about your sister?"

Absently, she began to rub the back of her forefinger against the inside of his arm, slipping the surface of her nail up and down in a tiny caress. His skin was soft and supple over firm muscles.

"My grandparents begged to keep her, so my father let her stay. It was a wise thing to do.''

He closed his eyes and focused for a second on the small movement of her finger, wanting her to touch him more fully, craving the warmth of her palm and the excitement they could create between them.

"Was it difficult to be separated from her?" Genny asked quietly.

Gus's palms opened under her arms, and he slid his thumbs under the edge of the blanket she had wrapped around her, so that his hands cupped the sides of her breasts. Genny tensed, covering his palms with her own as licks of fire shot through her, making her breasts feel heavy and aching.

"Gus," she began, a warning note in her voice.

He kept his hands where they were when she pushed at them.

"I was only five, *istatowin*. I missed my mother keenly, and then my sister, but once we were away from everything that I had known, I adapted quickly. In Montréal, my father was reunited with his family after having been gone for more than fifteen years. Despite his failure to communicate even his whereabouts during all that time, they welcomed him back. My grandfather insisted he take a position at the bank. Eventually we moved into our own house and my father remarried. From that point on, the story of my father's family becomes desperately insipid. I have a younger half-brother named Marcel, whom I haven't seen in more than ten years." He purposely didn't go into the events that followed his father's second marriage. It didn't matter anymore. He'd chosen his way in life, left the Renard family behind, and he didn't want to dredge up the past. "Basically, the Renards are a completely typical, dull as dry toast, white family."

With a mixed-blood eldest son, Genny thought, they were hardly typical. Again, she was aware of undercurrents of emotion in Gus. He was leaving a great deal unsaid, but she decided not to press him.

"Your father doesn't sound dull at all. He sounds as though he's had a fascinating life. You take after him, don't you?"

She wished Gus would move his hands away from her breasts. She felt caught in a whirlpool of unfamiliar sensations, as if she were being pulled into an unexplored realm without experience to guide her. It wasn't unpleasant, but she wasn't ready to go. Not with Gus, and not now, when their very existence seemed precarious.

He moved his hands, but not away. Instead, he looped his forefingers inside the blanket, loosening the tuck she'd made under her right shoulder, and touching her lightly.

"What makes you say that?"

He stroked the top of her left breast with one long finger. Her pulse leapt at the touch and she grasped his hand and held it tight, trying to push it away. "Your mother sounds far too sweet to have bestowed her temperament on you."

"I can be sweet," Gus assured her, brushing his lips across her shoulder as he clasped his hand around hers and nestled both of them together against her breast.

She caught her breath. "I don't think you could maintain it for very long. You'd be bored silly, and you know it."

"You're right," Gus sighed dramatically. "It's more

fun to be dangerous than sweet.'' He squeezed her hand, and part of her breast under it.

Genny rapped his hand sharply with the knuckles of her other hand, but that didn't stop the liquid rush that flooded her breasts and shot straight through to her core.

"You're putting my patience to the push, Gus. You know, I might like you better if you practiced up a bit with being sweet.''

"No, you wouldn't. It's more fun to play with fire and dangerous toys, *istatola*, something you learned long before I met you. Otherwise, you'd never have marched into a brothel. And in spite of your wicked behavior with regard to an Army of the Potomac officer last spring, I think I'm the one who's going to show you that men are one of those fires that make for dangerous excitement. Didn't your Henri ever kiss you?''

He lifted her and pulled in his legs so that she sat sideways in his lap, their heads on an even level, tenting the blankets over them. The blanket Genny wore caught under her hip and slipped a little lower.

"Of course, he did,'' Genny answered quickly, reaching for the blanket with her free hand.

"So what did you think?'' Gus caught her wrist in the darkness and raised it to his lips, placing a light kiss on the inside of it before releasing it.

"It was . . . pleasant enough.'' But it hadn't been the same as when Gus kissed her. Not the same at all.

"That's a pretty lukewarm description. Didn't you like his kisses?''

He brought her hand away from her breast, placed it on his shoulder, and returned his own hand, unencumbered, to the curve of her flesh. Her other hand clamped around his wrist, but he had started a throbbing in her breasts that made her yearn for his touch. She didn't push his hand away.

"I liked them,'' she told him, spreading her fingers so that they dipped into the hollows of his collarbone. His skin was warm now, and silky over the hard bone and muscle beneath. "But . . .''

"But nothing,'' he said, low and emphatically.

"Kisses should be like taffy or caramels or divinity fudge. You should love them so much you want to make yourself sick on them, only to discover that the most glorious thing about kisses is that you can never have so many you can't enjoy a thousand more."

He pushed his hand inside her blanket, cupping her breast fully, feeling her nipple bead against his palm.

"It wasn't like . . . this," she gasped softly, still holding his wrist.

The ache in her breasts intensified, radiating throughout her, and the rough texture of Gus's hand was both comfortable and exciting. It felt too good to stop him. She caught her breath again when he brushed his cool fingers over the crest, sending a tumult of sensation straight to the center of her. In the darkness, her whole consciousness seemed to focus in her breasts, and she waited breathlessly for him to touch her again.

"But I'm not kissing you, Genny." He spoke into her ear, sending tingles of feeling down her neck, hardening her nipples further. He rubbed his thumb across one, testing the weight of her breast in his hand.

"I don't believe you have to. Why is it so different when you touch me, Gus?" She felt heavy, as if her blood had thickened and slowed, pooling close to her skin so that every touch was intensified, heightening her pleasure and building a deep anticipation.

"I wish I knew," he murmured, raising his hands to cup her face. "I wish to heaven I knew. But I think I'm going to be your wildfire, ištatola." His mouth closed over hers and she turned in his arms, the blanket falling to her waist. Soft, moist, and hot, his lips moved, exploring gently.

A tiny moan escaped from the back of her throat, as she placed her arms around his neck and pressed her bare breast against the hard muscles of his chest. Her nakedness was strangely liberating, and she marveled at the sensations she felt as she breathed deeply, pushing the soft weight of her breast into the unyielding flesh of his. An exquisite vulnerability overcame her, accompanied by the desire to let his strength envelope and protect her, even as the woolen blankets that caught on her hair and brushed her shoulders did. With a sigh, she moved her lips under his, abandoning rational thought in favor of physical sensation and the waves of untapped emotion that his touch drew forth.

The scent of musty wool was overlaid with the cool, rain-clean scent of Gus's cheek, and the damp, salt smell of his wet hair. His lips were full and soft, and never still. His nose and chin brushed her with kisses of their own, light, grazing touches that extended the range of pleasures in his kiss, before he teased her lips apart with flickering strokes of his tongue. He surged forward to meet the soft swell of her mouth, coaxing her to match his intimate caress.

Lightning shot through her, and she flexed her hips, squeezing her thighs together in an unconscious movement that sent fire into Gus's loins. He rocked up against her, his flesh hard and aching, and she answered his demand with the bold thrust of her tongue against his.

Pulling her to face him fully, Gus ran his hands down her neck and across her chest until he covered both her breasts with his palms. Genny groaned, pressing forward, accepting both his hands, and the seductive thrusts of his tongue into her mouth. When he massaged her breasts, once again rubbing his thumbs over her throbbing nipples, she instinctively rolled her pelvis into him. The bunched material of the blanket between her legs was not barrier enough to keep her from feeling the hard length of him.

She backed away. He was going too fast for her, but it was as he said. His kisses were like candy, sweet and tempting her to more. Much more. With a whimper, she rocked back against him.

Gus drew his mouth from her, running a line of soft, sucking kisses down her neck. He was breathing heavily, his muscles taut and ready for the movements that would bring him into the most intimate embrace of all. With an effort, he tried to relax, reminding himself who she was. His mind screamed for him to look at what he was doing and stop, but he didn't heed it. There was still time. Time to touch her breasts, to kiss her, to glory in the pulse of life that quickened his heartbeat and hardened his body. He touched his lips to her breastbone.

"I want to see you," he whispered against her, flinging back the blankets over their heads.

It had stopped raining, but the sudden wash of cool, moisture-laden air made Genny gasp. When she opened her eyes and looked down at Gus she froze.

He was gazing reverently at her breasts. She was high, full, and firm, her flesh rounded and crowned with rosy-brown peaks that tightened under his regard and the kiss of the cool breeze. He touched her lightly, circling one aureole with a dark finger.

Genny stared, transfixed by the sight of her lover's hand caressing her intimately, and by the gentle smile on his face. His eyes rose and caught her gaze. The fierce desire that lighted his dark eyes complemented his quiet smile, creating an expression that promised passionate excitement and tender demonstration.

Gus saw fascination and confusion in Genny's face. Her gaze darted over his features, lingering on his mouth and returning to his eyes, and her eyebrows raised in a silent question. Her lips parted as if to speak, but no words issued forth. Whatever was between them was strong and vital, as unmanageable as the storm which had so lately passed, and at times, as easy as the soft breeze that flowed over them now.

In a flash of self-honesty, Gus knew he wasn't pretending to seduce Genny anymore. He'd begun a game that he wanted to play to only one conclusion.

"You're lovely, *istatowin*," he breathed, bending his head to one breast.

"No!"

Genny pushed him away abruptly. In the afternoon sunlight, filtering through the breaking clouds, she saw herself, nearly naked, with only a red blanket haphazardly wrapped about her waist, sitting atop a naked man, her knees spread on either side of him, his swollen flesh pressing intimately against her. She grabbed for her blan-

ket, pulling it rapidly up over her breasts, and tried to
back away.

Gus's arms came around her, pulling her firmly into
his embrace. He tucked his own blanket over his legs,
then held Genny's head against his shoulder with one
hand while he draped the other blankets around their
shoulders.

"Relax, Genny," he sighed, willing his hands to be
still and his groin to stop throbbing.

"I can't believe I let you do this," she groaned. "I
can't believe I did this! Please, let go of me."

"In a minute." He exhaled slowly. "There's something I want to say."

Genny waited in silence. Gradually, the tension in him
eased and he dropped his arms to rest lightly around her
waist.

"It's been a long time since I've been with a woman,"
he began. Genny winced, not at all pleased at the thought
of Gus doing what he'd just done with her with anyone
else, and even less pleased with her own jealous reaction.
"And you're obviously a little overripe yourself."

"I hate the way you talk," she said tightly. "We are
not a pair of rotting melons. Get to the point."

"You need to make a decision about this."

She lifted her head to stare at him. "About what?"

"The time is at hand for you to decide if you want a
little love in your life."

Genny flamed scarlet from her breasts to her hairline.
"You're talking about lovemaking, not love."

"Weren't you?"

She wasn't honestly sure what she'd been talking
about. "No. Let me up, Gus." She pushed, but he didn't
release her.

"Tell me what the difference is."

"I know I'm not in love with you. I don't even like
you."

"But you feel something. Something powerful. It
might be love," he said huskily.

"You feel something, too. Are you in love with me?"

A cheeky grin spread across his face. "I already told

you I don't know what love is, but I know I want you
like all bloody hell.''

Genny looked away in embarrassment. "You have
such elegant ways of expressing yourself," she bit out.

"I wasn't doing so badly a few minutes ago." He
paused, tipping her chin up with his finger so that she
was forced to look at him. "You want me, too, *istatowin*,
just as much as I want you. I see it when you look at
me, and I can feel it when I touch you."

She resisted the sudden urge to trace the line of his
eyebrows with a finger. He was right; she did want him.
Quite simply, she lusted for him, and she couldn't dress
it up as any more noble sentiment. Admitting as much,
however, even to herself, was flying in the face of the
training and values of a lifetime. She couldn't say it
aloud.

"I thought you didn't get involved with white
women," she reminded him.

Faint lines appeared between his eyebrows. "That
bothers me, and normally, I don't. There's something
about you, though, that's cracked my resolve, and I've
never been much good at self-denial. I've got a feeling
that if the weather doesn't kill us first, I'm about to break
with long-standing tradition." There was a note of bitterness in his voice that surprised and annoyed Genny.

"Don't sacrifice your principles on my account,
please," she snapped, pushing to get out of his arms.
He caught her wrists and held her.

"Think about it, Genny. Think about what you really
want, because I'm giving you fair warning. You know
what I want, and I don't feel like fighting my desires.
You've already said you don't want to get married, and
that you're not unduly concerned about your reputation.
So be forewarned. If you don't oppose me directly, I'm
going to show you territory that will make Nebraska look
tame." He released her hands, but held her gaze with
confident certainty.

"You're asking me to consider taking you as a lover?"
she gasped. "Just like that?" She snapped her fingers.

"Just like that." He snapped his fingers back at her.

"Think about it," he said, smiling at her horrified expression. "Right now, we need to find some clothes and see to our more immediate problems. Up you go."

Most of their gear was damp but otherwise undamaged. Genny dressed in her brown twill winsey skirt and a boy's blue work shirt that she'd worn often on the trail west. Gus donned a second pair of buckskin trousers and a blue wool shirt identical to the one that had gotten drenched. He wrapped his extra pair of moccasins around Genny's feet, binding them with leather strings to take up the excess room, and told her to leave her boots behind. They ate soggy crackers, cheese, and raisins, Gus sharing the last without complaint, then repacked the saddlebags. Gus tied the bags into packs that could be slung over their shoulders, rolled the blankets and tied them on, and handed Genny her rifle.

"We'll leave the saddles here," he said, acting as if nothing out of the ordinary had transpired between them.

Genny tried to match his nonchalance. "What do you suppose happened to Harv and Trixie?" she asked, fearing the worst.

"They might have gotten out of the worst of it. If they did, Harv will find us. If not, we're in for a long walk."

"Won't we need the saddles if they come back?"

"We've got the blankets, and they'll have to do. Harv is fine without a saddle, and that mare of yours isn't much good to us with or without one. Are you ready?"

She nodded, and they started walking, skirting the lake to the west, and assuming a northerly course.

"How long do you think you can walk?" Gus asked, glancing at the shafts of sunlight streaming from behind the clouds in the west. "There are about four hours of light left. Can you make ten miles?"

"I can walk as far as we need to go," Genny said. "Do you have a particular destination in mind?"

"There's a river about ten miles north," he replied. "The valley there would give us some protection from the weather, and there are small areas of timber and good water. I'd sure appreciate a fire tonight."

"So would I," Genny agreed, shifting her pack a little higher. "If you can guarantee me a fire and a cup of coffee, I'll walk twenty miles."

Gus grinned at her, a wicked twinkle lighting his eyes. "I could promise you a lot more comfort than that, if you're of a venturesome mind."

Genny's nervous smile belied both wariness and grudging amusement. "You can always dream, but don't get your hopes up, handsome," she shot back, striving to emulate his carefree tone. "I've had similar offers before and never consented to any of them."

"Henri?" Gus guessed, grin in place, but eyes narrowing.

"Among others," Genny said lightly.

"Well," Gus said with mock seriousness, "I'll just have to work that much harder at showing off my unique charms. Did you happen to notice this . . ." With his free hand, he started to pull his shirt bottom up from where it hung over his hips.

"Don't you dare!" Genny exclaimed, skipping ahead of him.

". . . little scar on my stomach. It's shaped exactly like a fishhook. It's very distinctive," he finished, chuckling.

She laughed back at him. "I'll take your word for it. Now if you really want me to seriously consider your proposition, you're going to have to be silent so I can think," she told him, blatantly using the only means she could think of to gain a little peace.

"You've got a deal, *istatowin*. I'll be as quiet as a mouse."

Chapter 9

Gus was as good as his word, and much as she tried not to, Genny did mull over the possibility of entering into a romantic liaison with him.

For all of one minute.

It was too ridiculous to consider. This was the man who had faced her down with a rifle and shot a hole the size of a saucer into the wall not three feet from her! Little more than twenty-four hours later he was claiming he couldn't keep his hands off her, suggesting they become lovers. It would have been laughable but for the sorry fact that she was almost tempted to consider it. But there was her reputation to consider, though that really was a laugh. If her past foibles had not been enough to put her beyond social acceptability, it was only because she had never been involved with any hint of romantic scandal until the incident involving Nicholas Mercer. Even that wasn't half so bad as it appeared. Her adventure in France was a far more serious breach of decorum, but no one in Philadelphia knew a thing about it.

For the first time, Genny saw that leaving White Rock Spring with Gus might prove a formidable obstacle to realizing her dream of a serious art school for girls. Stories of women taken captive by Indians made dramatic newspaper copy, and it was possible that her adventure could be thus construed. People always assumed the worst sort of humiliation and degradation was visited upon white women at Indian hands—and while there might be pity for the victims, Genny had noticed that they were still held in contempt by much of society. She could easily become one such victim, regardless of what actually befell her on her journey.

She could end up a ruined woman. Respectable women would not entrust her with the least fraction of their daughters' educations.

Unhappily, Genny understood that she might have dashed her hopes for the future on the stones of impetuosity and stubborn pride. The consequences of not following Roger and Martha Rivier to the safety of an army encampment could well reach far beyond her year on the frontier.

There was always the possibility that no one would find out what had happened, but with Paul bound to learn most of it at some point, Genny didn't put a great deal of hope in that eventuality. She had a foreboding sense that it would be hard to keep her adventure a secret, in which case she would simply have to make the best of things.

But was allowing Gus Renard to make love to her the best thing? She doubted it, but she was unable to dismiss the idea. With no question of marriage to complicate matters, he wanted her to accept from him the most intimate of attentions. She had to admit that her curiosity was great. Never before had she felt the way she did when Gus touched her. And if this was only the beginning, how much further could passion carry them?

As a lover, Gus had definite attractions.

Shocked at where her line of reasoning had led, Genny retrenched and called herself a fool for thinking such a thing. With sudden clarity, she knew that however much or little the idea of being Gus Renard's lover struck her fancy, she would not do it. No matter how attractive she found him, she was not in love with him. They weren't even friends!

Friendship might prove a starting point, however, a place from which to explore the very powerful attraction between them. Perhaps if she and Gus made an effort to put their irregular start behind them, she'd gain a better idea of whether or not she wanted to be his lover. In all good conscience, she could offer him nothing more.

The sky was still gray, deepening into evening violet, when Gus and Genny came to the edge of the valley of the Niobrara. The hills fell away in a steep, rounded bank that dropped more than a hundred feet. Small stands of cottonwood and willow dotted the shadowed river bottom, and the sound of the flowing water drifted up to them in the calm that came as the sun set.

Gus dropped cautiously to his stomach and crawled to the edge of the hill overlooking the narrow valley. He signalled Genny down as well. After long minutes of watching, he seemed satisfied that it was safe to descend.

"What were you looking for?" Genny asked, following Gus over the edge.

"Pawnees, mostly, but other enemies, as well," he said softly. "Watch your step. The ground's wet."

"Other enemies? Such as?" She angled her feet to accommodate the steep slope, elbows spread to help her balance with the unaccustomed load on her back.

"Cougars, bears, ostriches, elephants," he said with a straight face.

"Elephants? There aren't . . ." she started to retort before she realized he was teasing. "Ostriches aren't dangerous," she finished with a short laugh. Looking unhappily at the muddy section of decline in front of her, she hesitated.

"When you find them in Nebraska Territory, they are," Gus insisted, turning and holding out his hand to her. She took it and he guided her down the slippery slope.

Together they skidded to the bottom.

Genny laughed, coming to a sliding stop beside him. "You have quite an imagination."

He smiled back. "Keeps the ladies' minds off the rigors of frontier travel."

She glanced back up the hill. It was much steeper than it had looked from the top.

"Thanks, Gus," she said simply. "I'd have to admit

that after today, I know what the pilgrims along the trail mean when they say they've 'seen the elephant.' "

A wide smile creased Gus's face. "Oh, Genny, today was mild happenings compared to what a lot of those farmers and shopkeepers endure on their travels, and less yet than what my mother's people have come to accept as commonplace."

Genny sniffed. "What's the dividing line between mild and severe happenings, then?"

"Whether or not you come out alive and sane at the other end. Lose either one, your life or your mind, and you can say you've 'seen the elephant.' "

"I doubt I'd be saying much in either case," she pointed out.

Gus chuckled softly. "You know, it's kind of nice not to have to stop and explain what an ostrich is," he said, almost to himself.

She looked at him blankly.

"Nobody out here's ever seen one," he explained, shrugging.

"Neither have I," she replied, glancing back out at the valley before them. "I've only seen drawings in books."

"Nobody out here reads books."

Something in the soft intensity of his voice made Genny look up at him. He wore a wistful smile that didn't touch his eyes, and she was reminded of Martha Rivier. The trader's wife had worn a similar expression when she saw the straw sunbonnet trimmed with Brussels lace, sprays of silk violets, and black satin ribbons Genny had given her in thanks for her help in getting settled.

Gus reached over and swatted Genny smartly on the behind, effectively destroying the moment.

"Come on, *istatola*. Let's see what we can find to make that fire."

He strolled toward the river, Genny following, and muttering imprecations as she went.

They made camp near a thicket of gray-green buffalo berry bushes, working hard to collect fallen wood before the light faded. When the wood was piled in a heap close by, Genny unpacked their wet clothes to spread them over the bushes, tying them to the thorny branches so they wouldn't blow away. The blankets were likewise left to dry in the light wind, draped over the scraggly bushes and weighted with river rocks.

By the time it was dark, Gus had a small blaze going and had put several small rocks from the river into it to heat. He brewed their coffee in a small, collapsible tin pan by filling it with water and dropping the rocks into it when they were cracking hot. Then he added the coarse grounds that Genny had made by beating the beans between two rocks. While they waited for the coffee, Genny melted a chunk of cheese on a green stick, and ate it with damp pieces of cracker, then accepted a piece of buffalo jerky from Gus. She gnawed at it a while, unable to get her teeth through it to bite off a piece.

"Did you lose your dagger or are you just too lazy to get it out and cut that leather into something you can chew?" Gus asked, handing her his knife.

Genny clapped her hand to her ankle where she normally wore the dagger. Feeling only the soft top of Gus's moccasins and no boot or dagger, she gasped. "I didn't even think about it! What rotten luck! It must have fallen out of my boot in the lake."

"We can get you another knife when we get to camp," Gus told her.

"Oh, but you don't understand," she said. "I've had that dagger since I was fifteen, and it was special. And lordy, Paul's going to have fits."

"It was just a knife. Why should he care?"

"That's what he wanted if he wins the wager and I don't make it a full year on the frontier," Genny explained. "I can't believe I lost it!"

"Why does Paul want it?" Gus asked, holding out his hand for his knife and her jerky. When she gave them to him, he cut the dried meat into small chunks and dropped them back into Genny's lap.

"It was his originally. I won it from him in a horse race. He got it from a Pawnee medicine man, I think, who told him it was the key to a great treasure. It was very old, of Spanish design, and Paul is convinced it's connected to the legend of El Dorado and the mythical cities of gold.''

Gus's soft laughter filled the cool night air. "Then why didn't he hang on to the blasted thing himself?"

"It wasn't until after I'd already won it that he met another medicine man who had a similar knife and a piece of an old doubloon. Then he decided there might be something to the story after all, but I wouldn't give it back. If there is a treasure, Paul certainly doesn't deserve it. What do you think, Gus? Could the dagger really have been the key to a hidden treasure?"

"If it is, I doubt it's a chest of gold. El Dorado is a figment from an ancient time. Come to think of it, though, I've seen a few warriors from different tribes wearing old Spanish coins as medallions. I know of one Cheyenne holy man who has a helmet from a soldier who came into the country south of here with Cortéz, hundreds of years ago. Old artifacts abound, but there isn't any treasure. The Spaniards came to discover Indian treasure and take it with them, not to leave their own gold behind in the wilderness."

"How can you be so sure there's no treasure?"

"If there ever was, you can bet some trapper found it years ago and squandered it all on cheap whiskey. Those men were into every nook and cranny of the country between the Mississippi and the Pacific, and they were after fortune. If there was an unattended treasure lying about, one of them would have snapped it up."

"What if it was well hidden?"

"They'd have looked hard and found it."

"It's a big country, Gus, and there weren't that many trappers. If there was a treasure, it could still exist."

"There wasn't a treasure, though. It was Spanish dreams of wealth and immortality that spawned the legend. They were told stories they didn't understand about treasures they didn't value. It's always the same between the red men and the white. Take my word for it, *istatola*. There's no hidden treasure hoard of gold."

Genny decided there was no point in arguing further.

"I didn't think there was, but I'm sorry I lost the dagger. It was in the case you left me. That's gone, too." She paused, remembering the circumstances under which the knife case had been given, then plunged ahead. "About that case . . ."

Gus chuckled.

"Now don't you start laughing. It was inexcusable, what you did."

"Aw, come on, Genny. I took a few raisins, a couple of jars of jam, and your book, and I left you the knife case as a fair trade." He stretched out his legs and leaned back on one elbow, watching the fire instead of her face.

"That's not what I mean, and you know it. Whatever possessed you to do such a thing?" She tried to put a sufficiently righteous tone into her complaint, but it was hard when Gus sat next to her with a pleased smile quirking his lips and his eyes dancing.

"I don't know what you're talking about, but I'll spare a word of advice. Never ask a man to explain his transgressions, *istatola*. My motivations defy rational thought and mystify even myself," he said, lifting one shoulder in an eloquent shrug.

"Aha! You admit it! And I don't accept that hogwash for a second." She fixed him with a reproving gaze.

"How'd you come to the conclusion that any transgression had occurred?" he said, trying hard not to laugh. "Not that I'm admitting anything, mind you."

"You left a large dent the size of your head on the pillow and the scent of strawberry jam on the pillow slip," she informed him. "I was so taken aback, I threw that pillow right out the window into the mud."

"Heavens!" Gus exclaimed, his eyes laughing. "Such dramatics, Miss Stone. But I maintain my innocence. You lack incontrovertible evidence that it was my head upon that pillow, or my *parfum de fraise* scenting it."

"What would your father say about you inviting yourself into a lady's bed in such cavalier fashion?" she demanded sternly.

Gus's smile broadened. "He'd tell me to choose the

lady carefully and avoid getting caught. Are you ready for some coffee?''

Genny shook her head in exasperation. "You can be a trying conversationalist, Renard. You drop topics others haven't finished with, and you don't answer questions directly. That's impertinent. However, to demonstrate how it's done, I shall answer your question without ambiguity. Yes, I'm ready for some coffee, to the point where I think I would die for a cup.''

Gus sat forward and grasped the handle of the saucepan with a corner of the blanket Genny was sitting on. She toppled backwards a little when he tugged it out from under her.

"Even if you have to share that cup with me?'' he asked coyly, swirling the coffee to settle the grounds.

"After everything I've been through today, I'd share a cup with a billy goat and do it happily. Hurry up and pour.''

Genny accepted the tin cup of coffee from Gus's outstretched hand, and took a sip. "Oh, this tastes good,'' she sighed, feeling the hot, bitter liquid slide all the way down her throat and into her chest.

They sat quietly, passing the cup back and forth between them until it was empty. Gus refilled it and threw a couple of more cottonwood branches into the flames.

When the coffee was gone, Genny fished her comb from her saddlebags and started valiantly tugging it through her tangled hair. She winced when she hit a snarl that wouldn't work free.

Gus put the empty cup down beside the fire and moved to sit behind her.

"Let me do that,'' he said, taking the comb from her hands.

"No, I can manage,'' she protested, but he pushed her hands away.

"I know, but you've had a long day, and you're tired. You'll get impatient and pull all that pretty hair out rather than ease the knots out.'' He pulled her hair back so that it fell down her back and started working with the comb.

His touch was pleasant and firm, yet gentle as he

patiently unraveled the tangles. It was intimate, she decided, but not threatening.

"Do you know that when the sun shines on your hair, it looks as soft and warm as a fox's coat, with hints of red and gold?" Gus said, drawing the comb from her scalp all the way down to the ends of her hair, lifting the length in his hands.

Genny smiled. It was not a good sign, she told herself, that she was beginning to enjoy his compliments. As she relaxed under Gus's ministrations, her mind began to drift toward sleep, and each brush of his warm hand against her neck increased the comfortable lassitude that claimed her. Listening to the crackle of the flames in their small fire, she gave herself over to the simple pleasure of having her hair combed.

Gus looked down at the woman in front of him, her head tilted back, eyes closed, mouth turned up a little in perpetual smile, and wondered at what he was doing. It was a husband's right to tend his woman's hair. It was a personal task that no Lakota man would dare engage in with a woman he had not lived with for years, and with whom he didn't share a high level of affection and respect. Yet here he sat, enjoying the cool caress of Genny's hair over his hands, plying the comb through her fine hair long after he'd removed the snarls and knots.

She was a white woman, not a Lakota, and she was a lady. She would have no idea what his action signified for the Indian part of him, and she would have no understanding of the degree to which he was torn in his feelings about her. The desire he felt for her and the bitter anger that came welling up out of the past were inextricably bound together. It bothered him to consider taking a respectable white lady as a lover; it went against his principles entirely, for he knew all too well the consequences of such actions, both for himself and her. Perhaps it was fate, as his father had been prone to say, for Gus doubted that what he wanted was the will of God. He wanted Genny with an unparalleled intensity, and he couldn't see his way around denying it. Even now, he was hard and wanting, touching only her hair.

The anger she made him feel came and went; the desire was always present and growing stronger. Perhaps if he eased his passions, he might purge himself at last of that old anger. He could seduce her, yes, and probably easily, but if Genny accepted him of her own will, he might be able to set to rest an old specter that had dogged him for nigh on a decade. Perhaps then he would be free to leave the past behind, and to accept the only future he could have without regrets.

Glancing at her hair spilling over his hands in the starlight, he suddenly remembered that he had never done this for White Shell. He had tried to act fully as a Lakota with his wife, and he had failed miserably in his role as husband. It was little consolation to him that White Shell had been as deficient a wife as he had been a husband. His marriage had made him relive old failures. The years had not dimmed his sense of dissatisfaction with his inability to set aside his white upbringing. Much of the time he told himself he was Lakota, and stayed busy so he didn't have time to fret over irrelevant questions and expectations long laid aside. With Genny, however, he was constantly reminded that he still wasn't sure who he was, or even who he wanted to be.

"I thought about what you said earlier," Genny said sleepily, interrupting his musing.

Gus slid his hands from her hair to cup her shoulders. His casual tone belied the fine tension that straightened his back and slowed his breathing, and his melancholy fled in the face of anticipation.

"Then tell me, Genny Stone. Are we going to be lovers?" he asked softly.

Chapter 10

∽◦◦∽

"**D**id I say that aloud?" Genny sat a little straighter, and lowered her head to stare into the curling flames. "Well, I thought I might consider . . . what you suggested," she said slowly, hardly able to believe her own ears. "If . . ."

"Go on." He found himself holding his breath.

"I couldn't do it now," she continued carefully. "But if we were friends first . . . perhaps I would think differently."

Gus frowned and drew his hands back to rest on his thighs. "Genny, men and women don't need friendship to have a satisfying . . . rapport."

In the darkness, he ripped the tops from a cluster of junegrass that grew at the edge of the blanket, and threw them away from him.

"I know that," she said patiently, eyes fixed on a smoldering twig. It burst into flame as she spoke. "I'm fully aware of what goes on in brothels, and that it isn't based on mutual regard and affection. I also know that few of the marriages I've seen included friendship between partners. But that merely strengthens my point. Overwhelming urges and financial security may serve most people tolerably as the basis for their liaisons, but if I'm going to think about taking a step that will have repercussions through the rest of my life, I'm not going to take it with someone who isn't my friend. And right now you're not."

"I think you're placing a little more importance on this than is strictly necessary," Gus said testily. His fingers found a small, round pebble in the grass, closed over it and picked it up. He tossed it over Genny's shoulder to land with a sharp pop in the fire.

She glanced back at him over her shoulder and frowned.

"I disagree." She held his gaze for a moment, then turned back to the fire. "I thought about my reputation and I'm afraid it may be past repair if anyone discovers that I left White Rock Spring in your company. Of course, you realize that everyone—even the most charitable of souls—will assume the worst. For now, I see nothing to be gained by fretting over this, but neither do I wish you to use that as an argument to sway me."

He yanked up another handful of grass, and sifted it through his fingers. "So you're saying that if we become friends, you'll consent to follow our 'overwhelming urges' to their natural conclusion?"

Both of them sat motionless, Genny staring into the fire, Gus looking fixedly at her rigid back.

"I'm saying that should we become friends, I will consider . . . the other."

"That's not good enough," Gus replied quickly, shooting another pebble into the fire. Genny started when it flew past her temple. "If I put in the effort to be your friend, I want to know what I can look forward to."

Her back stiffened further and she angled her chin toward him without actually looking at him. "That is a typically male reaction. Might there not be adequate reward for your troubles in the estimable virtues of friendship, in and of themselves?"

His hand came to rest on her arm again, sliding down to cover her hand where it rested in her lap.

"No, Genny, there isn't. Men and women aren't friends. It just doesn't figure when stronger urges, as you call them, are at play. It isn't even necessary to like each other a whole lot."

The calluses on his palm raked over her knuckles, and

even that small contact drew her attention from what she'd been going to say. After a distracted pause, she persisted in her argument.

"Haven't you ever had a lady you were friends with?"

Gus chuckled at her unintended meaning.

"Well, there was one, but I don't think you'd want to hear about it. She didn't start out as my friend," he answered. "She was had before that happened."

Genny blushed when she realized what she'd said.

Gus reached for her hand where it rested on her thigh and took it in his own. He turned it palm up and stroked his thumb in a circle at the center, smiling when she caught her breath. "Why would you want to be friends with a man like me, Eugenia Stone?"

"I don't know," she said, watching his hand curl around hers, the pads of his fingers touching the tops of her fingernails. Her wrist looked pale next to his, and the firelight intensified the pink and gold tones in her flesh, the brick and amber tones in his. "You're a rake, and you've been married and divorced, if you could call it that. You shot at me, and forced me to come with you on this ridiculous trek, and I just don't know."

He ran his thumb over the inside of her wrist, wondering if she had deliberately misunderstood him. "So you aren't out to find an Indian lover? You aren't just another white woman fascinated with the idea of being taken by a savage?"

"How could you say such a thing?" Genny snatched her hand away from him. "Is that what you think?"

Her shock was genuine. Gus schooled his features and kept his tone neutral. "I don't know what to think. It wouldn't be the first time."

Genny looked away into the night. Her voice shook when she finally spoke. "You have been the one to pursue me, Gus Renard. I never sought your attentions, and I'm not the one who asked you to consider becoming my lover."

Gus sent another pebble rocketing into the fire. "For Christ's sake, Genny, are you saying it doesn't matter that I'm a half-breed?"

"I didn't say it didn't matter. I don't know you well enough to know if it matters or not," she managed tautly. "Does it matter to you that I'm not Lakota?"

"Yes, it does."

"Why?"

"Because you can't understand the things that are important to me, the things I care about," he said harshly.

"Like *Great Expectations*?" she asked softly.

He stared up at the stars in silence. He couldn't even begin to explain to her. "There's so much you don't know about me," he warned softly. "I'm not a white man, Genny. That's only part of me. I'm also Lakota." He paused, knowing she didn't understand what he was telling her. "There are no simple answers as to why I didn't want to get involved with you, any more than there are as to why you want to be friends with me. But I know a big part of the answer to why we are going to get involved, no matter how foolish it is."

"I don't," Genny whispered. "I don't understand this at all."

"I think you understand more than you'll admit. What do you feel like when I touch you?" he asked, leaning closer and taking her hand again.

Every measure of her awareness sprang to life as he moved toward her, and warmth tickled up her wrist and through her body at his light caress.

"It makes your heart speed up a little, doesn't it? And your stomach tingle, low and deep inside you," he continued.

She didn't respond as he came up on one knee and moved so that he faced her, still cradling her hand in his.

"When you touch me," he said, drawing her hand to rest on his chest so that her fingers slid into the deep vee in the center of his shirt, "I feel the same way. A little breathless, keenly aware of the pleasure to be found in simple movements, and waiting with a fine anticipation for greater pleasures. We find each other exciting, and we like this kind of excitement, Genny. Both of us. I think you know it leads to just one end, and that hasn't got anything to do with being friends.''

He spread her fingers over the swell of his pectoral muscle. Genny felt the strong pulse of his heart through his smooth, firm flesh, and she was tempted to let her hand roam freely over his chest. She stared at her hand, fully inside his shirt now, and her lips parted.

Gus's eyes burned with desire and certainty. "I don't think it could get much better, *istatowin*, whether we were both white, both Indian, or friends,'' he said huskily.

She took a deep breath and tried to pull away. Large and hot, his hand closed over hers again, keeping her palm over his heart. The fire popped, and Genny looked past him to see a shower of sparks rising on the updrafts into the black night.

''Gus, there's too much I don't understand. I need to know why you shot at me, why you lay on my bed the way you did. Why do you insist that you don't get involved with white women, then tell me a short time later that you'll make an exception with me, and look as if saying as much has cost you your salvation? Why do you dress like an Indian and act like a white man, all the while denying that part of you? And,'' she took another breath, and looked away into the flames, ''why do I feel so scattered and alive and breathless when you touch me that I forget all those other things and let you do things I've never let any other man do?''

Gus moved to the side, pulling her with him so that the firelight illuminated her face more fully. When she looked at him, the confusion and honesty in her wide, blue eyes touched something deep inside him. Every minute spent with her made him want her more. Carefully, he lifted her hand to his lips and placed a kiss on her palm, then closed her hand in both of his.

''All right, *istatowin*. I don't know that I can answer all those questions for you, and part of me doesn't want you to ask, because you probably won't like the answers I have to give. But I'll offer you a deal. I'll try to be your friend on two conditions.''

"What are they?" She wasn't sure she wanted to hear.

Gus's eyes glowed dark against the bronze of his skin, and shadows flickered over his features in the firelight. "First, give me one chance to show you that we don't need to be friends to be lovers. Let me try to convince you that what's between us has a power all its own. If I can give you an experience that's beyond anything you've ever known, I want your word that you'll come to me willingly. Without delay. Whether or not we're friends."

"I don't know what you're talking about, Gus," she said uneasily. "Are you going to try to seduce me?"

He avoided a direct answer. "I won't hurt you, and I won't sully your virtue. I want to tempt you, but I won't corrupt you. If I can make you feel things you've never dreamed of, you won't make me wait. Let me show you that you don't need more time. Give me your promise."

"I don't know." She hesitated, and he raised her hand to his cheek. "You're asking a lot." When she tried to pull away, he pressed her hand more fully to him. Of their own will, her fingers spread to his jawline tentatively, and he lowered his hand to her wrist.

He waited, willing her to agree, as he stroked the fine skin on the inside of her wrist. "Where's your spirit of adventure?"

Her eyes flashed in response. "If I don't like what you do, you won't press me further?"

"That's right." He lied blatantly. He intended to push her until she was his.

The determined confidence in his eyes told her he wouldn't give up easily, and she didn't entirely trust him. Nonetheless, curiosity prodded her forward.

"When?"

"Anticipation heightens certain experiences." He reached out to touch her parted lips with his forefinger. Tracing the bow at their center, he fingered the swell of her lower lip. Her breasts rose with a rapidly indrawn breath, and Gus probed her lip, moistening his finger on the pink flesh within.

"One chance, Genny. That's all I'm asking for. Say yes."

The butterflies rioting in her chest made it difficult to breathe, much less speak. His eyes promised so much, dark both with passion and the knowledge that he had thrown her into an internal contest of divided will.

"Say it," he insisted, the tip of his finger dipping into her mouth to touch her tongue.

"Yes," she whispered, unable to take her eyes from his, and aching for his lips on hers in a more satisfying kiss.

Triumph glowed in his expression. "You won't be sorry," he said with quiet certainty. "There's still the second condition." He cupped her cheek in his palm, and slid his hand down her neck, running his thumb over her throat to rest against the pulse at its base.

"Which is?" He had dropped his hand from hers, leaving it on his face, and she let her fingers glide over the crease his smile caused.

"I want you to sleep beside me until we reach camp."

"But that's . . ." She withdrew her hand abruptly.

"Nothing you haven't already done," Gus finished for her, leaning closer to her, and capturing her hand again, placing it on his shoulder.

"Yes, and look what happened!"

"You liked what happened. Come on, Genny."

"We should forget the whole thing," she said sharply, but she didn't look away or move her hand. It was as if he held her in a spell she didn't want broken, a spell of warmth and pleasure that would not be denied.

Gus shook his head. "Neither one of us wants to, *istatola*, and as long as we're together, it won't go away. This is my offer. I'll talk, and listen, and try to become your friend, an effort that will take a lot of waking hours. In return, you give me one chance to win your acquiescence, and your sleeping hours until we get to camp. Do we have a deal?" His eyes challenged her before he leaned down to press his mouth to the pulse point where his thumb had been.

The pressure of his kiss drew her flesh into his mouth,

his tongue flickering against her in tantalizing promise. Genny's heart sped, and she arched her neck in unwitting encouragement. Gus groaned deep in his throat, and continued his kisses, girding her neck with a seductive necklace. Genny braced her hands on his shoulders, gripping tightly. The feelings he aroused were too vital to resist. There was only one answer she could give.

"We have a deal," she whispered, sliding her hand to the back of his head, running it under his hair, and holding him to her. Some detached fragment of her consciousness wondered fleetingly if Dr. Faustus had been tempted half as convincingly to seal his pact with the devil.

Gus nipped her throat. She gasped, and felt his triumphant chuckle through her hands as much as heard it. Then his lips covered hers swiftly, his tongue laving hers in a motion that sent a current of pleasure streaking through her. Almost as quickly as it began, the kiss was over, and he was smiling down at her.

"Let's make up our bed, *ïstatowin.*"

Fifteen minutes later Genny lay stiffly under her blankets, achingly aware of Gus, scant inches from her. It had been strangely intimate arranging their bed together. Gus had retrieved the blankets from the bushes, and spread them next to the fire. He insisted that their heads point west and their feet to the east so that the rising sun would fall on their faces to awaken them in the morning. Then each of them had slipped into the shadowed depths of the night to attend to personal needs, before meeting back at the fire. Without a word, Gus had stripped off his shirt and trousers, leaving only his breechcloth on, folded the clothes neatly and set them down as his pillow, placed his rifle beside him, and slid between the blankets. Stacking his hands beneath his head, he had watched Genny as she stood a distance away, nervously plaiting her hair.

"Come to bed," he'd urged, flicking back her side of the blankets.

His words were those a husband spoke to a wife. Simple, unadorned, and flush with meaning. They were not words Genny would have expected to hear in the middle of an empty prairie without so much as a roof over her head, nor from a mixed-blood Sioux Indian she had known for only a few short days. Yet in all her adult life, Gus was the only man who could have made her want to accept the invitation.

Her hair braided, she approached the bedroll, uneasily fingering the folds of her skirt. After a moment's hesitation, she dropped to her knees, sitting back on her heels to settle the saddlebag that would serve as her pillow on the very edge of the bottom blankets, as far from Gus as she could get without being in the grass.

He turned on his side to watch her, propping his left elbow under him so that his shoulders lifted off the ground.

"Aren't you going to take off your skirt and stockings?" he asked solicitously. "You'll be a lot more comfortable. That tight waistband won't let you breathe."

He was right, of course. And her drawers and petticoat covered her as thoroughly as the skirt, but she hesitated. Instead, she removed his moccasins and sat on the edge of the blanket, giving him her back as she unrolled her stockings. Once they were stowed in her saddlebag, she rose to her knees, furtively unhooked her skirt, and wriggled out of it. She made quite a production out of folding it and tucking it over her saddlebag as a pillow cover, smoothing out the wrinkles and ensuring that no corner of the leather pack underneath peeked out.

Gus caught her wrist in mid-fold. She lifted her startled gaze to his face, blushing when she caught his knowing smile. He let her go, pushing the blanket back a little further.

"Lie down beside me, Genny."

His softly spoken invitation stopped her heart and set her nerves to jangling. Gingerly, she eased onto the blankets, her eyes never leaving his shadowed face. The scratch of the heavy wool against the fine cotton of her petticoat sounded loud against the low hiss and crackle of the dying fire and the silence of the night. When she was prone on her back, her head rigid on her makeshift pillow, Gus pulled the top blankets up to her breasts. He leaned over her to tuck them between her arm and her breast, a lazy, satisfied grin etched on his face.

"Don't hog the blankets," he whispered, dropping a chaste kiss on her forehead.

She closed her eyes. His lips were hot and soft on her brow, and warmth radiated from his body as it brushed against her. He drew back, and still the heat from him warmed her across the small space between them.

Genny lay with her eyes squeezed shut, waiting for him to touch her again, wondering where his hands would stray first. Perhaps upon her cheek, maybe her neck, or perhaps her shoulder. Then his fingers would wander over her chest to cup her breasts, and his breath would fan her face, followed by his lips on hers, warm, wet, and demanding. She tensed, readying herself for the sensual onslaught to come, willing herself to set her fears aside and allow this one foray into the untasted delights of the flesh. He had said he wouldn't hurt her, and that he wouldn't sully her virtue. What was he going to do, though, and what temptation would he work that could convince her to become his lover now?

Genny realized that several seconds had passed. Opening her eyes, she expected to meet Gus's wry expression, evidence that he was enjoying her torment. When she didn't see him at all, she rolled her head to the right. He lay on his side, facing away from her, his shoulders rising evenly with the deep breath of sleep.

"That's it?"

She cringed. She hadn't meant to sound disappointed.

"Mmmm?" he mumbled sleepily. "What's wrong?"

"I thought . . ." she stammered. She turned abruptly onto her left side and faced the fire. "Never mind."

Gus rolled over and draped his arm across her waist, snuggling close against her. She stiffened in his arms. "Soon enough, *istatowin*. Soon enough," he whispered.

Within a minute he was sound asleep, warm and heavy beside her. His presence was almost as comforting as it was disturbing. For now. Softly, she placed her arm over his at her waist, and by slow degrees, she too, fell asleep.

* * *

Gus stared out into the predawn darkness, listening to the night sounds and thinking. As usual, he'd fallen asleep early, despite the temptation Genny offered, and awakened long before it was necessary to arise.

The ache in his shoulders from the bruises he'd gotten when the hailstones had hit him wakened him, but now he was preoccupied with a more insistent discomfort. His groin throbbed with frustrated need for the woman sleeping next to him, and he turned once more onto his side to cup her slight body in the curve of his. In her sleep, she had moved toward him, away from the edge of the blanket, and she snuggled comfortably into him as he drew her into his arms. He wanted to join his body with hers, and badly, he thought, pulling her a little closer, and savoring the soft press of her bottom against him.

But he also realized that part of him wanted more than that. Their kisses had moved him in ways he would never have expected, awakening feelings he hadn't known existed. The intense longing that had come over him when she kissed him this morning was like nothing he'd ever known. Yes, he wanted more from Genny than to ease his body's needs, however foolish that might be. And he needed her precisely because she was white, because she knew what ostriches were, and because he had discovered *Great Expectations* on her bookshelf.

Something soft brushed across Genny's cheek, then along her neck, coming to rest lightly between her breasts. She wrinkled her nose and waved her fingers weakly at the intrusion. Her hand landed on her chest, closing over long, warm fingers. As her eyes fluttered open, she caught a glimpse of the pale, apricot light of dawn before Gus's handsome, smiling face filled her vision.

"Good morning," he greeted, leaning closer.

She stretched, simultaneously aware of his hand between her breasts and a dull ache in her shoulders. Raising her head, she winced.

Gus brought his hands up under her arms and lifted

her, rolling her toward him and laying her on her stomach.

"Hey . . . !"

"Shhh." His hands moved across her back in slow, easy circles. "Your shoulders are a little bruised from the hail yesterday. Any bumps on your head?"

She tried to concentrate on her head, but Gus's light touch commanded all her attention. "No," she mumbled, resting her cheek against the blanket and closing her eyes. A low murmur of content escaped her throat.

For many minutes he rubbed gently along her shoulders and down the center of her back, lulling her into a torpor of stirring desire. Genny thought she might fall asleep again when the tips of his fingers skimmed the sides of her breasts as he ran his hands over her. Her blood leapt to a hammer pulse, and a quiver of deep response tugged at her insides. She stiffened, but his hands moved to her shoulders once again, and she relaxed. Then, a little guiltily, she wished his hands would stray again.

Gradually, the circles Gus outlined became lines that followed her spine from waist to neck. Ever so slowly, he began dipping below her waist, running his hands smoothly over the tops of her hips, then up her sides to her shoulders, and back down to her hips again. Genny found her breath coming faster. She unconsciously spread her arms further from her body, inviting him to touch the sides of her breasts again. The thought intruded that his hands would feel so much nicer on her bare skin, as they had when he'd held her yesterday after the storm. Caught in languorous equilibrium, it was difficult to assert even to herself that he shouldn't be touching her at all.

But he most definitely shouldn't be. She summoned the strength of will to roll onto her back.

His right hand dropped immediately onto her stomach and continued the easy stroking motions. Muscles deep within her opened, and desire surged with liquid warmth. She grasped his hand and held it still against her.

Opening her eyes, she found Gus staring at their joined

hands. In the faint, early light, his eyes glowed with firm intent.

"Let me touch you, Genny." His breath played over her cheek, warm and soft. "Let me show you passion."

Chapter 11

Genny's pupils darkened, and she tried to pull away from him. "Now?" she breathed.

Gus's smile gentled and intensified at the same time. "Now," he affirmed, drawing her toward him. "Relax, *ĭstatowin*, and let yourself go. No protests. No thoughts. Only feelings."

She clasped his hand tighter. "This isn't going to be very proper, is it?"

He didn't answer, but extracted his hand from her grasp and deftly caught her wrists in his left hand, raising them over her head. Her breasts thrust upwards into his chest, and she inhaled sharply, but didn't struggle.

"How do you decide what you want to paint when you go to make a picture?" he asked.

"What?" She looked past him into the middle distance, knitting her eyebrows at the unexpected change of topic. "I suppose I see something that catches my eye and I remember it."

"So art begins with your eyes."

"Sometimes." She looked at him. "Or with a feeling." His eyes were as dark as the centers of the black-eyed Susans that peppered the prairie sand dunes around them, their pupils barely distinguishable from the irises.

"The expression of passion between a man and a woman starts the same way," he said, one thumb rubbing her wrists, the other toying with the buttons of her shirt. "With a look, and a feeling."

Genny's eyes roamed his face, and she thought of the portrait she had attempted of him and Walks in Thunder as she had first seen them. She hadn't been able to get the feeling right in that painting.

"Do you remember the first time we saw each other?" It was as if he'd read her mind, and their eyes locked.

"I saw a windblown wisp of a woman with silly goggles on her face, her skirts blowing back against her legs, and her hair falling out of a loose braid in long strings. Then you took the goggles off and I caught my breath." He paused, eyes glancing to her mouth, then back to her eyes. "I saw the most beautiful, clear, and wide blue eyes I've ever seen. Eyes as clear as summer skies and as soft as winter shadows. They made me feel like smiling."

"You did smile," Genny reminded him. "You always smile."

"And it made you nervous."

"Yes."

"What did you see, Genny, that made you so nervous?"

She glanced away from him. "The most handsome man I'd ever seen," she admitted. "Looking at me as if he'd as soon have me for supper as bread and jam."

Arrogant satisfaction deepened the creases in Gus's cheeks.

"Lovemaking begins the same way acquaintance does, and the same way as art. Naturally and easily. With a look or a feeling. And a smile." A melting smile creased his face as he spoke. "Smile for me, *istatola*."

Genny couldn't help it. She smiled.

"The next step you're already familiar with," Gus murmured. "We bring our other senses into play. First, with touch."

Slowly, he brought his right hand up and touched his forefinger to her cheek. Tracing her cheekbone, he moved back toward her ear, circled her lobe and slipped his finger down her neck. She shivered as tingles ran down her arms and through her center all the way to her toes. "You like that. Every time I touch your neck you get gooseflesh."

"I know," Genny said softly. "I can't help it."

He retraced his path backwards, taking satisfaction in the reactions his fingers generated.

"And I can't help touching you," he replied, bringing three fingers to rest lightly on her mouth. "First I touch you with my hands."

He parted her lips, dragging his fingers over her lower lip.

"And then with my mouth."

He dipped to press his lips to hers, fingers gliding up to stroke the hair back from her temple.

"And then we taste," he whispered against her, darting his tongue out to touch hers.

Fire shot through her in a wild stroke, and a small sound of disappointment caught in her throat when he pulled back. She felt his smile for a second, and then his open mouth touched hers again. Soft at first, his lips slanted over hers with increasing hunger. He outlined her lower lip with his tongue before deepening the touch. Warm, sweet, and velvety, he explored the hollows of her mouth, gently challenging her to match him touch for touch.

Genny melted under his kiss. Tugging at her hands, she wanted to twine her hands into his hair, but he held her firmly. Deep breaths sent her breasts into his chest, and she arched her back, holding the contact.

He ended the kiss, lifting a handful of her hair to his face and burying his nose in it. "You smell of wind, and rain, and fire," he told her. "You taste of summer sun and prairie wildflowers. Your breath sounds in your throat like grass sighing before a storm wind." He gave her another lingering kiss. "And there is much more of you to see, taste, and touch."

His free hand dropped to her throat, and he slipped her buttons free. Genny lay motionless, reminding herself that she'd given her word to allow him this. When he lowered his head again to nuzzle her neck and nip at the flesh he'd bared above the top of her camisole, she lost the thread of her fears in a shuddering surge of feeling. His mouth claimed her attention as he tugged her shirt off her shoulders and ran his hand beneath her, lifting her, and pushing the shirt up. Releasing her hands, he pulled the sleeves from her and flipped it away before grasping her wrists again. Kisses tumbled over her shoulders and down her bare arms as strong fingers pulled at the white ribbon ties of her camisole.

Cool and moist, the morning air touched her breast briefly, followed by the dry warmth of Gus's palm. She sucked in her breath audibly.

His lips plucked a scorching line of kisses from her collarbone, over her chest, and lower to the breast he held. Pushing her flesh into a mound, his lips closed over its hardened tip. When he suckled, a bolt of yearning satisfaction rocked through Genny, lifting her shoulders, raising her knees, and drawing forth a ragged, gasping cry. Had her arms been free, she would have held him to her.

Gus shaped her nipple with his tongue and lips, savoring the velvety peak, and the heat that flowed between them. Unwilling to stop himself, he moved his hips against her in a small movement that served to increase his excitement and his frustration. This time, and only this time, he would forgo his own satisfaction. As Genny arched beneath him and tugged impatiently at her hands, her restless movements spurred him to increase her pleasure.

He raised his head and returned to kiss her mouth hungrily, his fingers circling the damp center of her breast, then pushing the thin material of her camisole away to bare the other breast. She was so soft, as soft as a puppy's ear, and he wanted to touch every inch of her.

His kiss was hot and more demanding than it had been, not allowing Genny a moment to think about what he was doing. She could only feel. Heat and sensation engulfed her. His mouth was succulent, wet, and pulsing, his tongue dancing in and out of her mouth. His hand was dry fire, burning her sensitive skin with alternately firm and light caresses, moving between her breasts, keeping each nipple peaked and aching. And against her thigh was the firm and building pressure of his aroused flesh, pulsing like his tongue, yet unfamiliar. All this and more set desire thrumming in her blood, pooling with aching sensitivity between her legs.

He broke away from her mouth and forced himself to leisurely attend the breast he had just bared, teasing the rosy nipple with his tongue before drawing it into his mouth to suckle it as he had the other. She gasped. Her response ignited wildfire in him, and he strove to maintain his intention to go slowly, enhancing her anticipation and pleasure. He laved her breasts thoroughly with his tongue, one after the other, and his hand roamed wherever he wasn't kissing her. When the straining motions of her arms against the hand that held her wrists moved in sensual rhythm with the slight movements of her hips, Gus kissed her mouth again, thrusting his tongue against hers in a matching, seductive cadence.

"This is hard for me, *istatowin*," he breathed, pulling back a little. "I want all of you." He ran his hand over her stomach and Genny tensed, flexing her thighs tight together.

"Let me hold you, Gus," she whispered. "Let me touch you."

He shook his head. "Not yet. If you touch me I won't be able to stop." His breath was hard and fast, gusting against her throat before his mouth closed over hers again. She opened to him, drawing him deep into her mouth.

"Then touch me again," Genny pleaded between wet, open kisses.

Lightly, his hand settled over the mound at the juncture of her thighs. Through the layers of cotton cloth, she felt a small caress that shot streamers of bright sensation through her. She writhed beneath him, pressing her legs close.

"I'm going to touch you here, *istatowin*," Gus breathed, shifting so that he leaned heavily against her side. He burrowed a finger into the material of her petticoat and drawers, searching out the sensitive skin underneath.

"No, Gus. You can't." She fought to free her hands, and now she knew why he held them. As she bent her knees to pull them up, he threw one leg across her, holding her still.

He kissed her until she was still beneath him. "You said yes last night. Now let me please you, * istatowin*."

She whimpered once, then moaned when he covered one breast again with his palm.

"Feel the fire build, Genny. Feel the tension." She strained into his hand, and he increased the tempo of his touch and kisses. With fierce abandon, he drew her back into the rush of fevered anticipation, paying no heed to his own spiraling need. He rained kisses over her face and throat, thrusting his tongue into her mouth like lightning, only to back away, then come again. Heat sparked through her breasts as his hand rubbed over her and his fingers tugged and fondled.

As his kisses slowed and deepened, and incoherent murmurs rippled from both their throats, he dropped his hand to her loosened waistband and slid below it to rest on her stomach. He spread his fingers and crept lower, marking delicate circles and curves on her skin, absorbing every tremor and flutter of her muscles, and every shudder of her breath. Part of him wanted to linger, learning her body, and testing his desire. Another part wanted to claim her now, in an instant, first with his touch, then with his kiss, and finally, with the thrust of hard flesh. He wanted to lose himself in her, to carry them both to the heights of passion, to become as one, consumed wholly in ecstasy. The very force of his wanting labored his breathing and tautened his muscles. More than that, it set his chest to aching with a long felt, ill-defined, and frustrated need. Hope tumbled through him, mixed up with longing and fraught with fears, and he closed his eyes against the racking emotions that were so tightly bound to his raging desire.

His fingers met soft curls and stroked lightly, grazing sweet, swollen flesh beneath. He groaned when his middle finger advanced into moist heat, evidence of her arousal and her readiness for more than he would give this morning. Cupping his hand between her thighs, lightly teasing her with the tips of his fingers, Gus pressed hard into her mouth with his tongue, seeking to absorb all of her, to draw her as fully into himself as two bodies would allow without full consummation.

"Open your legs for me, *ištatowin*," he said thickly.

Genny whimpered as his hand tucked lower and nudged her thighs apart. The brush of his fingers glided over the most sensitive part of her, and her muscles reacted from feet to jaw, arching, straining, and lifting. After a quick squeeze, she opened her thighs a little, tilting her hips upward to receive Gus's sparkling caress again. All vestiges of resistance evaporated, and she was overcome with an almost frantic need for him to touch her again as he had.

"Please," she begged raggedly. "Whatever you did . . ."

Gus touched and pressed, slipping his fingers into the folds of her satiny flesh. Genny thrust instinctively against his hand, tightening her thighs, and heightening the stabs of pleasure. When one finger slid deeper, penetrating into slick heat, she cried out and jerked away from his kiss, panting, eyes shut tight, clinging to the wild excitement. He continued to kiss her jaw, then her neck, all the while stroking her intimately, in and out, up and down, pressing, rubbing, grazing, with delicate finesse and driving tension.

Genny's breath came harder as Gus fanned the fire in her, pushing her toward a breaking point she couldn't fathom. He murmured words she didn't understand as he kissed her, speaking in low, rasping tones, his breath tearing from his lungs in harsh bursts. Vaguely, she was aware that he was pressing himself rhythmically against her hip. More fully, she felt the force of his will overtake her in the glory of loving expression. She felt in her blood that he was fighting his own desires to focus upon her pleasure. Through the iron clenching of his arms, the swift thrust of his tongue, the way his groans matched

her small cries, and in his shuddering breath, she knew
he was caught in the same magic that held her.

The grasp he maintained on her wrists tightened as the
motions of his hand intensified the pulsing waves of
feeling thundering through her. Heat flushed her body,
and she was suddenly so hot she wanted to tear her clothes
away. As she thrashed under Gus's touch, reaching with
screaming muscles for the heights of sweetest tension,
her world shattered. She froze motionless for an instant;
then a deep throbbing broke through her, rapid, trembling
flashes of release that loosed and then united rippling
flesh with shattering emotion. Tears sprang into her eyes.
Yearning for something she no more understood than
heaven, and touched to the quick by something more
than passion, Genny wrenched her hands free from Gus's
grasp and wrapped her arms around him, clinging
fiercely.

Gus surged over her possessively, reveling in sharp
appreciation as her nails dug into his back and she drew
his mouth to hers for a searching kiss. He ached to bury
himself in the heated heart of her passion, to ease the
pounding of his blood and the heavy throbbing in his
loins. When her tongue met his, his flesh leaped and the
fire in his blood exploded, his control disintegrating.

He flung himself away from her, onto his back, with
one arm over his face. Frustration screamed through his
body, urging him to complete what he had begun.

"Sweet Jesus!" he gasped.

"What's wrong?" Genny managed, still breathing
raggedly.

"I want you too much, Genny. It's . . ." He exhaled
slowly. "It's too hard. I'm too hard," he whispered
unevenly. "I can't wait, *ištatowin*."

"Does it feel the same for you?" she asked, eyes still
closed. Tiny pulses ticked through her, and she savored
them.

"Like a catherine wheel going off inside you?"

She smiled. "Mmmm. Like nothing I've ever felt before."

"Then we have a deal." He rolled back on top of her

and pushed her loosened waistband down.

Genny's eyes opened, her gaze still soft with passion's aftermath. "What?"

"You agreed that if I could give you an experience like you'd never had before, we would become lovers immediately. Friends or not."

"I didn't say that in so many words." She stiffened under his efficient hands. Her garments were falling away rapidly.

"No; I did, and you agreed," he said soft, but implacable. "You gave me your word."

"But . . ."

He shook his head. "I can't wait, Genny. I've never wanted a woman the way I want you, and I have to have you. I need you. Now." His voice cracked as he lifted her to strip off her drawers.

"Gus . . ." she whispered nervously.

"It gets better, *istatowin*. Hotter, brighter, sweeter, and stronger," he promised, ripping off his breechcloth.

Genny caught only a glimpse of his bare flesh before he covered her, pressing insistently into the juncture of her thighs. He wedged one knee between her legs, settling so that the tip of his aroused member pushed against her intimately.

"Kiss me, Genny. Touch me," he demanded, lifting her arms to his shoulders, and sliding his tongue into her mouth.

She panicked for a moment, struggling to get away from his weight and the unfamiliar press between her thighs, but his kiss captured her. There was nothing she could do but accept him, his kiss, his touch, and the thrust of his hard flesh. Her breath caught when he slipped inside her, and she tensed when he met the barrier of her maidenhead.

"You feel like heaven, *istatowin*," he groaned.

And then he thrust hard, burying himself in her. He took her gasp into his own mouth, and shook his head in mute apology as he thrust again, and then again. He lifted his head and thrust powerfully into her one last time.

As Genny took a shuddering breath, he tensed, lifting his torso over her, and pressing deep within her. She felt the liquid rush of his seed as she watched his face contort as if he were in pain. And yet she knew he wasn't. His primal roar of satisfaction assured her of that.

Gus collapsed over her, his head dropping beside hers, his breath gusting on her shoulder.

Genny was a little stunned. Tentatively, she raised one hand to his head and smoothed his long hair back over his shoulder.

He kissed her cheek and smiled, chuckling in sated release. Happiness radiated around him in a tangible aura.

Genny smiled uncertainly. "I had no idea making love was a matter of mere seconds for men," she whispered.

"Oh, Genny," he groaned. "I'm sorry. It will be better next time. Like I promised. Hotter, sweeter, and stronger."

"You forgot brighter."

He laughed. "And we'll take more time to savor the feelings."

"I'm sorry it wasn't better for you. I've never done this before," she said, feeling some apology was in order.

Gus lifted his head and looked at her. Tiny lines of worry wrinkled her forehead. "It was wonderful. You're wonderful. I haven't been this hot for a woman in years." He clapped his mouth shut. This was no way to talk to a lady.

"Is that a compliment?" she asked doubtfully.

"Yes," he replied firmly. Then he laughed again. He shifted his weight to his elbows and looked down at Genny. "Are you all right?"

Her eyes were wide and her lips were swollen from his kisses. She looked vulnerable and uncertain. "I think so." She didn't smile. "It didn't hurt as much as I thought it would," she added thoughtfully.

Gus kissed her gently, brushing the hair back over her ear. "It'll be better, *istatowin*. I lost control this time. But thank you, Genny." He kissed her again.

The smile he gave her was unlike any she had seen before. For once, it reached not only his eyes, but his heart.

The day grew warm and a dry south wind picked up mid-morning, rustling the grass and cottonwood leaves. The slightest movement of the air set the round leaves to chattering and shaking like rattles as Gus and Genny walked northeast along the river. There was no sign of their horses, and they pushed to cover as much ground as possible. By tacit agreement, they didn't discuss what had taken place at daybreak, but Genny could think of little else. By late morning, she couldn't remain silent a moment longer.

"Gus?" she began hesitantly. "What do we do now?"

"About what?" He sounded cheerful and relaxed.

"Don't be obtuse. About what happened this morning."

He shot a sideways glance at her and grinned. "Do you want to do it again? Now?"

"No!"

"We could, you know. Any time you want."

"What if I don't want to at all?" She swatted at a gnat.

Gus slung his arm across her shoulders casually and matched his step to hers. "Well, you will, you know, and I thought we had an agreement."

"That's what I'm wondering about. How long is that agreement good for?"

That was a good question. Gus didn't have an answer.

"How about until we reach your camp?" Genny suggested. "How long will it take to get there on foot?"

"Depends where it is," Gus answered casually, trying to buy a little time.

"Don't you know?"

"I know about where it should be, but there's no fixed location. We won't have any trouble finding it," he assured her.

They continued on in silence. Gus began thinking about having Genny in camp and how his friends and family were going to react to having a white woman in camp in the midst of a war against her people. There was bound to be some resentment, and depending on how many had lost relatives in the attacks along the trail, there might be a great deal.

"Well?" Genny asked. "How long does this agreement stand?"

"I guess that depends on you."

"Do you mean when I want to end it I can?" After his insistent efforts to get her into his bed, she couldn't believe he'd let her go so easily.

"Not exactly. I'll give you a choice. You can enter the camp as my captive or as my lover. What'll it be?"

Genny shrugged off his arm. "What kind of a choice is that? We're alone out here now, and it's bad enough what we've done without anyone else knowing. I'm not going to openly proclaim an illicit liaison in front of anyone!"

"Then you prefer to be a captive."

"I am not your captive," she stated firmly.

"That's debatable." Gus started walking again. "I did force you to come with me, and I'm a lot bigger than you are. I could make you my captive if I wanted to. But I'll let you choose. You should know that captives have a harder time with the other women than wives do."

"Wives?" Genny hustled after him, grabbing his arm to stop him. "Who said anything about getting married? You said captive or lover! I didn't hear anything about marriage!"

Gus shook off her hand and kept walking. "I already mentioned that Lakota marriage customs are a little less formal than you're used to. We will not be getting married, so don't panic. I'm not any more interested in taking you as my wife than you are in filling the position. But if I openly claim you as my lover, you'll be treated as my woman. Call yourself a wife, call yourself a mistress, or whatever you like. The bottom line is that you'll be treated with a lot more respect than you would be as a captive."

Genny shuddered at the idea of being any man's mistress, and she certainly couldn't think of herself as a wife. She was well and truly caught between less than savory options, a circumstance that was becoming far more familiar than it was comfortable.

"Why can't I be a simple visitor?"

Gus laughed. "Why can't I be a bank president in Montréal? Honey, my mother's people and yours are engaged in a war. You expect people to believe you decided to pay a neighborly visit just now?"

"Why not? I could have decided to do that," she insisted.

Gus didn't dignify her with a response.

"Are captives treated very badly?" she asked.

"Not always." Genny's face lit up. "But it's pretty much hit or miss. It depends on how high feelings are running against the *wašicus*, which is usually a direct result of whether there have been recent hostilities."

"Oh." She caught her lower lip between her teeth.

An amused grin tugged at the corners of Gus's mouth. "I think you're beginning to get the gist of things."

She sighed. "It would appear so."

"So what'll it be?"

"I believe you have just acquired a temporary wife, Monsieur Renard," she bit out in terse resignation. "But don't think I'm happy about this. You're going way too fast for me."

Gus grinned broadly and glanced over at her. "When I was a child, that was my name. Too Fast. I'm too fast for everybody, *ištatowin*." For the life of him, he didn't know why her scowl irritated him so much, but he was certain he wasn't going to let her see that.

"I must be losing my mind," she grumbled. "Don't look so smug. How long am I going to have to endure this farce?"

"Not more than a couple of months. Things are almost certain to settle down before the cold weather starts."

Genny frowned. Two months was a long time. A lot could happen in two months. "Gus, what's going to happen if . . . ?'' Despite the heat and her sunburn, Genny flushed even darker.

"If what?"

"If I were to conceive."

"A baby?"

She nodded, but avoided his gaze.

He should have thought about this earlier. The only white women he'd slept with had been prostitutes, and though he knew Lakota women sometimes used herbs to discourage pregnancy, he didn't know which ones.

"You don't know what to do about that?"

Genny shook her head, eyes still averted.

Gus appeared not to notice her embarrassment. "You can talk to my sister when we get to camp. In the meantime, we'll take our chances. If you get pregnant and you don't want the baby, my sister will take care of it. There's always a place for another child in Lakota families. Don't worry about it."

Genny's eyes flew to his face. Sometimes she simply couldn't believe his careless attitudes! "Don't worry about it? How can you tell me to not worry about it? You're not the one who would have to bear a child alone in the middle of nowhere without even a midwife! And how could you think I would ever leave any child of mine?" She stalked ahead of Gus. "How much longer until we reach your camp?"

"It shouldn't take us more than a week." He lengthened his stride to catch her.

"Then our agreement is on hold until we get there. And that is not negotiable!"

She stomped ahead again, leaving him chuckling in her wake.

"Don't bet on that!" he couldn't resist calling after her.

Chapter 12

The rest of the afternoon was spent in silence or desultory conversation about wind shifts and cloud formations. Genny was growing too tired to talk or get Gus talking, the last chaotic days having depleted her energy. By the time Gus called the day's travel to a halt, there was less than an hour of daylight left, and Genny was exhausted. When Gus disappeared to gather some firewood, leaving her sitting in a tired heap on the ground, she rallied the energy to collect her soap and towel, and headed for the water, hoping she would feel better.

She made her way back upstream a short distance to a sheltered pool they had passed, then quickly shed her clothes and slipped into the river. It was heaven to feel the water on her bare skin, cool and silky after the heat of the summer afternoon. First she rinsed out her clothes and spread them on the bank, then she ducked beneath the shallow water and proceeded to soap her hair, taking care not to tangle it too much. After rinsing it, she washed her limbs, then sat on her heels in the water so that it just covered her breasts. She closed her eyes. The water flowed gently around her, and she thought she could have gone to sleep right there. That set her to thinking about sleeping tonight beside Gus, and gooseflesh rippled over her.

He'd been a good companion today, keeping her amused, asking her questions, and, as always, teasing constantly and laughing as easily as other people breathed. This morning they had become lovers. In the course of the day, they had begun to be friends. There were many things about Gus that bothered Genny, such as his far too casual approach to the possibility of her becoming pregnant and his refusal to take anything seriously unless he was angry with her, but he really was engaging when he wanted to be.

She could hardly believe that he'd seduced her into becoming his lover in a few short days. Engaging wasn't the word for Gus. He was right; he was like a wildfire! And for the life of her, she didn't seem to be able to resist him.

Genny smiled at the irony of having succumbed to the wiles of a rake after years of having resisted similar assaults of charm and sensual temptation. All Gus had to do was catch her eye and smile one of his nicer smiles, and her stomach went silly on her. When he touched her, she lost all ability to think clearly. Whatever his faults, there was definitely something special about Gus Renard.

Gus returned to where he'd left Genny with a load of branches and driftwood slung across his back, and his rifle under his arm. It was a good thing there was no one around to see him doing this women's task, he thought, with a wry smile. Walks in Thunder would never let him hear the end of it, and his cousin Hawk Dancer would have told him they should have let him die alone on the prairie as a child rather than see him come so low in life. His smile disappeared promptly, however, when he discovered Genny was gone.

Stashing the wood under a tall cottonwood, and checking their bags, Gus found that Genny's bag was light. A quick look inside verified that she'd taken her toilet items and most likely gone to bathe. He threw the bag down and stalked off to find her. This time, he was going to tell her what he should have on their first night out. It was simply too dangerous to wander off alone.

Gus hurried upstream, and soon stood in the shadows of the cottonwoods and box elders, gazing at Genny where she sat in the water. Her clothes and her rifle were strewn out along the bank, and she was facing away from him, looking at the red and purple splendor of the sunset in the west. Thin tatters of clouds flushed in crimson lines against the blue evening sky, while below them, the glowing sun sank into an indigo bank of cumulus, gilding its edges with golden lace.

Gus untied the belt at his waist and stripped off his shirt and his britches, before walking to the river's edge. The water reflected the red light in the sky, shot through with gold streaks. He stooped, picked up a small rock and tossed it in Genny's direction.

A small splash behind her sprayed a few drops of water onto her shoulders, and Genny whirled, half-rising from the concealing water. Gus stood on the bank behind her, and he looked as angry as he had the other day in her cottage. She dropped immediately back into a crouch and folded her arms across her chest protectively.

"What the hell are you doing?" Gus ground out, taking a step into the river.

"What's it look like? Bathing!" He advanced through the shallow water. "What do you think *you're* doing?"

He stopped in front of her and glowered, his mouth compressed in a narrow line and his eyes reflecting the last light of the sun.

"Administering orders," he said, reaching for her shoulders. He hauled her upright against him in a spray of water, clamping his arms around her and pressing her naked flesh against his.

"Hey!" she exclaimed. "What . . . ? Oh!" His chest was warm against her wet skin, and her breasts flattened against him. The leather flap of his breechcloth caught between her stomach and his groin, and she could feel the bulge of his flesh beneath the folded leather.

"I warned you the other night, but you don't seem to have heeded the message," he continued, in spite of her sputtering protests. "This time I don't want there to be any question. Don't go off by yourself without asking me. Under any circumstances. The further east we get, the more likely we are to run into Pawnees. The river isn't always safe. The bottom can look solid and mire

your feet, gradually sucking you into itself. This isn't
Philadelphia, Genny. You can lose your life out here.
Look at the bruises on your shoulders and back, for God's
sake." He ran a hand over one discolored streak and she
winced. "Didn't you learn anything from that hailstorm?"

She started to retort, but Gus lifted his head suddenly
and shushed her with two fingers over her lips. The faint
sound of hoofbeats rose from the west, from beyond the
screen of trees.

"Damn!" Gus swore softly. "Don't talk now,
Genny," he said, pushing her ahead of him to the bank.
"Grab your stuff and follow me." He snatched up his
clothes and both rifles and headed into the trees. She
stumbled after him, her wet clothes held protectively
before her.

Gus took her hand, pulling her down beside him into
the musty undergrowth of scraggly bushes. Branches
scratched her bare skin, and she saw a spider scamper
out of their way as Gus pushed her head into the dried
and moldering leaves. The hoofbeats approached rapidly.

"There's not much cover," Gus whispered, "but it's
almost dark. Whoever's coming, they're riding fast, so
they may not be following our trail and they might not
see us. Stay as still as you can."

They waited in silence as the hoofbeats drew nearer.
Gus maneuvered his rifle into position so he could fire
if he needed to, and pushed Genny's into her hands.

"Can you shoot that thing?" he breathed.

She arched an eyebrow at him but didn't answer. Her
rear end was getting cold, and her dignity was suffering
sorely. How had it come about that Gus's presence always seemed to coincide with her in a state of undress?
Well, she was as naked now as the day she was born.
It couldn't get much worse.

The approaching riders slowed, and Gus cursed softly
again. As they reached a point parallel with the belt of
trees where Gus and Genny were hiding, they swerved
to come on through the timber. Gus levered his rifle up
to sight down the barrel. A few seconds later, two horses

broke through the trees and into view, trotting across the small clearing to stop not ten feet from where Genny and Gus lay.

Harv lowered his head and peered through the tangled branches, whickering questioningly.

Gus dropped his rifle and chuckled, low and a little wildly as the tension broke. Then he smacked Genny on her bare behind and scrambled to his feet.

"Don't do that!" she exclaimed. Trixie neighed in response to her voice, and Gus laughed again.

"Get out of those bushes and dress yourself," Gus called, swinging himself up onto Harv's back in a graceful motion. "Wait for me where we left the gear." Genny heard him give a series of high pitched yips as he rode off exuberantly, with Trixie following.

Genny emerged from their hiding place with damp earth clinging to her knees and elbows and feeling like creepy things were running all over her. She returned to the river to wash again, grumbling the while about Gus's warning her of dangers, then tearing off on horseback, yelling his head off, and leaving her alone. The man was as consistent as the shifting quicksands in the rivers he'd warned her of.

Genny had been back at their campsite for twenty minutes by the time Gus returned. She'd arranged their bedrolls, dressed in dry clothes, and started the fire. Gus walked into camp, flanked by the horses, whose muzzles were dripping with river water. Before he joined her by the fire, he carefully examined both horses, running his hands over their legs and flanks, inspecting their mouths and hooves. Then he wiped them down with handfuls of dry grass.

"Are they all right?" Genny asked, not bothering to keep her ire out of her tone.

"They seem to be," Gus answered pleasantly. "I really didn't think you two had made it when you didn't show up this morning," he said to Harv and Trixie. "This mare of yours probably took Harv off on an adventure or two, in imitation of her mistress. We got to watch out for these wild *wasicus*, Harv. They're set on complicating our lives." He gave each horse a final pat and walked to the fire. Genny sat on her blankets, scowling at him. "What's wrong with you? Aren't you glad to see them back?" He threw himself down beside her, and Genny could see that drops of water beaded his skin. He must have bathed while the horses drank.

"Of course, I am, but I didn't appreciate your getting so angry at me about going off alone, to the point of embarrassing me horribly, and then taking off yourself, yowling like a banshee, and . . ."

"Not many Indians would know what a banshee is," Gus interrupted good-naturedly, shaking his hair back over his shoulders.

Genny stared for a second, then resumed her complaint. "And what was I supposed to do if you ran into a dangerous situation? I didn't know where you'd gone, I couldn't have caught up to you, and you'd have been on your own," she finished, reciting the argument she knew he would throw at her if she gave him a chance.

Gus grinned and wiggled his eyebrows at her. "I can handle things. You have yet to demonstrate that you can."

"I don't know that you can handle anything," she retorted. "I haven't seen the evidence."

"I'm still alive, and most of my life's been spent on these plains. That's all the evidence you need," he said confidently, reaching for her arm. "Besides. Who saved your butt during that hailstorm? You didn't know what to do." His fingers closed around her elbow.

Genny cast him a sidelong glance. "You have an unfortunate penchant for crude language. What are you up to now?" she asked disdainfully.

"We have a bargain, *istatowin*," he said meaningfully. His wicked grin caused a riff of shivers to dance through her. "I'm going to turn your attentions in other directions and improve your mood substantially. Come here," he invited, pulling her into his arms.

Genny let him kiss her once. Then she grasped his chin in her hand and pushed him back.

"No, Gus. Not until we've reached your camp and

I've talked to your sister about certain matters we discussed earlier.''

''And I said we'd take our chances until we get there. It'll only be a couple of days, now that the horses are back.'' He turned his head to catch her fingers between his lips. When she tried to pull away, he trapped her wrist in a light grip and thoroughly kissed each finger, laving each one with his tongue, and testing each with a gentle bite.

''You're outrageous,'' she complained mildly. ''I want something to eat, and then I want to sleep. And I don't want a baby.''

''Ever?'' He set her hand on his shoulder and kissed her neck.

''Possibly some day,'' she qualified. ''Not now. Or in nine months. Or before I'm married.'' Warmth washed through her, radiating out from the places where his mouth touched her.

Gus sighed dramatically, his breath rushing over her throat. ''You forget so quickly, Genny. We're almost married. After a fashion. What's a day or two?'' He slid the top buttons of her blouse open and pressed his mouth to her chest.

She tried to push him away but he toppled her backwards, quickly stretching out atop her. His thighs slid between hers, and she was reminded of the things they had done that morning. Butterflies danced through her insides.

His mouth slanted softly over hers, probing delicately as he licked at her bottom lip.

''Mmmmm.'' That wasn't what she had meant to say at all. She tried again. ''Gus. Stop. I'm serious. I'm hungry.''

''So am I.'' He opened his mouth over hers, sliding his tongue against hers. His hips rocked forward, increasing the pressure that was building between her legs.

''I'm tired, Gus.''

''I'll revive you.'' He worked one hand between their bodies and cupped her breast, running his thumb over the already swollen peak.

It wasn't any use. He wasn't going to stop, and her body didn't want him to.

"I'm going to tease you, and touch you, and tempt you, Genny, until you stop thinking and start feeling. Remember what you felt this morning?" He pushed against her pelvis, squeezed her nipple, and sucked her lip into his mouth in the same moment.

"Ahhhh! Oh, heavens!" Her breath came ragged as her body froze to savor his handling. "I remember," she gasped.

Gus kissed her deeply, tasting her warmth and sweetness. He beckoned her tongue to duel with his, drawing her more fully into his passion. Beneath his fingers, her heartbeat accelerated within her breast, and he murmured his encouragement as she began to kiss him back.

"All right," she whispered hoarsely. "Just tonight. I guess it won't take very long, after all."

Gus chuckled warmly. "That's what you think, *ista-towin*. This time is going to be a little different from this morning." He lifted himself away from her to undo her shirt buttons. "To start with, we're both going to take off our clothes. Raise your shoulders."

In a moment her clothes lay piled in the grass beside them and Gus was kneeling astride her. Genny was grateful for the darkness. The fire had burned low and there was no moon. The night air was warm, but she shivered when Gus ran a finger from her chin to her navel.

"Now you help me," he instructed, guiding her hand to his waist where her fingers found the tie that held his breechcloth in place. "Pull."

She did, and the soft material fell onto her stomach. Gus swept it aside and held her hand so that it barely brushed the crisp hair at his groin. "I want you to touch me, *istatola*." He nudged her hand. "I want you to know my body the way I began to know yours this morning."

His skin was warm, and he was still damp from his bath. Breathlessly, daringly, Genny inched her way lower until her hand closed around his shaft. The sound of Gus's rapidly indrawn breath pleased her, and gave her the courage to explore the length of him. She was fascinated by how soft his skin was, and how hot, and by how different he was from her. With gentle encouragement, he coaxed her along, telling her where her touch pleased him most. His excitement resonated within her. After a moment, his fingers dropped between her thighs to bestow caresses of his own, and her concentration shattered. She gripped him firmly, and he arched his back, thrusting into her hand.

Gus pulled away from her. "That's enough of that for now," he gasped, lowering himself over her again. "Let me kiss you."

His fingers stayed where they were, and he began a rhythmic pattern of kisses and stroking caresses. Genny soon felt as though she was melting into the earth, lost to everything but a pulsing awareness of her blood coursing through her veins, and the driving, vital energy that cascaded through her wherever Gus touched her.

Her body arched and tensed, seeking satisfaction, but he wouldn't let her take it. Twice he brought her nearly to completion, only to ease her back from the edge of fulfillment.

"Stop teasing me, Gus," she begged. "I can't take this. I don't know . . ."

He stopped her words with his mouth, turning her head in his hands so that his lips slid from her lips along her jaw. "Now you know how I felt this morning. It could happen for you fast, now," he whispered against her ear. "Shall I take you over the edge, *istatowin*?"

Her answer was a low cry of inarticulate need. Tensed, ready, needing him, she wrapped her arms around him and arched against him.

He caught her in his embrace and lifted her, drawing her hand to hold him as he positioned himself to enter her. Slowly, he pushed inside, giving her tight body time to adjust to him, to accept him.

She didn't want time. Her pulse racing, her breath labored, she felt as if she were tightening into a coil that was about to fly apart into fragments. Thrusting her hips forward, she seated him deep within her, and she pulled his head down so that she could taste his lips once more.

He thrust hard and fast then, and this time it was she who lasted only for a few seconds. Her muscles clenched around him as throbbing waves of hot sensation engulfed her. Every muscle in her body strained to meet the demands of powerful release, and it seemed as if the tremors would never end.

Gradually, the intensity eased, though the pleasure remained. Genny had barely drawn a single deeper breath when Gus began to move inside her once more. Streaks of renewed pleasure accompanied his careful thrusts as he started slowly. Fires that had seemed to ebb returned with vigor, and this time she felt him with her.

This was no matter of seconds now, and it was exactly as he'd said it would be. Hotter, sweeter, brighter, and stronger. Because they shared the passion. Together they moved as one, spiraling higher through a fusion of heat and touch. After endless minutes of intent passion, cries of pitched excitement tore from both their throats, and together, their bodies damp with sweat, and taut with strain, they reached a pinnacle of mutual fulfillment.

"Sweet Jesus," Gus panted when it was over. He braced his forehead against Genny's and took a shuddering breath. "Sweet Jesus, Genny, but it's going to be hard to give you up."

Genny lay with her eyes closed, trying desperately to fall back to sleep. Next to her, Gus slept soundly, his breathing heavy and slow, one warm arm wrapped possessively around her waist. An hour ago, he had wakened her out of a sound sleep with soft kisses and roving hands, and they had made love again. It had been heavenly, starting slow and drowsy, then building into tension, ripe and sweet, like the first strawberries in June. When it was over, Gus had snuggled against her and fallen immediately into heavy slumber.

Now, tired as she was, Genny couldn't still her chaotic thoughts long enough even to drowse. The last three days could have been months, so completely had they changed her life. Sleep was impossible. She might as well get up and watch the sun rise over the river as lie here brooding.

Easing out from under Gus's arm, she slid from the blankets and tied on Gus's loose moccasins. At the last second, she remembered his insistence that she not wander off alone, but she hesitated to wake him. Instead, she picked up a cartridge clip, grabbed her Spencer, and made her way quietly to the water's edge.

There she settled herself against a fallen log, listening as the birds began to wake and sing their greetings to the new day. Soon a faint light streaked the eastern sky, and the birds became more active, hopping and flying along the banks of the rippling water. Their antics soothed Genny's troubled mind, diverting her. She smiled to herself as one raucous jay careened head first into a fellow.

Then suddenly, the birds fell silent and disappeared into the trees. Genny scanned the area on each side of the river, but she saw nothing in the predawn shadows. Frowning, she remembered that Gus had said there were cougars in these parts. Cautiously, she shifted forward and raised her rifle.

A horse neighed loudly, shattering the unnatural quiet. It was Trixie. Then a man's bloodcurdling cry rent the air. It wasn't Gus.

Genny was on her feet instantly, running the hundred yards back to their campsite. The sight that met her eyes froze her mid-step, mere feet from their campfire. Gus lay fighting for his life upon their bed, grappling with a strange Indian. Behind them, a second Indian held Trixie by the nose as he tried to slip a rope over her head. The newcomers were nearly naked and painted grotesquely, their hair standing up in a ridge above their shaved scalps. She had seen Indians like this in the eastern part of Nebraska, and the recognition struck dread in her heart.

They were Pawnees.

A flash of cold metal drew Genny's horrified gaze back to Gus and his opponent. Gus was reaching for his rifle, but the Pawnee kicked it out of reach. Growling taunts, he charged Gus and threw him into the ground. With a knee in the middle of his chest and his left hand at Gus's throat, he raised his arm. The long knife hovered aloft dramatically, then plunged downward.

Gus bucked and rolled, but the blade caught him, ripping into the fleshy part of his upper arm. He broke away from the Pawnee with another bucking jump, and scrambled back toward the trunk of an old cottonwood. The attacker followed, arm raised to drive home his knife once more.

Genny never said a word. Lifting the Spencer to her shoulder, she wished the light was better, but there was no time to wait. She aimed quickly and fired a single shot.

The Pawnee's knife dropped to earth, and the warrior clutched his wrist to his chest as he turned to look at Genny. Her attention had turned to the other intruder. Before the first could shout a warning, she had slapped the hammer back to full-cock, jerked the lever down and up again to move the next cartridge into position, and fired a second shot. This time the man leading Trixie into the trees collapsed, a bullet tearing into his thigh. The horse reared and broke free, running back toward Genny.

Gus lunged for his rifle and brought it up inches from his attacker's chest. The man stopped, looking him square in the eye. There was a moment of taut silence before the man spat a single angry word. Then both of the Pawnees turned and made for their horses. Within seconds, even the sound of their horses' pounding hooves had faded.

Genny ran forward, dropping her carbine and hurtling herself at Gus. She caught his shoulders and her eyes dropped to the gash in his left arm.

"Oh, my lord," she whispered. The cut was a good four inches long, deep and spreading. Torn muscle gleamed pale beneath the blood that dripped over his forearm and down his hand.

"Where the hell were you?" Gus shouted in her face, oblivious to his wound. "Jesus!" He pulled her into his arms and hugged her fiercely. Then he let her go abruptly. "By the love of every saint in heaven, I thought they'd killed you! Pick up your gun!" A string of French curses the likes of which Genny had never heard issued from his lips. "Didn't I tell you not to go off alone?"

"This is one time when you'd better be glad I wandered off, you ungrateful lout!" Blood from his arm stained her sleeve and breast. "I just saved your life, in case you failed to notice!"

Gus looked at her like she was a three-headed goat. "Damned if you didn't," he said in a stunned voice. "Where'd a Philadelphia society girl learn to shoot like that?"

"I wasn't well supervised as a child. A neighbor boy taught me. But I've never shot anything besides birds and squirrels before this." Her voice shook with delayed reaction.

"You're either good or you're damned lucky." Then he saw the blood on her shirt. "God, you're bleeding!"

She shook her head and pointed to his arm. He looked down and stared. His mouth tightened and he paled.

"It looks bad," she said, swallowing hard. She'd never tended a wound in her life, but she'd learned a few things by listening to Nicky Mercer's ranting about the horrors in army war hospitals.

Gus closed his eyes and took a deep breath. "It looks worse than it feels. It'll need to be cleaned and stitched, but we don't have time for that. Those Pawnees must have followed Harv and Trixie's trail. And unfortunately, Indians rarely travel in such small groups. These two are probably scouts for a larger party. *Istatola*, if there's a Pawnee war party around, we've got to get away from here, *now*. Catch the horses."

"What about your arm? You can't ride with it like that!"

"We can bind it. There's no time to do anything else. Give me one of your petticoats."

"Sit down," she ordered. "I'll do it."

When she finished wrapping clean strips of material tightly around his wound, he yanked away from her. "Hurry, damn it! We have to get out of here!" His urgency spurred her on. "Get the horses!" he called, rapidly tying their saddlebags back into packs and rolling their blankets together. He pulled on a shirt, breeches, and belt, slung his rifle over his right shoulder, and began emptying cartridges into a pouch that hung from his waist. He glanced up to see Genny stooping over something on the ground near where the second Pawnee had fallen. "Hurry up!" he shouted again.

Genny straightened, and quickly led Harv and Trixie back to him. He had already collected all their gear and eradicated any evidence of their fire.

"Look what I found," she said, holding out a knife with a bone handle. "The Pawnee taking Trixie must have dropped it."

"Great. Take it. You'll need it," Gus said, hardly looking. He spun her around and looped her pack over her shoulders. He had tied a length of rope to her rifle, and he slipped that over her arm, as well.

"How are we going to do this?" She cast a worried look at Trixie.

"It's a good thing that Pawnee left his rope on Trixie," Gus said. He removed it and rapidly fashioned a halter and leads, which he slipped over Harv's head. "Can you ride bareback?"

"Yes."

"Your hidden talents are coming in handy this morning. I'm going to put you on Harv and start you ahead of me. Go north of the river. Hopefully, Trixie will follow. Are you sure you can hang on?" He boosted her up onto Harv's back.

"I don't think I have a choice this time." She took the leads from Gus.

"Not a very pleasant one." He reached up and pulled her head down to kiss her quickly on the mouth.

She caught his jaw and looked into his eyes. "How will you stay on Trixie with your arm hurt? You should use the halter, not me." She couldn't see the bandage under Gus's shirt, but she was afraid it was still bleeding. If by some chance it wasn't, a wild ride on Trixie would surely start the blood flowing again.

"It won't do any good. I'm a lot stronger than you are, Genny, even with a bad arm. Trixie and I will manage. Now get going!'' He slapped Harv's flank. ''I'll be right behind you!''

Harv trotted off, splashing through the shallow river and up the north bank, where he broke into a gallop.

Gus turned a leery eye on Trixie. She was nervous, flicking her ears and stamping skittishly. In no mood to dally, Gus approached from the right side, favoring his injured arm. Tangling his good hand in her mane, he vaulted onto her back from the right, Indian fashion. The jolt of landing shot licks of pain through his arm, but he gritted his teeth and hung on for dear life.

Which was a good thing, because Trixie was off and running before his backside ever touched her.

Chapter 13

Gus threw himself forward over Trixie's neck, digging his hands into her mane and clamping his knees around her sides. They flew through the river, water splashing high onto his legs, Trixie's mane blowing back into his eyes. His left arm burned in agony, but he didn't dare risk a one-handed grip. Resigning himself to the pain, he focused on keeping his seat.

Trixie's all-out stride quickly ate up the lead Genny had on them. In short minutes they had caught and passed Genny and Harv. In a futile effort to get the mare to match her pace to Harv's, Gus pulled back on her mane and barked a short command in Lakota.

To his utter surprise, she slowed. Genny caught up to them, and he glanced over at her. Eyes slanted against the wind, hair whipping back from her face, her expression was intent. Gus grinned at her. "Trixie doesn't like saddles!" he hollered.

Genny scowled at him as they hurtled along. "Look at your hand!" she shouted.

His eyes dropped. Dark blood dripped from under his cuff onto his hand. At the sight of it, his head began to spin.

"Can you stop her?" Genny screamed, panic flooding through her. If Trixie wouldn't stop, Gus was either going to faint and fall off, or stay on and bleed to death. Then what would she do? Dear heaven, she needed him! Alive and well enough to tell her what to do to get them to his camp! "Gus! Don't pass out! You've got to stop Trixie!"

He struggled to clear his head. No warrior would react to the sight of his own blood like a stupid *wašicu* girl, he chided himself. Then again, he was no warrior. Hadn't been since he was eighteen years old. The memory of a long-ago fight with other Pawnees filled his mind with vivid immediacy. He hadn't been hurt then. He'd been strong. So strong arrows and bullets couldn't touch him. He had been an uncontrollable storm of violence and destruction. There had been blood on his hands then, but it hadn't been his own. The awful image superimposed itself over the vision of his own hands wound into Trixie's black mane, the ground flying by beneath them.

"Gus!" A woman's voice shrieked. Genny's voice. "Gus! Don't faint! You have to stay on! Try to stop the horse!"

Responding automatically, he pulled back on his mount's mane, telling her in Lakota to stop. She slowed, but didn't stop. Then he remembered this wasn't his horse. Where had she come from? Everything seemed hazy. He tried another word, and pulled again. Her gait slowed gradually, until she dropped into a walk. Finally she stopped. Gus's eyes fixed on the stream of blood seeping from beneath his sleeve, running in a spreading rivulet over the base of his thumb.

Someone shook his good shoulder. "Let go of her, Gus. You have to get off now so we can stop the bleeding."

He shook his head, and it cleared. The pain in his arm seared up into his shoulder as he released his grip. He looked up, finding that they had stopped on a broad rise. They were completely exposed.

The world settled back into a coherent present. "You've got yourself a Cheyenne war pony, here, *is-tatowin*," he grunted, straightening his back slowly.

"And I'm going to have myself a dead Lakota if we don't stop that bleeding. I need you alive, Gus. Now get down here," she ordered frantically, pulling on his good arm. He obediently hiked a leg over Trixie's neck and slid to the ground. "Who would have thought an Indian warrior would be undone by the sight of his own blood?"

"I told you once. I'm not a warrior. I'm a hunter." He dropped his pack and stripped off his shirt. The bandage was crimson, soaked through with blood. "Shit," he muttered, looking away. "Find a small stick and prepare to sacrifice your drawers. I need a tourniquet and another bandage."

"I would think hunters would see enough blood to harden them to any ill effects," Genny said, shucking her pack to pull out her cotton drawers.

"Will you just shut up and get to work? We're still in sight of the river. If you want to live past this afternoon, you'd better hustle," he bit out harshly. "Now do what I tell you to, and don't worry about hurting me."

Gus instructed her in how to apply the tourniquet above the slash, then watched impatiently while she waited for the blood to stop flowing and bandaged it a second time. When she was finished, she made him drink some water from his water skin. Finally they were ready to go again.

"I think Trixie's problem, aside from being the most headstrong animal I've ever seen, is that she's been trained to respond to a bareback rider. She hates a saddle. She stopped immediately when I told her to in Cheyenne, so I'd bet she's only had one owner, some Cheyenne fighter, until recently," Gus said, stroking the black's side. "This helps a lot. Now we can try to disguise our trail to slow those Pawnees down." He looked back toward the river.

"They might not follow."

Gus snorted. "Yeah. And the wolves might not howl tonight, either, but what's your experience tell you?"

Genny blanched. "The wolves always howl."

Gus nodded grimly. "And Pawnee war parties follow vulnerable travelers. I don't like to say this, but if you have to shoot at them again, Genny, shoot to kill. We should have done that this morning."

She looked at him aghast.

Gus turned away, lifting her pack with his right arm

and settling it on her shoulders. Woodenly, she scooped up his bloody shirt and wrung the blood from his sleeve before holding it uncertainly toward him. He ducked so she could slip it over his head, carefully threading his injured arm through the sleeve. She wiped her hands on the grass, and they picked up their rifles.

"Can you handle my rifle?" It was longer and heavier than her carbine, but Genny nodded. "Then let me take your repeater. If we're attacked, I'll be able to make more efficient use of it than you will. You're sure you can shoot my Spencer?"

"I can shoot it. I don't know if I can kill anyone."

"I know, *ištatowin*. I can if I have to. Let's hope it doesn't come to that."

But he steeled himself for that eventuality. He'd already broken the most fundamental of the precious few principles he held as a result of bringing Genny Stone with him on this infernal escapade. He doubted this one would be any different.

They rode throughout the long day, resting only for water, and then only briefly. Gus led them east to a stream that emptied into the Niobrara, and this they followed for several miles, taking the horses up the middle of the shallow watercourse. Then they had raced all out over a flat expanse of plain before coming to another creek. Sometimes they doubled back, circling to leave a confusing trail, and Gus took the time to cover their trail carefully when they left the streambeds. Unfortunately, the Pawnees would know they had gone north, due to Gus's assumption that he wouldn't be able to control Trixie in any way but heading her in the right direction.

The terrain changed gradually, and there was more rock and less sand in the rolling prairie. The day was hot, but the winds were unusually light. By late afternoon thunderheads could be seen towering like mighty, sky-borne mountains in the west and north, though it was still clear where Gus and Genny rode. Long past the time when Genny's limbs began to ache with fatigue, Gus pushed them forward. Uneven buttes punctuated the horizons, and it was toward one of these that he steered them. There was only a pale wash of daylight left in the western clouds by the time they reached it. With a new moon, they would have to stop for the night.

Gus's arm was throbbing, and he was having a harder time keeping his head clear when they rode to the base of a square, steep-sided butte that lifted fifty feet or so above the open terrain. He stopped Trixie with the pressure of his legs and a guttural command.

"This is it?" Genny looked around at the inhospitable landscape. There wasn't a tree in sight. "We're stopping here?"

Gus grunted as he slid from his mount, landing on a large, flat rock. "We can't ride any farther. The horses are exhausted, and so are we. I know this butte. There are rocks at the top where we can hide. We can fend off an attack here."

Fear lanced through Genny. "What about the horses?" The sides of the butte were sharply inclined, covered with prickly cactus and spiky yucca plants. "Can they make it up that slope?"

"No," Gus answered shortly. "We're going to have to let them go. Try to land on rock when you dismount, and watch where you step. Don't crush anything if you can help it. If by some miracle our friends the Pawnees make a mistake, they may follow the horses' trail. Take the rope off Harv and come down easy."

Balancing her pack and Gus's rifle, with the rope halter in one hand, she put her feet down gingerly in the light spaces between the plants. Gus whistled Harv over to him. He leaned his head against the gelding's nose and whispered to him. Then he gave a low whistle and Harv moved away. Trixie followed.

"What if the Pawnees aren't trailing us?" Genny asked, her eyes on the retreating horses. "How will we get to your camp?"

"We'll walk, and be grateful," he said, making his way over to her. "But they're back there, Genny. I can feel them."

Genny prayed he was wrong as they picked their way up the butte.

At the top they found a jagged crown of large, flat-surfaced rocks at the south edge of the butte. Below them, the drop was almost vertical. Gus led them into the cracks between the rocks and shrugged off his pack, grimacing when the rope caught on his injured arm.

Worried about his arm and unable to do anything about it, Genny gave vent to her frustration. "I thought Indians were supposed to be stoic and bear pain in silent dignity." She dropped her pack and quickly took his, setting them against the rocks. She balanced their guns alongside.

"You thought wrong, *istatola*." An irrepressible smile hovered on his lips. "Indians are smart enough to know that letting a woman know you're hurting can gain better treatment. Here," he said, handing her his blankets, "shake these out. It may get cool tonight."

Genny obliged, then folded one of the blankets and laid it down to sit on. "You'll get the same treatment from me as before you were hurt."

"Well, I guess I couldn't complain too much about that. Not if it was how you were treating me in bed last night that you're thinking of."

Heat flushed her cheeks. "I don't know how you can even think about that right now. You're hurt—and this may be our last night alive!"

Gus sank heavily to the blanket and grinned up at her. "Then what better to think about than something so pleasurable? Besides actually doing it, that is. You must have figured out by now that I always think about that when I'm with you. And you know what else I think?"

She snorted. "No, and I don't care to."

"You're getting to think the same thing about me. A lot." He leaned back against the rock and sighed, ignoring her sputtering denial.

That he was right irritated her all the more. "Why you think I'd be thinking indecent thoughts about a man who's dragged me into the worst experience of my life is beyond me. I think we should take a look at your arm. I've got another pair of drawers to make another bandage.'' She wasn't going to fall for his baiting tonight. Kneeling beside him, she tugged his shirt up over his stomach.

"See? I knew you were thinking about last night,'' he chuckled. "You can't wait to get me out of my clothes and you're just itching to toss your drawers to the winds.''

"That's right, handsome. I can't wait to get your sweaty, dusty, bloodstained clothes off so I can run my fingers over your sweaty, dusty, bloodstained skin.'' She leaned close and took a delicate sniff, wrinkling her nose. "Not to mention.''

"All right, I get the picture,'' Gus groaned. "But for the record, the fact that you are also sweaty, dusty, musty, and your hair is a tangled mess, does not diminish my desires. I still want you.'' He caught her wrists against his chest and strained forward to touch his lips to hers. "Mmmmm. Dry and a little chapped, but lovely,'' he whispered.

His tongue snaked out to lave her lips gently, probing at the corners, before he sucked her lower lip into his mouth. Then he backed away, lightening the pressure of his mouth on hers to a mere wisp of a kiss. "Now you can look at my arm.'' He wore a quiet, satisfied smile.

His arm had bled more during the day, but it wasn't infected. Still, it needed to be stitched closed or it was going to leave a gaping scar. "Do you have anything to sew this up with?'' Genny asked as she washed carefully around the wound, using what little water they had sparingly.

"Yeah. There's a needle and some thread, along with a small flask of whiskey in my bags. Have you ever done this sort of thing before?'' He sounded wary.

"No. How long can it be left alone?'' She didn't want to try to stitch the ragged wound together, poking a sharp needle through his skin. But she would.

"It should be done soon. Do you have the stomach for stitching me up?''

She nodded grimly. "I'm willing to try. You'd do it for me.'' She said it offhandedly, but as soon as the words were spoken, she knew them for the truth.

Their eyes met. Gus reached for her hand, covering it with his own. "Okay. Might as well be now while there's still a little light. Hand me my saddlebag."

"I hope you don't regret this," she said, pulling his bags toward her. The white background of the quill work design on their sides glinted in the sunset.

"I trust you, Genny."

She smiled tremulously, but his words lightened her heart.

He flipped open his bag and extracted a nearly flat leather case, which he handed to her. "Pour some of the whiskey into the cap and soak the thread and the needle in it." Genny did as he instructed. "Now give me that piece of leather next to the flask." She handed him a tough length of thick hide. "Have you ever sewn leather?"

She shook her head. "I've only done needlepoint and embroidery."

"Use a firmer touch than you would on cloth. Don't prod around, trying not to hurt me. Clean, fast, firm strokes." He grinned. "Kind of like when I . . ."

"I understand!"

"And talk to me, Genny. Keep my mind off what you're doing. Tell me why you got shipped off to France." He watched her thread the needle.

"Do you want to drink the whiskey? For the pain?"

He shook his head, and wedged the piece of leather between his teeth. "I don't drink. Makes me sick. Pour some over the cut. It'll deaden it a little," he mumbled around the gag.

Fire burned through his arm when she did. He closed his eyes, lids flinching when she pushed the edges of the wound together and took the first stitch.

"France," he reminded her tightly. "Tell me."

Genny's stomach rebelled when she pushed the sharp needle through Gus's arm. It took all her concentration to force the bile back down her throat.

"Talk!" Gus ordered harshly.

"I got sent to France for retaliating against Paul!" She

pulled the thread through the hole she'd made and doggedly pierced a second one. "After my mother died, I was discouraged for months. That was about four years ago." The first stitch was complete. "How close are these supposed to be to each other?"

"Doesn't matter," Gus ground out. "Keep talking!"

She poked the needle in again as close as she could get it to the first stitch. "I'd realized that I wasn't a truly great painter, and only just given up that dream when Mama got the wasting disease that killed her. It was so difficult to watch her die slowly. And after she passed on, I wasn't myself for a long time. In the midst of that, Paul came home for the winter after a very profitable year freighting supplies to the new mines in Colorado. My cousin has always found immense pleasure in annoying other people, me in particular, and this visit proved no exception." Another stitch was finished. She took a deep breath and started a third. Gus looked like he was bearing up, but he was starting to sweat.

"Paul decided it was time I married, and he assumed the responsibility of finding me a husband. To make a long story short, he rounded up every unsavory, unbalanced, unattractive, and unlikable rogue in three states and paraded each one through my father's parlor, displaying me like some sort of second class baggage that he needed to discharge immediately." Her voice shook with a combination of nerves and remembered indignation, and she began to stitch more quickly.

"Tell me about the suitors," Gus grunted.

"There was Hiram Boatman. Fifty years old if he was a day, bald as a turkey's wattle and quite as red, and already a grandfather several times over. Then there was Philaster MacMarty of the shifty eyes and dirty neck."

Genny glanced up at Gus. His jaw was rigid, and a sheen of moisture glinted on his forehead and chest. She looked back to her task and dipped the needle once more into his flesh. Her nose began to prickle, but she kept talking. "Paul left me alone with the beast, and Mr. MacMarty chased me around the sofa. When he caught me, as he was very strong, I was obliged to clobber him with a candlestick. I know he had a dirty neck because I saw it as he slid past on his way to the floor. Later I learned that he made a living at a slaughterhouse and kept his living quarters next door. Can you imagine anything so unpleasant?''

Gus growled deep in his throat and his eyelids flinched.

"I'm sorry, that was a thoughtless remark." A neat line of dark stitches showed against his skin now, but there were many more to go. "Those two gentlemen were among the more congenial of the collection. Eventually Paul came back west and left off tormenting me, but not before I resolved to get revenge. As soon as he left, I enlisted the help of a childhood friend, Tommy Danvers, a boy who lived nearby us in the country. Together, we came up with a plan."

Gus made a strangled sound and his breathing grew increasingly labored.

Working efficiently now, Genny continued. "In short, we signed Paul up for several companies of army enlistees in southeastern Pennsylvania and southern New Jersey. Tommy had his college friends at the University of Pennsylvania help out. Since Paul didn't ever show up at any of the companies, there began to be people looking for him. It really wasn't all that bad, because Paul was hauling army contracts here in the west, and he knew a great many people in Washington. It was only a minor inconvenience to straighten matters out, but we ruined his Christmas."

An inch or so remained to close now. In and out, she punched the needle through Gus's skin, gradually closing the wound. "Then we stole his prize stallion and took him out to a farm near Lancaster. That was a severe blow, for Paul dotes on that beast as if it were his firstborn son. And finally, we dressed up like highwaymen and robbed Paul as he was on his way to a party we were all attending. We got a little carried away and made him strip down to his drawers. When it started raining, he was forced to go to the house where the party was for shelter. It made quite a spectacle. Unfortunately, I couldn't resist gloating, and I returned Paul's purse to him the next day with a full account of my deeds. There was a real row, and the result was that I accompanied an old friend of my mother's, who had been recently widowed, back to her home in Paris. There I managed to engage a good painting master and I ended up staying until last winter." She finished the last stitch and made a neat knot in the thread, clipping it close with Gus's knife. "We're finished," she said, nearly sobbing with relief.

Gus was breathing heavily, and his eyes remained closed. She thought he had passed out, but after a minute he spoke.

"Thanks." It was more of a grunt than a word.

Genny wiped his brow with a clean piece of her now-shredded underdrawers before binding his arm back into a bandage. After removing the leather strip from between his teeth, she offered him water and folded everything back into the case.

When she was finished, she sagged down beside him. Both of them were as limp and worn as a pair of peddlers' nags. For many minutes they sat quietly, and beneath her hand, Gus's heart gradually returned to a slow, steady beat. His breath stirred the hair at her temple, and she thought he was finally asleep.

He wasn't. Capturing her hand in a weak grip, he carried it to his lips and pressed a tiny kiss to her fingers. "You've got some courage, Genny Stone," he rasped, low and soft. His good arm stole around her, drawing her close. "Pull those blankets up around us, will you?"

His compliment nestled into her heart with the warmth of sunlight streaming through a winter window. She smiled as she dragged the blankets up, tucking one corner around Gus's injured arm and the other under her own shoulder. Rolling her head back upon his breast, she looked out between a crack in the rocks to the night sky. "Are you all right?" she asked.

"Yeah." Far in the west, a flash of light sparked yellow-orange through a distant thunderstorm. "Heat lightning. *Wakinyan*," he breathed, muttering an indistinct sentence in Lakota.

"What did you say?" As she watched, the lightning flared again, far beyond the reach of sound.

"A prayer, of sorts. Or as close to prayer as I'll ever come. To the Winged Mystery in the Clouds, Wakinyan. He brings the powers of life with the cleansing rains." He sounded exhausted.

"Or the powers of death with destructive hail and lightning and wind," she countered.

"They're the same power, *istatowin*. All part of the same whole."

"I prefer to live."

Gus smiled. So did he. "Then live we shall. Perhaps Wakinyan will favor us tomorrow when our enemies come."

"If you knew they would follow us, why didn't you kill the men who attacked us?"

Gus closed his eyes. "Force of habit. I swore a long time ago that I wouldn't kill anyone I didn't absolutely have to. It was a mistake this morning, though, to let those men go."

"Why did you swear not to kill anyone? Not that I disapprove," she amended quickly. "It surprises me, that's all."

"Because you weren't brought up to think that Indians hold life sacred." It was a statement, not a question.

"That's not . . ." She stopped. He was right. And somewhere during today's grueling flight she had passed the need to lie to him. Or to herself. "I'm sorry, Gus. I didn't think. We shouldn't be talking. You need sleep."

He was silent for a minute, and she thought that he had drifted off when he spoke again, low and barely audibly. "The power of the Wakinyan is in all of us. The power to give life and nourish it, or to destroy it. I killed once. Pawnees. Two of them, in a battle when I was young. First I counted coup for the glory, but the blood lust took me, and even though they were defeated, I didn't stop. Not until both men lay dead and mutilated at my feet."

Genny stiffened against him, but he held her tighter, squeezing his eyes shut to blot out the memory of that day. "I was only eighteen. The others in the war party didn't want me to go with them at first, because I had no spirit helper, no visions. I've still never had a vision. But after we ran into the Pawnee party, they sang songs about me. They said I was a great warrior, that I would be among the best as I grew in strength and power.

"But my actions sickened me. In the excitement of the fight, I forgot that life is precious. That it should be taken only with the greatest respect." He opened his eyes and watched the lights in the west, flashing, jolting streaks of tremendous power, reduced by distance to pretty drama. "It was too easy, Genny. Too easy to kill. It made me feel invincible, like a raging storm. But when the tumult passed, I was left to face myself. To face the knowledge that I had deprived two families of their men. Afterwards, no visions came to ease my burden. It wasn't like the power of the Wakinyan. It wasn't whole. No life came from the deaths of the men I killed."

Genny was uncomfortable with his confession, unsure why he had revealed the darkest side of himself to her. This was a different Gus from the man she had come to know.

Or maybe not. He presented a constantly changing array of reactions and feelings, drawing forth strong responses from her. As usual, she was left divided. Admiring his honesty, she was also shocked by it. He was frightening, a cold-blooded man who relished war. Yet he was noble, recognizing evil in himself and striving to change.

"Weren't you defending your people?" she finally asked.

"No. We were a party of hotheaded young men seeking adventure and honor. The Pawnees we fought were the same." He sighed, shifting uneasily.

Wanting to comfort him, wanting to run, she said nothing for a while. Finally she voiced the question his confession prompted. "But now? What will you do now, Gus?"

His chest heaved under her. "I'll do what I have to. I'm not a boy out for glory now. I'm a man, and I'll do what I think is right. No Pawnee wolf will take your life from you,'' he promised. ''Rest now, *istatola*. There's time enough to fret tomorrow.'' Even as his words died, his breathing slowed, and he succumbed to pain and exhausted slumber.

Genny straightened and eased Gus down so that his head rested in her lap. Rearranging their blankets around them, she smoothed the dark hair away from his face, and wondered what the morning would bring.

Chapter 14

Genny woke the next morning before dawn, her neck stiff from her awkward posture, wedged as she was between the eroding limestone boulders. In the east, the morning star shone bright above the horizon. She looked around for Gus. He was crouched to her left, listening intently.

He turned and met her gaze, setting a finger to his lips. Silently, he handed her a piece of jerky and the water skin. Close beside her, hunkered down in the rocks, he spoke in her ear, his voice a mere breath of sound.

"They're out there. I heard one of their scouts signalling the others with a wolf's cry. I think they must be camped over that rise to the south. They'll wait for light to break before they do anything, and they may not be aware how close we are yet." He slipped a handful of cartridges into her lap. "We've probably got better guns than they do, and your repeater may make this a fast fight. Don't shoot until I do, and then choose your shots carefully. Make them count, and we'll be fine."

She nodded, her mouth as dry as a dandelion puff. She dropped the jerky into her pocket and took a sip of water. "Can they hear us?"

Gus shook his head. "Not yet. The wind's out of the south, so we'll be able to hear them first, and we've got the advantage of height. They won't be able to sneak up on us. All we can do now is wait and hope for the best."

Genny pointed at his arm. "How is it? Shall I change the bandage?"

"Not now. It's okay. Just sit tight."

They waited nearly an hour in silence. The sun breached the horizon in a golden, reddish haze before it lifted into a bank of clouds low in the eastern sky. Lying on his stomach at the edge of the butte, Gus scanned continuously with his spyglass. Scant minutes after sunrise, he tensed.

He gestured with his chin. "There. To the left," he whispered.

Genny couldn't see anything. A moment later she caught a tiny shift of movement on the rise Gus had pointed out.

"Don't move, Genny. Keep your rifle barrel down, and keep under that overhang." They remained motionless until the scout disappeared. At length Gus crept forward to find a position among the rocks. He signalled her to stay where she was.

"I can't believe this," she grumbled fifteen minutes later. Her neck was kinking up and she was dirty, cold, hungry, and scared. "I'm sitting on a pile of rocks waiting to kill or be killed by a bunch of wild Indians."

"You're not going to be killed. I don't get killed. I survive, and so will you. But I agree this is a pretty stupid place for a woman like you. Paul Conrad ought to be drawn and quartered for bringing you out here. No Indian would ever treat a relative the way he's treated you." Gus sounded stronger than he had last night, but Genny barely noticed for her irritation.

"Paul? You blame Paul for my being here? That's rich!" She wriggled her elbows into the dirt and flexed her legs. "He probably wasn't even in the territory when you decided you couldn't live without my company on this stupid trip. Don't you go blaming anyone else!"

"Conrad's the one that brought you out here in the first place," Gus maintained in a loud whisper. "So it's his fault."

"It is not!" she hissed. "I came because I wanted to. And it's not my fault we're in this predicament now! The responsibility rests entirely on your shoulders!'' She glared at him, but his eyes were focused on the plain beyond.

"We're going to have to finish this debate later, *is-tatowin*. Here they come.''

"Where?'' She edged up beside him.

"That puff of dust. Now get back. And for God's sake, keep quiet. I don't think they know where we are.''

In a few minutes the low sound of horse hooves striking the soft prairie ground rose on the morning breeze. Genny swiveled her head around to look. A moment later, a line of riders broke over the ridge to the south, charging forward. There were eight of them, small in the distance, but closing fast.

On they came. Soon Genny could see the colors of their paint and horses clearly. They were following the path Gus had taken the night before. As they drew closer, Genny's heart began to pound so that she heard each beat thrumming in her ears. She glanced at Gus.

His dark eyes followed the Pawnees' every motion, flicking back and forth among them as if weighing each man's measure. Every muscle in his body was taut with excitement, and Genny saw no fear in him. He was alive and ready, sure and waiting.

His words from last night came back to her. It was easy to kill, he'd said. Too easy. The realization that at some primal level he was enjoying their dangerous predicament slammed into her. It was beyond her comprehension.

The Pawnees rode close below them now, their leader intent upon their trail from the night before. Genny could see the colored paint on the horses' flanks and chests, hear their gusting breath, and the clicks and rattles of their tack. The musty smell of horseflesh rose on the breeze, mingled with the dust their passage stirred. But it was the riders who commanded her attention. Dressed in leather breechcloths, and adorned with the teeth, claws, and feathers of bears, wolves, panthers, and eagles they looked wilder than any beasts. The paint upon their faces, arms, and chests made them look like ghouls, and their bare heads, glinting brown in the morning sun, lent the warriors a cruel, heartless aspect. They terrified her, and Genny's heart raced and her breath stopped as they reached the place where she and Gus had dismounted.

The lead rider, his tufted ridge of hair bobbing with the motion of his red and white pinto, slowed his mount to a walk and leaned down, examining the ground. He lifted his face, eerily painted white on top and black on the bottom, to scan the side of the butte. Dark eyes flicked up to the rocks where they lay hidden, passing over them unseeing.

He rode on. The line followed him.

Genny dropped her forehead to the earth. Air rushed into her lungs in rapid draughts, and sweat erupted on her palms.

They were safe. The Pawnees had fallen for the ruse. Relief shuddered through her. After a quick prayer of thanksgiving, she turned to look at Gus, beside her in the dirt.

A shadow crossed her face and fled across the rock above her, and then another.

Gus cursed graphically. Genny followed the direction of his gaze, looking up. High above them, two large, dark birds circled slowly. As she watched, a third joined the graceful, descending spirals. She recognized the birds immediately, and had she not been a lady, she would have echoed Gus's disgust. They were vultures.

One of the birds uttered a harsh cry. The sound punctured the morning quiet, settling on Gus and Genny's ears with the finality of death. Before the cry had ended, the Pawnee leader, only a few hundred yards past the butte, wheeled his mount. For a moment he studied the birds. Another man turned. And then another.

"This is it," Gus whispered. "Betrayed by a bunch of damn vultures! Get ready to fire." He spared a quick glance at her even as he positioned the repeater on the rocks. Incongruously, a smile flashed across his features. "Move around behind that rock and stay low. Shoot to kill. These warriors will die hard, and try to take us with

them if they can. Don't let them.'' He reached out to
rub her cheek with the backs of his fingers, and his smile
became pensive. "You know, I . . .''

A high, piercing cry erupted from the plain below
as eight mounted warriors plunged their horses back
toward the butte. More cries lifted as they thundered
onward.

Whatever Gus had been about to say was lost. He
pushed Genny deeper into the cleft between the rocks to
a point where she could still shoot down on their attack-
ers, then looked toward the Pawnees.

"Here they come," he breathed. Sighting down the
barrel of the Spencer, he picked out the lead man. He
fired, the retort echoing among the rocks, ringing in
their ears. The Pawnee jolted backwards, clutching his
chest. In another second he slumped over, then tumbled
to the ground. "And there they go! Shoot, Genny!
Keep up the fire! Take the one on the black and white
horse!''

Her throat was so dry she was choking, but she lifted
the rifle to her shoulder and sighted the man he told her
to. With her heart slamming, fighting terror and tears,
Genny fired. A second later the man flung back one arm,
lifting in his seat, but he didn't fall. In the same instant,
two other warriors loosed their bows, and arrows clat-
tered into the rocks around her.

Gus fired the next six shots in the Spencer's magazine
rapidly, hitting two more men in the shoulders, one in
the chest. The last toppled from his mount and lay still
upon the ground. Three of the Pawnees slowed, confused
by so many shots coming so quickly, but as Gus paused
to load the second magazine, the air filled with the sounds
of battle. Guns exploded, bows twanged, and bullets
cracked among the rocks. The sweet scents of crushed
grass and broken earth mingled with the acrid tang of
gunpowder and the sickly scent of blood.

Adrenaline sped through Genny's veins with the realization that she was fighting for her life. She reloaded
and aimed again, this time for a warrior's chest. Forcing
her mind into a space where the men ceased to be any-

thing but targets she must hit at all costs, she fired with a precision born of years of practice. This time, she hit her target dead on.

Five of the Pawnees reached the base of the butte. Arrows landed in the dust atop the butte, shattering in the hard ground, or falling uselessly on the rocks, and bullets careened into the rocks, ricocheting dangerously, but none hit them.

Gus peered down through a cleft in the rocks and carefully chose his shots. Three of the Pawnees were dismounting, while the remaining pair spurred their horses back to approach the butte from the other side. He took a bead on one of the retreating riders, noting that it was the man who had attacked him yesterday morning by the river. Gus pulled the trigger.

By the time he had thrown the lever down to eject the used cartridge and rammed it back up to load another, the Pawnee was dead, dragging alongside his pony, his feet tangled in the traces as the terrified horse bolted across the prairie. Gus fired again, hitting the second rider low in the back, and then again, a second later. The warrior pitched from his seat, and his horse ran off after the other one.

Genny watched in fascinated horror as Gus turned his sights to the three men scrambling up the slope toward them. They were close, and the next bullet from the Spencer blew one young warrior's head half off. In another second the fourth Pawnee lay dead with a gaping hole in his chest. The last warrior looked at his fallen friends in disbelief.

Lifting both arms, he let out a chilling cry. Harsh and anguished, it grew in volume until it became a furious roar. Genny shivered, clapping her hand over her mouth to still her own cries as the last Pawnee snatched a loaded rifle from his dead comrade's hands. Charging up the butte, he raised the gun to his shoulder.

Gus paused, jaw tight, nostrils flared. With a guttural shout, he pulled the trigger of the Spencer.

The bullet crashed into the Pawnee, the force of it sending him reeling back down the hillside. His rifle discharged when it fell to the rocky ground, a last violent echo to the battle.

Unnatural silence followed. Three horses milled aimlessly at the foot of the butte, while five more wandered across the plain. Eight men lay dead. Somewhere in the grass below, a meadowlark broke into lilting song.

Genny rose unsteadily, her eyes riveted to the carnage before her. She had killed a man. Dear God in heaven, help her! And Gus Renard, her smiling, laughing, teasing captor and lover, had killed seven warriors. Suddenly she whirled, falling to her knees, bent over at the waist. She retched uncontrollably.

Gus watched her, wanting to go to her and comfort her, but he couldn't move. He stared in frozen horror at the scene below him. An eagle plume tied on one of the Pawnee's arms fluttered in the breeze, and a ground squirrel poked his head up out of a hole near another man's foot. The vultures returned to circle overhead.

Slowly, both hands in the dirt, Gus came to his knees. He left the Spencer on the ground, pushed himself to his feet, and walked out of the rocks into the small flat area of grass at the north end of the butte. With deliberate steps, he turned clockwise to face the west.

Genny glanced over her shoulder when she heard him move. Unable to go to him, she watched.

He threw his head back and his arms out and he began to sing. High and piercing, his song opened on the same note upon which the last Pawnee warrior's life had ended. Shivers ran down Genny's spine as she listened. The fury, the grief, and the futility were the same. Gus's song was the Pawnee's song, and Genny clutched her sides against the wave of revulsion that crashed through her.

Gus paid her no heed. Brave and fearless, he sang to the west, driving the words Genny could not understand and the same emotions that rocked her with the violence of that terrible hailstorm into a fervent chant. His throat worked each syllable. His chest rose and fell in uneven breath. The morning sun glowed bright upon his back, upon the dark hair that hung limply over his shoulders, but left his face in shadow.

His rich voice rasped over a final note and he turned to the north. Again he sang the song, stronger this time. His words were the same, but now it was his song and no longer the dead Pawnee's. He sang now for himself. How she knew this, she couldn't say. Now he sang a plea, a protest, and it found an echo in Genny's aching spirit.

Then he faced the east. Genny saw the bloodied bandage on his upraised arm, and the morning sun threw his features into bold relief. He paused as he surveyed the broken bodies below. Closing his eyes, he raised his voice once more, and it was a dirge now, full of agony and despair. Tears sprang to Genny's eyes and he faltered once, but he sang on.

He faced the south, where she stood, but he didn't see her. Singing loudly, almost shouting the strange words, he stared into the sky. Now he demanded, he begged, he cried with his voice, with the same words he had used before. And then he softened, ending in an almost crooning whisper that made Genny long for a peace she doubted she would ever feel again.

He turned again to the west and he sang a fifth time, the same song. He looked down and sang again. At last, he lowered his arms and stood quietly, in a throbbing silence.

Then one hand lifted, his left. He reached toward her without looking, his palm turned upward.

"Genny." His voice was low and deep with need. "Come."

She didn't move. How could she go to him? How could she ever forgive him for what he had put her through? And yet, how could she not? She needed comfort and safety now and he was all she had.

"Please, Genny."

With stilted steps, she approached him. Dirt and black powder streaked his fingers, and blood oozed from a cut on his thumb. Trembling, she placed her hand in his palm.

Gus squeezed his eyes closed and wrapped his fingers tightly around hers. Shaking as badly as she was, he pulled her to his side.

"I've never been a praying man," he said softly. "But I'm praying now, Genny." His voice broke. "Stand with me. Honor the spirits of those whose lives we took, and seek to leave them here upon this field. Stand with me in regret, facing the home of the Wakinyan, and be grateful for life. Will you sing with me?"

She nodded, tears spilling from her eyes. She didn't know what else to do. As Gus took a deep breath and sang again, she struggled to sing his song. Forcing sound through her swollen throat, she tried. Voice unsteady and breaking, she followed him as best she could, hesitating over the unfamiliar words. Half a note behind him, she finished the halting words. Gus closed his eyes and dropped his head.

Hand in hand, they turned to the north. He lifted his head and sang again, carrying her with him, urging her to sing with him with convulsive jerks of his chin. She sang with him, stumbling over words, and notes, but stronger. The descending melody spoke her conflicting grief and anger as articulately as any words. The song carried her emotions up from her gut and flung them into the boundless sky, an eruption of destructive hurts.

They turned east, and the sight below them brought sobs to her throat, but Gus sang and she stayed with him. Facing the horror of what they had done, of what he had brought her to, she cast a wary glance up at him.

He was crying. Tears threaded over his cheeks. His chin shook, his song wavered. Genny looked away, into the sky. Their voices died.

Gus tugged on her hand and they turned to the south. Now their song pled for healing. For forgiveness. As before, his voice grew fuller, stronger. The force of his prayer engulfed her, and it became her own. Her heart cried out for absolution and peace, but she doubted it would come soon.

Finally they faced the west again. Gus sang again, and as he did, his grip relaxed and his breathing became less

harsh. His tears ceased, though his cheeks remained wet.
Genny stopped singing, listening to him end the song,
looking up at him. As the last notes died on his lips, his
energy changed. Without moving at all, he settled into
himself, and a sense of calm radiated from him. It seemed
suddenly that strength flowed down from the summer sky
above and up from the earth below to hold them fixed.
Light shimmered over the plains, pulsing like the beating
of a heart, surrounding them, filling them with the awareness of their own existence.

Gus drew Genny into his arms and held her close. She
reached to place her arm around his neck. Dropping her
forehead against his chest, she pressed her face to his
hot, damp skin. She didn't want to need him this way,
but there was no denying it. She did.

One of his hands came up to cup her nape, and he
leaned down, burying his lips in her hair. "I'm so sorry,
ištatola. I never meant to bring you to this." His sigh
was more a groan. "Please believe I never did."

Gus rounded up the Pawnee horses, choosing mounts
for Genny and himself, and they rode northeast, quickly
leaving the battle sight behind. To Genny's mingled dismay and relief, they left the bodies of the Pawnee warriors where they had fallen. She had not liked to leave
them as prey for carrion fowl and wolves, but neither
had she wanted to approach them. When she had begun
to fret about it, Gus stilled her protest.

"Warriors expect to die this way," he'd said. "It
happens often enough. Sometimes there's no one left
alive to retrieve the bodies. It's happened to friends of
mine, Genny. Perhaps someday their relatives will come
to retrieve their bones. But those men are gone. They
don't care anymore, and we have to move on."

The day was warm and humid, with great white cumulus clouds sailing in a milky sky. They didn't speak
as they rode, and afterwards, Genny never could recall
what her thoughts had been that day. Numb, she simply
rode, following Gus's lead, not thinking, not questioning, not feeling.

Early in the evening, long before the sun was down, Gus made camp beside a small spring on the south side of sloping rise of prairie. There was scant timber, just a few chokecherry bushes that the birds had stripped of their fruit, some scraggly cottonwoods, and a box elder tree. To the south, storm clouds flickered periodic lightning, but they were far away, and no rain threatened them.

As soon as the horses were watered, staked and tended, Genny made for the spring. Her need to wash away the filth and grime of the past two days was as much of the spirit as of the body, and she longed to immerse herself in the clear, refreshing waters of the spring. Gathering her few remaining garments, all of them now soiled, stained, or torn, she walked to the edge of the shallow pool below the seep.

Gus met her there, his face uncharacteristically solemn. Exhaustion deepened the lines around his eyes and the creases in his cheeks, and he looked older, and weary. His dark blue shirt was stiff with dried blood and sweat and caked with dust, and long strands of hair that had escaped their ties straggled forward, framing his face. Genny knew she wasn't in any better shape.

He walked to her side and took the clothes from her arms, dropping them on the grass. Then he stripped off his shirt and pants, so that he was dressed only in his breechcloth and the bloody bandage on his arm. A habitual smile curved his mouth, but his eyes looked empty as he placed his right hand on her shoulder.

The weight of his hand was oddly comforting. "I was going to bathe," she said, looking away from him into the pool. "But I'll wait if you want to go first."

Gus shook his head, and his hand slid to her open collar, toying with the buttons. "Let me bathe you. Let me strip away these dirty clothes."

He brought his left hand up and undid her shirt to the waist, tugging it free of her skirt. With a whisper, it fell away from her shoulders, gliding to the ground. Her skirt followed. Standing in her camisole and torn drawers, Genny let him undress her. She could not deny the need she saw in his eyes, nor the need she felt in her own soul. What she felt, and what she sensed in Gus right now, was far deeper than lust.

Tonight, they needed each other. They needed warmth, and they needed to touch. They needed to feel the blood throbbing in their veins and to feel an answering heartbeat in another's breast.

They needed life.

"Let me take away the dirt," he repeated softly, loosing the tie at her breasts. He whisked her underthings away and caught her in his arms. Lifting her against his chest with his good arm, he stepped from the bank into the water. In the center of the pool, it reached her waist. He set her a little away from him. "Let me cleanse you, Genny." There was a question in his eyes, and he waited.

Eyes lowered, she nodded her assent.

Gus reached for the bar of soap on the bank and brought it through the water. Rubbing it between his hands, he worked it into a lather, releasing the scent of lilacs, sweet and soothing. He took Genny's hands again, and gave her the soap. Then his hands went to her waist, slippery, warm, and wet, running up her sides to lodge under her arms, grazing the sides of her breasts.

She tilted her head back and closed her eyes, sighing. Soapy hands slithered down her sides, crossing over her stomach where they traced slow circles, dipping below the water and back up, carrying cool water over her belly. Then he placed his hands on her shoulders, dripping rivulets over her breasts and back, and pushed her down into the water.

Crouching before her, Gus pulled a once blue ribbon, now stained brown and fraying at the ends, from her floating braid, and tossed it on the bank. He spread her hair through the water, then laced his fingers behind her neck, kneading tense muscles with his thumbs.

"Let me give you ease," he whispered, bending so that his lips brushed her forehead. He took the soap from her clasped hands and worked it again, then gave it back. "Close your eyes." She did, and his fingers whispered over her face and down her neck like soft spring rain.

Gooseflesh shivered down her arms and back, and a breathy exclamation caught in her throat. Following the pressure of his hand on the top of her head, she ducked under the water to rinse and he stood her up and turned her. Gathering her wet hair in one hand, he pushed it over her shoulder.

He stroked her back and shoulders with wet palms. Taking the soap again, he washed her back gently. Then he lifted each arm, and ran one hand down each limb until he held her hands. In a smooth caress, his warm palms slid back to her shoulders, where he began lathering her arms. He worked until they were encased in fragrant gloves that flowed down over her elbows, wrists, and hands. Then he took each finger, starting with her thumbs, rubbing, squeezing, caressing. His long, supple fingers glided over each nail and across each knuckle in light, stroking whispers, catching in the webs between her fingers, dragging slowly across her palms, tracing soapy circles over the backs of her hands. Every touch was a delight. Her muscles relaxed, and she felt boneless, wrists weak, fingers useless, attuned only to the small, sensual pleasures of her bath.

Cupping water in his hands, Gus rinsed her arms. Water sluiced down her fingers, running white and cloudy into the clear pool. "Your hands are clean again, *ištatola*," he said. "Turn back to me."

Genny hesitated. Looking over her shoulder, she caught the invitation in his eyes. Like a magnet, it drew her to him.

Before she had fully turned, his hands, hard and callused, yet slick with soap, closed over her breasts and washed them. She felt heavy, swelling under his touch, her nipples hardening into points. The familiar ache of desire joined the deeper needs the last days had opened within her spirit, and she moaned, leaning into him, pressing her breasts into his hands.

She stood compliantly, savoring the slippery rasp of his hands as he washed all of her. He led her into shallower water and his hands moved over her hips and thighs. Kneeling before her, he braced each foot upon his thigh to clean her legs and feet as thoroughly as he had the rest of her, dipping his soapy fingers between her toes and behind her knees. When he had rinsed her, he leaned down to press a kiss against her right knee where a pink scar marked the wound she had received at their first meeting. His tongue explored the healed skin lightly, and more shivers skittered through her. Her toes curled, and her muscles tensed.

When he ran his hands up her legs to slide his fingers between her thighs, she accepted his touch, and let him wash her there. His hand was hot in contrast to the cooler water, and the press and movement of his fingers made her feel hotter yet. Eyes closed, her bottom lip caught between her teeth, she would have had him linger, but he withdrew, leading her into deeper water again. Below the surface of the pool, he rinsed her, pushing her this way and that, turning her and finally lowering her backwards over his arm so that her hair spread over the water. He cupped her mound and bent to kiss her throat.

Then he lifted her and took the soap again to wash her hair. Genny sighed and turned so that he could reach her better, but the ache between her legs did not subside. As his hands massaged her scalp and lathered her hair, anticipation ignited need into a raging, though strangely static, burn. Her heart thudded, and she leaned forward to watch the steady way it lifted her breast. The image both soothed and fired her. Motionless, her blood coursed thick and molten, nerve endings quivered, and muscles strained. Her cheeks burned hot, and her lungs tightened painfully. When Gus ducked her head to rinse her hair, the water seemed warmer, as if her body had heated it. With single-minded focus, she lost herself in the moment.

Gus raised her from the water and waited while she let the water stream away from her eyes. When she opened them, he stood mesmerized. Her gaze was hot with wanting, yet soft with emotion. He saw the reflection of his own needs and desires, of his hurts and the deep chasms the last days had reopened in his soul, and he drew a ragged breath.

"Wash me, Genny. As I have you." He closed his eyes. "Make me clean."

Chapter 15

Genny reached for the string that held Gus's breech-cloth in place and released it, pulling the wet leather away from his body, her eyes never leaving his. Tossing it on the bank, she untied the bandage on his arm, and the wet cloth came away easily from his stitched wound. As naked now as she, he stood motionless. With slow precision, she rolled the soap in her hands until bubbles dripped into the water, floating in tiny rafts to lodge against his stomach.

He exhaled, blinking with relief. She hadn't refused him. To hide his reaction, he ducked under the water and rose again, shaking his streaming hair back over his shoulders. Before his eyes had opened, she pushed the soap into his hands, and he felt her fingers at the crown of his head.

In that moment, as the first soap bubbles dribbled over his forehead and down his nose, he felt as if he had won a greater battle than had been waged with the Pawnee warriors that morning. Genny wasn't sure of him. Now more than ever, he knew she didn't want to care. But she did. She didn't just want him. She didn't just need him. For all his flaws, and in spite of everything he'd put her through, she was coming to care for him.

Genny moved closer to wash his hair. Water spiked his lashes, and the sun glinted off the drops of water that clung to his dark skin. He was beautiful to look upon, his even features relaxed in groaning pleasure as she laid her hands upon his head. She sank her fingers into his hair, her touch firm and gentle as she worked the soap through. Her forearms bumped against his ears and jaw, and he turned his cheek into her, dropping a swift kiss on the inside of her elbow. Warmth shuddered up her arm as his breath flowed over her sensitive skin, and she had to concentrate to keep her hands moving. They stood very close together. Her breasts brushed his chest, and she felt the cake of soap and his fingers against her waist. Lower still, the tip of his aroused member grazed against her belly.

She fought the inertia in her drugged limbs, willing her hands to move. As she had warmed under his ministrations, she felt Gus do the same under hers. Laving soap over his face and neck, she washed the dust and grime from him, feeling his smooth skin slip beneath her fingertips. She explored the bones of his cheeks, jaw, and nose, finding them fine, hard, and solid. The corded muscles in his neck stretched and twisted under her touch, and the pulse in his throat pounded in concert with her own. Unable to resist, she brought the length of her body up against his, and circled her arms around his shoulders.

"Lean down so I can rinse the soap away," she whispered against his ear, as he had so many times done to her. Satisfying shudders rippled down his neck, and gooseflesh pebbled his shoulder as he complied with her directions.

Genny bathed him as thoroughly as he had her, gliding her soapy palms over his broad chest, molding the bones of his shoulder blades, and tracing the many small scars that marred his upper body. Carefully, she washed his most recent wound. Her hands felt small on him, delicate and fragile. She picked up one of his hands and held hers flat against it, palm to palm. Their fingers twined, soapy bubbles squishing between them. The dark bronze of his skin contrasted vividly with the pink of hers, and the strength of his long fingers was apparent next to hers. Both hands had killed. Yet both could bring pleasure and healing.

"Your hands are clean, too, Gus," she whispered, carrying them into the water.

His reply was a soft, knowing smile.

He left his hands trailing in the water as she took the soap from him again. After a moment he stepped toward the bank and the water fell away from him, revealing everything that the soap-clouded water had hidden. It was the first time she had been able to appreciate the sight of him standing fully naked before her, his desire for her unashamedly exposed. He was glorious, she thought. Long, brown legs showed hard muscle, and narrow hips and firm flanks drew her eyes to his genitals. She remembered the excitement she had felt when he had held her, thrusting into her, deep and hard, and she wanted him again. She wanted to touch him, to have her touch her again, and to affirm life. And she didn't want to wait.

Wading through the cool water, Genny went to him. Their eyes met, and from the intensity of his expression, she knew he wanted all she sought, and perhaps more. Throwing the soap cake onto the grass, she set her hands on his hips, and began to rub, slipping and sliding over his firm flesh, back to front, over the mounds of his buttocks, and down his thighs. Kneeling, she ran both hands over one leg and then the other, kneading his thighs and calves, gliding over the indentations behind his knees, pressing down the flat bones of his ankles. The feel of him was exquisite. He was warm, hard, and smooth beneath her slick hands. Sensual greed quickened her motions, and her nails dug into his thighs as she stroked him. Soap bubbles slid down her wrists, dripping from her elbows onto her stomach as she stoked their desires higher.

Reaching the tops of his thighs, she ran her hands up over his hip bones and closed them in an arch framing his manhood. She stopped, not quite sure what to do. She wanted to touch him, and his short, excited breaths told her he wanted her to, but she hesitated. This was still so new, to touch a man, to look upon him. Finally, she closed her hands over him.

Head thrown back, a silent cry parting his lips, his hand came to rest on her head. Slick with water and soap, she rubbed and stroked him, squeezing gently, feeling the tug of his response. Her own insides contracted and heat engulfed her; she was flushed and ready. Her breath rasped in her throat, blowing over his thighs.

It was too much to endure. Gus jerked out of her hands and flung himself into deeper water, scrubbing the soap from himself. Genny bent to quickly rinse her hands. Before she could rise, he scooped her into his arms and thrust against her belly, hard and impatient. She arched against him, winding her arms around his neck and holding tight. Everything except the feel of him and the driving need to take him into her body faded into oblivion.

When his mouth closed over hers, his tongue plunging wet and silky against hers, she groaned aloud. It felt so good, so right. His kiss purged her, drawing all the tense emotion of the last days into him, draining her of fear, grief, weariness, and anger. And still it wasn't enough.

Without knowing how she got there, Genny felt the grass beneath her back as Gus lowered himself over her. Her thighs parted instantly and he came to her. As easily as their soap-slick hands had slid over shoulders, arms and breasts, he slid into her waiting heat.

This was what she needed. This was what she craved. His weight protected her and his arms warmed her while his body filled her. There was no room left for grief and anger. There was only the mutual gift bestowed between them. They took one another in passion, and in the tangle of questing hands and hot surrenders, a ragged joy burst the ropes of anger and regrets that bound them.

Gus withdrew and thrust again. Genny cried out and surged against him, pulling him back to her, rocking, thrusting upwards, straining as pleasure and emotion jolted through her.

He thrust again and again, hard and fast. Each time, it was as if lightning exploded in her body, hot, bright, and searing. Each time she cried out, ragged and wild like the west winds. Upwards they spiraled into tension, and Gus gasped each time she tightened around him until he, too, shouted out in passion. His body drove him faster and faster, like a spinning twister, pushing him to completion.

Genny threw her hips forward, back arched and thighs taut as she pressed into his fevered thrusts. Her arms fell back, her fingers dug into the grass, and the muscles in her neck strained with effort. The burning fire in her sex raged beyond control. It flared, retreated for a heartbeat, and flared again. Then it burst in a fire storm, consuming her in white-hot release. A cry tore through her, carried up from the soles of her feet through the crown of her head, giving vent to emotions she could no more name than will away. Her muscles clutched and quivered, closing tight around Gus, rocking her with an intensity that left her gasping.

When he felt her pull hard upon him, he froze, then drove into her, fingers buried in her hips. Hot and liquid, his seed erupted, spurting life from his loins into the depths of her womb. Long and hard, his climax and the unacknowledged emotions that raged between them shook him violently. When he finally collapsed over her, limp and panting, his throat was tight and his eyes burned. He rubbed them absently, still caught in a riptide of feelings he was unable to sort or understand.

His fingers came away damp.

Neither of them spoke when they finally rose to set their camp to rights, and to rebandage Gus's arm. He had torn two of the stitches open and started bleeding again. Physically exhausted and emotionally drained, they combed each other's hair in quiet contemplation, knowing there were many things they could have said, but finding more comfort in their silence. Genny washed their clothes, and Gus scrubbed the war paint off the Pawnee horse she had ridden. They ate dried apples, and jerky, and fell asleep in each other's arms.

Halfway through the next day's travel, Gus and Genny ran across Harv and Trixie grazing alongside a dry creekbed. Genny wanted to abandon the Pawnee horses. They reminded her forcibly of the brutal attack the day before, but Gus insisted they were too valuable to let go. He promised she'd never have to see them once they reached his camp.

That evening they entered a heavily wooded river bottom as the sun was setting in an orange and pink glow. A haze of blue-gray smoke hung in the air, and the scent of cooking meat tantalized them as it wafted past on the breeze. The grass around them was cropped close, and the ground bore testimony to many passing hooves. Genny looked ahead through the trees with more dread than anticipation.

The day had been taxing. Both of them were tired, Gus's arm hurt, and the previous day's experiences cast a somber pall over both of them, despite the passion they had shared beside the spring. Genny sensed a withdrawal in Gus that upset her. She needed him now. He was coming home, but she was facing another major challenge. Her nerves were fraying more with every step they took toward the Lakota camp.

Now, with the smoke from many campfires in view, Gus tugged on Harv's mane to get the horse to stop. "We're almost there, Genny. The camp will be spread out alongside the river up ahead. It'll be easier tonight if you let me do the talking. There are sure to be a lot of questions, and I may not be able to translate everything for you." He looked at her, flexing his arm gingerly.

"What am I supposed to do?" Nervously, she pushed her hair back.

"Don't stare at people, especially men, and try to remember that while things may seem completely foreign, we're just people. We're not so different from white folks. Be quiet and cautious."

Genny's fears fueled her defensive reaction. "So I'm supposed to stand meekly by and not say anything?"

Gus shook his head, glancing around. No one had come out from the camp yet to meet them, but they would soon. "That's not what I meant."

"Then why do you want me to keep quiet and not look at anyone?" Genny watched Gus carefully. His posture was suddenly straighter than it had been, and there was an excited glint in his eyes. He was glad to be coming home.

He didn't look at her. "It looks better that way." He sounded distracted.

"What is that supposed to mean?" Her eyes narrowed.

"It looks more respectful. More natural." He shifted forward a little on Harv's back.

"I am not your squaw," she said tightly.

Gus turned sharply to look at her. Anger flashed in his eyes. "Don't use that word. That's a white man's word, and we don't call our women squaws. And there's nothing degrading in respect between a man and his woman. That's all I'm asking for. And make no mistake, Genny. While we're here, you're my woman. Unless you've changed your mind and prefer to come as a captive taken in war."

Genny stared at him. "How can you talk to me like this after what we've been through? What you've put me through? Yesterday morning I killed a man! Because you dragged me away from my home, out into this heathen wilderness. I have to live with that for the rest of my life, so don't you dare threaten me now, Gus Renard! We've come too far for that. I'm not Lakota, and you can't expect me to act like an Indian."

Gus flipped his hair back over his shoulder, and frowned. "I know that. And I know you can deal with this. But I don't want you to judge my mother's people before you know them. It's easy to do, and you're right. You've been through a lot, and I've already told you once, I never meant for it to be this hard. Yesterday morning just happened, Genny, and it was as hard for me as it was for you. Maybe harder. Don't make this harder yet. Remember that in coming here, whether by your own will or because I forced it on you, you'll be the one judged harshly if you aren't careful. Keeping quiet tonight is being careful. Will you trust me?"

"I don't have any choice. You never leave me a choice, Gus."

He opened his mouth to reply but no words came. He frowned and tried again. "Have I let you down yet?"

She didn't answer.

"How you behave tonight will set the tone for how people respond to you while you're here. Among the Lakota, if you act as though guided by generosity, courage, integrity, and respect for others, you'll be fine."

She nodded once finally and looked away, not at all certain she liked Gus in a moralizing mood.

"Let's go, then," he said softly, with a last, contemplative look at her.

In a few minutes two men on ponies charged through the trees ahead of them. They were dressed in brown leather breechcloths and leggings, and their long braids flew back over their shoulders as they came. Gus raised his arm and called out to them, and they answered with shouts of greeting. When they drew closer, Genny saw that both men were obviously happy to see Gus.

After a nod to him, though, they looked curiously at Genny. A few words from Gus ended their perusal, and they brought their ponies into pace alongside Harv and Trixie, ignoring Genny. Gus was all smiles, laughing merrily as he caught up on news and exchanged barbs with his friends.

Genny felt like a maiden aunt at a church social for all the attention they paid her, but she kept quiet and didn't stare at Gus's friends. More than anything in the world, she would have liked to have been riding through the gate at Riverwood, safe and sure of her place in her own family. Even Aunt Augusta would have been a welcome sight.

It was half an hour before they reached the main part of the camp. In spite of her poor spirits, Genny looked around with interest at the dun-colored tipis that lay scattered on one side of the river, their smoke-darkened tops bristling with pointed poles and sporting streamers of colored cloth, feathers, and horsehair tassels. Some were decorated with colorful paintings of horses, deer, eagles, and other birds and animals. The tang of wood smoke filled the evening air, and the sounds of dogs barking and children laughing and shouting rang throughout the clearing. A pair of fat, black puppies tumbled into her ankles, then scampered away, bringing a faint smile to her face.

There were people everywhere. Men and women were gathered in front of most of the tipis, some standing, some sitting on the ground. Iron kettles were suspended over cooking fires, and clouds of steam rose when dark women with long braids ladled food into bowls for hungry men and children. Genny's stomach rumbled as she inhaled the fragrance of boiling meat.

It took a few minutes before the people of the camp were aware of the new arrivals. Gus spoke briefly to an older man who strode off calling something aloud to any who cared to listen. In his wake, curious eyes began to turn their way, but not before Genny had time to look at the people around her.

Most of the men were dressed as their escorts were, in clouts and leggings, their hair carefully arranged in braids or tied up with feathers and other colored ornaments. Only a few of the younger men wore shirts, and it was startling to see so much bare flesh. At least the women were fully clothed in wide-yoked leather or woolen shifts that fell to their knees or lower. Most of the smaller children were naked, or nearly so.

And everyone was dark. Their complexions spanned a range of browns, from creamy, lighter tones, to deeply bronzed, sunburned hues. Everyone Genny saw had dark hair, either brown or black, and as people began approaching, she saw that all their eyes were dark.

Gus handed the horses over to a boy of about twelve and stepped closer to Genny, though he didn't touch her. Slowly, a semicircle of onlookers formed around them.

More than a little nervous, Genny glanced down at her hands, clasped tightly before her. She looked sideways to where Gus's hands hung at his sides, and could not help noticing again how pale her skin looked compared to his. Her eyes rose to his face.

For the first time since she had discovered him reading on her sofa, she saw him fully as an Indian. He belonged here. These people were his friends and family. He had grown up among them, and this was his home. As he had told her repeatedly, he was Lakota.

Dear Lord, what had she done? She didn't belong here. Not with these people. Not with this man.

He caught her gaze and held it, his eyes knowing. In her mind, she heard again the question he had asked not so very many nights ago. Why would you want to be friends with a man like me? With a half-breed Indian. A Lakota. An Indian like the savage Pawnees they had killed yesterday.

Gus tensed, and a muscle ticked in his cheek as he watched her. Wariness crept into his eyes.

Genny saw evidence of internal struggle in the firm set of his jaw and the tight line of his lips. Suddenly she understood why he left white women alone.

He was avoiding moments like this, and the pain of trying to bridge two very different worlds.

Right now, she saw his fear. He was afraid that she would turn away from him, rejecting his people and that part of him that was Lakota. And afraid that she would inadvertently shame him, embarrassing him in front of his mother's people. It startled her to recognize his fears, for she had come to think of him as fearless. She had seen him wary, even cautious, but never frightened until now.

Genny didn't want to see his uncertainty. She needed to see him smiling to reassure her. And intuitively, she knew she had to reassure him first.

So she smiled for him. Slowly, uncertainly, and a little shyly.

Her reward came in kind. The relief she felt when Gus's eyes lit up and his lips lifted at the corners was palpable. Unexpectedly overcome by emotions she couldn't easily fathom, she lowered her eyes and ducked her head.

Genny looked at the ground as Gus began to speak in Lakota. She assumed he was explaining who she was and why she was there. She didn't care.

In a rush of the same conflicting feelings that had overwhelmed her last night when they made love, it dawned on her that if she wasn't very careful, she just might find herself in love with Gus Renard.

If she wasn't already.

Genny followed Gus through the camp until he came to a group of people he seemed to know better than the others. She assumed they were his family and she began looking for his sister. None of the women looking curiously at her resembled Gus in the slightest. Shortly, Gus informed her briefly that his sister wasn't in camp. A small boy riding up on a bay pony interrupted him, and Genny got no more information. She tagged along behind him as he circulated among his relatives and friends, feeling increasingly inconsequential. When Gus handed her a bowl of thin soup, she accepted it gratefully. Doing as he did, she sipped it, and found it bland, without salt or seasoning. Nonetheless, it was hot, and her stomach was too empty to be particular. She smiled shyly at the woman who provided the soup, receiving a curt little nod in reply.

Learning that his sister and her family were gone, Gus had taken Genny to Brings It Along, Hawk Dancer's wife, to get some soup for their supper. They drank their soup standing up outside the lodge, and Gus noted that there seemed to be more boys about than usual. He asked Hawk Dancer about it.

"Those three are my wife's nephews," the tall, angular man answered, nodding toward three boys ranging in age from about seven to fourteen. Hawk Dancer was a holy man, not very experienced yet, but still young, and far closer to Gus than his own brother would ever be. "Her brother came through camp a few weeks ago and these boys wanted to stay a while, so we're keeping them."

Gus nodded. It was a common enough occurrence, but with his sister, Good Shield, and her husband and children not expected back from a family hunting trip for a few days, Gus needed a place for Genny and himself to sleep. Since Hawk Dancer's lodge was so full, he reluctantly led Genny to his aunt's tipi.

He scratched at the hide covering that served as a door, and waited. A shrill voice called out and Gus lifted the cover, ushering Genny inside.

They were met by a blast of hot air and a strong musty odor as they stepped in. It was nearly dark outside, but the tipi glowed with a warm orange light from the fire at the center. Smoke was collecting in a cloud at the peak of the conical structure, and an old woman sat at the back of the lodge, across from the door, fanning ineffectually at it. She shouted something at Gus, motioning him back outside.

Gus muttered a disgusted word and pulled Genny out with him. "She forgot she closed the smoke flaps. Take that pole and carry it around to the back," he directed in English, pointing at one of two pine lodgepoles leaning against the front of the lodge.

Genny did as instructed, pulling open one of the smoke flaps at the top of the hide tent as she maneuvered the long pole around to one side. She met Gus at the back of the lodge, where he commenced a shouted conversation with the woman inside. After a series of adjustments, the smoke began to draw through the top of the tipi. Gus anchored the flap poles firmly.

The old woman continued to shout at Gus without bothering to leave her seat inside the lodge. Genny had no idea what she was talking about, but she sounded upset.

"My aunt," Gus said tersely. "She has stiff joints. They bother her less with a fire, even in summer. We're staying here tonight. She has more room than anyone else in the family," he added, guiding Genny back into the sweltering lodge.

"Is this what you call a sweat lodge?" Genny asked under her breath.

Gus erupted into laughter, then spoke in Lakota to his aunt. Genny thought he repeated her question because he laughed again when the old woman started a high-pitched harangue that lasted several minutes. She waved at Genny in a dismissive gesture, and shook one hand at Gus in a scolding fashion.

"Is it?" Genny demanded, frustrated with her inability to understand what was going on.

Gus laughed again. "No. A sweat lodge is used for religious purposes. I'll explain it later." He put his hand on her shoulder. "Sit down. With your legs tucked under you to the side."

"I know how to sit," Genny muttered in irritation.

While Gus spoke to his aunt again, Genny looked around the lodge. It looked disordered, with hides heaped haphazardly on the floor and a number of rectangular, painted leather containers piled up on one side. Gus's aunt looked as if she were in her late sixties, and her most striking feature was her hair. It was very long and thick, mostly gray, but still streaked much darker in places. She wore it loose, so that it flowed over her small frame, like a cape. From her seat against a triangularly shaped backrest suspended from a pole, she scrutinized Genny while she listened to Gus.

The old woman turned suddenly to her nephew and began arguing with great energy. Gus maintained a cheerful smile and bantering tone, but when he reached to pull something from the pile of heavy robes his aunt was hunkered down upon, Genny held her breath, expecting the worst.

Gus's aunt shrieked and jumped back, knocking a painted leather bag off one of the lodge poles. Gus grabbed for something with both hands, nearly landing in the fire before he captured his prize. Triumphantly, he held aloft a tiny field mouse, swinging by its tail. The old woman waved her hand in disgust when she saw her inconsequential guest.

Genny covered her mouth with one hand to keep from laughing as Gus headed outside with the creature. As he passed Genny, he tripped over one of the hides that lay bunched on the floor, landing half in and half out of the entrance. The mouse disappeared. Genny hoped it was outside the lodge. When Gus picked himself up and came back in, his aunt seemed more amenable to guests for the night. She tossed him a couple of sleeping robes and settled down in her own bed, close by the fire.

Gus caught the robes, deftly snatching one corner away from the fire.

"Are they clean?" Genny whispered doubtfully.

He nodded, arranging the robes. "Pretty much. Put one of your blankets on top of them. You won't want a blanket over you tonight," he told her, shaking out one from her bedroll.

"What's your aunt's name?" Genny asked, kneeling on the bed. It was surprisingly soft, and it didn't smell. Genny wondered where the musty odor came from.

"Mni Sapa Win. It means Black Water Woman. You should call her *tonwin*," he whispered, rolling onto his back beside her. He tugged her down to lie with him.

"What does that mean?"

"Auntie." He flexed his shoulders and settled back into the buffalo robes. "I don't care how hot it is in here, I'm going to sleep like a baby," he sighed. "Come here, Genny Stone."

"Gus!" she whispered furiously when he pulled her into his arms. "Stop it! Your aunt's not even asleep yet! She's watching us!"

"So?" He kissed the tip of her nose. He glanced up. Sure enough, his aunt was looking at them, her dark eyes sharp and alert from across the fire.

"You can't seriously want to . . ." Genny was interrupted as his mouth closed over hers. The kiss ended as abruptly as it started.

"Well, I do," he whispered in her ear. "But I also have a few sensibilities, so you're safe. For tonight." He kissed her again, then reached to unbutton her skirt. "You should undress or you'll die of heat stroke. If you lie down, my aunt can't see you over my shoulders." He obligingly leaned up on one elbow to shield her from view.

"Why don't you have your own tipi?" Genny asked as she struggled out of her clothes.

"Most men don't. The lodges belong to the women." He ran one finger along the edge of her camisole, dipping lightly into the valley between her breasts.

Genny pushed him away gently. "Are we going to

have to sleep here every night?" she asked, flopping onto her back. She could see stars through the opened smoke flaps. "Maybe you should see about making arrangements for a little more privacy."

"Why?" Gus lowered himself to lie on his back as well. They lay close, not quite touching.

"Because I'm not used to dressing and undressing and sleeping with people I don't know," she whispered primly.

"That's all? What about making love?" he queried suggestively.

Genny didn't bother to answer.

"Living in close quarters as we do, no one notices what anyone else is doing. We learn to give each other privacy within the lodge. You'll learn, too, *istatola*."

"That may well be, but I'm not going to . . ." A low chuckle broke from his lips. "Well, I'm not!"

"I've heard you say that before, Genny," Gus taunted quietly.

She flipped onto her side, facing the wall of the tipi. That seemed like a very long time ago, though it had only been a few days. "I mean it this time!"

"You meant it before, but you know how I love a challenge. You don't stand a chance, *istatowin*. Tonight, and only tonight, you get a respite." He reached over to pinch her lightly on her backside.

Swatting his hand away, Genny sincerely hoped that whoever they ended up staying with were sound sleepers.

"Genny?" Gus caught her hand. He paused and she turned her head, waiting. "About earlier. In front of everyone . . ." He stopped again, and the silence stretched between them. "Thank you." He squeezed her hand, then tucked it against his breast.

His skin was warm and his heartbeat steady beneath her palm. She wondered if he realized the depth of feeling that was growing between them, and if he understood where it was taking her. Or where it was taking him. If she didn't miss her guess, both she and Gus stood poised on the brink of learning what it meant to love. She sighed, turning to rest her cheek on his shoulder, wishing she could stop what was happening, hoping nothing would stop it, and knowing without doubt that they were moving into an impossible course.

Chapter 16

After Genny fell asleep, Gus slipped from her side to meet with his cousins, Hawk Dancer, Bad Arrow, and Walks in Thunder, along with the camp elders. The incident with the Pawnees concerned everyone and had to be discussed immediately. It was unlikely that there would be any retaliation, since none of the attacking war party had survived, but there was a chance a scout or a boy caring for the horses had stayed back out of the way. Gus didn't think so, but the camp leaders had to know what had happened. With so many warriors off fighting the *wašicus*, all threats, however remote, were taken seriously. Long past midnight, he returned to Genny, and fell contentedly asleep, his body curved around hers like a shell.

In the morning Gus and Mni Sapa Win awakened early, and Gus was able to talk his aunt into letting Genny sleep as late as she would. He noted the older woman's speculative expression, and he knew she was wondering what kind of a woman slept the day away as if she were a lazy child. He didn't say anything. Soon enough, Genny would prove her mettle, and he was sure she'd acquit herself well. He wandered off to find his cousins, confident that Genny was more than capable of dealing with his crotchety aunt.

He couldn't have been more wrong.

In the middle of the afternoon, Gus was returning to camp with Hawk Dancer, Walks in Thunder, and several other men after an impromptu horse race, with Trixie as the star attraction. Gus was laughing and gloating over the prizes he had won, including one rumpled gray felt hat, uncannily like the one he'd lost in the hailstorm, when one of Hawk Dancer's boys came racing up, shouting for him.

"*Tuṅska*! You better hurry! Your woman is causing trouble with *Uṅčiśi*! Nobody can talk to her," No Hair called. "Hurry up!"

Gus handed Trixie's leads to one of the other men and dug his heels into the sides of the mare he was riding. Within minutes, he'd reached the edge of the village, dismounted, and was running after his young cousin. As they neared the part of the camp where his family had their lodges, he saw a crowd of women and a few children clustered in front of his aunt's lodge. There was much shouting and gesturing, and over the ruckus, Gus picked out his aunt's shrill voice.

"You stupid girl!" Mni Sapa Win screeched. "How could you do this! I worked for weeks to gather those roots! They were my medicine! Now what will happen? Tell me that, *waśicuwin*! The spirits are going to be angry, and something bad will happen. Something very bad, mark my words!"

Gus pushed through the ranks to find Genny and his aunt nose to nose. Genny's hands were on her hips, and his aunt was flailing her arms in agitation. The air was heavy with a musty, acrid odor that Gus recognized at once.

Genny must have burned his aunt's rare and meticulously cared for supply of bear medicine. He had smelled the roots in the lodge last night, and seen them drying on the ground near the fire when he'd captured the mouse.

"All I did was to try to clean up your filthy tent!" Genny yelled in English. "What was wrong with that?"

Gus cringed as a murmur swept through the onlooking women in response to Genny's disrespectful tone. However unpleasant Mni Sapa Win was, she had the privilege of age on her side. Genny's outburst was an affront. What's more, Mni Sapa Win was considered a wise woman, the mother of an up-and-coming holy man who had a little medicine of her own. The spirits favored her. Her bear medicine had helped several women with minor ailments, and while not very many of them liked her overly much, she had earned their respect.

Mni Sapa Win straightened to her full height and shook her long hair back over her shoulders. "You have much to learn, *wasicuwin*. I am sorry my nephew brought you into my lodge, and the people of this camp will be sorry he brought you into our midst." The crowd fell silent as Mni Sapa Win's voice dropped into a barely audible chant. "The spirits will be angry. It is not good for you to be here. It is bad. Something bad is going to happen. Then all will see that I am right, and that you must go back to your own kind. You should not have come here. The spirits will be angry."

His stomach in knots, Gus stepped forward, hoping to break the thrall his aunt had created. When Genny turned to look at him, he spoke softly and rapidly in English.

"Don't talk, don't move, don't argue." His eyes shot daggers at her. He wheeled to face the crowd. "She did not come," he said loudly in Lakota. "I brought her here. She's my woman. She didn't know that she burned your medicine, *tonwin*. She thought to help you in the lodge. Her people don't have your medicine, and she didn't know what it was. If you're angry, be angry with me."

"That girl was rude. She shouted at me," Mni Sapa Win told him haughtily. "I will not be treated thus by a skinny white girl."

"She was frustrated, *tonwin*, because she can't understand our language. She needs time to learn. She needs our patience. Would you treat a child who didn't know better this way?"

"She is not a child." The women surrounding them murmured in agreement.

"When I explain to her what she did, she'll be sorry."

"Tell her now, so I can see," his aunt demanded.

Gus fixed Genny with a warning look, willing her to respond properly. "Those roots you burned were my aunt's special medicine," he said in English. "She worked hard to gather them. With her swollen joints, it's difficult for her to dig them, and they're hard to find. You burned up her year's supply, and many of the women whom she helps are upset, as well. My aunt is saying that the spirits are going to do something bad because of this."

Genny held her head high. "That's ridiculous. Tell her I'm sorry I burned her medicine. If she'll tell me where to look, I'll dig some more roots for her."

Mni Sapa Win huffed at Genny's clipped tone.

"I wish you'd said that with a little more humility," Gus said flatly.

"I have my pride," Genny snapped. "This has been a horrible day! I haven't done one thing that pleased your aunt. I think she's an evil woman. Do you know what she did?"

"Hush!" Gus bit out. "Everyone is listening! All these women will carry tales home that you . . ." He glanced around him and trailed off. Every woman in the circle was glaring at Genny, and Genny was glaring at him. "Shit!" He straightened his shoulders and took a step toward Genny. When he spoke, his voice was menacingly soft. "That's it. Don't ever argue with me in public again. And apologize to my aunt right now. Make sure you sound like you mean it, or no one will be satisfied, and you'll be paying the price until you leave. Which isn't going to be soon."

Anger flashed in Genny's blue eyes, and she tilted her chin back to look Gus straight in the eyes. "Don't talk to me this way! I didn't know I was doing anything wrong!"

He took another step closer, reaching out to snare her elbow. "Apologize. Now."

Their eyes held and his fingers bit into her arm. Gus was vibrating with anger, and Genny knew from experience that he was unpredictable in such a state. "I didn't do anything wrong!" she told him one last time, before turning to his aunt.

"Lower your eyes when you talk to her," Gus commanded.

With an effort, Genny did so. "I'm sorry I burned your plants," she said, her voice shaking, "and I'll get you more if I can."

She stood motionless while Gus translated her words. Mni Sapa Win scowled, but retreated back into her lodge. A moment later, Gus's and Genny's saddlebags came flying out the door.

"And I'm sorry I ever came here," Genny whispered bitterly.

Gus grabbed her suddenly by both arms. He spun her away from him and pushed her through the throng of women toward the river.

He hustled her along until they were nearly a mile upstream from the camp. Skittering ahead of him, Genny shrugged his hands away from her. Somewhere along the way tears began to cloud her vision, but she refused to give in to them. It was, however, a losing battle.

When a constricted sob escaped her lips, Gus halted as if he'd been shot.

Genny continued on, brushing the tears from her cheeks. It was no use. She stopped, unable to see where she was going as more tears took the place of those she wiped away.

"I suppose Lakota women don't cry about things like this," she whispered brokenly.

Gus shook his head. "Not often. The Lakota are raised to be strong. To resist emotional displays that would embarrass others."

She sniffed loudly, but the tears kept coming. "I'm not Lakota. I cry, and I'm still strong. And I've seen you cry, and I didn't say anything mean to you when it happened!"

Gus didn't respond, and Genny turned away, heading for the riverbank.

He followed. In two quick strides, he caught her and pulled her into his arms, hugging her fiercely.

"Damn it, Genny," he muttered angrily. "Don't cry. Not about my aunt yelling at you. It can't be that bad."

Genny wanted to argue with him, but she couldn't get any words past her constricted throat. She tried to break away from him, but he held her firmly. Finally she buried her face in his shirt and let her sorrows take her. Didn't he realize how much she'd been through since she'd discovered him thieving in her pantry a week ago? His aunt's hostile behavior was only part of why she cried. Cataloguing the dramas of the past few days made her tears run all the freer, and before she could stop herself, she was sobbing convulsively.

Gus was at a loss. Unfamiliar guilt niggled at him, bidding him to accept Genny's tears as a natural reaction to the chaos into which he had plunged her. Awkwardly, he eased his hands over her back, patting and smoothing the material of her shirt over her shoulder blades.

She cried for a long time, but finally her tears abated, the sobs ceased, and her breathing returned to normal. Gus tipped her chin up and looked down into her face, tracing one wet streak from her eye to the corner of her mouth, before rubbing his finger across her bottom lip. Then he touched his finger to his tongue, tasting the salt of her tears as he watched her eyelids close, shuttering her bleak expression.

"Are you all right now?"

"You shouldn't have brought me here," she told him quietly. Her eyes opened, taking on a rebellious glint. "I don't fit in. And I will not tolerate being treated the way you've treated me since we got here. I've been through hell this past week because of you, and I've had about all I can stand. I want to know what's going on, who people are, and how I'm supposed to act. Don't ever leave me alone like that again! And how dare you shout at me and push me around in front of your relatives and friends? I gave you better treatment when you dropped in at my house out of the blue, frightening me and casting insulting looks in my direction. Is this how you treat your guests?"

All Gus's gentler inclinations fled. "Genny, there's a lot you don't understand . . ."

"Then tell me! In English, in a polite manner, and

before I bungle into any more transgressions!''

"It isn't that simple."

She pushed out of his arms and spun to face the river. "Why not? How difficult can it be?"

"For one thing, you aren't here as my guest, but as my wife."

"As your drudge, you mean!"

"No, damn it! That's not what I mean!" He grabbed her arm and yanked her back to face him. "Look, Genny, everything is different here. Customs are different. Expectations are different. It takes time to learn. Words alone can't explain it adequately."

"I'd like to be the judge of that. I feel like I've spent the day playing a game where everyone knows all the rules except for me, and they've all agreed to keep me in the dark," Genny said angrily. "Including you. It can't be so hard for you to tell me what to expect and how not to offend!"

Gus clenched his jaw and flung his hand from her arm. He thrust out his right arm, displaying a series of small scars on the underside of the upper part, just above his elbow. She'd seen them before, he knew. When he spoke, his voice was like a knife, sharp and brutal.

"Then see if you understand this. My cousin, Hawk Dancer, now a respected holy man, held me on the ground while his brother, Bad Arrow, one of this tribe's most renowned warriors, dropped red hot coals on my arm to see if I would scream. For no other reason than to see if I was more Lakota or white. If I was more white, they thought I'd scream. If I was more Lakota, I'd be able to hold my tongue. Other boys stood around taking bets on how long I'd last. I was twelve years old. I had traveled all the way from Montréal by myself and gotten here in one piece, and that didn't matter a damn to them. I could hardly make myself understood, and the first thing I knew, my cousins, my own relatives, were torturing me to test my strength according to their standards. Bad Arrow and Hawk Dancer put twenty glowing coals on my arm, and I didn't say a word. I didn't even grunt.

"And when they let me up that time, do you think

they stopped? I can tell you they didn't, and I've got the scars to prove it. There's not a mark on my body from battle wounds except this slash I got protecting you. All the other scars I took earning my right to call myself a Lakota, earning my place among my mother's people. Do you think I don't know what it's like not to understand what people are saying or how to act? No one ever took the time to teach me the language when I came back. They laughed at me, and my cousins hit me if I said something offensive. To this day, my Lakota name is Śungila Eyeglaśna which means Bad Talking Fox, in honor of my clumsy attempts to relearn the first language I ever spoke.

"Here, among the Lakota, it's considered a matter of respect to allow you, or any other newcomer, to prove your worth. But in terms they understand. You learn by making mistakes, and people assume you're intelligent enough to figure out how to do things right the next time. Does that answer your question?"

Genny looked away at the water flowing bright and fast through the shallow river bed. The knot in her throat was as much in response to the pain of the boy Gus had been as it was for herself, and she hated that. She didn't want to care about him. Not like this.

"The Lakota honor each person's right to do whatever he or she wants to, but behind that is an absolute demand for mutual respect," Gus continued. "It's that respect which made me ask you to be quiet yesterday. It isn't respectful to embarrass someone by drawing attention to the fact that they can't do something, like talk to their peers. And if I'd stayed with you this morning, that would have implied that you needed help. I didn't think you did. God, Genny, I've seen you cope with things this last week that would have broken a lesser woman. I thought you were strong enough to handle things on your own."

"I am. In my own world," Genny retorted rigidly. "But I need your help here, Gus. I'm not here to make a permanent place for myself. You forced me to come. I'm not really your wife, and you can't expect me to act like I am. I don't want to upset anyone, and I'm willing to learn what I can about the Lakota people, but I'm not here to become an Indian. You know that.''

Gus stared at her a long moment before releasing her arm. "You're right," he said softly. He opened his mouth to speak but no words came.

What had he been thinking? Had he unconsciously transferred to her the feelings he remembered from his own long-ago return to the Lakota? He must have. He'd been trying to save her the griefs he'd suffered then, trying to help her fit in to a place where she had no desire or intent of staying any longer than she had to. This camp was not her home, and it never would be.

The realization that he had forgotten that slammed his heart down into his gut. It felt like someone had strapped a brace around his middle and was slowly tightening it, squeezing the life out of him.

Genny watched him throw himself to the ground and set his arms on top of his upraised knees, dropping his head to rest against them. Anger drained out of him as suddenly as prairie winds can die at sunset, and he sank back into the earth as if he were part of it, hunkering low.

She didn't know what to think. Frustrated, she started to walk away.

"Come back," Gus said flatly, lifting his head. He couldn't let her go. He needed to help her, as she'd asked. If he could. "Tell me what happened besides burning *tonwin*'s medicine. We've got to get this straightened out."

"Why can't you just take me home?" Her voice was thick with longing.

Gus thought of all the men who were still absent from camp, away with war parties, and of the stolen payroll buried in Genny's pantry floor. "It's too dangerous. I won't keep you here any longer than I think necessary, but that'll be at least until the weather starts to turn. Then the war parties will make their way home and things along the trail should settle down."

Genny knew she wouldn't sway him by arguing, and

there was no way she would strike out for White Rock Spring on her own. Not after everything that had happened getting here. She was going to have to make the best of circumstances. Like it or not—and right now she didn't like it a bit—she needed Gus's cooperation and help. Walking over to where he sat beneath a tall spruce, she fervently wished that she had gone with Roger Rivier to Julesburg.

"All right. I'll tell you what happened." She dropped to her knees near him and began a listless recitation. "Your aunt prodded me awake about mid-morning and handed me a tin pail. I didn't know what she wanted. When she pushed me to my feet and out the door, I was still at a loss, and her hollering didn't put me in a very good frame of mind. She did finally point at the river, so I went and fetched a pail of water for her.

"When I got back with it, there was another old woman in the lodge with her. I crossed the floor to give your aunt the water, and both women stared at me as if I had the pox. Your aunt began lecturing me again. I have no idea what I did wrong."

"Did you step in front of the other woman? Between her and the fire?" Gus interrupted.

"Yes. So?"

"Bad manners. The Lakota equivalent of blowing your nose in your sleeve."

Genny gazed at him levelly, lips pursed. "You could have told me that very easily." He shrugged. Biting back an angry remark, she continued. "After that, I disappeared as quickly as possible for a bath. That didn't go well, either. No sooner had I submerged myself in this infernally cold river, when a group of boys appeared on the bank. They took great delight in examining my clothes quite thoroughly, and I couldn't do a thing to get them to leave. Fortunately, they only took my stockings.

"After I returned to your aunt's lodge, the worst thing happened. Gus, you must believe I'm not lying to you. Your aunt grabbed one of those cute little pups that are running all over camp, and she strangled it. I swear she did." Genny shook her head in horror. "And then . . ."

She broke off, unwilling to go on. She forced herself. "Then, she put it in the fire and started to singe its hair off. It was horrid to watch. But the worst is that I think she put it into the soup pot. I'm not absolutely certain, because I left. I was too upset to watch any more. But when I came back, she had a pot boiling on the fire, and the pup was nowhere in sight. Gus, I'm almost sure your aunt is cooking that puppy for supper."

Try as he might, Gus couldn't contain the laughter that bubbled in his throat. A chuckle escaped, and Genny looked at him with a combination of dismay and revulsion. Then her face crumpled and she looked as if she was going to cry again. "Did she really put the puppy in the soup?"

Gus reached for her hand and laced her fingers through his. "I'm afraid so, sweetheart. We eat dogs. *Tonwin* is cooking for a feast a friend of hers is having to honor a son's first coup."

"How can you eat dogs?"

"People eat what they have. We have a lot of dogs."

"It's barbaric."

"No," Gus corrected tightly, "it's just not what you're used to. It's different, not barbaric." The pressure of his fingers increased painfully.

Genny looked shocked, but Gus had made his point. "I won't have to eat the puppy, will I?"

"No. I think it would be best if you keep a low profile tonight." He looped one arm around Genny's shoulders and drew her closer. If she would let him, Gus wanted to comfort her.

"Gus, you shouldn't have brought me here. I'm not like you. I shouldn't be here. I can't fit between these worlds."

"You don't have to, *istatowin*. As soon as it's safe, you'll be going back to your own." There was an unfamiliar bitterness in his words, and his hold on her tightened. "What made you burn *tonwin*'s bear medicine?"

Genny squirmed to loosen his hold. "I remembered what you said about being generous and respectful. Last night I noticed that her tipi smelled musty, and what with the mouse, and the general disorder, I assumed housekeeping was difficult for her. You said she had painful joints. Things had gone so badly, I thought it would help if I did something nice. When I discovered that it was those roots that smelled so bad, I threw them in the fire. I thought they were molding.

"Your aunt must have smelled them burning, because she came running in, screaming at the top of her lungs. She chased me out of the tipi, and all the noise she made brought those other women running over to see what was wrong. I stood there taking as much as I could, and when I couldn't stand it another minute, I snapped back at her. That's when you came. You know the rest.''

She stopped talking, and Gus maintained the silence between them for several minutes. Very lightly, he began to play with the wisps of her hair that had escaped the knot at the back of her head. The sunlight dappling through the cottonwood leaves shifted over her head, intermittently gilding her hair with clear, golden light.

"What's going to happen to me now, Gus? Your aunt was terribly upset. I don't want to stay where I'm not wanted.''

"*Tonwin* is only one person. She's hard on a lot of people. Don't let her bother you.''

"Gus, I need your help if I'm going to be able to stay here without causing more problems like the ones today. Will you give it to me?''

He didn't answer immediately. His sister would be able to help more than he would, but she was gone. In the meantime, it would be awkward to keep her with him all day. Men had things to do and women had things to do, and they rarely coincided.

"Is that a no?'' she asked incredulously, interpreting his silence negatively.

Gus pulled away from her and rose to his feet, snapping off a branch of the spruce tree as he stood. The scent of resin filled the air. She wasn't going to understand this.

"It isn't that I don't want to, Genny, but . . .''

Chapter 17

A woman's cheerful voice interrupted him. *"Misun! Le tuwehe?"* Who is this?

Genny looked up and Gus turned. Behind him, a tall, attractive Lakota woman in her middle years stepped forward, smiling. She looked curiously at Genny, then back to Gus.

"Mitawin," Gus said baldly. My wife. He looked at Genny. "This is my sister. Talk to her," he told her in English.

Then he fled through the trees away from the camp.

Startled and angry, Genny jumped to her feet and stared after him, opening her mouth to protest. He was gone so fast there was no point. Slowly, she looked over her shoulder at Gus's stepsister.

The Lakota woman looked as startled as Genny felt. Casting a look of disapproval after her brother, she finally looked at Genny and smiled, shrugging.

The two women regarded one another in silence. It was plain that Gus got his expressive disposition from his mother. He and his sister shared the same easy smile and snapping eyes, though his sister's features were more Indian. Her cheekbones were higher, her skin was a darker tone, and her hair was midnight dark. Though no longer young, she was a striking woman, and her smile made Genny feel at ease instantly. She wondered how they were supposed to talk.

"I speak a little French. I learned when I was a child

from my brother's father. Do you understand?'' Gus's sister volunteered hesitantly in halting French. Genny smiled nervously and nodded. ''Good. My name is Wahaćanka Waste Win. That means Good Shield. But we will call each other *stepan*, I think, if my brother is right. You are his woman?'' She sounded doubtful.

Genny frowned. ''Umm, yes.''

Good Shield laughed. ''But he is already making you wish you were not, hmmm?'' Genny assented with a tilt of her chin. ''I am surprised he would bring another woman into camp after . . .'' She broke off, with a questioning glance.

''I know about White Shell,'' Genny stated evenly.

Good Shield looked surprised. ''My brother told you?'' Genny nodded. ''That's good. Maybe he will be a better husband this time. I hope so.'' But she still sounded doubtful.

Genny debated telling her that her ''marriage'' to Gus was only a temporary arrangement, but decided to leave it to Gus to explain matters. ''My name is Eugenia Stone,'' she said, hoping to curtail any further discussion of her supposed marital relationship.

''I will call you *stepan*,'' Good Shield repeated. ''You must call me this, also. It means sister-in-law. Perhaps you'd like to come to my tipi. My girls are there, and they will want to meet their new aunt. They will have some soup cooking by now, and we can have a nice bowl of hot broth. Come with me. Don't worry about my brother. He'll come back when he's ready.''

Genny followed Good Shield back to camp, still seething over Gus's refusal to help her adjust to life in the Lakota camp. At least she had finally met someone else with whom she could communicate, and by this point, she was more than grateful.

Gus Renard did not endure either frustration or uncertainty gracefully, and in the past week he'd had his fill of both. He bolted from Genny, leaving his sister to sort things out, and headed for the steep sides of the valley. Tearing up the wooded slopes, he ran to purge himself of the restless energy that churned inside him like so many aimless dust devils.

Nothing was working out like he'd thought it would. He'd buried that payroll in Genny's pantry expecting a quick dash back across the sandhills to his camp, followed by a pleasantly uneventful couple of months hunting and gambling with his cousins while they waited for things to simmer down in the south. Instead he'd kidnapped a white woman—and a lady at that—nearly lost his life and his best horse in a hailstorm, seduced the woman, killed an entire Pawnee war party, and ended by bringing Genny into camp as his wife.

Gus had lived with only three fast rules in his adult life: Leave white women who weren't selling their company alone, avoid killing at all costs, and leave prayers to holy men and priests. After more than ten years without a slipup, he'd broken all of his tenets in the course of one short week. With a vengeance. All for the price of indulging an idle curiosity to see the man who had built a house at Bad Spirit Creek.

But the man had been a woman, and everything had spiraled out of control from the minute he'd looked at her. Gus ripped a handful of feathery gray-green women's sage up from the ground and inhaled the sharp fragrance. He'd thrown years of careful avoidance aside when he'd gazed into Eugenia Stone's wide, cornflower eyes. Why hadn't he been able to put her out of his mind as he had countless other women?

Climbing over the edge of the canyon, Gus strode onto the rolling plain above. He walked beyond the last scraggly pines and cedars along the bluffs until he was the tallest form on the prairie. Above him a red-tailed hawk circled lazily, and Gus's thoughts flicked back to wonder what it must have looked like to ride in a hot air balloon across the fields and forests of France. He knew what this land would look like. He knew this country and its people, and he knew that this was where he belonged. There wasn't room for him anyplace else.

And Genny wanted no part of it.

A figure on horseback rode over the edge of the valley,

veering toward him. Gus recognized the buckskin horse as one belonging to Hawk Dancer. Good Shield must have sent their cousin after him. Raising a hand in greeting, Gus waited.

"Your sister is worried about you, *tahaṅsi*," Hawk Dancer said, pulling his horse to a halt beside Gus. Only a year older than Gus, and neither as tall nor as handsome, Gus had always looked up to his cousin. He possessed a strength of character that Gus envied. "She sent me to find you. You know, people are asking themselves why you brought a *waśicu* into camp as your woman. The mothers of many young girls are relieved, but most of the others heard you say you wanted nothing to do with wives after the trouble last year. They wonder," Hawk Dancer continued, referring to White Shell's departure. He slid from his horse, and he and Gus started walking across the plain.

"I wonder, too," Gus sighed. "I've messed up this time, *tahaṅsi*. Worse than with White Shell."

The two men walked in silence, listening to the wind rustling through the grasses and the plod of the horse's hooves.

After fifteen minutes without a word out of Gus, Hawk Dancer cleared his throat quietly. "You've been quiet for longer than any time since you were twelve years old. Even when you couldn't speak the language well, you never stopped talking. I'm getting worried, *tahaṅsi*."

Gus had to smile. "No, you're not. But you're dying to know what's going on and you're too polite to ask outright. Do you remember when Walks in Thunder and I separated from the rest of you coming back from the council at Fort Cottonwood?" Hawk Dancer nodded. "We went to Bad Spirit Creek."

His cousin stopped in his tracks, his face solemn.

"The *waśicu* woman lives there."

"That's not good," Hawk Dancer said with characteristic understatement.

"Yeah, well, it gets worse," Gus told him, gazing off toward the horizon. "A lot worse."

He related everything that had happened from the time he had met Genny. His cousin let him finish without interruption, but by the taut line of his cousin's mouth, Gus knew Hawk Dancer was disappointed with him. Even after Gus finished talking, Hawk Dancer said nothing.

Gus spoke to relieve the silence. "I shouldn't have taken the Overland Trail Company's payroll, and I should never have gone back to Genny's house. Once there, I should have left her alone to face whatever fate awaited her. If she'd found the payroll, I would have lost nothing I had rightful claim to in the first place." Hawk Dancer remained impassive. "But I did take her with me, and I seduced her. I put her into a situation where she had to kill a man and see seven others slaughtered while she watched. And on top of all that, I brought her here as my woman. All with blind regard to the ramifications of my actions.

"She faces a difficult and uncertain future because of me. She thinks she knows what it'll be like when she goes back, but she hasn't got any idea how hard it will be. So I suffer little or no consequence as a result of the past week's adventure. In fact, I'm up eight horses and twenty thousand dollars. But Genny pays with her dreams."

Gus sank to his haunches and watched a spider lower itself from one grass stalk to another, scurrying to protective shelter under the petals of a tiny prairie rose. One fading pink blossom crowned the little plant, its petals brown and drying at the edges. Genny's tears had made him feel that way, like the very edges of him were curling and shriveling with the knowledge that he had changed her life forever. There would be no shelter from the wrongs he had done her.

"After taking so much from her, *tahansi*, I have nothing to give in return. My actions do me no honor, and they shame my family. I've ruined a woman, a white woman whose people won't want her after what I've done to her."

"Then you know what your responsibility is," Hawk

Dancer said. "No one needs to tell you what to do."

Gus thought about the grief he'd caused his family with his first marriage. Hawk Dancer wouldn't say so, but Gus knew he'd acted irresponsibly then, too. In fact, in his adult life, he couldn't think when he had acted responsibly where women were concerned.

"Somehow, I'm going to have to make things right," he whispered, shaking his head, "but, heaven help me, I haven't got a clue where to start."

It was a week before Genny saw Gus again. After he ran away from her beside the river, Good Shield escorted her back to her tipi, where she introduced Genny to her daughters, Blue Bird and White Hands, along with their father, Big Elk. Good Shield told her the relative terms she was supposed to use for them, but Genny was past attending carefully. After the promised bowl of soup, the first food Genny had tasted all day, Good Shield arranged a bed for her on the women's side of her lodge, and Genny promptly went to sleep.

When she awakened the next morning, Gus was nowhere to be found. "Don't worry about him, *štepan*," Good Shield told her, "our cousin, Hawk Dancer, says he's all right and will be back soon. He's got some things to do. It's just as well he's gone. It will be easier for me to explain a lot of things to you, since we're both women. Did you know women speak a little differently from men? Gus wouldn't be able to teach you how to speak correctly as a woman."

Genny began to understand what Gus had been trying to tell her the day before, but she remained angry with him. When he didn't appear for the second day in a row, she pestered Good Shield to tell her what he was up to, but to no avail. Good Shield didn't seem to know exactly, nor did she seem to find anything amiss in his absence.

Good Shield took much of the sting out of what looked to Genny like an abandonment by engaging Genny in her family life and in helping with household activities. During the course of gathering chokecherries and pounding them, seeds and all, into a mash that they formed into small cakes for drying, Good Shield, Blue Bird, and White Hands began teaching Genny Lakota. They were gentle and kind, and when they teased her, Genny was able to laugh along with them. She saw no sign of Gus's aunt, Black Water Woman, though her tipi was not far from Good Shield's. Gradually, she began to feel more comfortable in the Lakota camp.

On the morning of Genny's third day in camp, her monthlies started, and Good Shield explained that women in their moon time lived apart from the rest of the camp in their own little lodges. Women were too powerful then, she told Genny, and the spirits would not come for the medicine men where their power might be eclipsed. For the sake of the well-being of the tribe, the women secluded themselves during their periods. Genny felt insulted at first, but she found the quiet time in the *isnati* lodge a balm to her spirits. All her needs were seen to, and she did not have to talk to anyone or try to understand them. She was able to rest and think alone about everything that had happened to her.

Gradually, she was able to think less about what had happened at the rocky butte and the horror of having killed a man. Under no illusions that she would ever forget the incident, or that it would not cause her nightmares and regrets for years to come, she occupied her thoughts with her continuing dilemmas. Gus Renard was at the top of that list. Unfortunately, she came to no conclusions about how to proceed with him. Powerless to stop feelings she didn't want to have, she ended up passing most of her time daydreaming about making love with him. It was a foolish thing to do, but she couldn't help it.

After two days, as Genny was starting to feel her confinement, Blue Bird joined her in the *isnati* lodge, the younger girl's own courses having started. Blue Bird began teaching Genny how to work dyed, softened porcupine quills and glass beads into colorful designs on the moccasins she was making for her mother's cousin's husband, Walks in Thunder. He had given a horse in her sister's honor at White Hands' buffalo ceremony, in celebration of the girl's first menses. Now Blue Bird, a pretty seventeen-year-old with her mother's and her uncle's saucy smile, would return the honor. Slowly, and with much patience, Blue Bird and Genny began to talk. By the time Genny left the *iṡnati* lodge, two days later, she counted the Lakota girl as her friend.

The first morning back in Good Shield's tipi, Genny was greeted upon waking with a great commotion. As she exited the lodge, dogs and horses were everywhere, and several tipis were partially dismantled, their hide covers slumping inelegantly down the tall poles. Women were calling orders to children and packing household possessions onto travois.

White Hands came running up to Genny, an excited gleam in her eyes. "*Pte!*" she cried, followed by a long string of words Genny didn't understand. But that one word was one of the few Genny had learned and it was enough.

Buffalo.

Genny knew scouts had been out looking for the herds. They had been found, and the camp was going after them. The next hour was one of intense activity, as Good Shield and White Hands packed everything in the tipi into leather containers and onto their travois. Genny was astounded at how quickly the tipi came down, and how efficiently the women handled the heavy cover and awkward poles.

The day was spent traveling in a long, dusty caravan that stretched out across the prairie, heading northwest toward the Smoky Earth River. The buffalo were two days' march away. Since it was warm that night, Genny slept under the stars with Good Shield and her family. The following night, they would pitch the tipi again in the camp circle.

Good Shield told Genny that Gus was riding ahead with the scouts, making sure there were no enemies in their path. Other scouts rode far off to each side and to the rear, to insure the safety of the column. Genny saw Gus only once during the two days of travel, early in the morning and at a distance.

Tall and proud, he sat his mount with grace, dressed only in a breechcloth, and with his face painted red against the burning sun. The feathers in his hair danced in the morning wind, and his brown body radiated fluid strength. Genny caught her breath at his virile beauty, overcome by a rush of longing and desire that surprised her in its intensity. Remembering the warmth of his kisses, and the gentle coaxing of his hands upon her body as he had urged her to experience sensual delights, she wanted to feel him in her arms again. It puzzled her that he could hurt her and yet she still wanted him, that she could know they had no future together, yet yearn for his lovemaking. And why was he avoiding her?

Good Shield walked up beside her, placing her arm around Genny's waist. "Be patient with my brother, *stepan*," she said, reading Genny's thoughts. "He'll do the right thing by you, but he needs a little time. Some men take longer than others to come into themselves."

Genny wasn't at all sure what Good Shield was talking about, but she did know that, much as she wished she didn't, she missed Gus very much.

"*Stepan*, come along with us!" Good Shield called to Genny. "Come see the dancing!"

Genny glanced up from the beaded sash Blue Bird was showing her, then scrambled to her feet. Already the steady beat of a drum and the high-pitched, wild melodies could be heard soaring over the usual camp sounds of barking dogs and laughing children. She and Blue Bird trailed Good Shield and White Hands to the center of the camp circle, where the drum had been set up and the dancers were assembling.

The sun was well down, and only a rosy streak of light in the west remained of the day. With the moon not yet risen, a large fire cast a moving cape of light and shadow on the men crowded around the large drum. Families appeared at the edge of the circle, separating into clusters of young people, children, old men or women, hunters, warriors, and mothers. Blue Bird bobbed her head toward a group of girlfriends, and her mother nodded. The girl left them standing well back in the crowd where they could watch unobtrusively. White Hands, too, found her friends, and Big Elk walked past them to await a seat at the drum.

"The dancers will come a little later," Good Shield explained. "They're singing a love song now, but soon they'll begin singing of past hunts and brave deeds. They will sing and dance to ask the spirits to help with the hunt tomorrow. Look." She pointed with her chin to one of the singers. "My brother is singing tonight. We're lucky. He's one of the best in all the camps of the Lakota."

Genny saw Gus among the singers, dressed in leather britches and a fringed leather shirt with red and blue beaded strips that came down over his shoulders. He brought his padded leather drumstick down energetically in time with the other men, his eyes squeezed shut in concentration. The expression on his face was one almost of pain.

"What are the words to the song?" Genny whispered. Everything was foreign; the music, the firelight dancing on the tipis beyond them, and the lilting cadence of women's voices around her, speaking quietly in Lakota.

"They sing of a man who loved a girl but was too slow in pursuing her. Another man brought beautiful horses to her father, and she accepted him, though she loved the other one. It's a sad song, but beautiful," Good Shield told her. "Listen now. My brother will lead."

Gus threw back his head and his voice rose alone above the rest, piercing, haunting, filled with wracked emotion. The melody carried high, drifting through an unfamiliar scale in wild melancholy. Other voices joined, repeating the phrase, as Gus raised another. Then all sang together for several lines until the next round began and the lead passed to the next man.

The drumming built to a tension point, faster and faster, carrying Genny with it, her eyes never leaving Gus. When the last powerful beat ended the song in abrupt silence, she found herself leaning forward, her fingers pressed to her palms.

Gus raised his head and looked straight at her, his dark

eyes aflame with emotion. Genny read his desire, but also sadness, and a fierce possessiveness that both surprised and thrilled her. His regard left her breathless.

Then he smiled a slow, winning smile that sent her heart tumbling. It was a smile of renewal, an offer of reconciliation, and an acknowledgement of hurts unintentionally inflicted. It also held a question, faint and tenuous. Genny had never known a man who could put so much or so little into a simple smile, and she couldn't help responding. She smiled back.

Throughout the evening Genny watched Gus, realizing that he was not simply Gus Renard. He was also Šungila Eyeglašna, Bad Talking Fox, a Lakota. When the dancers came, enacting their deeds in past hunts, Gus disappeared for a time, returning in paint and stripped to dance. When he moved, knees and back bent to mimic a hunter approaching his prey, spinning and hurtling himself into an imaginary fray to capture his prize, his arms lifted to wield an unseen bow, he was as impressive as when he sang. Genny watched in single-minded fascination.

Many of the women around her murmured comments about the dancers and singers, and Good Shield made certain Genny understood every glowing reference made to Gus. "Horn Bowl says my brother is a skilled hunter who provides well for his family," she whispered in broken French. "And Runs With A Robe mentions that his sister always has hides and meat to give away. Which is true," she added with a giggle. "Now the women are saying that my brother's acts of generosity to old people and the less fortunate are commendable and that he's the best singer tonight."

Genny suspected there were a few comments that Good Shield didn't relay, for she already knew that Gus's reputation with women was far from spotless, and she knew this bothered his sister and other women in camp. More than once, Good Shield had alluded that she thought Gus should have settled down years ago and provided her with nieces and nephews, and once she had let it slip that mothers with marriageable daughters warned their girls to beware of his smooth talk and fancy ways.

For tonight, though, the mood was generous, and there seemed no end to Gus's virtues. As popular as a war hero and as entertaining as an actor, he appeared casually oblivious to all the attention he generated. Women brought him cups of herbal tea to ease his throat, and little boys squeezed between him and his neighbors to look over his shoulder as he sang. Older boys mimicked his dance steps along the perimeters of the gathered circle, and little girls told their grandmothers that when they were grown, they were going to find a handsome man just like Good Shield's brother. Most impressive of all, Hawk Dancer, the holy man presiding over the evening's more serious purpose of asking the spirits to aid them in the hunt, was so moved by Gus's singing that he gave away a horse to a poor woman in his cousin's name.

Gentle pride lighted Good Shield's face as she explained to Genny all that was happening, and more than once, Genny wondered if Šungila Eyeglaśna and Gus Renard were the same person. She, too, found herself gazing at him with proprietary pleasure, and every time he caught her eye, her stomach fluttered. Foundering in a confusion of feelings that contradicted logic, Genny had trouble seeing the thoroughly Indian Gus before her now as congruent with the man who had lain in her parlor eating jam and reading Charles Dickens. He was unlike any man she had ever known, more fickle than the prairie winds, yet as appealing as a meadowlark's song on a clear summer morning. Talented and accomplished, he was also unpredictable and unsettling, and Genny wondered for the thousandth time if any good would come of their odd alliance.

Then Gus turned toward her with yet another smile, assuring her that he was her lover, her man, no matter his name, no matter his guise, and no matter her doubts. The certainty of his desire slipped past her defenses, warming her heart. He was one man: Gus Renard and Šungila Eyeglaśna, a mixed-blood Lakota, a cavalier frontiersman. A man of complex contradictions.

Above all, Genny had to admit that he was a man she wanted to know better than she already did, however inappropriate or dangerous he might be. She walked back to Good Shield's tipi that night wondering how much longer she would have to wait until he came to her again.

Genny woke out of a sound sleep when something warm closed around her ankle. There was a scuffling noise on the other side of the tipi cover, which was unpegged and pushed up a foot or so to catch whatever breeze there might be on the hot August night. A moment later, a shadowy form appeared a few inches from her nose, beckoning her outside.

"Gus?" she hissed, rising on one elbow.

He held his finger to his lips and held the tipi cover higher so she could roll underneath it, between the poles.

Genny groped for the moccasins Good Shield had given her and slipped them on before ducking outside.

"I thought you were one of the dogs," Genny whispered once she was out. "I was afraid they'd come in with the bottom rolled up like that."

"I got the wrong end of you," Gus admitted, also in a whisper. "There's something I thought you'd like to see. Follow me." He took her hand, leading her through the silent camp and up away from the shallow river beside it. Hand in hand, they walked until they reached a small hill, where Gus guided Genny up through the dark.

At the top she turned to look at him. He approached, halting so close she had to tilt her head back to meet his gaze.

"I wondered when you were going to talk to me, again," she said softly. She could smell the clean, fresh scent of soap on him, and she noticed a spot of white in the hollow beneath his ear. Automatically, she reached to touch it.

Gus's eyes closed and he released his breath in a sigh when she drew her hand back, looking at her finger.

"It's paint," he said softly. "From the dancing."

She nodded, smearing the sticky substance between her thumb and middle finger. More than once in the last week she'd wished she had a sketchbook and at least some pencils with her. She looked at her streaked fingers thoughtfully.

Gus brought one hand up to cup her cheek and captured her paint-smeared fingers with the other. "I've missed you, *ištatowin*," he breathed. "I've missed touching you. And being touched by you. Tonight, every time I saw you, I wanted to walk away from all those people and take you with me."

She smiled. "I know."

He grinned in return, caressing her cheek. "I thought you might." He leaned into her, catching her close to his chest, and placing a gentle kiss on her mouth. Both of them groaned, low, deep, and needy.

When Genny tried to deepen the kiss, Gus pulled away, pushing her head into his shoulder and hugging her tightly. "Oh, Genny," he murmured. "You taste so sweet. By all that's sacred, I've been a real bastard to you. But I'm going to make things right. As right as I can." He released her, setting her away from him.

She looked up, questioning. Humility and promises of restitution were not what she expected. Even in the shadowy darkness, though, there was no mistaking the intensity in his expression. "Thank you," she said, ready to accept his apology. "But . . ."

He interrupted, hardly aware she had spoken. "I'm sorry I was so hard on you when you burned *tonwin*'s medicine. It was an honest mistake, and I overreacted. But something hit me when you said you weren't here permanently, and it's taken me a while to come to terms with it. Have you been all right?"

Genny wanted to hear more about whatever it was he was coming to terms with, but she answered his question. "Yes. Your sister's been very kind. I like her. She and the girls are teaching me Lakota."

"I wish she'd been here when we arrived." He swept his hand over her brow, lifting her hair and tucking it behind her ear.

"So do I." They fell into an awkward silence, and Genny wished he'd touch her again. "Everyone admired your singing and dancing tonight," she finally volunteered, not sure how to respond to his serious mien.

"Did you?" She nodded. "When I was younger I learned it was easier to fit in by participating. I was lucky I have a knack for singing."

"I suspect you have a knack for a lot of things. All I heard this evening were glowing reports about your many talents. You're quite a favorite."

Gus chuckled. "Yeah, as long as I keep folks entertained. I'll bet that wasn't all you've heard this week, though, was it?"

"No. Your sister thinks you're irresponsible with women," she said directly.

"She's right." He looked away, into the western sky.

"She also thinks you ought to settle down, that it isn't natural for a man your age to remain single. How old are you, Gus?"

"Thirty-one. Look up, *istatowin*. There," he directed her toward the western part of the sky. Lightning lanced to earth in a blue-white streak. "Did you see it? That's what I wanted you to come out here for. There are storm clouds in every direction, too far away to hear, but they're putting on quite a light show. I brought a blanket so we can sit and watch."

They sat, eyes fixed on the heavens. Genny wanted to move closer to him, but his uncharacteristic reserve made her hesitate. Finally she placed her hand on his knee and fingered a rough spot on the leather legging. When he accepted her touch, she scooted across the six inches between them.

"I'd like you to hold me, Gus."

Chapter 18

Gus opened his arm to her, and she slid back against him, resting her head on his chest so she could watch the sky. One heavy hand dropped onto her stomach, and she cradled it in the crook of her arm. Warmth flowed from his body over her back, and Genny relaxed. It was good to sit quietly like this with him. Very good.

He must have thought so too, for many minutes passed and many jagged flashes of lightning split the early morning sky before he returned to their conversation.

"You were right when you said I shouldn't have brought you here," he finally said, as if he didn't want the comfortable silence to end. Genny turned to look up at him. His arms shifted with her so that his hands cupped her shoulders, and he met her gaze. "I don't know what got into me. I don't know why I went back to your place, and I don't know why I didn't leave you there." He wasn't going to tell her about the payroll just yet. It would only complicate matters, and there were other issues he needed to address first.

"You were angry," Genny offered. "You let yourself get carried away too easily."

Gus released her and rolled onto his back. "That's part of what I don't understand too well. I don't usually have such a temper. Not like what you've seen. You bring out things in me that scare me, Genny. I feel things I haven't felt for so long I can't remember . . ." He broke off. He did remember when he'd felt this way. All too clearly. "You make me feel things I thought I'd put aside. That temper is one of them."

"Are you saying it's my fault when you lose your temper?" She raised her knees and rested her chin on them, looking down at Gus.

"No," he responded quickly. "No, it's not your fault. Oh, Christ, this is hard to explain." He flung one arm up across his face, then abruptly lowered it. "Do you have any idea how beautiful you are?"

Genny looked at him quizzically, surprised by his question.

"When I see you, I see a princess. An incredibly beautiful, desirable princess with a serene smile and an aura of unshakable happiness. You look like no ugliness or hurt can touch you, like you . . ." He closed his eyes, unable to find the words to tell her how she made him feel.

A long-forgotten memory leapt to mind. Words tumbled out behind it. "My stepmother in Montréal had a tiny set of carved and painted nativity figures when I was a boy. My favorite was a little angel with flowing blond hair, a white robe, and golden wings. She looked so clean and perfect, hanging from a little hook at the peak of the stable. The Christmas I was eleven, though, I took the angel and painted her hair black, so she'd look like an Indian, like I did. I don't know why I did it. One minute I was looking at the angel, admiring her, and the next thing I knew, I was in the stable with a can of paint and a brush in my hand.

"My grandfather noticed immediately, and he walloped me a good one, saying I'd defiled something precious and lovely, something that had been cherished for many years. He told me I'd willfully ruined a piece of art, and what's more, something that didn't belong to me. I was so angry with him, I snatched up the angel and threw her in the fire. I did destroy her, then." He sighed deeply. "Completely."

Genny's heart got trapped in her throat and her nose prickled in warning, but she refused going to cry in front of Gus again. Instead, she reached out and took his hand, linking his fingers through her own. When she could talk, her voice was thick. "I'm not an angel, Gus. I'm a woman."

"You're a white woman, Genny. A lady. And I've ruined you as surely as I destroyed my stepmother's Christmas angel." She tried to interrupt, but he gripped her hand tightly, stopping her. "Please. Let me say this. It isn't easy, and it's taken me a long time to get up the courage. Don't stop me."

He sat up, taking both her hands in his. "When I saw you, when I see you, I want you. I crave your beauty the way I craved the beauty in the nativity figurines when I was a child and I wanted to be . . ." He struggled again for the right word. "Included. I want to be included, Genny.

"Once, I went back to Montréal when I was nineteen, and there was a girl. A white girl. The daughter of one of my father's friends. We saw each other several times, and then there was a party at her house. She pulled me into the garden and kissed me. And when her father discovered us, he used the same words my grandfather had when I'd painted the angel's hair dark. He said I'd destroyed his daughter, that I'd defiled a beautiful woman, something precious and lovely. Something that wasn't mine, and that I had no right to. Because I touched her, no white man would want her."

Releasing Genny's hands, he braced his arms on his thighs and spread his fingers wide, staring down at them. He hated this. When he'd returned to Indian country all those years ago, he'd vowed he would never repeat any of it, not one word. But there was no other way to tell Genny why he'd done what he had to her. Or why he needed her now.

"After that, my father, who taught me to be proud of who I was and who loved the Lakota people, finally admitted to himself what I had learned a long time before. I couldn't live the life he'd envisioned for me as his heir. There was no place for me in an office where men managed finances and investments. No place in salons where white men drank brandy and discussed business ventures

and politics. And especially, there was no place for me
in the bed of a woman whose father or brother was white.

"My father finally acknowledged that I had to return
to my mother's people if I wanted to be treated as a man.
And I did, Genny. I wanted to be a man. So I came back
and set aside my books and the few wasted dreams that
had survived my years away from my father. I tried to
be a man, a Lakota, as fully as I could. Which meant
that I would take my women from my own people, from
a people who weren't ashamed of me." He paused a
long moment. He had so prided himself on his resolve
in this matter, and now it lay like ashes on his heart.
"For more than ten years I honored that principle. I met
lots of white ladies, and I left them alone, no matter how
beautiful or exciting they seemed to me. And then I met
you," he rasped, gripping his thighs.

"I'm sorry," she murmured indistinctly. As ridiculous
as it was, his agony made her feel she'd failed him
somehow. "Why was I any different?" He was different
for her, too, and she didn't know why.

He shrugged, meeting her eyes. "Maybe it was the
absurdity of your being in Nebraska Territory at all, in
your pretty little white house, with your paints and easels
set up like in any eastern lady's garden room. Maybe it
was your books. A whole case full with no one but
illiterate soldiers, freighters, and Indians in the whole
territory." Looking up, he watched another flash of lightning pierce the sky. He laughed bitterly. "*Great Expectations*, indeed. If I'd picked up anything but that, you
might not be here now. Have you read it?" She shook
her head. "Well, whatever the reason, Genny, you're
here, and I'm responsible. You won't have anything to
go back to once it becomes known what's happened to
you. You know that, don't you?"

"It's won't be that bad," she said with more conviction than she felt. "No one may ever find out about it.
Besides, I participated in the decision to allow this to
happen, Gus. I'm as responsible as you are, and I'm
willing to live with the consequences of my choices."

He shook his head. "You don't realize how bad it'll

be, *istatowin*. You'll never have your art academy after this."

His words sliced into her heart.

"And your family won't take it well. There's every chance that you'll be left completely alone, and that's a hard life for a woman. Don't forget that I know what it's like to be shut out of your world. At least I had another one to come to. You don't have anywhere else to go."

His words carried the bleak ring of fact, and the picture they painted resisted any hopes Genny tried to pin on them. She tugged her hands from him and tucked them close to her body. "My family would never abandon me," she insisted. She couldn't face this. Not now, when there was nothing she could do about it.

"They let Conrad bring you out here. They sent you to France. I'm not sure they'd openly shun you, but they might find it convenient to ignore you, to just forget about the embarrassment of a daughter who let herself be taken by an Indian."

"Stop it!" Genny whispered fiercely, pressing her knuckles against her lips. "Don't speak as if you're less because of your heritage! Besides, my father would always provide for my material needs. With adequate resources, I can manage, no matter what happens. I can go back to Italy or Spain, somewhere no one knows me. It isn't completely your fault I'm here, and I can deal with my own life as best I can!"

"For God's sake, girl, I forced you to come with me at gunpoint! I shamelessly seduced you, knowing you had no intimate experience of men. And because of me, you've killed a man. What in the name of heaven are you talking about? Do you think you're going to go back to Philadelphia the same woman you were before?"

"I didn't go with Roger and Martha when I could have. You couldn't have forced me to leave White Rock Spring if I hadn't been at least partly willing to go." Gus snorted in disbelief, but she continued. "And you could not have made love to me if I hadn't allowed it."

"How the hell would you have stopped me?" he demanded. "You didn't even know what I was doing!"

"I had a pretty fair idea, and I could have stopped you," she repeated. "I wouldn't have let you touch me in the first place if I hadn't wanted to know what it would be like to be with you. Like that. Like lovers. Once it started, no, I couldn't stop it. But I let it start. Because I wanted to. And if I hadn't, you would have stopped."

"You don't know that."

"Yes. I do."

This time it was her certainty that reached past his doubts and self-recriminations. Her misplaced faith touched him to the quick. "Genny, what the hell is going on here? I'm trying to do the right thing by you. Will you let me?"

Genny's heart slammed in her chest as she suddenly realized what he was leading up to. She should stop what was coming, but her throat closed.

"I can't put things back the way they were before we left your house. I can't give you your art academy, or balloon rides over Paris, or your lost innocence, but I can give you more respectability than you'll have alone."

"You can't mean . . ." Don't say it, she prayed. Please don't say it.

"I want you to marry me, Genny. For real. Legally. I'll take care of you. I can provide for you here, and . . ."

"Here?" Her eyes widened, and she held up one hand. "Gus, stop. Now. You don't have to marry me."

"Not strictly speaking, no. But I want to. It's the right thing to do."

"No." She shot to her feet, stumbling over a clump of bunch grass.

He surged after her, catching her by the hem of her skirt. "No?" He sounded stunned. "Why not?"

She leaned away from him, straining the cotton material against her hips. "I can't stay here, Gus. I don't belong, and I want to go home. And I wouldn't ask you to live with me where you'd feel less than a man. We don't belong together. You know that."

"I'm not so sure," he said, hating her plaintive tone. He wound her skirt around his fist, and drew her back to him. "I think I could be happy with you, Genny."

The simple honesty of his statement caught them both by surprise.

He touched the small of her back with the tips of his fingers. "I know it wouldn't be easy, but don't you think you could grow accustomed to Lakota life? Maybe we could run a supply ranch, like the Riviers', if you don't like camp life. We could work something out."

She shook her head. "There are other reasons not to marry." She laid her hand upon his cheek. "I don't love you," she whispered brokenly.

A crushed feeling, like being caught between a pair of buffalo bulls in a stampede, rolled through him, making him want to drop his arms and pull up his knees, shielding his middle. This was what he had been avoiding all these years. He fought to shake it off. Why did he care, anyway? He knew she didn't love him. He thought she cared a little, but he knew it wasn't love. He was only trying to do the right thing by her.

But he argued anyway. "You might come to love me. You already care for me. Some. More than you'll admit. I know you do. I can feel it."

She managed a sad smile. "Yes, but you don't love me."

His eyes snapped up to hers and he blinked hard. Something strong and vital crashed through his gut again, freezing his lungs with the suffocating pain of long-denied emotion. He backed abruptly away from her.

"I think I might, Genny," he whispered hoarsely, stunned by the realization her words forced on him.

"What?" She couldn't have heard him aright.

"I think I might," he repeated slowly, "love you."

He closed the distance between them and swept her into a fierce embrace. It felt better. The pain eased a fraction.

"What does love feel like?" he gasped, rubbing his chin feverishly along her jaw.

"I don't know," Genny answered breathlessly. His desperate grip found her heart, and she melted into him, hugging him back with all her might.

Burying his face in her neck, Gus groaned. "It hurts, *istatowin*. It hurts too much to be anything else. I get so mad I go crazy." He kissed the pulse point at the base of her throat.

"I get so hot I burn just thinking about you." His tongue darted along the sensitive cord in her neck up to just behind her ear, and she made an inarticulate moan of pleasure.

"My stomach knots up when I think about what kind of a life you'll face because of me. I've never had an attack of conscience in my life, *istatowin*. At least, not one that lasted more than a few minutes." Sharp teeth nipped over her earlobe, and he rimmed the shell of her ear with his nose before following the same path with his tongue.

"But when I have you in my arms, Genny, it doesn't hurt any more. When I feel your skin hot and soft next to mine, your mouth under my lips sweeter than strawberry jam, and your breath on my neck in short, excited puffs, I don't hurt anymore." He growled deep in his throat, giving vent to the rich torment that rioted in his breast.

His mouth met hers fully, wet, hot, and demanding her response. She gave it gladly, opening her lips to admit his tongue, chasing when he retreated, drawing him back into her. Their passion leapt full-blown between them, fiery, impatient, and beyond control.

"Genny, you quench a desperate thirst in me," he groaned between thrusting forays into her mouth. "I thought if I could have you, that if you'd accept me in your bed, I'd be free from the past." His hands cupped her breasts, thumbs running up to graze her peaked nipples. "That I could put it all behind me, all the regrets, all the longing for things that would never be." His tongue slid along her jaw to tease her earlobe. "But I can't. That's not enough. Because I want you more than anything I've ever wanted." He rasped his cheek over hers, speaking so that his lips moved close beside hers. "Because only when I'm in your arms, my flesh buried deep inside you, do I finally feel safe and free. Nothing else matters then. Accept me, Genny. Be my wife. Let me love you.'' He sucked her tongue into his mouth, abrading with his teeth, swirling with his tongue. ''Try to love me. Please.''

''It wouldn't be hard to love you,'' she gasped, pulling his hips into her abdomen, lifting and rubbing against him. But even in the midst of passion, she knew they had no future together. They didn't belong together.

''Love me now, Genny,'' Gus demanded, pressing into her. Tracing slow circles, he dragged hard and hot over her stomach. He thrust, grabbing her tightly, his hands gripping her buttocks, his mouth sucking and licking in the curve of her neck.

She reached to untie his belt, but she pulled the knot tight in her haste. One of Gus's hands flowed down over her thigh, reaching up her skirt until he felt bare skin. There his fingers found the Pawnee knife that she wore in a new case, tied with a strip of cotton, and he pulled it out, running the smooth handle along her leg and up over her naked hip.

Cool metal caressed her, leaving gooseflesh in its wake. Then Gus flipped his hand from beneath her skirt and brought the dagger to her palm. She took it, and in a trice, his belt fell away, sliced through. Pushing up his shirt, she trailed the handle of the dagger across his stomach. Groaning, he took it back, slipping under her skirts again to retrieve its case. Long fingers slid beneath the cloth band that held it, dancing over her skin with delicious familiarity. He slid the blade in and pulled the tie that held it free, casting it aside and riding his hand higher.

Genny's fingers encountered his flat male paps at the same moment his fingers curled around the top of her thigh, pushing into moist heat. Grinding her hips, squeezing his hand between her legs, she moaned. He did the same when she pinched him. His nipples beaded and she flicked her nails over them.

''What happened to your drawers?'' he rasped, probing deeper.

''They're all ruined,'' she answered, pushing his shirt

up under his armpits. Leaning forward, she touched her tongue to his nipple, licking tentatively. "Do you like that?"

"Yes," he growled.

"So do I." Her lips closed over him and she sucked, swirling her tongue over him as he did when he suckled her. He drew a sharp breath.

His hand left her to peel off his shirt. His leggings and breechcloth followed, along with Genny's shirt. They kissed again, bare breasts together, and Genny felt the moisture from her mouth on his skin. He was so exciting, so alive, so sensual. He was the wildfire he had promised her he would be, and he sparked fires in her blood that rivaled nature's fiercest.

He roamed her back and hips with greedy hands and his member burned between them. Genny let one of her hands drift down his side, dipping low to touch him. He throbbed against her palm.

"Ahhhh," he gasped. "Do that again. Hold me."

She did, rubbing him against her stomach, sliding her fingers over his smooth length. Soft and hard, hot and pulsing, she stroked her fingers over him. His fingers dug into her shoulders, and he threw his head back, murmuring words Genny didn't understand.

Still stroking him, she began to kiss his throat, skimming over the straining muscles, sliding her tongue into the hollows of his collarbone. He was all sharp angles, firm flesh, and silky skin. She'd never known a man's skin would feel so soft and velvet, almost like her own. Yet there was nothing feminine about him. Her tongue traveled over the slight swells of his breast, once more leaving hot, sucking kisses on his nipples. She laved the dip below them, bending to explore his stomach with her mouth, until she reached his navel. Dropping to her knees, she brushed her nose across his belly, then her tongue. He was salty, faintly smoky, and very warm. Almost burning. The first time they'd made love he'd said she tasted of fire. She knew what he meant now. She had discovered fire in his skin.

With one hand still grasping his member, Genny

backed away to look at him. In the intermittent flash of distant lightning, she admired him, stroking both hands back over him.

"May I kiss you here?" she asked, her breath warming him.

He cupped the back of her head and urged her forward. "Yes, kiss me, Genny. Please."

Feather light, she touched the tip of him with her lips. "More, *istatowin*," he begged. "Give me more."

Opening her lips this time, she wet him with her tongue. His hand tightened in her hair. After a few more tentative kisses, he thrust toward her. "Take me, Genny. Take me."

She did. Swirling her tongue around him, she pulled him into her mouth. His hips began to rock, thrusting gently. She sucked on him, feeling his skin tight over his swollen flesh against her teeth. He felt like he would burst, so taut and full was he. Her hands slipped to hold his hips, and she rubbed her chin against his thigh as she teased him with her lips and tongue. The few hairs on his leg were crisp against her cheek. She explored him, gradually taking more of him into her mouth while her hands circled him, stroking, squeezing, pulling.

Abruptly he pulled away from her. "No more," he panted. "Not yet. I want you with me." He collapsed to his knees before her and kissed her, savoring the taste of himself in her mouth, smelling himself on her cheeks. It aroused him so much he started shaking with the effort to control himself.

Genny felt his tremors and kissed him back, slipping her tongue into his mouth when he withdrew from hers, her hands still intimately stroking him against her hipbone. It pleased her to know she could affect him so, that what they shared was equally powerful for each of them.

Gus backed up, dragging his mouth from hers. "Slow down a minute, *istatola*," he said, trailing kisses down her neck. "Let me get your skirt off." He fumbled with the ties. Then he yanked the material out from beneath their knees and pulled the skirt over her head. "Oh, yes. Let me see you."

His eyes roamed over her, his fingers following, driving in an unerring line down her middle to wedge between her legs. "Open for me, Genny. Let me feel how wet you are for me. Let me feel your excitement."

Her knees slid apart and she let him touch her. A single firm caress sent lightning shooting through her, forcing her eyelids closed and wringing a moan from her lips. He stroked again. When she opened her eyes, all around her lightning lit the sky, stabbing to earth in the same shattering bolts that were coursing through her. Her blood felt thick and her breath was labored. His hand picked up a fast rhythm that brought her arching into him, jerking her hips and tensing her thighs.

"Gus! Now! Come into me now!" she cried.

He fell back, pulling her with him. After spreading her legs astride him, he held himself straight with one hand and guided her down over him with the other. She gave a shuddering cry as he rose to fill her.

Her body arched and lifted instinctively, and she moved quickly, driven on by desire. Gus held her at the waist and by the shoulder, and she braced her hands on his sides, riding him hard. With each drive down she felt him deep within her. A rocket of feeling exploded up through her womb, ripping through her belly and her chest to come blazing forth from her throat in cries and moans that she barely knew she made.

It was more than physical. She felt bound to Gus with all her being. They moved together, transcending the bodies that defined them separately, even as they created a raging physical storm. Genny felt more herself than she ever had, yet as much a part of Gus as the water is of the rain. When her climax came, he was with her, shuddering, clenching muscles, screaming in release. It lasted longer than any of their times together, hard and intense, draining in its fullness. With a groaning sigh that ended in a ragged chuckle, she finally collapsed on top of him.

Her breasts scudded against his damp chest, and he

pushed a moist curl behind her ear. Contented laughter rumbled in his chest, and when he kissed her forehead, she felt his smile.

"This is when I know," he whispered. "This is when I know I love you."

"Gus," she whispered, not wanting to let go of the moment. "Don't . . ."

"Ssshhh." He dropped his fingers over her lips, rubbing lightly. "I know, *ištatola*. We don't have to make any final decisions now. We have some time. Just tell me you'll think about marrying me. Tell me you'll consider letting me love you for the rest of your life."

She placed a wet kiss on his fingers and pushed them gently aside, wondering what it would be like between them if she had met him in Philadelphia or in France. If he could live with her in her worlds. And she wondered if she would ever meet another man to whom she responded so completely. She looked up, meeting his shadowy gaze thoughtfully.

"All right, *mon cher*," she said more easily than she'd thought she could. "I'll do as you ask. I'll think about marrying you. For real."

"Forever." He smiled gently. "Say it."

"Forever," she conceded. But she wouldn't offer false hope. "If."

He kissed the tip of her nose and folded her into his embrace. He held her tightly, afraid of that last word. But if he had anything to say about it, "if" wasn't going to be a problem.

Chapter 19

As the sun rose in a murky wash of dull reds tinged yellow-brown, a hot wind started from the south, blowing fine dust that soon obscured the dawn sky. Gus and Genny lay dozing in each other's arms when the first sifting rain of grit settled on their bare skin.

Gus bolted upright. "Get your clothes! Fast!"

"What's wrong?"

"Dust storm." He tied his breechcloth into place and slipped into his moccasins, draping his shirt over his head like a turban and his leggings over his arm. After helping Genny into her skirt and blouse, he shook the blanket and draped it over them.

"Shield your eyes," he ordered, half pushing, half carrying her down the hill. At the bottom he tucked the blanket firmly around her shoulders and grabbed her hand. "Run while we can still see the camp!"

They darted through the trees along the river. Genny coughed when her lungs filled with hot, dust-laden air, but Gus pulled her steadily forward. The tipis ahead, rapidly disappearing into a dark haze, were hard to make out, but Gus reached the village. Everywhere men and women were tying down the flapping lodge covers, shouting instructions over the rising wind, and closing smoke flaps that had been left wide open on the sweltering night. By the time they reached Good Shield's tipi, the sides were down and Big Elk was driving more stakes into the ground to keep the dust from blowing up under the cover. Gus pushed Genny inside and went to help him.

Her lungs burning, Genny found Good Shield and the girls hanging a leather curtain around the inside of the lodge. It was about five feet high and made of buffalo hide like the outer cover, and they were tying it to the insides of the lodge poles. In the near darkness, Genny could see dim painted patterns on some of the panels.

"Where have you been?" Good Shield asked over her shoulder as she slipped in. "We were worried."

"With your brother. *Nisunkala kin*," she repeated, using one of the few Lakota phrases she had mastered. She wasn't ready to call him her husband, but she knew using a proper term of address was important to Good Shield.

Blue Bird giggled. "I told you I heard them leave together," she said in Lakota, but with a knowing tone that Genny understood perfectly. Her mother hushed her.

Big Elk and Gus entered with a gust of gritty wind. They lashed the door tight to the nearest poles and moved to help with the curtain.

"Why are you putting that up?" Genny asked Good Shield in French.

Gus answered her in the same language. It was the first time she'd heard him speak it, other than to curse. "In the winter the curtain keeps the lodge warmer. Now it'll trap the dust that slides down the lodge poles and drifts in from the top, keeping it confined to some extent. It won't catch all of it, but it helps. Sit down by your bed and get something to put over your face in case it gets worse." His French was as fluent as his English. By either Philadelphia or Parisian standards, he was a talented linguist.

So thinking, Genny sat and pulled out a torn square of what had been her drawers to drape across her nose and mouth. The tipi cover slapped noisily against the lodgepoles. They, in turn, creaked and moaned as they shifted in the heavy wind, and the sand hitting the south side of the tipi made a soft hissing rattle. Inside it was dim, hot, and airless. In another minute Gus joined

Genny on her bed, sitting cross-legged beside her.

"What happens now?" she asked, sliding over to make room for him. It seemed strange to have him come to her so openly in front of others. How odd it was that these people thought of her as his wife. Odder still that he wanted her to be.

Despite the heat, Gus snuggled close to her, and Genny found she didn't mind. Big Elk and Good Shield and their daughters settled back into their beds across the fire pit.

"Now we wait," Gus said, raising his knees and pulling Genny into the space between them. He guided her head back to rest on his bare shoulder. "Can you breathe okay?"

She nodded, her cheek rubbing his skin, and relaxed into him. His arms were draped loosely over hers, and her hips were flush against his groin. She felt safe and protected. A warmth that had nothing to do with the temperature filled her, along with an almost giddy happiness. She had no idea where it came from or why, but it was wonderful.

"This reminds me of another storm we weathered," Gus breathed into her hair. "You didn't snuggle up to me so fast then." Silent laughter shook his chest.

"A lot's happened since then."

"Yeah," he agreed softly. He seemed about to say something, then changed his mind. Instead, he asked a question in Lakota.

His response was a chorus of murmured encouragements from his family. "I asked if they wanted to hear the story of how we met and about our trip," he told her. "It'll keep everyone's mind off the heat and dust. Do you mind if I tell them?"

She smiled at the excitement in his voice. She knew by now that he loved to entertain people and that he was good at it. His nieces were already shifting around in anticipation, cajoling him to start. "Go ahead. But don't exaggerate."

He chuckled. "This is one story that doesn't need exaggeration, *istatowin*."

With that, he launched his tale. Not able to understand most of what he said, Genny fell into a sort of waking sleep, conscious primarily of the man who held her and the cadence of his mellow voice. Almost dreaming, she relived their dramatic journey across the sand hills through the emotions that stirred him as he spoke. She could feel his exhilaration and unease, his pleasure in teasing her, his fear when the hailstorm hit, and his grief over the supposed loss of Harv. Vaguely, she was aware that Good Shield and the others were engrossed, laughing, offering low comments, and gasping at the high points of the tale. She wondered how much he was telling them about the course by which they had become lovers, hoping he was exercising a little discretion, but knowing him well enough to know his notion of discretion didn't coincide with hers.

In the midst of his tale she ceased to try to follow him and became lost in the memories of their lovemaking. She recalled the words he had spoken the night before the Pawnee attack along the river, a night which had been spent exploring a world as new to her as these wide plains, and her heart echoed the sentiments he had voiced in the aftermath of their loving.

It was going to be hard to give him up.

The dust storm lasted a couple of hours before the wind shifted into the east. Within minutes, the dust settled, and the temperature dropped by at least ten degrees.

"I've never seen a climate so contrary!" Genny exclaimed, emerging from the darkened tipi into the bright sunlight. The cottonwood leaves rustled softly in the newly gentle breeze, and the drifts and lines of fine dirt on the south sides of the lodges and a faint haze were all that remained of the storm.

"But it's a beautiful country," Gus said reverently. His sincerity surprised her. "Remember the lightning last night? It was all colors. Blue, white, green, yellow, even pink. Before you came here, I'll bet you didn't know lightning had colors, did you?"

"I didn't know a lot of things." She swatted at the

lodge cover, dislodging a cascade of dust. "The beauty here is harsh, Gus. Too harsh for me."

Gus looked at her with a smile in his dark eyes. "It's subtle, not harsh. You're just not used to it. Give it a little time." His eyes said, give *me* a little time.

That was the question she answered. "I said I would."

He picked up her hand and held it in both of his. "Good."

Big Elk came out of the lodge behind them, glancing at their linked hands before looking pointedly away. Gus let go reluctantly when Genny tugged. "I have to go with the scouts to see what's happened to the buffalo during the storm. They could have stampeded off. I'll be back tonight." He leaned forward to kiss her mouth. Big Elk cleared his throat, but Gus paid him no mind. Only when Blue Bird and White Hands came out and began giggling did he let her go. "Tonight, *istatola*," he promised.

Genny spent the morning cleaning up with Good Shield and the girls. The dust had sifted into everything. Even the clothes in her saddlebag were streaked with dirt in the creases.

Good Shield watched her shake out her remaining shirt and underthings. "You need some sturdier clothes," she commented. "Those are nearly rags, and they're so plain. I think you must have some new dresses, *stepan*."

"I think you're right," Genny agreed. Good Shield had restored her leather split skirt with a coating of a special clay and a vigorous brushing, but most of her wardrobe wasn't up to the rigors of camp life. And her clothes did look plain next to the finely decorated quill and bead work that adorned Good Shield's own clothing.

"My daughters and I have more than we need. You can wear this for now," Good Shield said, pulling a dress from a leather case behind her backrest, "and we can choose from my hides and material to make you some others."

The dress she handed Genny was made of finely tanned elk skin. It was light in color and trimmed with narrow beaded strips along the shoulders and yoke. Genny recognized the familiar red and blue beaded pattern on a white ground as one of Good Shield's signature designs. It matched the knife case Gus had given her after their first meeting, and many of his clothes bore the same design. Fringes hung from the sleeves, back, and hem, and large pony beads had been threaded onto some of the narrower strips.

She took off her own clothes and immediately pulled the dress over her head. When she stood to smooth it over her legs, Good Shield brought her a belt to tie around her waist.

"It's a little long," the older woman said, arranging the long end of the belt to fall gracefully down Genny's side. "If you pull the dress up over the belt, you can take up some of the length here." She bloused the soft leather over Genny's waist. "Where's your knife?"

Genny found it inside one of Gus's leggings. Blushing, she handed it to Good Shield, who only smiled as she attached it to the belt. Then she helped Genny tie her hair back.

"My brother treats you well," Good Shield said thoughtfully. "I never saw him so relaxed and happy with that other woman."

Genny was getting used to the often vague references the Lakotas made to people. She knew Good Shield was referring to White Shell.

"They stayed in their lodge most of the time, never coming here, or to any of our other relatives. We made her nervous. She missed her own family. It happens often enough. But now I think maybe it was for the best. *Misun* is different with you. Are you going to try for a child soon?"

Genny was flustered by the direct question. "Nooo," she said slowly. Gus obviously hadn't explained the true nature of their relationship to his sister. "I—that is, *we*— think it might be better to wait."

Good Shield nodded wisely. "I agree. It's easier if you get to know each other first. And," she said, smiling conspiratorially, "you have more time to enjoy one another. Once the baby comes, it can be hard to go a long time without the pleasures between a man and his woman.''

Genny looked at her goggle-eyed. It had never occurred to her that lovemaking stopped after a baby came. ''How long?''

Good Shield laughed. ''Sometimes a couple of years, if the baby is sickly and needs a lot of care. Haven't you noticed that Lakota children are usually three or four years apart?''

She hadn't noticed. ''What about first babies? Can't you do anything else to stop them coming? Besides not . . . you know.'' Gus wasn't going to stop. What's more, she didn't want him to, but she didn't want to become pregnant. In her heart she knew that if she did, she would never be able to leave her child. Neither did she think Gus would let her leave, taking their child away from him. In the short time she had been among them, Genny had seen how the Lakota cherished their sons and daughters. A child belonged not only to his parents but to it's aunts and uncles, grandparents, and cousins. They were loved and welcome in any lodge. She knew intuitively that Gus would welcome a baby, and that he wouldn't be above using a child to hold her with him. He understood the impossibility of her leaving a babe behind.

Good Shield watched the play of emotions across Genny's face before answering. ''Oh, yes, there are other ways to avoid a baby. There are plants that can help. But they aren't as reliable. You don't know about these plants?'' Genny shook her head. ''Then I'll get you some. There's one plant that's similar to mint. If you make a tea from it and drink it every morning, it should work. I'll show you this afternoon.''

''Thank you,'' Genny said, relieved. After last night, she only hoped she wasn't already pregnant.

On his way out of camp, Gus caught sight of his sister getting water beside the river. He turned back, galloping up the low bank until he reached her. Good Shield smiled up at him.

"I have to ask something of you," he said, sliding from Harv's back. "It's about *mitawin*."

When Gus didn't return her smile, Good Shield grew more serious. "Is something wrong? I thought it looked like you two had settled your differences this morning."

He did smile a little then. "Some of them," he admitted. Looking away, he ran a hand down his thigh. "Has she talked to you about preventing a baby?"

"This morning."

He nodded. "*Tanke*, I'm going to ask you to do something hard. I want a child. I want her to bear my children. She's afraid." He didn't say of what. "But I want this badly."

Good Shield looked at the lodges behind them, frowning. "It's not my place to interfere. This is between the two of you, but if you want me to, I'll talk to her."

Gus hesitated. What he was about to do was underhanded and dishonest, but he plunged ahead. "I'd like you to do more than that. *Tanke*, she won't stay with me without a child," he said baldly. "I don't want her to leave. I need her. I love her. If she left, I don't know what I'd do. But she'd never leave a baby behind or keep me from my own child. I know this about her."

Good Shield rarely looked directly into his eyes, but she did now. "What are you asking me to do?"

"Give her the wrong herbs. Give her something harmless that won't stop her from conceiving. Allow her to give me a child."

Good Shield shook her head angrily and turned away from him. "You shouldn't ask me to do this, *misun*. You shame me."

"No, *tanke*. I shame myself with my weakness. But I can't bear to lose another woman." That was a lie. White Shell's loss had been of little consequence to him, but he knew his sister would respond to the plea. "Please, *tanke*. This woman is my heart, and she'll not stay with me unless I bind her to me. A child is the surest way. Please. You're my sister. You have to help me."

Her angry expression let him know she knew she was being manipulated. "You shouldn't do this. You should talk to her. Convince her in other ways. I think she cares deeply for you, *misun*." She paused, her resolve wavering.

"Please, *tanke*." He took her hand lightly. "Help me in this."

She snatched her hand away from him and clasped it with her other at her waist. Staring at the ground, she said nothing. Gus waited. Finally she exhaled a long, slow breath. "If you're sure you want me to do this . . ."

As he'd expected, Good Shield wasn't proof against his begging. Lakota children were raised to do anything they could for their brothers and sisters. Gus had been good to her, and she couldn't refuse him, even if she knew that what he wanted was wrong.

"Thank you, *tanke*." He closed his eyes, partly in shame, partly in relief. "I will give a horse in your honor for this."

"Do not honor me for lies, *misun*." She stalked away, the water skins swinging at her sides.

Late that afternoon, Good Shield took Genny for a walk along the river east of the camp, leading her to a hollow where a spring had formed a tiny seep. It was filled with plants, high green grass, and wild plum bushes.

"Here," Good Shield said, stooping to snap the top off a straight, arrow-leafed plant with tiny purple flowers close to the leaves. The scent of mint rose into the air. "This is the plant I told you about. There's enough here to last for several weeks."

"What's it called?" Genny asked. "It looks like mint."

"It is a kind of mint," Good Shield agreed, busying herself with clipping the stalks. "It's called *ceyaka*."

Genny and Good Shield picked a large pile of the plant and lashed it into bundles which they tied to the pack Genny had carried out with them.

"We should hurry back," Good Shield said when they were finished. "It's late and *misun* will be looking for you when he returns."

As they walked back to camp, Good Shield was uncharacteristically silent, but Genny was content with the quiet. It was a peaceful afternoon, for once not too warm or too cool, and with no winds tearing through the vast, cloudless sky. Genny concentrated on the unaccustomed swish of leather fringes around her knees and let her worries drop away.

As the two women approached the camp circle from the east, a small party of horseback riders breasted a rise to the west. Genny recognized Gus and his cousin Bad Arrow as part of the group, and pointed them out to Good Shield. They watched the men ride into camp and head directly for the large central lodge where the elders and the men of the camp gathered.

"Something's wrong," Good Shield said. "Look how fast they walk, and how they scowl."

They proceeded to their lodge, where they hung the mint to dry on a loop suspended from one of the lodge-poles. Coming back out of the tipi behind Good Shield, Genny heard a voice that made her cringe. Mni Sapa Win was advancing toward them from the council lodge, strident words issuing from her lips.

Genny tried to duck back inside, but Good Shield took her arm and held her. "Face her, *stepan*. You faced a Pawnee war party with more courage. Don't run away from an old woman."

"She hates me," Genny whispered. "And I can't even talk to her. What did I do this time?"

"She doesn't hate you. She doesn't trust you."

Mni Sapa Win came to a halt in front of them, her black eyes skewering Genny with withering intensity. She began a scathing harangue, speaking in a singsong chant that sent shivers up Genny's spine. Good Shield stood straight and calm at Genny's side, lending strength and support. At length, the old woman ceased talking and settled into a triumphant silence that had Genny baffled.

Good Shield began to translate. "She says she knew you would bring bad luck. Because of you, something terrible has happened, just as she said it would."

"What happened?" Genny asked.

"I don't know, yet." As she put a question to her aunt, Gus and Big Elk came running up. Gus barked a command to one of Hawk Dancer's sons who stood among those who had collected to watch the proceedings. The boy caught a nearby pony and raced off toward the horse herd in the distance. Gus came to a careening stop at Genny's side. His arm automatically went around her back, and he edged her away from Good Shield, transferring her to his protection. Mni Sapa Win eyed his action with disdain. She turned and spoke to the assembled people at her back.

Gus ignored her. "I got here as fast as I could," he said, a little short of breath. Then he spoke rapidly in French so both of them could understand him. "The buffalo are gone. They vanished. We thought they might have bolted in the duststorm, but we couldn't find any trace of their passage. Hawk Dancer's setting up a sweat so he can pray, and people are upset." He turned to Genny. "*Tonwin* is blaming it on you. She thinks this is the result of your burning her medicine."

Many people in the crowd around them murmured unhappily as Mni Sapa Win finished talking at the same time Gus did. They looked at Genny accusingly.

Genny was aghast. "I had nothing to do with this! How can she think that? Is she crazy?"

"Hush," he said softly, holding up a hand in warning. "She's not crazy. For all I know, she may be right. I don't understand her spirits any more than I understand steam engines. Let me talk to her. By the way, how attached are you to Trixie?"

Genny's stomach plummeted. "What have you done with my horse?"

"Nothing." He tried to pat her back but she shrugged him off. He let her go and stepped toward his aunt. "Yet," he muttered under his breath so that Genny couldn't hear him.

Gus assumed his most winning tones and began talking to his aunt. What lies he was telling, Genny couldn't fathom, but she didn't doubt he was fabricating left and right to calm the woman. He cast her a few furtive glances that made her wary.

When No Hair, Hawk Dancer's oldest boy, appeared at the edge of the circle leading Trixie and carrying a heavy saddlebag, she straightened her shoulders and reached a hand toward Gus's elbow.

Good Shield pulled her back. "Let him talk," she hissed in Genny's ear.

"Tell me what he's saying," Genny insisted.

Gus glanced back in irritation. Genny shot him a piercing look, and Good Shield jerked her head meaningfully. Gus nodded shortly before turning back to his aunt.

"He's telling *tonwin* that you're sorry about the roots, and that he doesn't think anyone should be upset with you," Good Shield whispered in Genny's ear. "He's telling her how generous you were when he and Walks In Thunder, who is married to her daughter, visited your home. And how brave you were against the Pawnees at the river. He says you saved his life. He thinks the spirits wouldn't let you sleep and led you to get up. Because of this, they didn't get your horses, and *misun* wasn't killed."

More people were gathering to hear Gus talk, and Genny suspected that he was enjoying his audience. His voice became more dramatic, and he gestured freely.

"Now he's saying that you tended his arm, caring for him when he was hurt. He's *tonwin*'s favorite nephew, you know. He's trying to make her see how well you treat him. I think she may be a little jealous of you. She didn't like that other woman, either."

Genny wished Good Shield would stick to Gus's narrative. The crowd was murmuring approvingly, and she wanted to know why.

"*Misun* is saying that you're the bravest woman he's ever seen. He's telling how you hid atop a rocky butte where there were rattlesnakes and wolves."

Rattlesnakes? Genny blanched at the thought. Had there been? Or was he simply embellishing freely?

"And he's telling how you held still and silent while the Pawnees passed close below you, not even flinching when their leader looked right at the rock where you were hiding.'' That was no exaggeration.

Gus grew solemn, and his listeners scarcely breathed. "He says you fired upon the Pawnees, even though this isn't a woman's responsibility. You helped him when he needed you, and you killed a Pawnee warrior. Then you sang with him to ease his grief at having betrayed his vow never to kill again. You're brave and strong, and he's proud you're his woman. He wishes *tonwin* would feel honored that he's brought you into our family.''

Genny was astounded. She was flattered and embarrassed to hear Gus talk about her like this. But she was also a little hurt.

"Why didn't he tell her this before?'' she asked Good Shield.

The Lakota woman looked into Genny's wide blue eyes and shrugged. "Perhaps he didn't know it,'' came her enigmatic reply.

Before Genny could argue, Gus spoke again, motioning No Hair forward with Trixie and the pack.

"What's he doing now?'' Genny whispered, alarmed by Trixie's appearance.

Good Shield hesitated. "He's saying again how sorry you were about her medicine,'' she finally relayed. "He says you want the camp to know you meant no harm, and you bear *tonwin* no ill will. You want to give her something to express your regret and your hope that you will prove a good niece.'' Genny stiffened. "You brought little with you, only a good gun, which you have given to your husband, and this horse.''

Oh, you lying wretch, Genny thought. She hadn't bothered to take back the Spencer after the massacre. She hadn't wanted to touch the thing. But she hadn't given to him. And he wasn't her husband.

"Your most valuable possession is this black horse, a Cheyenne war horse, as fast as lightning and as strong as the mountains of He Sapa, the Black Hills. *Misun* says you would like *tonwin* to have her.''

Gus passed Trixie's leads into the old woman's hands. Genny held her face immobile as she watched Mni Sapa

Win squint up at the mare. However much of a nuisance Trixie was, the horse had been her steady companion at White Rock Spring. Now her supposed husband had given her away to a grouchy old aunt who could no more ride her than carry her to Omaha and back.

Mni Sapa Win muttered something under her breath, and Gus shifted his weight onto his left leg, his posture softening.

"*Tonwin* likes the color of the horse," Good Shield whispered.

She would, Genny thought. It matched her disposition.

Next Gus reached for the saddlebag No Hair held and offered it to his aunt with a casual comment. "He tells her now that she might like these roots. He had a dream and a bear told him where to find them. Actually, I think it was Hawk Dancer, but don't tell her that. *Misun* hopes she'll make good medicine with them."

Mni Sapa Win accepted the saddlebag, sniffing it suspiciously. Then she nodded, a satisfied look on her face, and turned to walk away, Trixie trailing behind her. The crowd parted to let her through, and she called out a shrill sentence.

Gus turned to Genny and grinned with the pride and sass of a cat dropping a mouse at its master's feet. He exchanged a triumphant look with Good Shield, then fixed his gaze on Genny.

"Well?" Genny demanded. "What did she say?"

"Go ahead," Gus prompted his sister.

Good Shield cleared her throat. "*Tonwin* says she thinks she may have heard the spirits wrong. After all, she's old. What can anyone expect?"

Chapter 20

Life in the Lakota camp was easier for Genny after Gus gave his aunt her horse and replaced the medicine she had mistakenly burned. The next morning, when she accompanied Good Shield and Blue Bird to fill their water skins, other women joined them, laughing and talking softly. Soon they were asking to see Genny's dagger, as Gus had spread the story that it had belonged to one of the Pawnees that had attacked them. A little to her dismay, the women referred to her as Pawnee Killer, and the name stuck.

Gus greeted her return to Good Shield's tipi with some surprises. He peered around the back of the lodge, crooking his finger at her, something held behind his back. Good Shield pushed her toward him.

"What are you up to now?" she asked, laughing when he retreated a few steps toward the trees along the edge.

"I have some presents for you, *istatowin*. Wedding presents, if you will. But you can only have them if you're my wife."

Genny stopped. "Gus, don't play games about this."

In a teasing mood, he refused to let her somber response deter him. He grinned engagingly. "Are you my wife?"

She didn't answer.

"My wife has brown hair and blue eyes. You might be her. My wife is an artist." He pulled a leather bound ledger from behind his back and a clutch of pencils. "My wife would be very pleased to have this gift.''

Genny's eyes fixed on the book and pencils. She hadn't seen a single sheet of paper since she left White Rock Spring. Forgetting that she was annoyed with him, she approached until she could reach out and touch the book.

Gus flipped it open, displaying the empty lined and numbered pages. Genny's tongue crept between her lips.

"Are you my wife?" he repeated saucily. "If not . . ." He snapped the ledger closed and held it out of reach.

"I'm your wife," Genny said immediately, reaching for the book and pencils. "For now."

"Good enough," Gus said, surrendering his gift. Genny smoothed a hand over the ledger reverently and smiled up at him.

"Than you." She slung her free arm up to clasp his neck and she pressed a warm kiss to his mouth. He caught her to him, crushing the ledger between them.

"Thank you?" he prompted.

She knew what he wanted. "Thank you, *mihigna kin*." My husband. For now, she added to herself.

Gus laughed with abandoned content, lifting her off her feet and swinging her in a circle. "I have something else for you. To replace something I took from you." He let her slide down his body, keeping hold of her free hand. "It's over by the trees."

Genny looked up and saw a pretty black horse with a white blaze grazing under the cottonwoods. Gus pulled her across the field to stand beside it.

"I've had this horse for a while, and I thought you might like her. She's not as fast as Trixie, or as big, but she's a good horse," Gus told Genny. "You'll probably get a lot more use out her than you ever would have out of Trixie."

Genny handed him the ledger and approached the mare, running a hand over her neck. "What's her name?" The horse nuzzled her shoulder and whickered softly.

"Wicanpila. It means star. I'll help you up." He boosted Genny onto the mare's back and helped steady her. "Take her for a little ride through the trees here. You'll be okay without leads on her."

He was right. Wicanpila was responsive and had an easy stride. An excellent mount, she was more suited to Genny than Trixie had ever been, and Genny returned to Gus with a smile on her face.

They walked back to camp, leading Wicanpila. When they reached Good Shield's lodge, Blue Bird and White Hands were hauling a bundle of hides from one of Gus's cousin's lodges.

"I have one last gift for you. Actually, this one's for both of us." Good Shield and Hawk Dancer's wife, Brings It Along, dragged some short lodgepoles to a point behind Gus's sister's tipi.

"What is it?"

"Watch. You'll see."

In a few minutes Good Shield and Brings It Along had raised three of the poles in a tripod, digging the pointed ends firmly into the ground, and expertly tying a strong rope around the top. Blue Bird and White Hands began laying in the other poles, while Good Shield wound the rope around them. Finally, she anchored the rope to the ground inside the frame, using a long stake. The resulting circle was much smaller than usual, but it was unmistakable.

"It's a tipi," Genny exclaimed. "A little tipi. Is it for playing in?"

Gus chuckled. "You could say that. How'd you like to play house with me, *ištatowin*?" He ran one hand over her hips suggestively.

"It's for us? Our own tipi?" She danced away from him.

He nodded, grinning wickedly. "It's a travel tipi for hunting trips. I got it from Brings It Along. If you don't mind, we'll still eat with my sister and her family, since there's not enough room to do much more than sleep in this little lodge."

Genny looked up at him, arching her eyebrows.

"Not that we'll be sleeping much," he conceded. "So

tell me, *ištatowin*. Which of your gifts do you like the best?''

A small smile curved Genny's lips. "They're all wonderful.''

Laughter boomed from Gus's throat. "I think you like the tipi best.''

She raised her chin primly and tried not to ruin it by smiling. "A lady,'' she said archly, "would never tell.''

August ended in the hazy warmth of late summer, and September began with a day so clear that buttes fifty miles away looked less than a day's easy march. As summer waned, Genny settled into a pattern of life that flowed with the camp rhythms. She tried to help Good Shield as much as possible, but she was slow in acquiring the skills necessary to be much more than a nuisance. Eventually, she came to spend most of her days drawing sketches of camp life and the people she was coming to know as friends and family. Learning to paint geometric designs on hide with bone brushes occupied her some, but she was more interested in capturing people's portraits. So many things caught her eye: a young mother scraping hides with her child strapped to its cradleboard beside her, old men smoking quietly by their fires, little girls playing with tiny tipis and dolls, young men draped in courting robes, hovering about a pretty girl's lodge. There was so much life, so different from anything she knew, yet much the same.

It was a constant frustration to be without materials. In desperation, she devised rawhide medallions upon which she drew portrait sketches in charcoal, thinking she could take them home with her to serve as a basis for her paintings. Then Blue Bird sewed a border of quills to some of the rounds, and Genny found she had created a much sought after memento. The children, in particular, would hang about for hours, watching her draw in her book or on the leather circles. When she gave away a few of the medallion portraits, those receiving them were so delighted Genny found it difficult to keep any of them. It became apparent she was going to have to rely on memory to bring life to the paintings she envisioned clearly.

However much she enjoyed her drawing, the time she spent with Gus quickly became the highlight of her days. Often they rode together over the plains or along the river bottoms where they camped. They hunted and gathered tiny wild plums in damp thickets along the creeks. Many of their expeditions were simply an excuse to escape the many eyes and ears in the camp, and they spent many warm September days in lazy lovemaking. The nights passed similarly. To Genny's intense relief, her courses came on schedule. Certain the herbs Good Shield had given her were doing their job, Genny had few worries to distract her from enjoying Gus's body to the utmost.

When she thought of it, though, the prospect of her coming departure brought her pause. She longed to return home, not to White Rock Spring, but to Philadelphia. Try as she might, after a month she had learned only a little Lakota. Without Gus's or Good Shield's help, she still couldn't talk to anyone beyond the rudiments of greetings and household matters. Even that was a chancy matter. She was lonely and tired of feeling so foreign. This wasn't her home and she didn't belong. She would never belong.

It had never been so hard in France. At least there she'd been able to talk to people, and she'd liked the food. Here, she wasn't fond of it at all, and she'd lost so much weight her hipbones stuck out like ships' rudders. Every meal, it seemed, was meat or soup, with an occasional fruit sauce to liven things up a bit. There was little salt, few herbs, and no bread. Some mornings she lay in her sleeping robes, nestled up against Gus, daydreaming about rising to a breakfast of toast and jam, eggs and hot coffee with lots of steaming milk. She no longer thought it strange that Gus had once eaten her jam straight from a spoon, and she forgave him entirely for helping himself to her stores. Now she'd have done it herself had the opportunity presented itself.

Gus—and his assurance that if she didn't want to stay when the snows came, he'd take her back—kept her going. Genny knew it cost him dearly to make that promise, and when he did so one day in front of an uncomfortable Good Shield, she believed him.

The greatest cause of distress in Genny's life was her growing conviction that not only had she and Gus become lovers, and later friends, as she had hoped, but that she was now hopelessly in love with him.

Under no illusions, Genny saw his faults. Yes, he was not above expedient lies. He had a tendency to exaggerate the truth if it would improve a story. He could be alarmingly single-minded in his actions, at times quite oblivious to other people's concerns, and his outrageous confidence, coupled with a certain amount of vanity, prompted him to show off more than she thought necessary. But all in all, she had come to admire him more than anything else. He had reason to show off, for he was good at nearly everything he set his hand to. He was a man of rare gifts and sparkling intellect, and Genny doubted she would ever meet another like him. As September drifted into October and the weather began to cool, the knowledge that they had so little time together added keen appreciation to Genny's days, and especially to her nights.

One morning Genny woke to find the lodge cover flapping irregularly against the poles. A draft of cold air met her exposed shoulder when she raised herself on one elbow to investigate.

Gus pulled her down, tossing the heavy buffalo robe over her head and burying his nose between her breasts. "Brrrrr," he growled. "You let all the warmth out."

Giggling, she fended him off and popped her head back out. "I can't breathe under there. Listen," she said, edging the robe off his head. "That doesn't sound like rain, but something's hitting against the cover. Do dust storms get this cold?"

Gus shut his eye and sighed. He groped for her hand and, finding it, bore it to his breast. "It's not dust."

"Then what . . . ? Oh." It was snow. The first sign of winter. Anticipation surged inside her, followed by biting sorrow. "Isn't it early yet? It's only October."

"Today's November first. For the plains, it's not that early." He gripped her hand tightly.

She didn't want to say what had to be said. "Do you remember when you asked me to think about staying with you? For good?"

He had been dreading this moment ever since. "Of course I do. I want you, Genny. I want you with me always. I love you."

She'd never said as much herself, thinking it would only make things harder. Now she couldn't stop the words.

"I love you, too, Gus." Tears slipped from the corners of her eyes.

"Genny," he gasped, rolling onto his side and enveloping her in a fierce hug. "Then you mean . . ." He couldn't speak through his relief.

Her heart constricted as she clung to him. "Stop, Gus." This was so very difficult to say. "I love you. I have for a long time. Probably since the day the Pawnees attacked us. But . . ."

His arms tightened around her. Despite his every effort, she wasn't pregnant. Only yesterday she'd come back from the *isnati* lodge. Her period had been two weeks late, and he'd been ecstatic. Then it had come, after all. He wasn't prepared for this. He'd been so sure he could get her pregnant before the first snow and that she wouldn't leave him with a child on the way.

"Genny, no. Don't . . ."

She felt him shudder in her embrace. "You have to let me say this." His mouth fell open to stop her, but she put her hand over his lips and gave a tiny shake of her head. "I love you, Gus Renard, and I can't imagine that I'll ever feel this way about another man, but I can't stay with you." Her voice cracked. "I want to go home. I want to belong, be a part of things. Here I only belong with you. I've tried, Gus, but I can't live this way forever. I can't even talk to people here. It's too different. Too hard. Even loving you can't change that. I'm sorry."

He dropped his forehead to hers and pulled his lips

into a thin line, eyes closed tight against the pain. Uneven breaths shook his chest, but with an effort, he steadied them.

"Don't be sorry, *istatola*. It's not your fault. I've always known inside that it was crazy to think we could be together, but I can't help my feelings. From the beginning, I haven't been able to control what's between us. It's stronger than our differences, Genny. Stronger than my being a mixed-blood Indian and your being a Philadelphia lady. Genny, it has to be."

"Can you live in Philadelphia? Will you come with me?"

He stiffened. "There's no place for me there. You know that."

"I have enough money for both of us. My father won't cut me off."

"I've money of my own if I wanted it. That's not the problem."

She eased back from him, cupping his jaw in her hand. "I know." Money wouldn't buy him self-respect or a place in white society. Not the way he wanted it. "But you have to understand that even if people here are willing to make a place for me, it's not a comfortable place. It would take years, Gus, and even then I might never be able to fit in. I see how the men look at me when they return from the fighting in the south. Worse, I see the anger and contempt in women's eyes when their men don't come back. And your aunt, however much she likes Trixie, still looks at me as if I carry the pox. But more than that, I don't think I could ever accept this as my home. It's just too different.

"Gus, if I saw any way for us to be together and for both of us to be happy, I'd hustle you off to the nearest minister, even if I had to walk all the way to St. Louis to find him. I'd make you marry me if I had to hold a gun to your head. But it wouldn't work. One of us would always be unhappy. We don't belong together."

"That's not true!" He thrust her away from him and threw back the robe, exposing both of them to the chill air.

Curled on her side, Genny made no effort to cover herself. "You know better than that, and refusing to admit it leaves me with the burden of making this choice alone. Do you think this is easy for me?"

He shook his head, unable to meet her eyes.

"Then don't make it any harder than it already is. You promised you'd take me back."

He felt like he was sinking. His lungs drained of air, and he didn't seem able to draw more. Very slowly, moving automatically, he pulled the robe back up over Genny's legs. Then he rose. After tying on his breechcloth, he walked out into the snow, not bothering to put on his moccasins.

Genny didn't notice. She had rolled into the warm space he had left in their bed, burying her head where his back had been, breathing deeply to inhale his scent. All too soon, memories would be all she'd have of him.

Gus burst into his sister's lodge. Everyone was seated around the fire, sipping porridge from horn bowls, their warm robes snuggled comfortably around their shoulders.

Good Shield knew at a glance what was wrong. "There is no child on the way and the snow has come," she said softly. "I wish it were otherwise, for your sake, *misun*."

Gus looked stricken. Unable to respond to his sister's compassion, he focused single-mindedly on his reason for coming in. "Do you still have Tunkasila's pipe?"

All four of them stared directly at him. "Yes," Good Shield said, her voice a mere breath.

"I need it."

Good Shield put down her bowl and rose. Kneeling behind her bed, she brought out a well-worn deerskin bag. A fine quill work design in red, yellow, and black adorned it, and long fringe hung from the bottom of it. She held it across her knees and turned to look up at her brother. "Are you sure?"

He nodded once and reached out for it. Good Shield stood and walked to him. "Please, be careful."

"I will, *tanke*." He received the bag into his hands.

"Tanhan," he said, addressing Big Elk, "can you show me how to prepare this pipe to present to our cousin? I am in need. I seek his guidance and any help the spirits might grant me."

Big Elk nodded, and his brother-in-law fell to his knees, cradling the pipe bag. He and Good Shield exchanged a worried look over Gus's head.

An hour later, Gus stalked through the driving snow, still dressed only in his breechcloth, though at Good Shield's insistence he now wore moccasins. Arriving at Hawk Dancer's lodge, he scratched on the door cover and waited a second. Then he entered, careful to protect the long stem of his grandfather's pipe from the flapping cover. The eagle feathers tied to it dangled over his arm, and the redstone bowl felt cold in his palm.

Everyone in the crowded lodge glanced up. When Hawk Dancer saw the pipe in his cousin's hands, he motioned for the children to be quiet.

Gus stepped toward the fire. *"Tunkasila,"* he said, addressing his cousin with the respect due a holy man, "I bring a pipe to you. Will you take it?"

Hawk Dancer remained seated at his place opposite the door and signalled Gus to come to him. "Our cousin needs to talk, boys," he said quietly. "Perhaps you have some stories you can tell each other over there." The boys moved away from the fire, giving the men as much privacy as they could. "So after all these years you bring a pipe, *tanhan.*"

Gus nodded as he came to sit next to his cousin. "I need help. I want to ask the spirits to help me. Will you tell me what to do?"

Hawk Dancer reached for the pipe Gus offered. "Let's smoke together first."

Gus surrendered the pipe. Hawk Dancer eyed it critically. "Pretty good for a beginner," he commented. Then he closed his eyes and was silent. After a moment he raised the pipe to the west, and then to each of the other directions in turn, north, east, and south. He lifted it to the sky and lowered it toward the earth, praying as he did so. When he finished, he nodded toward Gus. "Take that sage over there," he said pointing to a tight clump of dried wormwood. "Light it on the coals and let it smolder. Then do the same with the sweetgrass."

Gus followed his cousin's instructions. The sharp tang of sage filled his nostrils, then the musky scent of the sweetgrass.

"The sage chases away the evil spirits," Hawk Dancer said, not sure his cousin knew even that much. "The sweetgrass calls The Beautiful One who brought the pipe to the Lakota."

He broke the seal of fat in the pipebowl and brought a stick tipped with a live coal from the fire to light it. He drew strongly on the pipe, and clouds of fragrant willowbark and tobacco smoke puffed from his cheeks.

"This is a good old pipe." He smoked awhile before passing it to Gus.

When the pipe was empty, Hawk Dancer handed it back to Gus. "Why are you here?"

"I want a child. My wife is going to leave me, and I want a child to bind us together. I tried trickery, and it didn't work. I've made strong efforts to plant my seed within her, but so far it hasn't taken hold. I have perhaps two weeks more with her. I want to ask the spirits to help me."

"Maybe you should see my mother," Hawk Dancer said, smiling a little. "What do you think she does with her bear medicine?"

"Please, *tahansi*. Can you help me?" Only women went to Mni Sapa Win. He couldn't go to her. This was hard enough for him as it was.

"The spirits will require something of you. It may not be easy. Are you willing to make whatever sacrifice they demand?"

"Short of the lives of my wife, my family, or myself, I'm willing to make whatever sacrifice I have to to keep her with me. In happiness and good health."

Hawk Dancer nodded thoughtfully. "This afternoon we'll do a sweat. I'll talk to the spirits and see what they say."

* * *

Late that afternoon Gus emerged from the oppressive heat of the small sweat lodge into the bitter cold of an early winter storm. He didn't feel it. But though he was physically drained, his heart felt strong. Hawk Dancer had said the spirits had agreed to help him if he would honor his promise to take Genny back to Kills Plenty Water and pledge to go up on a hill for four days to seek a vision. Not certain how things would unfold, but desperate to keep her with him, he assented to both conditions.

Now he walked home through the snow, intent upon one purpose. All rational doubts were cast aside as he made the unfamiliar journey into faith. Tonight, perhaps tomorrow, or some other night in the next week, he would plant the seed that would find life in Genny's womb, binding them together for the rest of their lives. It could not be otherwise.

The weather cleared off the next day, but the snow remained through the week. Stalling as long as he could, Gus reluctantly made preparations to take Genny back to White Rock Spring. Several days were spent gathering information about the state of the war between the Indians and the U.S. Army down along the rivers to the south. Reports coming up from the Platte Valley indicated that sporadic raiding was still taking place, mostly along the southern fork of the river. The North Platte was reputedly deserted except for a few soldiers riding to or from Fort Laramie, and Gus heard that Roger and Martha Rivier had returned safely to their ranch. With the American soldiers killing mad about the raids and disruptions, most of the Lakota had moved their camps to the north to protect their women and children, but many Cheyennes were lingering further south in their traditional lands.

Even with word that the North Platte was relatively safe and that no Pawnees had been seen west of the forks for more than a month, Gus didn't care to put Genny at unnecessary risk by traveling with too small a party. Walks In Thunder, Bad Arrow, and Big Elk's cousin,

Afraid of Hawk were going with them, along with several spare horses. They would travel light, but fast, and with any luck, the weather would cooperate. The camp was now nearly due north of White Rock Spring, so the journey would be shorter than it had been in August.

On her last evening in camp, Genny packed her few belongings into her saddlebags. It was the middle of the second week in November, and after nearly three months of living in the Lakota camp, almost nothing remained of the things she had brought with her. Only her split skirt and her goggles remained in usable condition. She folded her newer things carefully, knowing the few dresses and pairs of moccasins Good Shield had given her, the ledger filled with sketches, and the few portrait medallions she had kept for herself were going to become precious in the years to come. For all that she could not stay in the Lakota camp, she treasured the time spent living with the man she had grown to love.

The door covering flew up suddenly, and Gus stepped into their tiny lodge, halting when he saw her packed saddlebags beside the fire. Their eyes met. She smiled at the passion she read there, knowing exactly how this last night in camp would be spent.

"You'd better close the door," she finally said. "All the heat's escaping."

"That won't be a problem tonight. You're going to have more heat than you know what to do with." He lowered the flap and tied it shut. He turned, dropping to his knees on their bed and coming toward her. "A great deal more, *istatowin*. You're going to remember tonight for the rest of your life."

She came up on her knees and waited for him. "So are you, *mon cher*."

He reached for her, and she leaned forward into his arms. Long fingers tilted her chin up, and he touched his lips to her. Barely. She felt his breath upon her more than his lips. Ever since she had said she had to leave, his lovemaking had taken on a desperate intensity that thrilled her even as it tore her heart. He was different tonight. Softer. Easier. Slower. Yet there was no less fire in him. Instead, he was controlled, measuring their love to make it last the night through.

He took her face in his hands and drew back, drinking in her features. "I love you, *ištatowin*. I love your beauty and your strength. I love you for accepting me into your heart and soul. If we can't be together always, let me give you a lifetime's worth of loving tonight."

His lips fluttered over her eyelids and down her cheeks, bestowing tiny, sipping kisses before settling gently against her mouth. Instead of bringing her his love with the wild fury of a prairie storm, his kiss built gradually, filling her senses slowly, like low clouds drifting before a day of gentle rains. His cheeks were cold, smelling of winter and campfires, and his mouth was warm, his lips soft and giving. Every shift he made as he slanted to tease her lower lip with his tongue resonated deep within her.

He was her lover, her husband, if only for a few more days, and she was secure within his love. Beneath his hands and mouth she felt her flesh swell and come to life. Shivers flowed through her, rippling like the summer grass in a gentle breeze.

Long fingers drifted down her sides and over her hips and thighs until they caught the bottom edge of her dress. With slow deliberation, he hooked the beaded hem under his thumbs and began sliding upwards, his palms open on the bare skin above her knees. Inch by slow inch, he uncovered her. When the dress rode high on her thighs he leaned back away from her to watch as his hands revealed her fair skin.

Genny watched him, her pulse racing when he raised her dress so that it just concealed the dark hair between her thighs. His lips parted as he stared intently, eyes riveted to the slow-moving line of her dress, and joy gathered in her breast with the knowledge that she could arouse him so by allowing him the simple freedom of looking at her body. When the soft leather caught and dragged over the curls covering her woman's flesh, lightning bolted through her, and her breath rasped in her throat.

Eyes as dark and soft as the robes they slept in flickered up to meet her gaze, and an enchanted, knowing smile lit Gus's face. No words were necessary. She knew that smile. It told her that he found her beautiful and exciting, and that he loved her. It also promised wanton pleasures.

Cool air whispered over her belly, and Gus looked down at her again, his eyes caressing her as surely as his hands. The calluses on his palms and fingers scratched lightly over her hips to come to rest in the deep curve of her waist, and Genny stilled herself, waiting in aching tension for him to undress her completely. Her breasts felt heavy in anticipation of the glide of his hands and her dress over them, and she closed her eyes to better savor each sensation.

Instead, she felt a gust of breath and Gus's soft lips low on her belly. She dropped her hands to hold his face to her as he kissed her with a tender reverence that made her wish for one small moment his child rested there within her. It had been the wisest thing to avoid a babe, but she couldn't stop the niggling regret that they would never share a family. A vision of herself holding a tiny, dark-haired child to her breast, with Gus standing at her side, brought another gasp to her lips.

"Oh, Gus," she groaned. "I wish . . ."

He smoothed his cheek across her stomach and looked up at her. "What do you wish, *istatowin*?"

"I wish . . ." She couldn't tell him. It would only make their parting harder." . . . things could be different."

"Perhaps they will be, Genny." His hands began their ascent once more, aided now by kisses. "The future may hold more surprises than we imagine."

He exposed one breast, his thumb skimming the side of it before his lips plucked gently at her distended nipple. Ringing it with nipping kisses, he then took it fully into his mouth, sucking rhythmically. She arched her back, pressing more fully into him, her hands once more tangled in his hair. When he pushed the other side of her dress up, she guided his mouth to her other breast, cupping his cheek in her palm. As he suckled her, he kept moving her dress upwards, lifting her arms from his head and easing it along them and over her head.

When she was naked, Gus sat back on his heels and looked at her, his gaze hot. Her limbs shone pink in the firelight, and their shadows wavered on the inner curtain that gave them privacy and held the autumn winds at bay. Wondering what changes a baby would bring to her body, Gus ran one finger from between her breasts to the flat plain of her stomach. She had lost weight since he had taken her from the house at Bad Spirit Creek, but a child would fill out her curves again, swelling her breasts and rounding her belly. Even now, she might be carrying the fruit of his seed. The thought brought a low growl of satisfaction rumbling from him, and his hand dropped lower to brush the curls that hid the entrance to her womb.

Leaning forward, he parted her with his fingers and bent, pressing his mouth to her. She shifted restlessly, hot and silky against his lips, a cry of pleasure breaking raggedly from her. When he darted his tongue in rapid, teasing flicks over the tiny bud within her soft flesh, she melted bonelessly into him. Reaching around her to support her back, he pushed her backwards and brought her down upon the heavy robes that made up their bed.

"Lie back, *istatowin*, and open for me." Spreading her thighs, he settled between her legs and kissed her deeply.

Her hands balled into fists as she tried to slow the fires he lit inside her, but the tension in her muscles only heightened the shivers coursing through her. "Gus, wait. You're not even undressed yet," she whispered.

"We have all night. This is how I want to start. Let me love you, Genny." He dipped his head to her again and his tongue dragged over her sensitive skin.

"Yes," she breathed. "Oh, yes. Love me. Always love me."

"I will, *istatola*. I always will."

Seconds stretched into minutes as he loved her with his soft mouth and roughened hands. She received his gifts with joy, her heart melting with a yearning that reached out to him, accepting the love they shared, wanting it to last, knowing that it couldn't. The climax that he brought to her exploded through her senses, streaming up her backbone, crashing into her heart, and releasing a wild cry of passion as it tore through her throat. Finally it burst into splintering fragments of light and pointless hope behind her eyes.

"Gus!" she gasped. "Oh, Gus. I love you so. How can I feel this way when I know I have to leave you?"

He surged up to take her in his arms, and she tasted herself in his kiss, sweet and salty on his lips. Then he laid his hands upon her cheeks and opened her eyelids with his thumbs. He met her gaze with wonder and sorrow, but also with a hope that baffled her.

"Think only of tonight, Genny. Think only of the love we share," he told her.

The sweet beauty in his smile tugged at her heart, banishing the cloud cast by their imminent separation, and she did what she always did when he looked at her that way.

Looking deep into eyes as dark as a sunflower's heart and as bright as its petals, Genny smiled back.

Chapter 21

On a cool November afternoon Genny sat astride Wicanpila overlooking White Rock Spring once again. Thin beams of sunlight angled through a lone cloud in the southwest, casting harsh shadows into the small valley. The leaves were gone from the cottonwoods and box elders surrounding the spring, and the grass had faded into winter's colorless palette of pale browns and ochres. Her white cottage looked sadly out of place amidst the sweep of empty prairie hills and sky.

A cold breeze rose from the valley, colder than the air around them as it whistled through the dry grass. Beside her, Walks In Thunder frowned and muttered something to Gus. Catching only a fraction of what he said, she understood that he and the others wouldn't ride into the valley. Uneasy lines had formed around the big man's mouth, and neither Bad Arrow or Afraid of Hawk looked comfortable. Even their horses shifted nervously.

"They won't go any further," Gus affirmed. His eyes fixed on a play in the light above the house. The shimmer of heat from a wood fire rose from the stovepipe. Someone was inside.

"Why not? I could give them supper. They must be cold and tired." She herself was so tired her bones ached.

"Did you ever wonder why Paul Conrad located you in this particular place?" Gus asked, eyes narrowed on the house below.

"He said it was safe. It's hard to see from the south."

"But not from here. Not from the direction a lot of Indians come from. He was right about it being pretty safe, though."

The wind rose, moaning softly as it slipped over the rise where they were standing. Afraid of Hawk made a clipped remark and moved to Genny's side. He shook her hand gently, waved to Gus, and turned his mount to the west. Bad Arrow followed, and Walks In Thunder after him. Genny murmured her goodbyes, barely understanding theirs. Within minutes the three men were galloping across the hills, the sound of their horses' hooves fading into the wind.

"What got into them? You'd think they'd been spooked."

A grim smile appeared on Gus's face. "The Indians around here call this place Bad Spirit Creek. About twenty-five, maybe thirty years ago, a Cheyenne war party was attacked here by a group of Pawnees. It made what we did at Rocky Butte look like a school picnic. Everybody says there are ghosts here."

Genny shot him a piercing look. "Except you. Why didn't you tell me this before?"

He shrugged. "I didn't want to scare you."

"You wouldn't have scared me. I don't believe in ghosts, but . . ." She thought back to the plain where she and Gus had left eight men dead. "Maybe we should go to Rivier's. Things like that can leave a bad feeling in a place. Funny I never noticed it." Her gaze drifted over the valley. It looked cold and lonely, but not sinister. When the wind moaned again, though, she shivered.

"We don't have to go down there if you don't want to."

She was being silly. This was her home. It had never bothered her before. Besides, she was too tired to ride another six miles to Rivier's. Her stomach was starting to ache, and she wondered if she was coming down with something. "No, it's all right. Gus, why did you come here in the first place? And how'd you get Walks In Thunder to come with you?"

Gus smiled feebly, remembering. "I came because I

was curious to see what kind of person would build a house here, and I got Walks In Thunder to come by bribing him with one of Wicanpila's brothers.''

"But why did you come back? If you knew Indians wouldn't come here, why did you force me to leave?'' Her question was deceptively soft, and she was watching him closely, her blue eyes alert.

He met her gaze. "I came back to see if you were gone. I kept thinking about you after that first visit. I made you come with me because I was angry, and worried about you. All bets on your safety were off with the fighting going on, and I didn't trust the U.S. Army anymore than I trusted angry warriors.'' He'd never gotten around to telling her about the payroll, and this didn't seem like the right time.

Genny accepted his answer. Looking at the lonely little house, she frowned and pressed her hand against her stomach as a twinge shot through her gut. "How long are you going to stay?''

He watched in concern. Her shoulders were slumped forward, and she looked pale. "I'm not sure.'' It was all he was willing to say. "Do you feel all right?''

She nodded. "I'm just tired. Let's go, then.''

"We'd better go in quietly. There's someone down there. Look at the stovepipe.''

Uneasiness straightened her shoulders when she saw the nearly invisible smoke.

"No need to panic,'' Gus told her. "It's probably someone Rivier sent up to keep an eye on things for you.''

"Or Paul,'' Genny said, voicing his own thoughts.

He hoped not. Genny looked like she needed rest and if it was her cousin, he was afraid she was in for a pretty rough evening.

Paul Conrad sloshed an inch of bourbon into the tumbler before him and held it up to the light, swirling it to watch it glide back down the sides of the glass. He sipped and smiled. This wasn't the homemade rotgut the troops along the trail concocted to keep their minds off boredom and the likelihood of being skewered by an Indian arrow, or the watered-down swill the traders bartered to the Indians. This was good Kentucky bourbon he'd purchased and socked away before the war. This particular bottle was from a stash he'd laid in the floor of Genny's pantry when he'd built her house last summer. Smooth and rich, it warmed his body all the way to his toes.

Unfortunately, it wasn't warming his spirits any. He glanced at the note he'd left pinned to Genny's cupboard when he'd found it there in late August, and at the splintered hole in the wall beside the stove. This was the second time he'd been back to White Rock Spring to see if she'd turned up yet, and he had the Riviers checking regularly, ready to wire him the minute she was back.

If she was coming back. That note made him wonder. It was brief, saying only that Genny was safely away from the hostilities along the trail, signed by one Auguste Renard. That was the part that worried him. He'd heard a few stories about the wild half-breed from some Lakotas who lived up by Fort Laramie. He was reported to have a taste for women and cards, and the devil's own luck with both. Between those tales, the bullet hole in the wall, and what he'd found in the pantry when he dug out his bourbon, he wasn't sure what the hell was going on, but he was damn certain he didn't like it.

A board creaked on the porch, and Paul rose to his feet, instantly alert, his Navy Colt in hand. Tossing back the bourbon, he was heading for the front window to take a look when the front door opened.

A tall, lithe Indian with a face that would make women weep stepped into the room. Behind him came a squaw dressed in a white blanket coat, her hands tucked up under her arms.

She looked up at him with wide, blue eyes.

"Hello, Paul," his cousin said with calm distaste. "Put that gun away in my house."

"Genny?" Paul gasped. His jaw fell slack, and shock glazed his expression.

She pushed Gus out of the way and closed the door, throwing her coat off and tossing it onto the sofa as she came into the room. When she'd recognized Paul's horse in the barn she'd wanted to leave and go straight to Rivier's. Gus hadn't let her. "Who else would it be? Put that revolver down," she repeated.

"My God, Gen, what's happened to you? You look like a damned Indian squaw!" Paul exclaimed, tucking the Colt into his belt. "Are you all right? Who the hell is this buck? What's he done to you?"

Before Genny could so much as blink, Gus lunged forward and slammed his fist into Paul's jaw. As he jerked back, Gus neatly removed the revolver from his belt with left hand and delivered another jab to Paul's chin. He fell backwards on the rug, too startled to retaliate. "You watch your mouth around my wife, you whiskey guzzling . . ."

"Gus, stop it!" She wrenched the gun out of his hand.

"What!" Paul bellowed over both of them. "What did you call her?"

He lurched to his feet and hurtled into Gus, catching him at the waist with his shoulder and wrapping his arms around him. The momentum carried them into the door at Gus's back. It wasn't shut tight, and they sailed through, landing with a loud crash in the middle of Genny's easels and canvases. They began to wrestle on the floor. Genny raced after them, hopping over a crock that had held paintbrushes a moment ago.

"You filthy savage!" Paul yelled, twisting his hands into Gus's coat. "If you've made my cousin your whore I'll kill you! If you so much as laid one of your stinking half-breed fingers on her, I'll shoot your balls off!" He tried to slam Gus's head against the floor, but they were very nearly matched in size and strength, and he couldn't get him down further than a couple of inches.

Gus wrenched out of Paul's hold and rolled on top of him. "Listen to me, you ignorant buffoon, if you don't stop insulting my wife, you're going to be the one scrambling around after your balls!"

Paul roared in outrage when Gus called Genny his wife again, and both men started pommeling each other indiscriminately. Grunting and huffing, neither was able to inflict much damage on the other, but Genny wasn't aware of that. She stared at them in fascinated horror. Then anger took over. Hand shaking, neck straining, blood pounding, red hot fury rammed through her. Raising the Colt, she fired into the ceiling.

At the thunderous explosion, the men stopped fighting and looked up.

She waved the smoking pistol at Gus. "Gus, get off."

Looking up at her pale, rigid face, he did as she asked, but slowly, flinging his hands off Conrad like he would a dead snake.

"Paul, on your feet and into the parlor," she ordered.

Her cousin got up, shaking himself as if he'd been contaminated. The motion only served to infuriate Genny more. Grabbing Gus by the arm, she pushed him through the door and Paul after him. Following, she slammed the bedroom door behind her and glanced at the two men.

Each had assumed a martial stance, legs spread, arms held away from the body, weight balanced forward on the balls of the feet. Both were flush with a livid hatred that was uglier than anything Genny had ever seen from either of them. Their eyes were locked in a visual combat that frightened her, and she wondered if she'd be able to stop them if they came to blows again.

Paul looked so righteously affronted that she almost didn't recognize him. The things he'd just said repulsed her, stripping away any willingness she might have had to tolerate his asinine behavior in the interest of family unity.

"Sit down," she ordered, stepping between them. "Both of you. And both of you listen to me. You will not tear up my house, nor each other. You may shout at one another until doomsday, but you will not hurt each other. Is that clear?"

Gus surprised her. He immediately backed up and sat on the sofa. Paul did what she expected him to. He argued.

"Gen, what is this nonsense?! Why are you dressed

like a squaw, and what the hell are you doing with this half-breed heathen?''

"Sit down!" She brought the Colt up and pointed it at his belly.

Paul retreated to perch on the edge of the wing chair, but he appeared ready to leap to his feet at any second.

Genny stepped back a little. Her heart was pounding, and the ache in her stomach was becoming more pronounced. Concentrating on her cousin, she ignored it. "We'll have time for questions after proper introductions. As you have no doubt surmised, Gus, this is my dear cousin, Paul Conrad."

Gus sneered, but held his tongue.

"And Paul. Meet Auguste Renard. My husband."

Paul jumped from his chair. In the second that he hesitated between targets, not sure who he wanted to throttle first, the grinning Renard or his idiot cousin, Genny brought his Colt up less that three feet from his nose and set the trigger.

"Stop right there, and sit back down. Slowly." In the face of a weapon he kept loaded and in prime operating condition, he obeyed. Gus lifted one foot to rest on the opposite knee and sat back, looking like a cat let loose in an aviary. Genny's eyes flicked between them. "If either of you says a word in the next five minutes I'll shoot something. Probably one of you." When neither of them made a sound, she dropped into the straight chair by the bedroom door, pressing her side with her left hand while she held the revolver up in her right.

The smile disappeared from Gus's face, replaced by concern. "Genny? Are you okay?" He moved to come to her.

"Hush! Stay there!" A spasm of sharp pain shot through her abdomen. After several deep draughts of air, she was able to relax her muscles and the pain eased. Both men regarded her silently, Gus with concern, Paul with more disgust than anything else.

Her cousin couldn't hold his tongue longer than a minute. As soon as Genny relaxed a little, he began badgering.

"I want to know what happened to you, Gen. I've wasted more than enough valuable time hieing my butt out here to see if you'd turned up dead with a clutch of arrows in your back and your hair missing. What the hell happened? And why in blue blazes do you think you're married to this half-breed scum?"

Before she could answer, Gus interrupted. "I'll tell him, Genny. Take it easy for a few minutes, all right?" He didn't know what was wrong with her other than exhaustion, and he was worried. She probably ought to be in bed, but with Conrad raving on like a lunatic, that wasn't likely to happen soon.

Gus, turned to Paul, and his tone became steely. "Can't you see she's not well? You watch what you say, or it's going to be you with the arrows in your back and your hair gracing some warrior's lodgepole. Do you think we came in here alone? If you know anything about Indians, you know we don't travel alone. Three of my relatives are waiting outside to see what happens in here. Three Lakota warriors the likes of whom you don't want to tangle with. One of them's got Genny's Spencer repeater, and the other two can fire arrows just as fast. Do you understand what I'm saying?"

Paul's face turned a deep red and the muscles in his neck bulged, but he nodded shortly. "Get on with it, then."

Gus started with a brief account of his visit in July, followed by what was for him an understated outline of what had followed when he'd come through White Rock Spring the second time. He managed to highlight the times he'd saved Genny's life, and he left out any mention of their more intimate relationship. Paul frequently looked to Genny for confirmation, which she gave with quick nods.

"So Genny's been safe with my family all this time. Now that winter's coming on and things are settling down along the trail, we decided to come back," Gus finished. "We mistakenly thought you might be concerned about her well-being."

"Don't get smart with me," Paul shot back. "There's

a few things that don't fit real well with this story. Gen, did he rape you?''

Gus made an incoherent growling noise low in his throat. ''I have never raped a woman in my life. Among the Lakota, men have no need to resort to violence with women. We prove our manhood honorably.''

Paul didn't spare him a glance. ''Did he rape you, Gen?''

''No. There was no need for him to rape me.''

Paul looked at her in horror. ''But you've had relations with him?''

She nodded once. ''I love him. I chose him of my own accord.''

''Christ, girl, do you realize what you're saying?'' Paul ran his fingers up into the hair at his temples in agitation. ''Think about it! You're throwing your life away! No decent woman would ever let a red bastard touch her! You're admitting you're no better than a whore if you claim you gave yourself to him. Tell me different, Genny, and I'll forget what you just said. No one will have to know. Don't be a fool.''

His words burned away any smidgeon of doubt that she was doing the right thing in claiming Gus as her husband. She didn't think past the moment. Anger surged through her again, and she stood, facing her cousin.

''I love him! He's my husband, and he's a better man than you could ever hope to be. He's loving and kind, loyal and generous. I will not deny him because our marriage offends your sense of propriety!''

Paul shook his head in disgust. ''He's got you snowed. Christ, Gen, I thought you were smarter than this. What happened to all those declarations that you were never going to marry? Here you up and fall for a pretty-faced half-breed liar who's put you through hell and back. You don't have any more sense than a mule!

''Look,'' he continued. ''I know you think I've given you nothing but grief—but Gen, you have to believe I'm looking out for you on this. Staying with this man is going to bring you more trouble and tears than you can imagine. I know his type. I've been out here a long time.

And I know there's no way you're legally wed to him if you've been out in Indian country all this time. You can leave what happened behind you. Nobody at home knows. I told them you were safe. If you insist on staying with him, he'll take off and leave you, and you'll end up a grass widow with everybody feeling sorry for you but nobody wanting to have anything to do with you. A woman who's been a willing whore to a half-breed pretty boy isn't going to be getting any invitations to afternoon tea, and you know it.''

Genny focused on Paul all her anger at the impossibility of living in peace with Gus in either of their worlds. ''My choices are none of your concern.''

Gus seized the opportunity to tie Genny to him permanently. ''We're to be legally wed. That's one of the reasons we came back. We're riding up to Fort Laramie to get the post commander to perform the ceremony for us. If we can find a preacher, so much the better,'' he said firmly.

''That's right,'' Genny agreed. ''We'll be married by the end of the week, and you can't stop it. If you cannot give us your blessings, then I have to ask you to leave. I will not stand for any more of your insolence and insults. Just for once, couldn't you let me have what I want and be happy for me?''

''This is what you want?'' Paul pointed his thumb toward Gus. ''You really want to be married to a wild Indian, living in a smoky tipi with dogs and kids crawling everywhere, bearing his brats out on the plains without friends and family to comfort you? What about your blasted art academy? You want to throw that away for him? To become an Indian?''

His questions hurt. They were the same ones she had asked herself time and time again over the past months, and her answer then had been no. It wasn't what she wanted, but she refused to back down in front of Paul. She'd show him she could marry Gus and they'd work things out. Just like she'd shown him she could take Nebraska Territory.

''We love each other, and we can make it work. We

will be legally married as soon as we can find someone with the authority to perform the ceremony," she reiterated carefully. Her stomach was paining her again. She needed to lie down.

Paul raised his head to heaven, muttering something unintelligible. "You're a damn fool, Gen, but if you're so set on this bastard, then I've only got one more question before I leave. Where's the twenty thousand dollars in the pantry fit into this mess?"

Gus bolted upright, and the satisfied smirk he'd been wearing for the past several minutes became a worried frown.

"What?" Genny's eyes flew to the pantry door. "Twenty thousand dollars? Where?"

Glancing between his cousin and her lover, Paul began chuckling. "Under the flour barrel. Neatly packed in a pair of saddlebags. Gold and greenbacks. Something tells me, your upstanding husband here might be able to enlighten us as to how it got there."

Genny stared at the pantry door, reliving the August afternoon when she'd discovered Gus walking nonchalantly out that door, stuffing raisins into his mouth. Her stomach cramped as she turned to face him.

"You lied to me! You didn't come back here to see if I was safe. You came back to hide that money. You're a thief and a liar!"

"Oh, Gen," Paul said with cruel delight. "I thought you said you loved him?"

"Shut up!" The pain in her stomach made her wince. Gus jumped to her side.

"Genny?" He took her arm.

Jerking away from him, she sat abruptly on the sofa. "You came here that day to hide that money, didn't you? You couldn't have cared less about me!"

"I did care about you," he insisted.

"I believed you, Gus. I trusted you. Where'd you get the money? It's stolen, isn't it?"

"I didn't steal it. I found it."

Paul snorted. "Probably at the Plum Creek Station atop the Overland Stage Company coach that was attacked by Indians. Eight people died in that attack, Renard. How many of them did you kill?''

Gus charged toward him, but stopped when Genny groaned and doubled over. The color drained from her face, and she broke out in a clammy sweat.

''Genny, what's wrong with you?'' He pivoted back to her, dropping to one knee beside her, his hand on her back.

''My stomach.'' Gus eased her shoulders up and put his hand on her midriff. She shook her head. ''Lower,'' she said. ''It's been hurting since just before we got here.''

Hope and alarm surged through him, and in his excitement he blurted out the first thing that came into his head. ''You're pregnant!'' He closed his eyes and whispered a few words in Lakota that Genny didn't understand.

''I can't be,'' she protested. ''I've been using the herb Good Shield showed me. I can't get pregnant.''

''Oh, yes you can,'' Gus informed her grimly. In for a penny, in for a pound, he thought. He might as well get it all over with at once. ''Before I tell you this or go any further, I want you to know that I never lied about how I feel about you. I love you. Do you believe that?''

''How touching,'' Paul said contemptuously. ''The lying half-breed renegade pledging his eternal devotion to his captive.''

''*Ištatola*, answer me. Do you believe I love you?''

Her eyes filled with tears, and the pain she felt was as much in her heart as her body. She wanted to cry out that she didn't believe anything he'd told her, but that wasn't true. She knew he loved her. Whatever else he'd done, the many nights she'd spent in his arms had demonstrated that without doubt. He felt more than simple lust, much more, and so did she. That had to be why she hurt so much now.

''Yes,'' she whispered.

Gus took a deep breath. ''*Tanke* gave you the wrong herb. You've been drinking mint tea all this time. It wouldn't hinder a baby being conceived.''

"No," Genny groaned. "She wouldn't lie to me. I know your sister. She'd never do that to me."

"I asked her to, Genny. She didn't want to, but I didn't leave her much choice. She was angry with me, but I've been desperate to keep you with me. I thought a child would do it."

Another spasm hit her and she brought her knees up sharply. "How could you, Gus? That isn't love. What about what I wanted? Ahhh!" Her hands curled into fists against the pain.

"We'll talk about this later. Right now you need to get to bed." He scooped her into his arms and levered himself to his feet. "Open the door to her bedroom," he told Paul. They exchanged a malevolent glance.

"I hope she loses your brat," Paul bit out, kicking open the door.

Gus was too concerned about Genny to respond, but he could have killed Conrad for that remark. "Genny, how far along do you think you are?" He didn't think a two-week pregnancy would cause this kind of problem.

"I don't know."

Setting her on the bed, Gus turned to shut the door on Paul. "I don't want you in here. She's upset and she needs calm. If she loses this baby, you can kiss any chance of fathering one of your own goodbye." He closed the door and sat beside her on the mattress. "Are you bleeding?"

She didn't answer, but tears leaked from her closed lids. She didn't struggle when he slid his hand beneath her dress, gently probing between her thighs. Panic seized him when he encountered dampness, but his fingers came away with no blood on them. "There's a discharge, but it isn't bloody," he told her. "Do you know what to do?" He felt helpless, frustrated beyond anything in his experience, and violently angry. Mostly with himself.

"Tell Paul to get Martha," Genny whispered.

Gus jumped up and threw the door open. Conrad had just taken another slug of bourbon and was wiping his mouth on the back of his hand. "She wants you to go get Martha Rivier,'' he said harshly. ''Tell her Genny may be losing a baby. She'll know what to do and what to bring. Hurry. If you care about her at all, hurry.''

Paul looked assessingly at the lines of strain around Renard's mouth. It would be better for Genny if she lost the child. He advanced toward Gus, intending to ask Genny if she really wanted him to go, but the movement of her hand reaching for Gus's stopped him. She twined her fingers in the half-breed's and gripped so hard that her bones stood out white.

''Gus?'' Paul heard her voice, low and thick with pain. ''Hold me, please?''

The Indian looked down at her, his features softening into a bittersweet smile. ''Of course, I will. You'll be all right, *ištatola*. I promise.'' He moved closer to her, casting a final pleading look at Paul.

Paul was not so insensitive that he didn't realize that that look cost Renard. A moment later, a blast of cold air shuddered through the house and the front door slammed.

Chapter 22

Martha Rivier came out of Genny's bedroom and found Gus Renard and Paul Conrad faced off across the kitchen table, palms flat on the oaken surface, chins jutting, and eyes flaming. The air reverberated with the final notes of their argument.

"Be quiet out here!" She marched across the room and yanked a chair around, shoving Gus down into it. She pointed across at Paul. "Sit down!" she commanded with so much authority that he did so immediately. "You two have got to be the sorriest excuses for men in this or any other territory. I ought to have Roger and my Cheyenne cousins teach you a thing or two about how to behave."

Her dark eyes swung back to Gus. "Your wife and *your* cousin," she turned to Paul again, "is ill and trying to rest. Both of you will be quiet and allow her to sleep."

"Why do you say she's his wife?" Paul asked testily.

"If she's carrying his baby, then I assume she's his wife. His relatives wouldn't stand for it any other way. Some people here in the west have high moral standards, Paul Conrad, and you'd do well not to forget it."

"How is she?" Gus interrupted. "Is she losing the baby?"

"She's exhausted and in need of some peace and quiet, but she's not bleeding. The baby is hanging on just fine."

"Then she's definitely expecting," Paul grumbled sourly.

"Yes, she is. I would think you might welcome a little cousin. You have the worst attitude toward family of any man I've ever seen, Paul Conrad, and considering the lowdown, dirty, filthy trail rats that have passed my way, that casts you in a pretty ugly light."

Gus would have seconded her opinion if she hadn't turned on him next. "And you! You irresponsible lover boy! What got into you that made you think you could carry off a white girl and marry her? How many times have I heard you say you'd never go back to that world? Did you think she would live in your sister's village for the rest of her life? You didn't think, Gus Renard. You didn't think at all, except with what God put between your legs." Martha swatted him on the shoulder and sent Paul a fulminating glance. "You two are the most puffed up pair of fools it has been my misfortune to meet!"

There wasn't much to say to that. "Um, how far along is Genny? If she isn't losing the baby, what's wrong with her?" Gus ventured.

Martha's angry expression softened a fraction. "From talking to her, I think she's in her second month. The child probably began growing about the end of September. She said she bled a little at the end of October, but that can happen even after a baby starts. As to what's wrong now, I've heard that riding a long distance can jar a baby loose early on. The trip south came at a bad time for her, especially as tired as she is. It takes a lot of rest and good food to make a healthy baby. Genny is exhausted and too thin. Weren't you feeding her up there?"

"She didn't like the food very well," Gus admitted.

Martha's eyes held silent condemnation before she turned back to Paul. "Paul Conrad, can you hunt worth a darn?"

"Of course I can," he muttered, sick of this day. Everyone was treating him as if he were some sort of villain when he only wanted the best for his cousin.

"Then get out there and find some meat. You've got an hour of daylight left. Genny needs a good strong broth and some fresh meat to help her build her strength. Prepared in some way she likes. Go on.'' She got up and prodded him.

"Fine. It will be a pleasure to get out of this madhouse.'' He grabbed his coat from the stand by the door and fled. This time, under Martha's watchful eye, he shut the door quietly.

"She wants to talk to you,'' Martha told Gus when Paul was gone, "and I don't think she's going to get any sleep until she has, so you'd better get in there. You'd also better say the right things, or you're going to be talking to my cousins.''

As he walked to Genny's door, Gus wondered how seriously to take that threat.

She was lying on her left side, back to him, when he entered her room. Her pose reminded him of the first time he'd seen her sleeping that way, in this very room. Now, like then, she wore a white cambric bedgown, and her hair was spread out across the pillows.

He walked around the bed and did what he'd done that summer morning. Gently, so as not to disturb her, he lowered his tall frame onto the quilt beside her. His weight shifted her toward him and her eyes fluttered open. They held a sorrow and disappointment that cut him to the quick.

"Well, Gus Renard, I always knew you were prone to exaggeration and tall tales, but I never figured you for an out-and-out liar. And not for a serious thief, either. It would appear I was wrong.''

Gus rolled onto his side and slid one hand beneath his ear. "Will you believe anything I tell you?''

"Experience has shown me to be pretty gullible,'' she sighed. "Give it your best shot and I just might. Or, of course, you could always try the truth.''

"Everybody lies sometimes, Genny. I'm not saying it's right, but it happens. Is it past hoping you might be able to forgive me?''

She couldn't begin to answer him. "Not everybody lies in quite the same way. I'm real tired, Gus. Why don't you tell me about the twenty thousand dollars in the pantry?''

"It's the Overland Stage Company's payroll. I didn't steal it, and I wasn't at the Plum Creek Station. I wasn't involved in any of the attacks anywhere along the trail. You of all people have to know that, after what I told you at Rocky Butte."

"Who's to say that wasn't another fine tale?" Her expression betrayed no emotion beyond her fatigue.

The breath ran out of him in a long, slow hiss that gave full vent to the pain her remark caused him. "It hurts to hear you say that, Genny. I've told you lies, but I've also told you more truth than I ever told anyone else. In your heart you know that."

She didn't say anything, and that hurt as much as her question had. Reminding himself that he'd asked for this, that he'd had plenty of opportunity to tell her everything long before now, he forged ahead.

"Anyway, about the payroll. When men started slipping away from camp in small parties, I was curious. I knew something was up, so I went to see what it was. Nobody told me in so many words, because they all knew I wouldn't fight. So I trailed one of the parties south, where I ran into Afraid of Hawk chasing a herd of horses down on the Platte, between the forks and Fort Kearney. He'd run them off from Plum Creek, but they were getting away from him. I stopped them, and when some of the party that attacked the stage station came through, they had the payroll with them. They were going to throw it away, since it was so heavy and they wanted to get away from the river quickly. I traded my share of the captured horses for it."

Despite the conviction that she shouldn't trust a word he said, Genny found herself believing him. Forcing habit aside, she questioned him. "Why? You told me you don't need any money. Or was that because you had the payroll?"

He gave a quick shake of his head. "No, I've got an inheritance from my grandfather, but I'd rather not touch his money. He always said I was a bastard because my parents weren't married in the church, and he preferred my stepbrother over me. My father's second wife's son, who was no blood relation to him. I still don't know why he left so much of his money to me. Indian bastards don't exactly need a lot of cash in their pockets."

He'd never mentioned this stepbrother before, and Genny knew it was because of the unhealed wounds of past rejections. He was no longer at pains to mask his hurts from her, however, as he marshalled all his resources to keep her from shutting him out. She knew there was a lot more that he'd kept to himself than she'd imagined, but she could only tackle one thing at a time, and she wasn't going to be manipulated into feeling sorry for him now. "Go on about the payroll," she said without energy. "Why did you bring it here?"

"I didn't know what to do with it. I couldn't turn it in without getting killed. No Indian was going to walk into a fort and come out alive after the attacks along the trail, much less one carrying a stolen payroll. And truth be told, I didn't much feel like giving it back. The Overland Stage Company has been responsible for a lot of the trouble out here between Indians and whites. Every year there are fewer buffalo, other game is scarce, and the Platte Valley has been razed from one end to the other by too many wagons, too many oxen and mules, and too many white folks. I won't lie about how I feel about this. I don't want to give that money back."

"Why here, Gus? Why my house?" she repeated.

"Because nobody was likely to come here. Most white folks wouldn't have known there was anything here, and most Indians would have kept clear because of what I told you earlier. But part of the honest truth is that I came back because I couldn't stop thinking about you. I figured you'd be gone, but it was a crazy impulse I couldn't ignore. You draw me like no other woman ever has. I've told you before that I wanted you from the minute I saw you. You knew it then, and you know it now. I freely admit I wasn't in love with you or here for any noble purpose. But I love you now, Genny, and I've never lied about how I feel about you."

She didn't say anything for a minute. "You made me

go with you because you were afraid I'd find the pay-roll.'' It wasn't a question.

"Mostly. Are you sorry now I did?"

"What do you think?" she responded bitterly. "You changed the course of my life to protect a bunch of money you didn't particularly want or need, just to keep it out of the hands of its rightful owners. That doesn't sound like the Gus Renard I thought I loved."

The stark lines around her mouth deepened and her lower lip trembled. Frustration, hurt, and disappointment charged the air between them, making reconciliation an unlikely outcome of their conversation. Gus gave in to his hopelessness and struck back at her. "Who did you fall in love with then? The bastard who forced you from your home and seduced you? The man who thrust a gun into your hands and had you kill a man? The man who stood beside you and shot seven men dead in the space of minutes? Or was it the man who thoughtlessly left you alone to fend as best you could with people you couldn't even talk to after having done all those other things to you? I don't know why you're surprised by a few lies. It seems pretty consistent with my character. If you could love me after everything else that I've put you through, why can't you now?"

"I didn't say I couldn't! But this hurts, Gus. A great deal. You hurt me."

"And you haven't hurt me? Do you think it pleases me to find that the woman I love and would have as my wife won't marry me of her own free will, but will sign a marriage paper in a minute to spite the cousin she claims to detest? Do you think it doesn't rip my guts out every time I remember hearing you finally say you loved me, only to add a few seconds later that you wouldn't stay with me? You're not the only one who's hurting!"

Genny closed her eyes and turned onto her back, one arm thrown up to shield her eyes. He watched the muscles in her throat move as she swallowed hard.

"There's the baby, Gus. That hurts the most. You tricked me. It was worse than a lie. Can you tell me what's going to happen to this child? You've been playing with people's lives. Mine and our child's.''

Remorse made him back off. "I know. Do you think I don't? Your cousin was right. I'm a liar and I manipulated my sister and you to get what I wanted." The anger surged in him again, mingling like acid with his guilt. Didn't she see what they would be losing if they weren't together? "But not only did I want it, I think it's the best thing for both of us to be together as a family. We need each other. We love each other. I don't think I can let you go. Do you understand how much you mean to me? Do you have any idea of the peace I've found in your arms? And just like so many things in the past, I'm going to lose you because I can't live at peace in either of my parents' worlds!" The desperation in his voice unnerved them both, but he couldn't stop. "I won't accept that this time. I'll take whatever terms I can get from you, Genny. I want you, and I want our child. Do you or do you not want to marry me?''

"No, damn you! I don't! Not now!"

He caught her hands, clutching them when she tried to slap free. "You don't mean that!"

She tried to sit up, but he leaned into her, holding her prone, and the chaotic energy of his emotions flowed over her in a swirling torrent. "I do mean it, but I don't have any choice any more. A child needs its father's name, so I'll marry you as soon as possible. What I'll do then, I can't say, and if you've any sense at all, you won't push me into making any decisions now.''

"Are you saying you'd leave me? With a child coming?" Stricken, he hadn't thought she could.

"I don't know anymore, Gus. I wouldn't have before. But if you can't be a husband and father who puts his wife's and children's wishes and needs on at least an equal footing with your own, I don't know. What I've learned today confirms doubts I've had for a long time. You've never given much consideration to what was best for me. A marriage has to be based on more than the feelings and the desire we've shared. It has to include mutual trust and respect and right now, I can't give you that, and I don't think you've given it to me.''

He lowered his head, pressing their joined hands to his brow. "Genny, we can make things work if we've come this far. We can. We can learn those things."

"You keep saying we can work things out, but all I see is you trying to force me to accept a life that frightens me. I know what *you* want, Gus. You've made it more than clear. But what about the life that *I* want? What about the things that are important to me? What's happening between us is what I always feared in marriage. My dreams, my plans, and the things I care about are shunted aside by a man who loves me, but who doesn't honor the very things that make me who I am." A sudden stab of pain brought her elbows close to her sides and stiffened her jaw. She gripped Gus's hands and a small moan broke from her.

"Take it easy, *istatola*," Gus breathed, his own gut twisting with a different kind of pain. There was a great deal of truth in what she said, but he felt helpless in the face of his suffocating need for her. With an act of conscious will, he released her hands and smoothed the hair back off her face. She needed to recover her strength, and he wasn't helping. "I don't think there's anything more either of us can say without making things worse right now. You need to rest. Do you want me to get Martha to sit with you for a while?"

She nodded, and he rose to leave. At the door, he paused. He wanted to tell her again that he loved her, but the words stuck in his throat. This time, words were not enough.

Genny slept nearly twenty hours straight, and Martha Rivier insisted that she be moved away from White Rock Spring as soon as she was able to travel.

"It's a bad place. Your cousin can stay here to keep an eye on things if he wants to, but you shouldn't be alone until you get your strength back," she said as she helped Genny pack a carpetbag. "A place where so many warriors met their deaths is a bad place to grow a child. You'll be better off at the ranch."

Roger Rivier brought a wagon to get her, and by late

afternoon of her second day back, Genny was riding out of the hills that sheltered her house, sitting next to Martha in the back of the spring wagon. She and Gus had left Paul and the payroll at the house, threatening him with all manner of horrors if he touched it. They had agreed to deal with it when Genny was better. They decided among the three of them that the fewer people who knew about the money the better, so they said nothing to the Riviers.

Gus, on Harv, rode ahead of the wagon leading Wicanpila, as they came in sight of the Riviers' adobe house and store.

"I see you got rid of that crazy horse," Martha observed. "Where did you get this one? She's a pretty thing. She looks every bit as smart as Trixie was, but a lot better mannered."

"Gus gave her to me," Genny answered, her eyes on his back. He was wearing a familiar navy blue shirt upon which Good Shield had stitched the beading that decorated each sleeve. She herself was dressed in her own clothes again, a forest green skirt and a beige and white striped blouse. She wore drawers and stockings again, and the feel of the soft fabrics against her skin was heavenly.

"The mare was a good gift. What did you give him in return?"

She'd never really given him anything. He'd simply taken whatever he wanted. "He got Trixie and my Spencer repeater." And me, she thought gloomily.

Martha smiled faintly. "I've been watching Gus. I think he'll settle down to make a good husband, Genny Stone. He'll take good care of you."

Genny glanced at her in surprise. She'd heard Martha rake Gus over the coals more than once in the past two days, and none too gently.

"He's changing. Growing up finally. Don't make hasty decisions about him," the mixed-blood woman continued thoughtfully. "He's been struggling for a long time, and it's worn him out. He has to find some peace within himself soon. You and this baby the two of you've made can help him.''

"What about my peace?'' Genny asked disconsolately. "What about the struggles he's put me through?''

"They're different struggles. Hasn't he already shown you what it feels like to have a man who cares what happens to you? To have a man protect you and keep you safe instead of throwing you in harm's way like that worthless cousin of yours has done? Men and women bring each other different gifts, Genny Stone. Your needs and Gus Renard's are not the same, but maybe you can help each other.''

"Gus's lies and scheming behind my back give me nothing of value.''

Martha didn't argue. Instead, she pointed out a rider approaching the ranch from the west. "That man must have some big news. He's going to land in the river if he doesn't slow down.''

In a few minutes, Roger had pulled the wagon up to the porch and set the handbrake. Stepping over the buckboard seat, he helped Martha down and stooped to lift Genny.

"I'm not helpless,'' she protested.

"You husband told me not to take any chances,'' Roger said, carrying her to the end of the wagon. Gus was there, lowering the tailgate, and ready to take Genny into his own arms.

"I can walk,'' she said as she was passed from one man to the other. It was funny how much more comfortable Gus's embrace was, how much warmer he seemed, and how her body fit so well against him.

"I know you can,'' he responded easily, carrying her up the steps. "Do you want me to put you down?''

"Yes.'' He lowered her feet to the floor, but his hand lingered on her back. "Thank you,'' she said, searching his eyes.

"Looks like Winslow Carr.'' Roger stood beside the wagon, squinting into the sun. "Must be important news to bring him all the way out here. Last I heard he was up at Fort Laramie.''

A small man dressed in dust-drab brown careened into the yard on a horse the same color. Almost before the horse had stopped beside the corral he was off, flipping the reins around a fence post and stumbling toward the house at a bowlegged trot. The Riviers' hired men and a few pilgrims who'd been stranded there until they could get a big enough party together to continue their journeys hustled over behind him.

"Hey, Roger," the man said, extending his hand and slapping his hat against his thigh, sending up a cloud of dust. Small and wiry, he was as bald as a baby's behind, while the lower half of his face was all but lost behind a stiff growth of gray and brown beard. "Wire in from the east yesterday at Julesburg says Lincoln got hisself reelected President."

A cheer went up from the men, along with several shouted questions. "That ain't all, folks," the messenger hollered above them. "General William T. Sherman has swung loose into the Confederacy! The heart of Georgia's burning, from Atlanta toward the sea! The war's got to be over soon. Now all we got to do is let these damned Injuns out here know who's boss, and the U. S. of A. and her territories will be united and at peace at last!"

More cheers greeted these announcements, but they died out into self-conscious silence. Neither Gus nor Martha reacted visibly to the last statement, both of them standing very still, their faces blank. Genny moved a little closer to Gus, but his hand dropped away from her back.

"Winslow, your tongue runs like thin syrup on a hot day," Roger said mildly. "You've got my thanks for bringing the election results and the war news, but kindly keep your opinions about the Indians to yourself in front of my wife. She's a lady, and she don't need to hear you threatening one half of her relations when you're about to partake of her hospitality."

"Sorry," Winslow muttered. "I see ya gots some more Abrigoins camped out by the river west of here, too. And another one on your porch." He nodded up at Gus with a grin that was at odds with his comments.

"Hey, isn't that Gus Renard? How you doing, Gus? I ain't seen you since last winter in Fort Kearney! Whooeee! That was a time! Whatever happened to that little gal you was spoonin' with? What was her name? Maybeth or Maybelle or something on that order?"

Winslow and the men seemed oblivious to the tension in the air. Martha moved to her husband's side, and Genny pursed her lips quickly before schooling her features into a mask of composure. "Well, boy, what happened to her? Did you ever talk her into . . . oh. Sorry, ma'am." Finally spying Genny, he put his hat on and took it off again. "I didn't see you there, right away, for the shadows. Roger's got a point there. I do tend to let my mouth run off a bit. My name's Winslow Carr. Pleased to make your acquaintance."

He stepped up onto the porch to get a better look at Genny. "Whoo! You're a pretty little gal, ain't ya? If you don't mind my asking, what's a fine lady like yourself doing out here in the middle of a country even the Almighty's forgot about?" He looked back at Gus, speculation arching furrows across his wide brow. "She's not another one of your fancy ladies, is she, Gus?"

"Winslow, you better watch what you say about my wife," Gus bit out.

The man's eyes nearly shot out of their sockets, and an audible gasp went up from some of the men behind Martha and Roger.

"Your wife, did you say?" Winslow croaked, his voice an octave and a half higher than it had been.

"That's what I said. And I'd be glad to accept your congratulations."

The man's adam's apple bobbed through several swallows before he found his voice again. "Congratulations, Gus. Mrs. Renard, I wish you all the best."

Hearing herself addressed as Mrs. Renard brought the blood rushing to Genny's face. In the Lakota camp she'd been considered Gus's wife, but her name had always been her own, and the designation "wife" had had little real meaning for her. In her heart, she'd never really thought of herself as his wife, with all the social implications that word carried. Being called Mrs. Renard by a man who was clearly startled by their relationship brought home to her the magnitude of what it meant to be married to Gus in her world.

"I'm pleased to meet you, Mr. Carr," she managed to respond. Her hand settled lightly on Gus's sleeve. "I need to lie down, Gus. Now."

"You'll excuse us, Winslow. Genny's expecting and she's real tired." His eyes scanned the angry faces on the other side of the wagon before coming back to rest on Genny. Rivier's men were impassive, but the visitors were openly hostile. He didn't miss that more of those men were glaring at Genny than at him. Glancing back to gage her reaction, hope slithered out of him as he watched her dawning realization of what they faced.

He feared she'd marry him for the sake of their child, but she was never going to stay with him. Taking her elbow and steering her inside, he didn't know how he was going to stop her.

Paul turned up at Rivier's the next morning shortly after breakfast, swaggering through the store to help himself to a cup of coffee from the blue enamel pot Martha kept on the stove. Genny was sitting in a rocking chair behind the counter, wrapped in a wool shawl, keeping Martha company while she unpacked several barrels worth of dry goods that had arrived the week before.

"I see those pilgrims who adopted you folks last month have finally broken camp. Word come through that parties that size are safe?" Paul asked, reaching into the cracker barrel.

Martha kicked the lid down from her perch on the ladder, nearly catching Paul's fingers. He escaped with only one cracker. "Winslow Carr brought word that Mr. Lincoln's been reelected and Sherman is destroying Georgia."

"Hey! That's news for celebration! Why aren't we having a party?"

Martha scowled down at him, and Genny leaned her head back and closed her eyes. Footsteps on the porch precluded any answer. A moment later a narrow shadow filled the door.

"Mornin', Mrs. Rivier." The speaker was one of the pilgrims, a gangly, sunburned woman in a faded yellow gingham dress.

"Hello, Mrs. Holdrege," Martha replied without turning.

"You folks heading out this morning?" Paul asked. The woman nodded. "Why? Speaking boldly, ma'am, that's not a wise course."

"The Bolger party's leavin' 'cause there's gettin' to be too many Indians in these parts. My husband decided to go on with them. It don't hardly seem safe here anymore. Mrs. Rivier, might you have any milk I could purchase to take with us for my baby?"

"Cow belongs to her," Paul said, slurping coffee and nodding toward Genny.

Mrs. Holdrege looked worn and tired, beaten dry by the wind and the rigors of a journey Genny doubted she had wanted to make. Martha had told her yesterday that the Bolger party was from Illinois, but the Holdreges were secesh folks from Missouri who'd been caught too many times between Union and Confederate raiders.

"Take what you want," Martha said, after Genny's quick nod. "Milk's in the springhouse, where it always is."

The woman stared at Genny. "You the one with the Sioux buck for a man?"

"My husband is Canadian and Lakota," Genny said tightly.

"Lakota means Sioux," Paul supplied, making sure there was no ambiguity.

Mrs. Holdrege's washed out features grew harsh and condemning. "I reckon I don't need that milk so bad. The boy's strong. Sorry to bother you, Mrs. Rivier." She turned back to Martha. "Don't think I think any less of you bein' a half-breed and marryin' a white man. I can understand tryin' to better yourself. But I'll never understand a white woman lettin' a man that dark touch her. It simply ain't right. Good morning to you, Mrs.

Rivier, sir.'' She walked out, the heavy soles of her boots echoing on the porch.

"Bitch." Martha didn't bother to look after her. "She isn't good enough for the dogs in my mother's camp."

Genny wrapped the shawl around herself tighter. Paul walked over to her, tilting the chair forward with one foot on the rocker. "How do you like your first taste of being known as that half-breed's wife?" His smile wasn't pleasant. "I wouldn't let him make an honest woman of you, if I were you, Gen. You'll spend the rest of your life regretting it."

Genny pushed out of the rocker and walked across the room. She'd reached the porch steps before she realized she wasn't wearing shoes. Leaning her forehead against one of the porch supports, she watched the pilgrims packing their wagons to leave.

Paul's boots clomped resonantly on the wooden floor as he followed her, and she raised her chin. He stopped just behind her, close enough for her to smell the coffee in his cup.

"Leave me alone," Genny said flatly.

"That's my intention," Paul told her. "Now that I know you're as safe as you're reasonably going to be, I've got to get back to work. I left a train to Denver at the forks, and if I hurry, I can catch them before my foreman sells all my goods out from under me. I stopped by to tell you I'm leaving that payroll where it is, and I expect it to be there when I get back. It's not right to keep money that belongs to honest businessmen. It's hard enough to make a venture fly out here as it is, and the overland Stage Company has done a lot to open the west to settlement. If you and that fool lover boy of yours don't return that money, I will. Probably save his hide by doing it, too, although why I'd want to do that has got me stumped."

"Then you won't say anything about it?" Genny was surprised.

"Nope. I won't turn that bastard in. Not while he can still give your brat a name. If you're smart, though, Gen, you'll get a marriage paper signed and filed, and then you'll turn your back on Gus Renard and go home to Philadelphia. You'll have proof of a wedding and you can establish yourself as a widow and still have your damned art academy. Nobody has to know Renard's a half-breed. The kid'll only be a quarter Sioux, and you can get by claiming his daddy was one of those dark French Canadians. There's lots of them out here, and it's not even a full-blown lie.''

It galled Genny to hear her cousin outline almost to the letter what she considered one of her best options. ''How'd you find that payroll, anyway, Paul?''

He tossed the grounds in his cup out into the dirt and grinned. ''I stashed a little cache of twelve-year-old bourbon where I figured even the most venturesome intruder wouldn't find it. Seems your handsome half-breed and I think along similar lines, Gen. There might be a telling lesson in that observation. You make of it what you will.''

He handed her his cup and clumped down the stairs, heading for his horse. ''See you in a month or so. If you're still here.'' Tipping his hat, he mounted and ambled off across the yard.

Chapter 23

Two days later, Genny stood with Martha on the porch again watching Gus and Roger Rivier ride away. The sun was barely peeping over the horizon, and the men disappeared quickly into the trees near the ford over the North Platte. They were on their way to find the nearest operating telegraph station to wire up and down the Platte in search of a preacher who could be convinced to brave hostile Indians to come to Rivier's Ranch to perform a marriage. Gus was willing to pay any legitimate man of the cloth the handsome sum of five hundred dollars for the wedding. He and Roger would go get the preacher, make sure he arrived safely, and give him a personal escort on to anywhere he'd care to go afterwards.

Gus and Genny were both grimly determined to make their union legal before the eyes of God and man, though neither was sure what sort of a marriage would ensue. As usual, Gus had hopes things would work out. Genny could see that he did, and she knew he wouldn't be Gus if he didn't. For all the tension between them, he still spoke of their future, of names for the baby, and of how pleased his sister was going to be. For herself, Genny was still exhausted and unable to think much beyond her disappointments with Gus and the moment at hand. She was relieved Martha had stoutly refused to let her travel, and she was looking forward to the time away from Gus to do some thinking. She'd be protected, by Roger's hired

315

men, a pair of hardened frontiersmen who couldn't have cared less about such trivial social breaches as mixed marriages, and also by Walks In Thunder, Bad Arrow, and Afraid of Hawk. So all Genny planned to worry about for the next week at least was regaining her strength.

Martha had other ideas, and it didn't take Genny long to figure that out. Before the dust from Gus and Roger's horses had settled, Genny found herself the object of one of Martha's dark, assessing looks.

"What?" Genny asked defensively.

"You didn't kiss him goodbye," Martha accused.

"I let him kiss me." She had allowed him a perfunctory peck on the mouth. No more.

"That's not the same. I saw the hurt in his eyes, Genny Stone. It was as plain as spots on a pinto."

"It's not as if he hasn't hurt me," Genny retorted bitterly.

"No. It goes both ways with a man and a woman. But how will you feel if Gus doesn't come back?"

Genny's eyes flew to Martha's face. "What do you mean?"

"These are dangerous times. What if he doesn't come back to you alive?"

Genny paled. She thought of Gus as invincible to the dangers that felled ordinary men. It had never occurred to her that anything could happen to him on this errand.

Martha marched into the store, returning moments later with a chair and a steaming mug of herb tea. She plunked the chair down and thrust the tea at Genny. "You sit out here and think about how you'd feel if something happened to Gus after that lukewarm farewell you just gave him. I've got work to do."

Genny sat, but she didn't have to think long. No matter how angry and disappointed she was with Gus, she knew she would be devastated if anything happened to him. Not merely upset. Life without him would be a torment.

At noon Martha rang the dinner bell that swung from one end of the porch. Fitz Ruby and Sid Enders, the

Riviers' hired men, and Gus's Lakota relatives made a beeline for Martha's kitchen, barely stopping to wash their hands at the trough beside the corral. The men had all been hanging around the corral for a couple of hours, watching Fitz work a new horse. Genny had watched them until she'd come inside to help with dinner. She was scooping mashed potatoes into a serving bowl when they trooped into the kitchen.

"Smells good, Martha," Sid said, inhaling the aroma of frying antelope steaks.

"Smells good, Martha," Walks In Thunder repeated, grinning.

Bad Arrow chuckled and cuffed his brother-in-law on the shoulder. "Smells good. *Waśte*," he repeated, trying out the phrase himself. "*Hankasi*," he said, acknowledging Genny, calling her cousin.

She nodded to Gus's cousins as she carried the potatoes to the table.

"Everyone take a seat," Martha ordered, repeating herself in Lakota.

As the chairs scraped back over the planks floor and the men settled down, Genny set the potatoes next to Walks In Thunder. "I didn't know you spoke Lakota," she said to Martha.

"I have to speak to my customers."

"Ain't been too many folks through these parts lately. Less than usual. These folks here's the first Lakotas we've seen in near on a month," Sid said, helping himself to coffee.

"Hey, don't put too much food down next to Walks In Thunder," Fitz interrupted when Martha set the platter of steaks on the other side of him.

Afraid of Hawk was also looking on with concern as the big warrior began loading his plate. "He eat everything," the younger man warned in slow syllables.

Laughter erupted when Walks In Thunder glanced up in baffled innocence. It was a look Genny had seen a number of times before under similar teasing circumstances, though usually it was Gus who ribbed his cousin about eating so much. She wondered where he and Roger were that evening.

The meal got underway amidst a comfortable clatter of spoons and forks against tin plates and an occasional comment. Whether it was offered in English or Lakota, everybody seemed to understand, and by the time Martha was passing out heaping bowls of molasses pudding, Genny had realized that there were times when whites and Indians managed just fine together. Meeting Martha's knowing gaze, she also knew her friend wasn't going to let her forget it.

In the next few days, Martha lost no opportunity to point out to Genny the degree to which Indians and whites could cooperate if they chose to do so. Genny found herself regaled with endless stories of white and Indian marriages that had transcended the boundaries of very different ways of life. Finally, after one particularly touching tale about a white guide's sorrow on learning of the death of his Indian wife, Genny couldn't stand any more.

"What about all the Indian women who were left alone to bring up children fathered by white husbands who decided to return to the east?" she snapped. "It doesn't always work, does it?" The women sat in the kitchen near the stove. The afternoon had turned cool, and the warmth was welcome.

Martha looked down at the shirt she was mending. "No, of course it doesn't. Many things can happen. Gus's mother died. My father's family came between him and my mother, and in the end he valued his career more than his wife and daughter. All I'm trying to tell you is that it doesn't always go wrong, either."

"None of the stories you've told me involved a white woman with an Indian man," Genny pointed out.

"There haven't been very many white women out here. And not many white women would want to live in an Indian camp."

"That's what Gus wants me to do. It's what his father did, and he wants me to do the same." Genny pushed the rocker into motion with her foot, then folded her hands over her stomach. It was hard to believe there was a baby growing inside her. Gus's baby.

Martha looked up, noticing Genny's protective gesture. "I think it's sometimes easier for men to make that kind of change. Especially if they're the wild sort, and by all accounts, René Renard was a very wild young man."

"I can't do it, Martha. I can't live as an Indian for the rest of my life. Gus's sister and her family were wonderful. People were far kinder to me than I ever expected, but it wasn't home. It was too different. If I wasn't with Gus I felt lost and isolated. I can't stay there, and Gus doesn't want to live in Philadelphia. I don't blame him, and I wouldn't ask him to."

Martha tied a knot as she finished stitching and bit off the thread, glancing at Genny impatiently. "Genny Stone, I've been trying to tell you that you have other choices besides living in Gus's Lakota camp or in your fancy house in Philadelphia. The west is going to be settled, no matter how many times our Cheyenne and Lakota relatives fight the soldiers and try to stop the wagons. Think, Genny. This war must end soon, and thousands more families will come pouring into Indian lands. Life here is changing. What do you think would happen if they put a railroad line through the Platte Valley? Roger says it's coming, probably within a few years.

"Nothing will be the same when that happens. There will be people, towns, churches, schools, and farms. Indians and white people are going to be together more than ever. There will have to be place for everyone. It won't be so unusual for a white woman to be married to a red man. Besides, Gus is half white. He's smart and he's educated, and he'll manage very well for himself, no matter what happens. If you stay with him, he'll take care of you and your child, and he'll protect you as much as he can from ignorant fools like Mary Holdrege."

Genny looked out the window. The sun was low in the sky and the light cast rich, golden tones on the November landscape, softening the barren hills. The air seemed to vibrate with the light, an effect Genny had noticed before. For a second, it was beautiful, but as she watched, the sun slipped below the horizon in the west and the warmth faded. Only the cold late autumn twilight lingered. "Why are you trying to talk me into staying with him?" she asked.

Martha put the shirt aside and picked up a torn petticoat. She stitched quietly for several seconds before answering. "Because you love him. Because he loves you. Because this country is going to need strong people like you and Gus who can serve as bridges between Indians in whites in the communities that are going to come." She smiled faintly. "Because I'm a silly woman who read too many smuggled novels in that convent school in St. Louis. I want to see a happy ending for you, Genny Stone."

"I don't see how," Genny sighed. "There have been too many lies."

Martha looked up sharply. "Do you think you're the first woman to be disappointed when she discovers the man she loves isn't perfect?"

"I never thought he was perfect," Genny insisted. "Far from it."

"Only because Gus is more open about his flaws than most. Consider that a blessing. You know what you're dealing with. With a face like his, do you think he has to display any finer qualities to get a woman? He could be the devil himself and one woman in a hundred wouldn't turn him down. Has he ever pretended to be anything other than what he is?"

"Not really."

"You knew what he was like from the first time you saw him. I shouldn't have to remind you that there a lot of men who are a lot less honest, both with themselves and with others. Genny Stone, you aren't going to find a man alive who won't disappoint you."

"Then I'd rather be alone."

"Would you? Would you rather raise your child alone and never share a smile with Gus as you watch your baby sleeping? Would you never miss sharing the joys of that child with its father? Would you never feel the comfort of your husband's arms again? Is that what you truly want?''

Vivid pictures flitted through Genny's mind at Martha's words, and she couldn't answer through the knot in her throat. Martha seemed to take that as a reply in itself.

"I didn't think so," she said. "You want the love and the sharing, Genny Stone."

"But I don't want the heartache," Genny choked.

Martha smiled gently. "Who does? It's all part of the same. Life doesn't come without death. Joy doesn't come without sorrow. Trite words, Genny, but true ones, and we make the best of life we can." She set the petticoat aside and rose to check the stew simmering on the stove. "If you love Gus, you'll find a way through the heartaches, but you'll never banish them. Ten years with Roger has taught me a few things."

"Has it been very hard to love him?"

Martha looked pensively over her shoulder at Genny. "Sometimes. But it's been worth it. I've seen a lot of men, both Indian and white, who aren't worth the trouble to love, but Roger is. Gus will prove worthy, too." She looked back into the stewpot. "That's enough of this talk for now. Supper's almost ready."

"Martha? Can I ask you a personal question?"

Martha replaced the lid on the stew and came to sit next to Genny. "After listening to all my advice, I think you've earned that right."

"Why haven't you ever had children?"

The older woman smiled, but a sudden tear slid from the corner of her eye. It came so fast, and Martha wiped it away so quickly with the base of her thumb that Genny hardly believed she'd seen it.

"That's been one of my disappointments, Genny. I lost a baby the first year Roger and I were married. A little further along than you are now. The spring after that, Roger took sick with a bad fever. I thought I was going to lose him, too. He was so sick for so long. We were lucky he's a strong man, and he was young. After many months he got better. But I never got pregnant again.''

"Did you want children?'' Genny asked softly.

"Very much, Genny Stone. I still do.''

"I'm sorry.''

Martha nodded. "Yes. So am I. My husband can't give me a baby, and there's nothing I can do about that particular heartache. You're lucky, though. You still have some choices. Hard choices, but choices nonetheless. Make the best of them while you may, for you never know when they'll be taken out of your hands.''

Genny tipped backwards in the rocker, watching Martha's dark eyes fade as she dwelt momentarily in the past. Outside the window, dusk lay deepening on the hills, bringing with it the dark chill of night, but in Genny's breast, the faint light of hope flickered into life. The love she and Gus shared was strong, despite the hurts and difficulties. Perhaps it was strong enough to enable her to face the challenges of a real marriage.

A small herd of pronghorn antelope grazed unconcerned as three riders galloped west from Blue Water Creek along the North Platte River. It had snowed in the past week, but the morning was warming up and the trail was clear, with no sign of other riders anywhere. Gus was tired and apprehensive, anxious to get back to Rivier's ranch and see Genny, but also dreading it. A scowl fierce enough to scare a bear from a honeycomb tightened his mouth when he thought about her reaction to learning about the payroll and discovering she was carrying his child.

Ahead of him, Roger and the Reverend Tobias Alton were slowing down, forcing him to ease Harv into a trot.

"What are we stopping for now?'' he bellowed, eyeing the minister with undisguised ire.

"Call of nature!'' Alton trilled. As soon as his mount was still, the young man slithered from the saddle, landing in a heap when his feet tangled with a yucca half buried in snow.

Gus and Roger watched as he jumped up, brushing

himself off as he ran a good distance from them.

"Do you suppose the Almighty gave that boy equipment we ain't seen before?" Roger muttered in a bored tone. "I swear the Reverend has to piss more than any man I ever met, and he's got to go further to do it than seems natural."

"Are you sure he's old enough to be a minister?" Gus asked for the hundredth time since he and Roger had picked Alton up at the trading post at Doby Town outside of Fort Kearney. He'd been stuck there for a month waiting for a party of a hundred or more westward-bound pilgrims to gather. "He doesn't look more than twenty. He doesn't even need a razor, for Christ's sake."

"Neither do you," Roger pointed out with a grin.

Gus straightened his shoulders and rolled his head on his neck, not deigning to respond. His muscles ached with cold and the long days on horseback, and he would appreciate a hot bath before his wedding. That was all he planned to wait for. "What do you think those Flatheads are going to think of their new missionary? Who sends these people out here, anyway?"

"You ought to just be glad somebody sent this runt. I can't believe you found a preacher who was willing to come with us," Roger replied. "What's the date, anyway? December first? We've been gone nearly two weeks."

They watched the gangly minister fasten his trousers and stumble back toward them. When he reached his horse, his oversized slouch hat slipped down over his eyes and his foot missed the stirrup. The horse shied away as he stomped awkwardly beside it.

Gus drummed his fingers while Alton calmed the animal. When he was finally mounted again, Gus caught up to him.

"If I was you, Reverend," he said, putting undue emphasis on the young man's title, "I'd try real hard to hold it from here on out. I'm in kind of a hurry, and every time you think you need to relieve your bladder, I want you to think about how many blankets and bags

of flour twenty-five dollars could buy for your mission
out there in Montana territory.''

"Quite a lot, Mr. Renard,'' Alton said with irritating
enthusiasm. ''But why should I do that?''

"Because that's what you're going to lose off the five
hundred dollars I'm paying you every time we stop.''
He urged Harv forward, leaving a surprised Reverend
Alton in his wake.

"They're back! Genny Stone, Roger, and Gus are
back, and they've got a preacher with them!''

Martha's voice carried up the stairs to the second story,
where Genny was making the bed in one of the ranch's
guestrooms. Her stomach fluttered and her hands grew
suddenly cold. Dear Lord, today was likely going to be
her wedding day! She sat down in the middle of the
freshly made bed and pressed her hands into the mattress.

Martha burst through the doorway. Her eyes were shin-
ing and her black hair was mussed from the wind outside.
"Come on!'' She reached out to Genny. ''Come downstairs to greet your husband.''

Genny took Martha's hand and rose. ''I'm scared,
Martha.''

"Gus probably is, too. You have to face this together,
so let's get you out there.'' She squeezed Genny's hand.

Genny followed the other woman down the stairs and
through the store onto the porch. Images flashed through
her head as she went: Gus holding her at gunpoint after
blasting a hole in her wall; Gus pushing her into a slimy
lake, with a towering hailstorm hurling bolts of deadly
lightning and jagged ice at them; a Pawnee warrior's
knife slicing into his arm; a rocky butte and a file of
enemy warriors passing below, and later, those same
warriors lying motionless after violent death. Both she
and Gus had been afraid, but he'd brought them through.
He'd shown courage and commitment, and she had relied
on him. He hadn't let her down. Would he now?

The three men had left their horses with Fitz at the
corral and were walking across the yard, but Genny had
eyes only for Gus. Dust covered him from head to foot,

dimming the bright colors of the beading on the seams of his britches and turning his once white blanket coat a dingy brown. His saddlebags were slung over one shoulder, and his slightly bowlegged gait was testamony to many hard days of riding.

Halfway across the yard he looked up and saw her, and his footsteps faltered. He stopped, his eyes riveted on her face.

Roger and the third man, whom Genny scarcely noticed, continued on toward the house. Vaguely, Genny was aware that Martha had thrown herself into Roger's arms, and that introductions were being performed. Another memory gripped her as she and Gus regarded one another. In her mind, she pictured the evening she had stood beside him in his camp for the first time, uncertain and needing his reassurance.

To get it, she'd had to give.

If she wanted a real marriage with this man, she was certain she was going to have to give a great deal more than she had that night. A smile had been all it had taken then. Even so, the price of that small smile had been the growing realization of how deep the bond between them had become. The stakes were much higher now.

Breathing deeply, she tried to sort out her feelings. Yes, there was still the fear that their differences were too many. But stronger than her fears, the longing to live in peace with him overcame her. Where, she couldn't begin to answer. All she knew was that more than anything else, she wanted to run to him, to take him in her arms and be taken in his.

The first step off the porch was the hardest, but when she moved toward him, Gus's face lit with a smile sweeter than a baby's kiss, and her feet took wing. His saddlebags landed with a thud in the dust, and he knocked his hat back off his head, spreading his arms wide.

Genny flung herself into his embrace so hard he stumbled backwards a step. Wrapping her arms around his neck, she buried her face in his shoulder, and his arms closed around her tightly. He smelled like dust and horses and the west wind. He was solid, strong, and familiar. His arms felt like home.

A rumble started in his chest as he chuckled with relief into her ear. "Don't I get a kiss?" he whispered. "A real one?"

She raised her head and took his face in her hands, her eyes roving over him. He looked wonderful. His brown eyes glowed and his mouth curved upwards in a gentle smile. If there was fine dirt in the creases on his cheeks and chin, and if his hair hung limp and flat, she didn't care.

"Yes, you get a real kiss." Leaning up on her tiptoes, she pressed her mouth to his. His face was warm and salty, his nose and cheeks cold from the November winds. She plied his mouth with her tongue, rediscovering the taste and textures of him.

One of his hands came up to cradle her head, his fingers sinking into her hair, and he pulled her even closer to him. He accepted her kiss, but it wasn't long before he thrust his tongue against hers in loving reciprocity.

"Hey!" Roger's thundering voice penetrated Genny's numbing senses. "What do you two think you're doing out there, going at it in the middle of the yard like that? We got a minister of God standing right here watching you, for Christ's sake. Where's your manners?"

They broke apart slowly and looked over at the house. Roger, Martha, and a skinny boy stood watching them from the porch.

"That's the minister?" Genny regarded the young man doubtfully.

"He's got a paper that says he's an ordained Lutheran minister," he answered as if he didn't find it any more credible than she did. He raised his voice and hollered back at Roger. "I don't give a damn what that baby-faced preacher thinks as long as he gets us married within the hour." He looked back down at Genny. "Are we still getting married?" he asked a lot more quietly.

She nodded. "Yes, we are. I keep my word."

"What about after the wedding?"

She stooped to pick up one of his saddlebags. "I

thought about that a lot while you were gone. It won't be easy, Gus, and I'd be lying if I said I wasn't scared. But I'd like to try to work things out."

Gus caught her free hand and carried it to his chest, covering it with his own. His breath came fast, and she felt his heart pounding underneath her palm. "You're sure? Are you going to be able to look beyond all the rotten things I've done to you? You can accept me with all my flaws?"

"If you can accept me with all of mine, I'm willing to try. You may not have noticed, but I can be a little inflexible and self-righteous at times."

Gus grinned. "Not to mention proud and impetuous."

"Please note that I'm not listing your shortcomings right now."

"We've been over that ground too often for me to forget, I think."

She ran her hand up inside his coat and hooked her fingers into the scarf he wore around his neck "We'd both have to work at this. Neither of us is exactly prize marriage material."

He nodded firmly. "I'm willing to work. I've said that all along."

"I know that." She looked at the ground.

"But you still have doubts."

"Yes. I have doubts. Especially about how the two of us can live in, or between, or alongside of both of our worlds. I'm not an Indian, and I never will be. I don't want to live in an Indian camp. That hasn't changed."

Gus looped his arms around her shoulders and blew a long sigh. "I don't know what to say, *istatola*. I did a lot of thinking as well, and while I'd like to think we can work this out, I know it may be rough." He paused, tilting her head up so that he could see her eyes. "I know I love you. I want you. But I don't want you to be unhappy. I was wrong to try to hold you to me with the baby, and I'm sorry. I'm just so damned scared we weren't going to be together." Emotion glittered in his eyes, and he took a deep breath. "If . . . if the differences are too big for us to make it, at least we'll have tried, and if it comes to you leaving me some time in the future, I'll understand that it isn't because you don't love me. Or that I don't love you. I'll do my best to look out for what you want, Genny. I'll try to respect who you are and the differences between us. That's the best promise I can give you about the future, and I wish it could be more.''

She laid her a hand along his jaw, running her thumb over the crease beside his mouth. "It'll have to be enough. For both of us.''

"Tell me you love me, *istatowin.*''

"I love you, Gus. Even if you are the dirtiest man I've ever kissed.'' She touched her lips to his.

"And I'm the dirtiest man you'll ever marry,'' he said into her mouth. Then he ran his tongue over her lower lip.

"Hey!'' Roger yelled again, this time coming out of the store and out across the yard to them. "What did I tell you about this? You're embarrassing me!''

"Roger!'' Gus hollered over Genny's head. "Get that preacher boy over here! I'm paying him for a wedding and I want it now!''

"You got to be kidding! Martha's heating bath water and . . .''

"Do I look like I'm kidding?'' Gus asked, placing another wet kiss on Genny's astonished mouth. His arms wound around her and he bent her farther back over his arm to drag his lips down her throat. "I've got one thing on my mind right now. If we don't get this wedding over with, this poor woman's going to be forced into all manner of grievous sins. Get him out here, and don't let him stop by the privy first.''

Roger hustled back off toward the house.

"What?'' Genny giggled.

"Long story,'' Gus said, nibbling at her ear. "Do you mind? We can haul the bath water upstairs and I promise I'll let you wash me clean before I make love to you.''

"You'll *let* me wash you?''

One hand covered her breast, kneading it through the

heavy wool of her dress. "I don't want to wait another minute to make you legally my wife."

"Well, I never thought I'd get married at all, so you won't be squashing any dreams I might have had of fancy lace and lilies." She pushed his hand to her waist. "Roger would have died if he'd seen where your hand just was."

"How about your dreams of a dusty, buckskin-clad, half-Indian wild man who can't get enough of you?" He clasped both her hands in his and pulled her forward for a kiss.

"What dreams?" Genny murmured, savoring the brush of his lips upon her own. "This looks real to me."

Martha came out onto the porch and across the yard, together with Fitz and Sid, Walks In Thunder and the other Lakotas, wandered in from the outbuildings.

"You don't leave much time for planning a celebration, Gus Renard," Martha announced. "If you'd wait a bit, I could at least get some biscuits made to go with supper."

Gus released Genny and grinned at his friend's wife. "Bet you never thought you'd see me wed by a preacher, did you Martha?"

"I'll bet you didn't, either," she retorted.

"I don't want to be anywhere near Miss Tolly's at Doby Town when word gets around that Gus Renard got hisself hitched to a lady, all legal-like," Fitz sighed, shaking his head.

Genny arched an eyebrow at Gus. "Is Maybelle or Maybeth or whatever her name was one of Miss Tolly's . . . employees?" she asked sweetly.

"I couldn't rightly tell you, *istatowin*. Seems last summer I met a blue-eyed girl who made me plum forget there was any other women in the territory."

Martha rolled her eyes and Sid and Fitz jabbed each other in the ribs, snorting in disbelief.

Gus assumed a wounded look. "You don't have to worry about other women, Genny. Ever," he said more seriously.

"I know that." She tucked her hand into his. "Is that

boy really a minister?'' she asked, glancing toward the young man being herded out of the store by Roger.

"If he's not, he's still doing our wedding,'' Gus said.

Reverend Alton stopped in front of them, and Roger stood beside Gus. Martha came to Genny's side, and the other men collected in a semicircle around them. The preacher held a prayer book in one hand, and he'd draped a stole over his black wool coat. The wind whipped his long, sandy hair across his forehead as he reached to shake Genny's hand.

"The bride, I presume?''

Gus answered. "Eugenia Stone, this is Reverend Alton. Or so he claims. How old are you, anyway?''

"Twenty-six, sir. Is that your full name, Miss Stone?''

"Eugenia Rittenberg Stone,'' she affirmed, smiling when the minister called Gus "sir.'' The poor man looked half-terrorized, if the nervous tick in his jaw was any indication.

"Have you got a ring?'' he asked, barely meeting Gus's eyes.

Gus reached into his shirt and pulled out a small pouch, from which he extracted a wide gold band. He handed it to Roger, then took both of Genny's hands in his.

"Make it fast,'' Gus ordered, his eyes never leaving Genny's.

"Dearly beloved, we are gathered this day to unite this man and this woman in the holy estate of marriage . . .''

Genny heard the familiar words with awe in her heart. She was actually being married. In the barren yard of a nearly deserted Nebraska Territory ranch station to a mixed blood Lakota with three of his Indian relatives, two grizzled frontiersmen, a French Canadian trader and his half-Cheyenne wife as the witnesses. And with love. Amazingly, she was marrying a man she loved. Almost before she realized what she was saying, she was repeating her vows, and in another minute, Gus had spoken his.

Reverend Alton's voice continued, surprisingly rich and full. "Then before the eyes of God, and according to the laws and statutes of the Territory of Nebraska, and the United States of America, I now pronounce you man and wife.''

"Go ahead and kiss her again," Roger instructed before the Reverend got the chance. "Get it over with."

A loud cheer went up from the men as Gus turned Genny into his arms. Long and hard he kissed her, and so lost was he in the warm sweetness of her mouth, he didn't notice right away when the minister tapped him on the shoulder.

"Excuse me, sir. I hate to interrupt, but there are some other guests arriving. They look a little wild. I don't know if they're invited." He broke off, staring over their shoulders.

Gus and Genny followed his gaze. Several horses were splashing out of the river two hundred yards away. Harsh cries carried over the distance, and when the riders were clear of the trees, Genny could see they were Indians.

Gus signalled the others to look.

"It's some of my cousins," Martha said, shielding her eyes as she gazed west. "That's Red Grass in the lead."

Suddenly the man pulled up on his mount, causing the horse to rear in protest. The horse's cry was joined by the man's plaintive howl, and agony pierced the aura of celebration surrounding the wedding party.

"Oh, Lord," Martha gasped, stepping toward the approaching riders. "Something's happened. Look at their hair! Look at the horses!"

Chapter 24

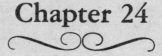

Martha began to run, with Roger close behind her. "What does she see?" Genny asked, straining her eyes.

Gus stiffened in her arms. "Their hair is cut. The horses' manes have been cut, and there's blood. Look at the brown stain on the buckskin." He dragged her with him after Martha.

Genny had spent long enough with the Lakota to know that the people cut their hair in grief over the death of a loved one, and often their own flesh. She had heard that some Cheyennes went so far as to cut off fingers in their distress over the death of family members.

"Gus?"

"Sshhh," he whispered, smoothing her hair.

The first rider reached Martha. Flinging himself from his horse, the man stood with hands outstretched at his sides. He threw back his head and gave another furious, sorrowful cry. His voice sounded the way Gus's had when he'd sung his pain atop Rocky Butte. The three men following him reined in their horses and dismounted, standing silently at his side.

Genny and Gus stood behind Martha with Roger, Reverend Alton, and the others. Red Grass began to speak in a language Genny didn't recognize as her eyes traveled over the Cheyenne warriors. Each man's hair had been raggedly hacked off, and their bare chests were scored with lines of dried blood. Likewise, blood had run from cuts on their arms, staining their elbows, wrists and hands. The horses had blood dried and matted on their hair—though whether it was their own or their rider's, Genny couldn't tell. Despite the cold, the men were nearly naked.

Genny gripped Gus's hand, and he returned the pressure, squeezing her fingers so hard she could hardly feel them. She glanced around her. Every face except the young preacher's had frozen into a mask of shock and revulsion.

When Gus began to tremble violently, she wrapped her arm tightly around his waist. He paled visibly, but suddenly her attention was drawn back to Martha. The half-Cheyenne woman fell to her knees, her arms held stiffly before her, keening in high tones.

Red Grass stepped toward her, drawing a long, wicked-looking knife. Martha reached for it, and before Genny's disbelieving eyes, she grabbed a handful of her hair and set the blade to it. Within seconds, her long, ebony tresses lay in scattered heaps on the ground, indiscriminately chopped from her head. Then she raised the knife to her shoulder and cut away her sleeve with sharp, jerky stabs of the knife.

Genny looked to Roger in alarm, her mouth opening to protest. He met her gaze, holding up a hand to stop her speaking. His eyes glittered with the sheen of tears.

Her sleeve in ruined tatters, Martha gave an anguished cry and quickly carved four long slashes in her upper arm. Blood welled red and hot, running quickly across her breast, staining her white blouse crimson. Genny lurched forward, but Gus's arms closed on her like a vise, holding her to him. She struggled, and he gripped her tighter.

"What happened?" No sound accompanied her whispered question.

"A massacre," he breathed. "The army killed almost an entire village of Cheyennes south of here on Sand Creek on Tuesday, two days ago. Women and children were shot as they tried to flee. Many were raped. Babies' skulls were crushed with rifle butts and their bodies thrown into the sand. Most of bodies were mutilated. Black Kettle, their leader, ran up an American flag to show they wanted peace, but the bluecoats killed them anyway. More than a hundred Cheyennes lay dead, and the soldiers remained through the day, searching for more.''

''Martha's family? Were they there?''

''Her mother lies with a broken back in a dry creek bed. Some of her cousin's children were with her. Red Grass lost two boys. He and his brothers were nearby.''

Gus was shaking so badly and clinging to her so tightly that Genny's teeth rattled in her head. Tears flowed openly down his cheeks, as they did from every other man there who had understood Red Grass's words. The horror of what had happened took several moments to sink in. Vivid pictures formed in her mind of women like Good Shield and girls like Blue Bird and White Hands raped, carelessly murdered and mutilated, their bodies broken and trampled by cavalry horses. Fighting the bile rising in her throat, she twisted in Gus's arms to look at Martha.

There was blood everywhere. Her face, her arms, her hands, and her clothes were streaming with red rivulets. They dripped into the hair and the dust at her feet, matting dark against the frozen ground.

Roger went to her as she collapsed over her knees, her mournful wailing rising on the wind. A dust devil kicked up along the river, swirling dry leaves erratically into the yard, whistling in eerie counterpoint to her keening. Roger knelt, gingerly draping one strong arm across his wife's back. As soon as she felt his touch, she lurched up, sobbing, to bury her face against his chest. Tears flowing silently from his own eyes, he held her tenderly, burying one hand through her shorn hair.

''Genny?'' he rasped. Gus released her immediately. ''I hate to ask it of you, but do you think you could help me get her to the house and stop her bleeding?''

Genny jerked her head in agreement. She looked back to Gus for reassurance, but found none in his stony stare.

Fear lanced through her. Never had she seen him such stark anguish in a man's face.

He pushed her toward Martha without looking up. "Go on." His voice was devoid of inflection. "She needs another woman now."

As she went to Martha's side, she saw him drift aimlessly out into the yard, his back to the ranch and the people standing there in horrified silence.

Eugenia Stone Renard spent most of her wedding night with Martha Rivier, offering what feeble support she could and crying tears of sympathy as her friend sobbed through her grief. After she had sponged Martha's cuts clean and helped her into a nightgown, they sat together in Martha's kitchen, hands clasped tight together. Following the customs of her mother's people, Martha keened aloud. The depth of her despair echoed through the house, sending shivers through Genny's limbs.

The men gathered in the store, where Fitz distributed the buffalo ribs, roasted potatoes, and dried apple pies that would have been Gus and Genny's wedding supper. Genny knew Gus wasn't with them. He was outside somewhere in the cold night, struggling with his pain. It wasn't an auspicious start to a marriage neither if them was certain had much chance of success to begin with.

A little after midnight, Roger came into the kitchen and sat down with Martha and Genny. Dropping a heavy hand over theirs, he gently disentangled his wife's and Genny's fingers, taking Martha's hand in both of his. She stared glassy eyed, but she gave him her other hand, as well.

"Thank you, Genny. I'll take her upstairs now. Her cousins are sleeping in the store, and more of their families will join them here in the next few days. It'll be easier for Martha when the women are here." He rose, pulling Martha to her feet and into his arms. "I'm sorry your wedding day was ruined. Bad Arrow was just in to say Gus is at the corral. Maybe you should go get him. He's been out there a long time."

"Thanks. I will."

As Roger lifted Martha to carry her upstairs, Genny picked up her shawl from the hooks by the door and slipped outside. The night was cold and clear, with a bright moon just past the full. The stars were thick and bright in the west, and she had no difficulty picking out Gus's form slumped over the fence rails across the expanse of the yard.

She hurried to him, desperate to hold him and be held, and to find sense in what had happened. If that wasn't possible—and she was afraid it wouldn't be, just as there had been no making sense of what had befallen them at Rocky Butte—there would be comfort in the shared warmth of their living flesh.

If Gus heard her approach, he made no sign. He wore the same clothes he had arrived in that afternoon, the same travel-stained buckskins he had been married in. Leaning into the fence, his arms draped through the rails at chest height, he stood with eyes closed, forehead resting on the top rail. His coat hung open, letting in the bitter wind, and when Genny placed her hand on his back, he didn't move.

Never having seen him unresponsive, she hesitated. Even in the depths of his anger and grief after Rocky Butte he had sought to connect with her, to touch her and be touched. Now he was colder than the wind and as still as ice.

She moved close to him, placing one arm over his shoulders and the other across his waist, but still he didn't move or acknowledge her presence. There was no warmth in him, and the chill began to penetrate her thin shawl.

"You should come inside now, Gus," she finally said. "It's cold. Too cold to stay out here." She tugged to pull him away from the fence.

His resistance baffled her. Like a rock, he stood unmoving on the fence, silent, motionless, and empty.

"Gus?" Her voice wavered.

"We made a mistake this afternoon." His words were flat and lifeless.

She tightened her arms around him, not sure how to respond.

"You were right before. When you said there wasn't any way for us to be together and for both of us to be happy, you were right."

He turned abruptly, breaking free of her embrace and leaning his head back against the fence, eyes fixed upon the moon. "It was wrong of me to try to tie you to me, Genny. What can I offer you and our child? An uneasy existence caught between peoples who don't understand each other and who won't live together in peace? A ranch station where every passing traveler feels justified to judge your moral worth based upon your choice of a half-breed husband? Or life in an Indian camp that may come to a brutal end one morning at the hands of a company of your own nation's soldiers?"

"Stop it! Don't talk this way." Anger she could have dealt with, but the lack of emotion in his voice frightened her. He was too controlled. Too cold.

"It *will* happen again, Genny, just like it's happened before. Ash Hollow isn't thirty miles away from here. The massacre there was nine years ago, and still the Sicaŋgu weep over what Harney did to our women and children. Many of our leaders lost their lives there, as well. Three days ago Colonel Chivington struck a like blow to the Cheyenne at Sand Creek, and it will happen again. How many times? The war will be over soon, and more soldiers will be posted here in the west. Battle-hardened, bitter men who've learned to take lives as easily as they take a drink of whiskey. All the Cheyenne, Lakota, Arapaho, Comanche, Kiowa, and all the other peoples of the plains put together will not be able to stop them from coming to into our very lodges and killing our families. America wants this country, and will stop at nothing to get it. Her soldiers will be named heros for killing Indian women and children.

"It was unthinkable for me to try to drag you into as precarious a life as my mother's people live, waiting for the morning when a bugle and rifle fire meet us at the dawn. Among the whites, the bitterness toward Indians will grow as more *wašicus* come into the land, and there won't be any place where we can be a family in peace. I'm sorry, Genny. I was so wrong.''

She pulled her shawl close and stared at the ground. "But you said we could work things out. You promised to try. We both agreed to try.''

"I was fooling myself because I wanted it to work between us so badly. I love you, Genny. And I should have listened to you and let you go without complicating your life with the baby and an unwanted marriage.''

"I want to be married to you, and I want your child.''

He braced his hands on his thighs, still gazing into the night sky. "I won't ruin your life. I'm leaving, Genny. Going back to camp. I don't want you to come. There are enemies I can't protect you from. You and the baby will have a better life without me.''

"I don't want you to go.''

He looked at her finally, but his eyes were empty. "I have to. There are things I have to do. Promises I have to fulfill.''

"You made promises to me, too.''

"Foolish ones I could never keep.''

"Damn it, Gus Renard, I love you. I set aside my fears and promised to be a real wife to you. Why are you doing this? Come inside and make love with me and sleep in my arms tonight. In the morning you'll see things differently.'' She extended her hand to him. "We need each other. You need me the way we needed each other after Rocky Butte. Let me love you. Love me. Come to bed, *mihigna kin*.''

"I can't,'' he whispered, jamming his hands under his arms. "If I do, I'll never be able to do what's right.''

"Don't leave,'' Genny pleaded.

He didn't answer. Instead he pushed off the fence and walked purposefully toward the stable. Genny went after him, nearly running to keep up with his long strides. When they reached the building, he went to a stall and brought Harv out. The gelding was already saddled.

He stopped to look at her silhouette in the stable door. With only the light of one small lantern, it was too dark to see her features clearly. That made it easier for him. "I made arrangements via telegraph at Fort Kearney to make my accounts available to you in case anything happened to me. I guess something happened sooner than I thought. Roger has the details."

"I don't want your money. I want you."

He made no comment as he kneed Harv's side and tightened the cinch on the light saddle.

"For a last time, Genny, no. I can't be the kind of husband you deserve, and I won't force you to live between these peoples, between the *wasicus* and the Indians. It can't be done easily. I've tried to do it all my life, and I still can't do it with any degree of real peace. Part of me is always yearning for something that isn't there. I'm not whole in either the Lakota or white worlds. You have a place where you can be whole. Go home, love our child, and forget about me." He set his foot into the stirrup.

Genny raced to his side, grabbing his arms. "Don't do this. Not now. Not when I want to make it work. Let us try, Gus. We have to try."

Looking down at her, he shook his head.

She flung her arms around her neck and kissed him. Coaxing and desperate, she tried to move him, tenderly touching her lips to his. She deepened the pressure of her mouth, urging him to join her, to kiss her back, but he didn't respond. He wouldn't kiss her back.

Instead he took her shoulders and set her gently away from him. Then he caught the stirrup and swung into the saddle.

She put her hand on his thigh and he looked down at her, his eyes filled now with haunting pain. "I'll wait, Gus. I'll wait here a month. If you don't come back or send word, I'll leave then, but not before. Do whatever it is you must, but then come back to me."

Infinitely gentle, the ghost of a sad smile curved his mouth. "I love you, *istatowin*," he said as he nudged Harv into motion. "I wish that was enough."

Genny refused to accept that he was leaving her. He had made such desperate attempts to get her to stay with him! Nonetheless, his form shrank into the distance. In a moment he was lost in the shadows beside the river. Tears burned her eyes and blurred her vision as the wind whipped her hair back from her face. She stood empty and alone in the cold Nebraska night.

Gus rode through the center of the Lakota camp at a walk. Children and dogs stared up at him, scampering out of the way at the last second, transfixed by the grim-faced man who was stripped to his breechcloth on a cold winter day. By the time he stopped in front of the holy man's lodge, he had acquired a procession of curious friends and relatives. He didn't see them, nor did he notice the boy who took his horse when he dismounted and went inside the lodge. Finding himself alone, he sat down by the fire.

A few minutes later, Hawk Dancer entered. He walked behind Gus and sat down at his place next to him. When Gus didn't say anything, his cousin began to fill a pipe.

The two men smoked in silence for nearly an hour. Gus had never before fully appreciated the quiet support his cousin gave without ever looking at him or uttering a word. It was an aspect of the Lakota world that had often made him uncomfortable. But now the silence calmed him and lent him the courage to break the silence.

"I want to go up on a hill. I need to seek my vision."

Hawk Dancer nodded, but didn't say anything.

"My wife is carrying my child." His voice broke. "It had already started growing before I made my vow, but I will honor it just the same."

"Why did you leave her now?" his cousin asked. "Winter's coming on. You should be together."

"It was wrong in thinking we could live together. She was wiser than I in that. Something happened that made me see how great the differences are between our peoples."

"Your blood is also of her people."

"But they make no place for me because of my mother's blood."

"Perhaps you have to make your own place."

"I don't know how. I have chosen to make my place here, but I would not ask my wife to live where she isn't happy. Or where I can't protect her."

"We protect our families well," Hawk Dancer reminded him.

"For how much longer?" Gus looked away from the fire and directly into his cousin's eyes. "I have a tale to tell, *tahansi*. With shame and sorrow that I share *wasicu* blood, I bring bad news from our friends the Shahiyela."

When he had relayed what had happened at Sand Creek, Hawk Dancer filled his pipe again and they sat a long time more.

"Well, at least we are safe for the winter. This isn't a good time to go up on a hill, *tahansi*. *I* would wait for warmer weather," Hawk Dancer finally said.

"I can't wait," Gus responded. "I have to do it now."

Hawk Dancer frowned. "It will take some time to prepare. You need to learn some things before you go out there alone."

"I know."

"Where do you want to go?"

Gus hesitated. A memory flashed through his mind, and he knew there was only one place he could go to seek his vision. There was only one place where he had ever prayed and felt some sense of acceptance of his prayer.

"Rocky Butte," he answered solemnly.

Gus spent his days at Hawk Dancer's side as he learned the prayers and songs he needed to get through his time on the hill. More than once he asked himself what he was doing, and it was often in his mind that the spirits whose aid he sought were little more than the figments of imaginations bored with the endless repetition of the rolling prairie landscape, but he had nothing else to do. When he concentrated on Hawk Dancer's teachings, he didn't think about Genny and their unborn child baby. He didn't think about what the army was planning next, or what raids his Lakota relatives had planned. All he thought about was building the strength he needed to survive alone outside while he sought his vision.

The worst times came in the nightly sweats Hawk Dancer made him endure. He dreaded crawling into the small, round *initi*, made of bent willow branches covered with hides and blankets, for he hated the darkness that pressed down close around him like a living thing when the door was shut. No night was ever so dark. Nameless fears gripped him as he huddled on the ground, staring at the faint glow the rocks gave off when they were first in. When the fiery blast of steam came off them as his cousin ladled water over them, many times Gus cried out in the effort to control his panic. Something in the dark heat brought forth every demon he had ever had to fight to challenge him again. Hawk Dancer wouldn't let him turn away. He had to face them, his only weapons the prayers and songs his cousin commanded him to sing. And as he did, Gus learned a kind of courage that he had never known before.

He learned to face himself with empty hands and no place left to run.

Finally he was ready. Along with Hawk Dancers, Big Elk, and one of his cousin's sons, he set out for Rocky Butte. Two days later they reached it. Hawk Dancer made Gus wait behind while he and the others went ahead. When Gus approached the butte, he saw no evidence of the Pawnee warriors he had left dead upon the ground last summer.

The weather was with him: warm for winter, and with no wind, though the nights ahead would be long and cold. Gus dug a square pit into the frozen ground atop the hill, and when he was finished, Hawk Dancer came to stand beside him. He set a buffalo skull on the mound of earth Gus had piled on the west side of his pit, stuffing its eye cavities with sweet grass and white sage, and painting a zigzagging black line down the center of it. Gus stood quietly while his cousin prepared the sacred space, then motioned Gus to strip down to his breech-cloth.

When Gus was naked, with only a buffalo robe to warm him through the days ahead, Hawk Dancer handed him his pipe, the one that had belonged to their grand-father. Together they prayed, facing each direction, the sky and the earth, and then Hawk Dancer withdrew, leaving Gus alone atop the butte.

For two days and nights Gus sang and prayed and waited. All his energy was focused on listening for any message that might come to him, but there was nothing. In the frigid early morning hours of the second night, he sat in his small pit, clinging to his pipe, singing wearily. Suddenly he stopped. It was no use. There were no spirits to hear his pointless prayers, and no ease for the sorrows in his heart. Abandoning Hawk Dancer's songs, he rose to his feet and clambered from the pit, letting his robe fall away.

In anguish, he shouted as loud as he could. Facing the west, he let the tears of frustration and disappointment fall. He remembered all that happened here before, and the song he had sung then. It was the first song he re-membered knowing, and he thought he had heard his grandfather singing it when he was very small. He had remembered it even through the years in his father's house in Montréal. It was a scout's song, but he sang it again now.

> I will walk anywhere.
> With courage, I will walk.
> For the people, I will walk.

He felt no courage, only sorrow, despair, and lone-liness. In his heart, he wasn't willing to walk anywhere. There were firm boundaries beyond which he was not willing to go. And who were his people? Still he sang on.

The sound of his own voice filled his ears and tears filled his eyes as gradually his song became a plea for the courage to walk anywhere—anywhere life took him, be that into fear, into sorrow, or into sacrifice. Facing west, he sang until his voice scraped raw and uneven over the notes. He didn't notice the cold or the darkness. Nothing existed except his song and the darkness.

At length he faltered, throat aching and eyes burning. Stepping back down into the pit, he dragged the buffalo robe over him, turning to the east so he would see the first light of the new day. He waited. His prayer was spoken.

Genny's face swam before his eyes. He wished she were with him. After they had fought the Pawnees, she had sung with him, and it had made his burdens easier to bear. He had been able to accept what they had had to do to survive, and helping her through the same fear and guilt that raged like a storm within him had helped to heal him. When they were together, he had more courage than he'd ever known. For her, he would walk anywhere, but he could no longer bring himself to push her down a path that would make her miserable.

Shadows appeared in the east as the cold light of pre-dawn crept onto the plains. The sun rising would signal the end of his *hanbleceya*, his crying on the hill. It was nearly over, and he felt drained. No spirits had come to help him through this. As always, he remained alone. He had lost a love he treasured above all else, and seen his dreams scattered on the winds of conflicts he could not control. Closing his eyes, he leaned his head back against the frozen ground. There was nothing left to do but wait for Hawk Dancer to come and get him.

"Who are your people?"

Gus heard the voice, but he couldn't open his eyes to look. It was very cold, and he didn't want to leave his bed.

"Who are your people?" the voice asked again. It was a man's voice, clear and strong.

"The Lakota," he answered. "I am Lakota."

"Where does your treasure lie?"

He thought of the payroll in Genny's pantry. No, he didn't really care about that. Not now. He thought of Genny, carrying their child within her body. She was his treasure. The finest he had ever known.

Something grabbed his feet and pulled hard, anchoring him in the ground. He could feel claws digging into his heels and the balls of his feet, but they were caught in the earth and he couldn't pull away. Blazing pain seared up his calves and into his thighs.

"Where does your treasure lie?" the voice repeated.

"In my family. My wife and the child she will bear." The claws dug deeper, scraping bone.

"Go to them."

"I can't. My feet are caught." He pulled frantically to free himself, but it was in vain. The pain only increased.

"Then cut them off."

Something hard and cold dropped onto his chest, and his hand closed over it. It was a knife. A small knife. The pain in his feet was excruciating, increasing every second. Blindly, he gripped the blade and reached for his ankles. With two swift strokes, he severed his feet. The pain stopped at once, and he fell back in relief. Then he realized what he had done.

"My feet!" he screamed.

"Go to them. Go to your people."

Gus gasped in frustration. "I can't! I don't have any feet!"

"Go anyway."

"I can't!"

"Then you will lose your greatest treasure. You will lose your heart."

"No!" He struggled up on his elbows. There were walls beside him. He could push himself up and support himself with his arms. He could crawl. He would go to Genny without his feet. "No! I won't lose her! I won't! I'll find another way to walk."

"Then go." The voice faded like the low rumble of distant thunder.

"What are you doing?" another voice asked. This one was familiar. It sounded like his brother-in-law.

"Walking without my feet," Gus answered. Something slapped his cheek and he found he could open his eyes. Big Elk stood before him, grinning from ear to ear. "What's so funny?"

"Look at yourself."

Gus suddenly became aware of his body. He was perched on his arms on the edges of his pit, dangling his feet uselessly below him. Self-consciously, he settled onto them, wincing as a few prickles shimmied up his calves. "My feet must have gone to sleep," he muttered.

"Your feet and your head," Big Elk chuckled. "We saw a bird up here a while ago. It was too dark to tell what kind, but we thought you must have got your vision."

"I didn't see a bird," Gus said, eyes still on his feet. A glint of metal shone among the tumbled folds of the robe. He stopped to pick it up.

In his hand he cradled a small dagger of antique design. Spanish, he recalled, and he would have recognized it anywhere. It was the dagger Genny had lost during the hailstorm.

Gus simply stared at it in awe.

Chapter 25

$\sim\!\!\!\sim\!\!\infty\!\!\sim\!\!\sim$

Genny looked north toward White Rock Spring as she handed the last of her paintings up to Fitz in the wagon. From the size, she knew it was the one of Gus and Walks In Thunder as she had first seen them, and she wondered where they were now. Walks In Thunder and the others had left the morning after Gus had left her, more than a month ago. It was January the third, and with the new year had come unseasonably warm weather and clear skies. Genny knew that if she had to leave, this was the best time to do it.

"I can't believe he didn't come back," she said to Martha. Her friend stood beside her, holding a satchel filled with Genny's pens and paints and sketchpads. "He did it again. He took all choice right out of my hands. If I wasn't so sick at heart, I'd be furious."

Sid reached for the bag in Martha's hands, and as soon as her hands were free, she gave Genny a quick hug. "I thought he'd be back, too, but with the baby to think about, it's best you return home while you can travel more comfortably. I know it's hard, but this is probably the best choice you can make now. This is a harsh place for a lady to raise a child alone."

"It's a harsh land," Genny agreed, but even as she spoke she found herself admiring the clarity of the light, and she hardly noticed the breeze that teased wisps of fine hair from her braid.

"Have you got everything?"

"Everything except my husband." Genny surveyed the inside of the covered wagon. At its far end was the trunk packed with her winter clothes and the leather dresses Good Shield had given her along with a smaller bag containing essentials. The only other things she had bothered to take from the house at White Rock Spring were her sketches and paintings, all carefully boxed in slat frames, and enough of her materials to occupy her on the journey back to Pennsylvania.

Fitz climbed over the buckboard seat and called back to them. "We'll be ready to go in a few minutes, Mrs. Renard."

Sid and Fitz were seeing her as far as Omaha, where she would cross the Missouri River to catch the train in Council Bluffs. The men's spirits were high for the trip, but Genny's were not. Throughout December she had waited expectantly, hoping to see Gus ride back into the yard at Rivier's Ranch any day. When it hadn't happened, Roger had advised her to take advantage of the lull in the hostilities along the trail and the clear weather.

She'd had no word from Paul, and decided he'd find out where she'd gone soon enough on his own. She had no desire to face him with her decision to leave Nebraska Territory, and she didn't even have the dagger she'd wagered on this misbegotten adventure. Her pride mattered little, now that there was her unborn child's welfare to consider, but she was glad she didn't have to deal with Paul immediately.

She'd also wondered if she should do something about the payroll buried in the pantry floor out at White Rock Spring, but in the end she had left it where it was. She didn't want to so much as look at it. Paul could give it back to the Overland Stage Company, or leave it buried forever for all she cared, and she doubted Gus would ever be back to White Rock Spring.

Roger came out of the store, carrying the basket of food Martha had packed for that day's meals. He handed it up to Fitz, seated now on the buckboard, as the two women walked to the front of the wagon. "Looks like this is it, Genny. You take good care of yourself and that little one.''

"I will. Thank you both for everything you've done for me.'' She hugged Roger and then Martha again. This time they held each other tightly. When they let each other go, Roger boosted her up onto the seat next to Fitz. "If you see Gus . . .'' she said. "Tell him I miss him. Tell him I won't forget him and that I'm sorry he left.''

"We will,'' Martha promised. "Good-bye, Genny Stone.''

"Good-bye.'' She tried to smile.

Then Fitz slapped the reins and shouted, and the wagon lurched forward across the yard. Roger and Martha waved from the porch, but Genny's eyes had already turned north for one last time, hoping beyond hope that she might see her husband riding hell-bent for leather toward her on a big dun horse.

All she saw were the drab winter hills and the azure sky. Far above, a single large, dark bird circled on the wind, and the land was as vast and empty as it had ever been.

"*Tahansi*, how long has it been since I came back without my wife?''

It was the first question Gus put to his cousin when they came out of the *initi* after his time on the hill. For the first time in his life, the sweat lodge had not been an ordeal. He had welcomed the darkness and the cleansing heat, embracing it, knowing that his prayers were heard, and that he wasn't as alone as he had always thought. He felt strengthened by it. Moreover, he knew where his heart lay, and there was no ambiguity about it.

"A month or so,'' Hawk Dancer answered, pulling a small square of hide marked with the phases of the moon from a pouch among his clothes. He pointed to one of the moons. "You came on this day last month, so that was,'' he paused to calculate backwards in his head, "thirty days ago.''

Gus couldn't remember ever having lost track of the date in all his years on the plains. He had to think a minute, counting the days from the last date he could remember, the day of his marriage. The day he had left Genny. "It must be January fourth." He stared at the moons on Hawk Dancer's calendar. "She's left. She said she'd wait a month, and it's been longer. It's too late."

"Go anyway," Hawk Dancer said, pulling his shirt over his head.

Gus blinked at him. "What did you say?"

"Go anyway. Wasn't that what the voice in your dream told you? You don't pay attention very well, *tahansi*. No wonder it took so long for you to hear anything from the spirits. But before you go, you need to come back to camp and share your vision. It's good for the people to hear these things if they can be told, and I think no power will be lost to tell your story. Will you do it?"

Gus thought a minute and then nodded. "I will. Another week won't make that much difference. I'll still find Genny, wherever she's gone. And when I do, nothing's ever going to separate us again."

Hawk Dancer grunted his approval, then directed Gus's attention up into the sky. "Look, *tahansi*. An eagle. Maybe it's the one that brought your wife's knife back to you."

"Maybe," Gus agreed, watching the bird with a sense of wonder. It drifted lower until it was almost directly over head. With a shrill cry, it veered suddenly to the east, gliding low over the plains. "That eagle knows where my future lies, *tahansi*. My feet are rooted here in prairie earth, but my heart calls me far away. The time has come for me to walk with my heart."

A dark-haired girl in a pale pink dress advanced into the bright studio, her blue eyes sparkling and her cheeks flushed from the brisk March wind. One or two fading forsythia blossoms clung to her blue paisley shawl and the ends of her hair. Her eyes lit upon a large wooden box in the middle of the floor.

"What's in the crate?' she asked, walking into the room. "It came while you were out riding, and Daddy had the men bring it up here. Should you be doing, that, Gen?''

Her sister was on her knees, bent over the box, using the claw foot of a hammer to remove the heavy lid.

A loud creak filled the room as Genny pried the last nail out. ''I'm fine, Beth. These are my paintings. The ones I did in Nebraska Territory last summer. Apparently, the box was taken off the train by mistake in Pittsburgh and the agent there finally got around to forwarding it. Come help me get the lid off.''

Together they lifted the top, setting it against the wall, and began to remove the carefully packed canvases inside.

''Here's the one I want.'' Genny's fingers closed over the largest one. She carried it over to an empty easel next to one holding a draped canvas of about the same size.

''Do be careful, Gen. You shouldn't be lifting all these things,'' Beth admonished, looking pointedly at her sister's belly. The paint-streaked blue smock she wore was old, and it stretched tight across her middle, emphasizing the round bulge caused by her pregnancy.

''Quit fussing over me and help me get this uncovered,'' Genny said, rapidly pulling much smaller nails from the frame Roger Rivier had made to hold her paintings during shipping.

She had been home for a little over two months now, and she was six months pregnant. One year ago this week she had left for Nebraska Territory with Paul. It had been a long year, she decided, and one she would never forget. Since her return, she had spent most of her time in this upstairs corner room at Riverwood, where the afternoon sunlight streamed through the banks of south and west windows. Surrounded by a familiar clutter of canvases, recently completed paintings, and tables covered with paints, rags, brushes, jars of water and oils, and other paraphernalia, Genny had been working constantly, recreating the events and landscapes she had experienced during the months away.

''I want to compare this painting to something I've

been working for a couple of weeks," she told Beth.
"Ouch!" She jerked her hand away when a splinter bit
into her forefinger.

"You mean the one you're hiding under that sheet?
Nicky's dying to see it. He says your work is much
improved." Beth nudged Genny aside and took over
prying the wooden slats from the painting.

Genny stood aside, sucking on her finger. "I still can't
believe you and Nicky are engaged. After what happened, it amazes me that he ever had the courage to come
back here."

"Well, you misjudged him from the start. I tried to
tell you he was serious in his intentions toward me, but
you simply wouldn't have it. The only reason he agreed
to pose for you was because he was impressed with your
portraits. If you'd spoken to him long enough to find out
that painting is one of his great interests, you might have
realized that."

"I'm afraid I embarrassed him horribly," Genny admitted. The bottom of the painting was visible now. Two
pairs of legs had appeared. "At the time, it never occurred to me that all those sidelong glances he was sending my way were the result of discomfiture. Now that
Nicky's opened up his own gallery in Philadelphia,
though, I have to concede he's a very good critic. He
knows what he's doing."

"Thanks for your vote of confidence, Genny." Ni-
cholas Mercer, formerly a lieutenant in the Army of the
Potomac, strode into the room and dropped a kiss on
Beth's forehead. "Hello, darling."

Genny smiled when she spotted a few telltale yellow
petals clinging to his trousers. "I hope you two weren't
doing anything too terribly improper out under the forsythia hedge. You know that's the first place Aunt Augusta goes when she notices the two of you missing."

Beth and Nicky exchanged the small smiles and guilty
glances that indicated that what they had been doing was
indeed improper. Genny felt a pang of nostalgia watching
them. How many times had she and Gus looked at each
other that same way when Good Shield had commented

that they had disappeared for yet another afternoon? Now secret smiles and lover's kisses were part of her past. They belonged to another place and time.

"What are we looking at here?" Nicky asked as he deftly began pulling tacks from the slats covering the top of the picture. "Something we can hang in my gallery?"

"Nothing for your gallery, Nicky. You're going to meet some visitors who dropped in on me one evening." Genny moved forward and took the sheet over the other painting in hand. "Are you almost finished?"

Nicky pulled the last slats away as Genny yanked the cloth down. Both paintings stood revealed, and all three of them stepped back to look.

"They're the same!" Beth exclaimed.

"No, they're not," Nicky corrected softly. "Are they, Genny?"

She smiled and shook her head, fighting back the tears that swam suddenly in her eyes.

"What's different, then?" Beth asked. "Each painting is of two Indian men leaning against a porch rail. They're the same men." She looked a moment longer. "Oh, no. They're not quite, are they? This is Gus, isn't it, Genny?"

She nodded, not trusting herself to speak.

"You painted this one shortly after this scene took place," Nicky stated, pointing to the picture she had done last summer. "The men in this painting are strangers. There's a stiffness here, almost an uncertainty. And look at that predatory expression on Gus's face. Heavens, Genny, you made him look like an absolute rakehell."

"He was." She smiled ruefully. Even Beth didn't know about their initial encounter in the middle of the night, or that Gus had dared to lie upon her bed as she slept. "He quite shocked me."

"He certainly got your attention, if you painted this from memory after one meeting," Nicky surmised astutely.

"He did at that," Genny agreed, staring at her painting. It was an extraordinary likeness, but something wasn't quite right about it. "Imagine me falling for such a flirtatious scoundrel."

"You thought Nicky was a rake too, but you were wrong," Beth reminded her.

Nicky chuckled, and Genny wondered why she had disliked him so. "Strictly speaking, darling, she wasn't wrong. Before I met you, I did have something of a reputation as a ladies' man. Your sister correctly interpreted the signs, if not my intentions, regarding you."

Beth grinned. "The right woman can bring any man to heel."

"How very unflattering, my dear. Don't get any ideas about relegating me to the kennels after we're wed."

Beth blushed becomingly. "I don't believe I will. But were you right about Gus, Gen? Was he really as bad as you thought at first?"

"Oh, yes. I'm afraid he was." She'd told her family some of what happened between her and Gus, leaving many of the details deliberately vague. "But in time I discovered that he had other sides, as well. From the first, I realized he had a certain amount of character. You can see a hint of it in the earlier portrait, but I never understood how much until it was too late." Her eyes drifted over the second painting, the one she was working on now.

"You love him very much now, don't you?" Nicky spoke softly, wrapping his arms around Beth's waist and pulling her back to lean against him. "And the man in this second painting. He loves you deeply, as well. The aggression in the first picture is absent. In its place is a rare honesty of emotion, and you aren't afraid of his desire for you anymore. It's very powerful." He paused, eyes fixed on the paintings. "Genny, why did he leave you if he loves you this way? If you love him? I can't understand it."

"We belong to different worlds. I'm not sure I really understand myself." She stepped forward, draping the sheet over both paintings. Beth and Nicky were looking at her with more compassion than she could easily bear.

"Gen, I wish you could be as happy with Gus as Nicky and I are together," Beth said quietly.

"So do I." She folded her hands over her stomach and felt her baby move. "Oh!" A smile bloomed on her face as she spread her hands. "The baby! He's kicking again."

"Eugenia!" Aunt Augusta's strident voice carried down the hall ahead of her, long with the staccato thunk of her heels. "Eugenia! You have a visitor!" Aunt Augusta stopped in the doorway and frowned at Nicky and Beth. "It is most unseemly to stand draped around one another like a pair of eels, whether or not you are betrothed," she pronounced.

"Who's here, Aunt Augusta?" Beth asked, trying to pull out of Nicky's arms.

Genny stifled a grin when he clamped his arms more firmly around her sister. He and Gus would have gotten along splendidly.

"Mrs. Milroy said he wouldn't give his name, but he mentioned that he knows Paul. The gentleman says he has some things of Eugenia's that he would like to return to her. He's in the library." Aunt Augusta turned on her heel and clomped back down the hall.

"I suppose I should go see who it is, although if he's a friend of Paul's it might be nice if one of you would pop your head into the library if I'm not out soon," Genny said with a shrug. "I'll see you at supper."

She heard Nicky grumbling to Beth on her way out the door. "I regret very dearly that a certain disagreeable party ever had occasion to see me in my drawers. It set her against me. I know it did."

Genny couldn't resist sticking her head back in the door. She was going to tell Nicky he should try giving Aunt Augusta his best horse if he wanted to win even her grudging acceptance, but she stopped short at the sight of her sister and her fiancé lost in a heated kiss. Beth's head was thrown back, her hands buried in Nicky's black hair, her eyes closed in rapture. He was kissing her neck with one hand tangled in her hair while the other pulled her hips close to him. Then he rocked his pelvis lightly into her and Beth groaned.

Genny slipped quietly down the hallway. At the top of the stairs she paused to look in the mirror that hung over a narrow mahogany table and cupped her hands over the child that grew inside her. "Your daddy and I used to kiss each other like that," she whispered. "He would hold me tight and I would melt against him. When he'd kiss my neck, shivers would run through me to my toes. If I try very hard, I can still feel his lips on my skin and the warmth of his arms. I miss him, *cincala*." She used the Lakota word for a little child to address her baby. "I wish he was here with us."

Then she turned and went downstairs.

Genny headed straight to the library, not bothering to change her clothes or wash the pigment stains from her hands. Unable to recall having lost anything, she expected the visitor awaiting her in the library was part of some practical joke Paul had devised. She knew her cousin had sent a wire and was coming home shortly, and she'd been on the alert since. All too easily, her imagination conjured any number of embarrassing charades he might attempt to enhance his enjoyment of her lost wager. Not in the mood for games, she opened the library doors and looked inside.

Late afternoon sunshine fell in bars through the French doors, leaving long rectangles of light on the red and blue patterned carpet. One of the doors was open, but Genny couldn't see anyone on the stone steps that led out to the gardens. She looked around the room, blinking to adjust to the dimmer light in the corners, but there was no one there. As the clouds passed before the sun, the light faded and she saw that the lamp on the sofa table was lit. She walked across to turn it off. Reaching to turn down the wick, she stopped suddenly.

There beside the lamp, resting on a well-worn book, sat a familiar beaded knife case, far too big for the small blade that protruded from it. The design of red and blue triangles and squares on a white ground was the same one she had seen on dozens of articles of clothing worn by Good Shield's family in the Lakota camp. An almost identical case sat upon her dresser upstairs. Genny reached for this one and slid the knife out.

Her heart faltered in her breast. In her hand she held the dagger she had lost in a nameless lake in the middle of the Nebraska sandhills last August. It was the same one. Every weathered nick and scratch in the ebony and silver handle was familiar. No two blades would have worn identically, and no one but herself would have recognized it. Who had found it? How had that person known to bring it here?

Her eyes darted around for any sign of a note, then settled on the book. She stared at it a moment before the letters formed into words. *Great Expectations* by Charles Dickens.

If her heart had nearly stopped before, now it raced so fast the blood surged in her veins. She picked up the book in her left hand and clutched the dagger tightly in her right. Paul couldn't have done this. He didn't know about the book. Or did he? No, only she and Gus knew.

Had he come? Had he truly come to her?

Booted footsteps rang out across the flagstone patio below the steps and a man's shadow fell into the square of light upon the carpet as he climbed the stairs. He stopped just outside the door and his shadow froze, as if in a frame. Genny's heart leapt into her throat as she stared at it, unable to look up.

Heart pounding, she gazed at it, unable to look up. What if it wasn't Gus? What if this was one of Paul's cruel tricks? But how could Paul have found the dagger? How could Gus, for that matter? She was going to have to look.

As slowly as a morning glory opens to the sun, she lifted her eyes and beheld a pair of gleaming black riding boots. One foot was set at near right angles to the other in a distinctly male pose that threw the man's weight back upon his left leg. A scuff of mud was visible along the outside edge of the right boot where the light slanted in over it.

Her eyes traveled up long calves until she encountered

dark trousers at the knees. They appeared to be brown wool, but the bright backlighting made it difficult to tell. Forcing her eyes up, Genny took in strong thighs, and at their tops, the hem of a gentleman's riding jacket. It hung open, and the lighter material of his shirt was shadowed above his waist. His hands were hidden, the right one in his pocket, the left tucked behind the fall of his jacket.

The man's pose and clothing registered abruptly as a coherent whole. Whoever he was, he was a gentleman, dressed carefully in fine clothes that he wore with the casual grace of accustomed use. This was no frontier mixed-blood Indian in buckskins and a breechcloth. Genny's mouth went dry as disappointment ravaged her, and she swung her gaze back to focus blankly on the dagger in her one hand and the book in her other.

The man halted in the doorway, transfixed by the sight of the woman standing across the room. A soft wash of golden light fell on her, throwing her classic features into sharp relief, and tinting her long hair with rich caramel and golden highlights. It hung in soft waves over her shoulders, with one strand curling forward over her breast. She had on a simple dark green dress with a paint-smeared blue smock over it that pulled tight across her belly. It was obvious she carried a child.

With bowed head and her arms extended, a book in one hand, and a dagger in the other, she looked like a medieval queen receiving holy benediction. She was the most beautiful thing he had ever seen, and the sight of her sent his heart soaring. He began to shake with the joy that blossomed in his breast, and he could barely contain the chuckle that fountained upward.

"Where did you find these things?" Her voice was small, bewildered, and almost frightened. "Who gave them to you?"

"I found them in a little white house at a place called White Rock Spring, a long way west of here." The chuckle finally broke, as wide and open as the Nebraska plains. "I took the book from a lady and left her the knife case like that one as a trade. The dagger's a little harder to explain."

Genny's whole body jerked as she looked up at him. His voice filled her like spring rain flowing into an empty rain barrel. "Gus?" She squinted into the sun. "My God! Gus? Is that really you?"

Stepping over the threshold, he carefully closed the door behind him before he crossed to stand before her. "Hello, *istatowin*."

"Dear Lord!" Genny gasped. "It's really you!" She was shaking visibly. All she could do was stare at him. He looked so different! Even his hair had been cut so that it hung just a little longer than his collar, and he looked every inch the gentleman. "Look at you!"

"I'd rather look at you," he said, and she saw that he was devouring each detail of her changed appearance just as she was his. His eyes dropped to her stomach. His hands came forward, spread to touch her, but he hesitated. "Jesus, *istatola*. You're so beautiful."

In her messy painting smock and with her big belly? He was crazy. "So are you," she choked. "What are you doing here? Why are you dressed like this?" She waved the book toward him. "Where did you find the dagger? What does this mean, your coming here? What do you want?"

"Slow down," he said, placing one hand uncertainly on his stomach while his eyes lingered on hers. Suddenly he felt as confused as Genny looked. "I don't know where to start." He glanced nervously back up to her face, then down at each of her hands.

She took a deep breath and closed her eyes. "Why don't you start," she said, not quite able to look him in the face, "with whatever is most important?"

He wanted to touch her. He was desperate to erase with kisses and sweet caresses the hurts he had inflicted. Most of all, he wanted to put his hands on her belly and feel their child within Genny's body.

"Then let me start where we left off. With a kiss. A real kiss." He took a half step toward her but she didn't move. "May I kiss you, Genny?"

Chapter 26

"Oh, yes," she whispered. "I thought you'd never ask."

Taking the book and the knife case from her, Gus tossed them on the table. Before the crash of the book had finished echoing in the cavernous room, Genny was in his arms, and for a moment, it was enough for them just to hold each other. Then, clinging as if their lives depended upon the other's touch, Gus turned Genny's head into his shoulder and brushed his lips to hers.

Both of them groaned. She sank her fingers into his hair, and pulled him closer, parting her lips for him. He traced her lips with his hot, silky tongue and nibbled softly. Then he slipped his tongue along the inner side of her lower lip and ran it over her teeth. As easily as butter sliding from a hot knife, he glided over Genny's tongue. Warm, wet, a little rough, and very sweet, his kiss claimed her.

Feelings she'd never thought she'd have again flowed through her, and she couldn't get enough of him. Tiny whimpers sounded in her throat as she sought to deepen the kiss, sucking on him, encouraging him to thrust boldly into her mouth. When he complied, she thought she would go wild, and her hands began to move in his hair and across his neck. On and on they kissed, sating passions too long denied, feeding hope in each other's hearts. Genny tried to press even closer to him, but when she did, the baby protested with a sharp kick.

Gus lifted his head at once, his eyes meeting hers briefly before dropping to her belly. "Was that the baby?" Awe widened his eyes. "It's already moving?"

She nodded proudly. "For more than a month now. He's very active."

"He?"

She shrugged, but he didn't see. His eyes were fixed on her round stomach. His hands came forward again, palms forward, and again he halted a few inches short of placing them on her. This time, she pushed her smock up and took his wrists, settling his hands over her belly.

"It's hard," he said, his eyes jumping to hers.

She nodded. "And big."

"Bigger than I imagined," he said, looking back at her.

She grinned. "But not as big as it's going to be. We have three months left to wait." She stopped, biting her lip. "Gus? Is it going to be 'we'? Will you be here?"

Guilt flooded through him at the uncertainty in her voice. "Maybe we should sit down," he said, straightening and taking one of her hands.

She let him lead her to the sofa, worried that he hadn't answered her directly. When they were seated, he pulled her hands into his own, and lifted them to his lips to kiss her palms. There was a blue stain on her thumb and he kissed that too. "Seeing you again, Genny, all I want to do is look at you and hold you. I want to undress you and see the changes in your body, and I want to make love to you for weeks on end. But there are some things that need saying first. And then I think I'll let you decide what you want to do."

The months without him had taught her what she wanted. Did she dare hope they both wanted the same thing at last? "Go ahead."

"It seems like I haven't done much right when it comes to dealings between us. It was harsh of me to leave you at Rivier's the day we were married, but now I think it was probably for the best. For me. Probably not for you, but I think I learned some things while I was back in camp that are going to make it possible for us to have a real future. One we can both live with. If you still want to try.''

The hope that had been percolating inside her erupted in a sudden geyser, along with the need to assure him that she very much still wanted to try. ''I've had a lot of time to think, too, Gus. After staying at the Riviers', I understood a lot better why you did the things you did. About why you lied about that payroll and forced me to go with you. I wouldn't have wanted you to hang for that, and if I'd found the money then, I can't honestly say that isn't what would have happened.''

Gus smiled quietly. ''It wouldn't have happened. You'd never have turned me in.''

A snippet of their conversation from the day he'd hidden the payroll in her house came back to her. ''I don't know how you can know that,'' she said. ''I don't.''

He laughed. ''Seems like I've heard that before, *istatola*.'' Wrapping one arm around her shoulders, he pulled her close to him and dropped a kiss on her forehead. ''Thank you for forgiving me for those lies.''

''I've forgiven you for the baby, too.''

His next kiss fell on her lips with a sigh. ''That's very good to hear. You're a generous woman.''

''Tell me why you're here.''

''I had a vision, Genny. I went up on a hill, and the spirits finally spoke to me. Before we left the camp to take you back to White Rock Spring, I was desperate to keep you with me. I was willing to try anything, even things I didn't think were real, so I went to Hawk Dancer and had him ask the spirits to help me keep you with me by giving us a baby. In return, I pledged to go up on a hill. That was part of why I had to go back. The other part was because, after hearing about what happened at Sand Creek, I knew you were right. It was unfair of me to try to hold you with me in a life that was so foreign and difficult, and which is becoming more and more dangerous with each year that passes.''

He ran one hand behind his neck, lifting the hair there and stroking through it as if surprised by how short it was. ''Since I met you I've wanted you because you made me feel whole. Having you by my side there in my mother's people's country made me feel like I could have everything I wanted. I could be a man among the Lakota, and I could have a beautiful woman who knew what ostriches looked like and who'd read the books I have. You brought everything together for me, and I wanted you like I've never wanted anything in my life.

"But then I came to love you, too. For who you are and not just for what you represented. I've told you in the past, you make me feel things I never thought I could. And yet all I seemed able to do was mess things up with my attempts to keep you from leaving me. Did you ever get around to reading *Great Expectations*?"

Genny nodded. "I read it when I got back here. It was the first thing I did."

"Do you remember the part where Pip says that there are days in our lives that change the entire course of things for us? That out of single moments we forge the chains that bind us throughout our lives?"

"I remember," she said softly.

"The day I took you with me out of White Rock Spring, I came to think of as the day I began to break the chain of thorns that I'd been weaving since I was taken to live in my grandfather's house. That's where I learned that my Indian blood marked me as not quite good enough. You transformed my thorns into flowers, Genny, but in return, I gave the thorns to you."

"Sometimes," she pointed out, replacing his hand upon her stomach, "thorns grow into roses."

The baby moved, a tiny thrusting under his palm. For several minutes, he couldn't speak.

"Tell me about your vision," Genny prompted when her own throat would allow.

"I went to Rocky Butte." She nodded as if she'd known he had. "It wasn't much of a vision. More than a dream, really, caused by my feet going to sleep." A wry smile quirked his mouth. "I sang the song we sang together after the Pawnee fight last summer. I never told you the words, did I?"

"No. Tell me now."

"It's just a scout's song I learned from my grandfather. It goes 'I will walk anywhere, with courage I will walk, for the people I will walk.' In my dream, a voice asked me who my people were, and where my treasure lay, and my feet got stuck in the earth. They hurt terribly, like burning claws were scraping away my skin, and I couldn't move. I said I was Lakota, and that my treasure lay with you and the child you carried. When the voice told me to go to you, I couldn't move, but then I suddenly had a knife in my hand and I just reached down and cut my feet off. Without even thinking about it. I had to stop the pain, and so I did it. But then I couldn't walk. Then the voice told me to walk with my heart.

"I am Lakota, and my feet are rooted deep in the earth where my mother's people have lived and died for generations. That's something I can never lose. It can't be taken from me, but my treasure lies elsewhere and I have to follow it. Even if I have to walk a little differently from how I have been walking. Finally, I have a place inside me where I'm whole, and where there's room for me to love you without demanding that you live a divided existence alongside me. Somewhere in my heart, Genny, lies the place we can be together in peace. It wasn't there before, but it is now. I've come to you to be your husband if you'll have me, to live wherever you can be happy, and to raise our children together in love."

Struggling to find her voice through the knot in her throat, Genny could only whisper. "I'd like that more than anything in this world." She picked up his hand and held it to her breast. "My heart has been lost without you, and the only home I want is in your arms. Take me home, Gus."

Gus lifted her into his lap, folding his arms around her. Cradling their child between them, they both were shaken by tremors of emotion, until finally they burst into uncontrollable giggles.

"I don't know why I'm laughing," Genny gasped, fluttering a hand over her mouth before finally settling it on Gus's chest.

"Because it's less embarrassing then seeing your husband burst into tears like a blubbering two-year-old," he chuckled, wiping a little telling moisture from his eyes.

"You still haven't told me where you found the dagger."

"It was in my robe when I woke up after the dream. Hawk Dancer said an eagle flew over just before I woke up, and he thinks the bird brought it to me. To lead me to a great treasure. To lead me back to you."

"That's impossible!"

"That's what happened, and I have witnesses to prove it. I also have more faith than I ever thought possible. Hawk Dancer advised me to just accept what happened with the dagger as a gift. Even he said he'd never seen anything quite like it. Especially after he heard where you lost the thing."

"I spent long enough with the Lakota to recognize wise words when I hear them. There's no reasonable explanation for this one. I can't get over it!" Eyes sparkling, Genny dropped her head onto his shoulder. "Then Paul's Pawnee medicine man was right. The dagger was the key to finding a great treasure."

"So it seems. But it's like I told you. White men never understand the sort of treasures medicine men are talking about."

"We'd better hide the dagger," she said, snuggling against him. "Paul's going to be coming home soon, and he'll want it if he sees it."

"I don't think that's going to be much of a problem," he said cryptically. Boosting her forward, he reached into his breast pocket and brought out a slim wallet. "Before I forget, we have a little detail to see to here. In the confusion following our wedding, it seems we neglected to sign our marriage papers. The Reverend Alton left these with Roger, and I brought them with me, hoping for the best."

Genny was off his lap in a second. "There's a pen on the desk."

Gus followed and spread the paper flat on the dark wood surface. When Genny handed him the pen, he signed with a flourish that made her raise her eyebrows.

He put the pen into her hand, and she signed her name in a neat, flowing script beside her husband's.

"Well, madam," Gus said, shaking their marriage paper to dry the ink, "I think we're really married, and I know what I'd like to do to celebrate." He grabbed her around the waist and swung her up into his arms. "Oof!" he exclaimed, pretending to stagger under her weight. "That kid's going to be a bruiser."

"Put me down! You're going to strain something!"

"Something's straining, all right," he agreed, "but I don't think putting you down is going to ease it any. We're going to have to do more than that." He strode as far as the sofa, where he collapsed with Genny across his thighs. "As I recall, the cure begins with kisses. Sweet, fiery, candy apple kisses from the woman I love." His lips sampled hers delicately. "Mmmmm. More," he begged. "Lots more."

In a few minutes, they were sprawled full length on the sofa. Her smock and his jacket lay on the carpet and Gus had found his way up through her petticoats to rest one hand high on her thigh. The tight collar of her dress had halted the progression of the line of kisses he was trailing down her neck, and both of them were working at the fastenings down her back.

"Did you go back to White Rock Spring?" Genny asked, lifting her hair to give him better access.

"Mmmhmm."

His lips tickled her earlobe, and she cringed with delight at the shivers that scattered down her neck. "What did you do with the payroll? Did you give it back?"

"Not exactly," he whispered, "but it's in . . ."

The door from the hall swung open with a loud creak, and both of them started guiltily. "Genny?" Beth's voice was tentative.

Nicky spoke from the hallway. "Is she in there?"

"There's a light on, but I don't see her. Oh dear, the outside door is open." Beth advanced into the room at the exact moment Aunt Augusta came racing in from the garden. At the same instant, both of them discovered Genny stretched out on the sofa with a strange man.

"Oh, heavens!" Beth threw her hands up. "Nicky! This man is attacking Genny! Hurry!"

"Elizabeth! Eugenia! Mr. Mercer! Quick! There's a naked man skulking about in the yews near the stable! What on earth is going on here?" Aunt Augusta screeched as the sight on the sofa registered.

Nicky bounded across the room and had Gus by the scruff of his shirt, dragging him away from Genny before either of them could say a word.

"Stop!" Genny struggled upwards, hampered by her stomach and the petticoats caught beneath her. "Nicky, let him go! It's Gus! Go help Aunt Augusta with the man in the garden!"

Her aunt's mouth flapped soundlessly as she gaped at Gus and pointed back out the garden door.

"Go on, Nicky," Beth said briskly, grabbing his hand and pulling him away from the tall, dark man who had been undressing her sister. "Go see what Aunt Augusta is talking about."

"Are you all right, Genny?" Cobalt eyes regarded Gus with obvious suspicion.

"She is clearly unhurt, Nicholas. Come along with me at once. There is a criminal loose on the premises." Aunt Augusta bolted back out into the twilit gardens, and Beth pushed Nicky after her.

Genny finally managed to sit up straight, though a strand of hair caught in one of the hooks at the back of her dress tipped her head at an angle as she wound it free.

Gus was staring out the door. "Nicky? As in Nicky Mercer? The army lieutenant you asked to take off his clothes for you? What the hell is he doing here?"

Genny had never seen Gus jealous, and the sight of his flushed face gazing malevolently toward the garden was more than a little satisfying.

Beth cleared her throat. "He's my fiancé."

"This is Beth, my younger sister," Genny said, suppressing a grin.

"You're going to marry that rogue? After what he did to your sister?" Gus demanded.

"You mean after what she did to him, and yes, I'm going to marry him. And you, sir, are not one to be calling anyone a rogue if half the stories my sister tells about you are true."

Genny laughed when Gus looked pained. She didn't heed the twinkle that quickly leapt into his eyes. "Ahh, Genny, what'd you tell her? Not about when I shot at you, I hope. Or when I snuck into your bed, or . . ."

She was off the sofa in a trice, her hand clapped tight over his mouth. Beth was staring at them with eyes the size of dinner plates. "This is Gus Renard, Beth. My husband. Gus, hadn't you better go help Nicky catch Aunt Augusta's intruder?" She tried to drag him toward the door, but he stood rooted to the carpet.

"Nope." He pushed her hand down and snaked his arms around her waist. "I'm going to wait right here for the good lieutenant to deliver his quarry on the doorstep."

He wore a smile that Genny didn't like in the least: Predatory, smug, and glittering with unholy anticipation. She was on her guard instantly. "What are you up to?"

Before he could answer, a resounding crash echoed through the house as the front door was thrown back on its hinges, slamming into the wall.

"I got him!" Nicky shouted. A series of grunts and scuffles sent Gus, Genny, and Beth running into the hall. There they found Aunt Augusta puffing in the doorway and Nicky lying atop a man dressed only in short, cut-off drawers and a black felt hat that had been pulled down over his eyes. Gus walked over to them and together, he and Nicky hauled the intruder to his feet. Gus yanked the hat off him.

"Paul!"

The three women gasped in unison. In another moment Genny and Beth were laughing uproariously, and Aunt Augusta looked like she'd swallowed a piano. Nicky looked confused, and Gus looked very pleased with himself.

"I needed a little time to myself with Genny before her got here, and your dear cousin refused to wait at the tavern in town. I'm afraid I borrowed a leaf from your book of tales, Genny, and enforced a delay,'' Gus explained.

"I'm going to kill you, Renard. You may be married to my cousin, but I'm going to kill you," Paul ground out.

"You were traveling together?" Genny asked in utter disbelief.

"Since January the twenty-first, I'm sorry to report. We ran into each other out at your old house, Genny and got stuck because of bad weather. Then hostilities flared along the Platte again, and we were forced to wait at Rivier's for nearly six weeks." Gus let go of Paul with a shake.

"What happened to the money?" Genny's tone was wary.

"Tell her, Paul."

"What money?" Beth and Nicky both wanted to know.

Paul looked like he was choking, but when Gus prodded him in the ribs, he spoke. "It was, uh, a large sum that Renard happened into."

"An inheritance?" Beth queried.

"My guess would be a lucky wager," Nicky said.

"More like an exceptionally lucrative trade," Gus supplied.

"What happened to it?" Genny was not interested in how many ways he could avoid saying it was a stolen payroll taken during a bloody attack on innocent people.

Gus looked pointedly at Paul. "It's in Chicago," her cousin finally said. "In the keeping of a garrulous priest who runs an orphanage." He looked disgusted at the very idea. "Get your hands off me, Mercer. If you will pardon me, Mother, I should like to dress for supper." Straightening his shoulders, he marched up the stairs and disappeared down the upstairs hall.

"Good heavens," Aunt Augusta muttered. She glanced around the hall, narrowing her eyes when they lit on Gus. "Genny, is this man truly your husband?"

"Yes, Aunt Augusta, he truly is."

"I don't like him."

Genny walked to his side, not bothering to hide the very pleased expression she bore. "Well, I do. Quite a lot." She stood on her toes and planted a noisy kiss on his mouth, before turning to the stairs, towing him after her. "I don't think the horse ploy will work on *this* aunt, sweetheart, and I don't think you can go outside and dig up a new son for her. More's the pity."

Gus stopped on the bottom step and whirled Genny around, neatly lifting her into his arms. This time, she didn't protest for a moment. Instead, she wound her arms around his neck and held on tight.

"A pleasure to meet all of you." He nodded to Genny's relatives. "You must excuse us, now, and please don't wait supper for us. We have some catching up to do." He hoisted Genny a little higher as he started up the steps. "Now, where were we, *istatowin*?"

At the top of the staircase, Genny caught their reflection in the mirror as they passed. To think that less than an hour ago she had looked into that same mirror, very much alone and wanting nothing more than to be where she was right now. Laughter spilled from her as joy bubbled through her heart.

"Where am I taking you?" Gus smiled into her eyes.

"Left at the end of the hall, then my room is the second door on the right," she directed. "And you were kissing my neck."

Soft lips brushed over her earlobe and down to her shoulder. Somehow, they made it into Genny's room, and in the hours to come, his lips found a great deal more of her than her neck.

Cool, moist air flowed in a soft current over her arm and Genny sleepily tried to burrow deeper into the blankets. They were heavily weighted, though, and she couldn't tug them over her. Thunder rumbled in the distance, bringing her more fully awake, and with waking came the knowledge that she lay naked in her bed, her feet tangled in the sheets, the pillows lost somewhere

among them. Reaching for one, her fingers closed instead
over a man's forearm.

Gus. He was with her. Tears of joy sprang into her
eyes, and she lifted one hand to her breast, sensitive and
still tingling from the effects of his loving. Sliding her
fingers down over the swell created by the child within
her, she remembered the proud, possessive wonder that
had illuminated her husband's face when he had finally
laid his hands and mouth upon her naked belly. As ever
with Gus, he had made no attempt to hide his emotions
from her, and his tears had made him no less a man in
her eyes.

Lower still her hand wandered until she tucked it between her thighs and felt the warm dampness there. Here,
too, her flesh still tingled, sensitized anew to loving
touches and the deepest kiss of all. It was so good to
have him next to her, to feel the solid weight if him on
the mattress, and to know that the morning would bring
more loving. Outside, spring rain had begun to fall, and
lightning flashed beyond the lacy curtains. Thunder
boomed a little nearer than before, and Genny thought
that the day's events had fallen into her life like the gentle
storm, promising sustenance and life. Unable to resist,
she went over them in her mind. The image of her dagger
upon the book would remain clear in her memory until
her dying day, she was certain.

Suddenly she bolted upright. "Gus!" She shook his
shoulder. "Gus! Wake up! We left the dagger in the
library. I have to get it before Paul sees it."

He groaned and rolled toward her, looping one arm
around her middle, burying his face in her hip. "Relax,"
he said, touching her with the tip of his tongue.
"Mmmmm."

"He's probably found it by now. We have to get it
back." She reached for his discarded shirt at the end of
the bed.

Gus ran his nose up her side, grazing the side of her
breast and sending shivers dancing through her. "He
won't touch it."

"Yes, he will. You don't know Paul like I do."

He raised her arm and began to kiss the underside of it, using his lips, teeth, and tongue in maddening combination. Gooseflesh erupted on her skin, slithering down her arm and up over her shoulder.

"I know him pretty well, *ištatowin*, and I learned a few things that even you don't know. Your cousin has secrets he doesn't want told."

Genny lowered her arm and took Gus's face in her hands. "I wondered how you got away with not returning that payroll. You're blackmailing him, aren't you?"

"That's an ugly word, Genny." He pulled her thumb into his mouth and bit it gently.

"You'd better tell me. Secrets and lies have cost us a lot already."

He eased her back down and pulled the covers up over them both, wrapping his arms around her so that his hands met over her stomach. "Paul's got a Cheyenne wife and a three-year-old daughter. They showed up at Rivier's with some of Martha's relatives after you left. Her name is Keeps the River, and she's a beautiful woman. A lot of her kin were killed at Sand Creek."

Genny tried to sit up again but Gus held her firmly. "I don't understand. What about all those horrible things he said to us when he found out I was carrying your child? And later? He told me to pretend you'd died and present myself as a widow. This is such blatant hypocrisy, I can't make any sense of it. Are you sure?"

"Oh, yeah. I'm sure, but you can ask him yourself. I told him I was going to tell you, because it seemed important that you know." His sigh wafted over Genny's cheek. "Paul's not an easy man to understand, but he's got a lot of company. I've seen plenty of others who keep an Indian family they never say a word about to their white friends and colleagues. They keep their secrets partly out of fear of judgement, partly out of the desire to protect the women and children from a harsh society, and partly out of selfish cowardice."

"Doesn't anyone else know about Paul? In Nebraska, I mean. How can you keep something like that a secret?" Rolling her head on his shoulder, she looked up into his face. Shadows lay deep across his mouth, but his troubled eyes were visible.

"It's not that hard. People come and go. Paul's freighting business gives him an excuse to be anywhere along the trail at any time. You know, Genny, after what you and I've been through, I have a certain amount of compassion for the bastard. The saints only know how well I understand feeling split between peoples and doing stupid things as a result.

"And I have to say in his favor in that he seems to love the woman and treat her and the little girl well."

"I did kind of wonder how he seemed to know so much about what it was like to live in an Indian camp," Genny mused, remembering how he'd tried to talk her out of such a life.

"They've been together over five years, and he spends a lot of his time out there with her in the Cheyenne camps. But he's not willing to live there all the time, and he doesn't want to bring her here. Keeps the River is a lot like you, Genny. She refuses to abandon the world she knows for one where she can't be sure of her place or what will happen to her and her child."

"What about you, Gus? Can you really leave your family and the Lakota way of life behind?"

"It's like I told you earlier. I am Lakota. That's with me wherever I go. I don't feel as if I'm leaving it behind, just as I was never able to leave the world of books and banker's sons behind me on the plains. I belong to two worlds, and it hasn't worked for me to pretend I don't. This is my world, too, sweetheart. I know what to expect. I speak the language. I know how to make small talk with ladies at tea parties, and I can chat about politics and business over brandy and cigars if I have to. This world isn't entirely comfortable with me, but I can fit in here a lot more easily than you could in an Indian camp."

She leaned her brow upon his chest and sighed. "I could never have asked you to do this, Gus, but I'm glad you can. Very glad indeed." Her arms tightened over his, holding him closer to her. "Where will we live?"

"We'll have to find a place we're both happy with.

Until the baby's born, I think we should stay near your sister, but I'm of a mind to get us our own house. Too many relatives can be a little wearing.''

"*Now* you say that," Genny laughed. "It's too bad you didn't bring our little tipi with you. We could set it up in the garden.''

He chuckled into her neck and nipped at her ear lobe. "And be prey to your aunt's snooping? No, thanks.''

"What about after the baby comes?" Arching her neck, she encouraged him to touch her again.

Speaking between the plucking kisses he peppered down her neck, Gus sounded wistfully. "Since I was a little boy, I've always wanted to see France. What would you say to an extended tour abroad? I know you've already done it, but you could show me the sights. Maybe even introduce me to Henri.''

"I'd like that.

"And your friend Mademoiselle Chermont." Long fingers captured a pouting nipple, teasing it to a point.

"Not her," Genny said decisively. Then she groaned in satisfaction, pushing her breast into his hand. "Ahhh, that's very nice. Do the other one, too. How are we going to pay for all this?''

His other hand closed over her neglected breast, and he heard her smile in the little gasp she made. "I've decided that it's time to accept my grandfather's inheritance. After all, I have a family to consider now.''

Warm and sleek, his tongue explored her collarbone while his fingers spun a languorous magic in her breasts. "Perhaps when we get back, we could take our child to visit his Lakota relatives. And his Cheyenne cousins, too, it would seem.''

Lifting his head, he met her eyes. "We can go anywhere you want to. What about your art school?''

"I'd still like to do that, but for the next couple of years, I want to concentrate on just painting. There's something different in my work since I got back from Nebraska, Gus, and I'm excited about it. And I can paint almost anywhere.'' Genny raised one shoulder off the bed and leaned up to kiss him. "You're not afraid any more." She spoke against his cheek and she felt the crease there deepen as he smiled.

"I'm still afraid of things. I'd be a fool not to be, but you give me a lot of courage, Genny, and with courage, I will walk anywhere."

Bright lightning split the room with flickering white light, the thunder cracking right behind it. A gust of wind roared through the open window, knocking over a crystal vase of lilacs on the sill.

Genny sprang up to shut the window. Gus bounded after her, catching her before the open window and holding her before him so that the wind spattered rain onto their naked bodies.

"Feel the power in the storm, *istatowin*. The power of life in all its fullness." His hands caressed her, gliding rough as they spread cool moisture over her breasts and belly. "This storm is nothing compared to Nebraska storms. Don't you miss them, Genny?"

She turned in his arms and lifted her mouth to his. "Not when I have you, Gus. Not when I have you."

She tasted the rain on his lips as his mouth twisted hungrily across hers. Against her belly, his hard flesh throbbed, bare, silky, and more insistent than the tongue he thrust into her mouth. He was hot on her rain-wet skin, and his mouth was sweet, and so bold he took her breath away.

His lips never left her mouth as he carried her out of the rain and back to bed. He fell back into the rumpled sheets and blankets, hauling her with him, pulling her legs up to straddle him.

"Then let the storm spirit take us, Genny," he whispered. "Anywhere we want to go."

Avon Romances—
the best in exceptional authors and unforgettable novels!

America Loves Lindsey!

The Timeless Romances
of #1 Bestselling Author

PRISONER OF MY DESIRE 75627-7/$5.99 US/$6.99 Can
Spirited Rowena Belleme *must* produce an heir, and the magnificent Warrick deChaville is the perfect choice to sire her child—though it means imprisoning the handsome knight.

ONCE A PRINCESS 75625-0/$5.95 US/$6.95 Can
From a far off land, a bold and brazen prince came to America to claim his promised bride. But the spirited vixen spurned his affections while inflaming his royal blood with passion's fire.

GENTLE ROGUE 75302-2/$4.95 US/$5.95 Can
On the high seas, the irrepressible rake Captain James Malory is bested by a high-spirited beauty whose love of freedom and adventure rivaled his own.

WARRIOR'S WOMAN 75301-4/$4.95 US/$5.95 Can
In the year 2139, Tedra De Arr, a fearless beautiful Amazon unwittingly flies into the arms of the one man she can never hope to vanquish: the bronzed barbarian Challen Ly-San-Ter.

SAVAGE THUNDER 75300-6/$4.95 US/$5.95 Can
Feisty, flame-haired aristocrat Jocelyn Fleming's world collides with that of Colt Thunder, an impossibly handsome rebel of the American West. Together they ignite an unstoppable firestorm of frontier passion.